2-2022

THE *Magic* OF FOUND OBJECTS

Center Point
Large Print

Also by Maddie Dawson and available from
Center Point Large Print:

Matchmaking for Beginners
A Happy Catastrophe

THE *Magic* OF FOUND OBJECTS

A Novel

MADDIE DAWSON

CENTER POINT LARGE PRINT
THORNDIKE, MAINE

To Jimbo,
who knows how to
make quarantine fun

PROLOGUE

I came into the world as both a surprise and a complication, which tells you everything you need to know about how things have gone ever since.

My twin brother and I were conceived at Woodstock. And by Woodstock, I mean the music festival. Summer of '69 and all that. The time of the moon landing, the birth of the gay rights movement in Greenwich Village, and half a million hippies converging upon a little town in upstate New York.

Woodstock: Peace and Love.

Remember that iconic photograph? You know the one I mean. The hippie couple wrapped in a blanket, embracing and looking bleary-eyed at the camera? When Bunny, my grandmother, was telling me the story when I was six, I asked her if those people were my parents.

Could have been. Looked a bit like them. Bunny didn't think so, though. She laughed and said she wasn't sure my parents had even had a blanket with them.

My mom, she told me, was different from anybody my dad had ever known. (I knew that part. My mom is different from everybody.) Back then, when he met her, she was a beautiful girl, an artist who wore silver amulets and bracelets and long skirts and tie-dyed shirts she made herself, *and* she practiced magic. She did batik and macramé. Her name was Janet, but she had switched the letters around and called herself Tenaj.

Was it love? It sounds like love, but maybe it was something else altogether. One of those mysterious moments in time.

She might have bewitched him, my grandmother whispered, with a little laugh. She put her finger to her lips and her eyes twinkled. Our secret.

My father isn't anyone you could imagine being bewitched. He was a regular farmer's son from rural New Hampshire, named Robert Greer Linnelle, and he was eighteen years old when he met her, and what I think is that he was bedazzled by everything he saw at Woodstock. He had graduated from high school two months before—and on a little whim, according to Bunny—he and his friend Tom drove a pickup truck to upstate New York to see the music festival. He was going to come back and settle down and work full-time on the farm after that.

But then—over the years, she has always lowered her voice for this part—somehow with the music and the mud and the secondhand marijuana smoke and the magic, he fell in with Tenaj.

Fell in were the words she used.

Fell in the mud?

Fell into her body?

Fell in love?

All of it, she said. She laughed. The full catastrophe.

And after the concert was over, he didn't go back to the farm that was waiting for him, back to his father who was counting on him and who was furious. My grandmother wouldn't say she was mad at him, too, but once she admitted she had been "a little disappointed." Scared for him. Still she understood how he felt, she said. She knew what love could do.

But mainly it was his back-home girlfriend, Maggie Markley, who was the maddest. She had been in agreement with the rest of the town that she and Robert had a relationship that was the sun, the moon, and the stars. She hadn't wanted to go to Woodstock with him because she was working, and that little decision turned out to be the worst mistake of her life.

That's how come my parents were pretty much strangers to each other when they got married, and they lived in Woodstock in a little tiny house together, no bigger than somebody's corncrib. And that next May, my brother and I came tearing into the world, shaking our fists and wailing out our own brand of music—we had our mother's eyes and our daddy's curled-up fists, my grandmother said—both of us probably fed up with the cramped quarters in my mother's little body and looking for some decent room where we could stretch out.

Were we welcomed into the world? I don't know. Bunny doesn't talk about this point.

I was named Phronsie, after a character in a book that my mother loved in childhood—*Five Little Peppers and How They Grew*. Phronsie was the youngest—a sweet, blonde, curly-haired toddler who was doted upon by the family. And they named my brother Hendrix, because well, guess why.

Hendrix and I are from the mud and the music; we are from Tenaj's silver bracelets and the New Hampshire dirt under Robert's fingernails, from marijuana smoke and cornfields. We were born to a witch and a farmer who had nothing in common. Sounds like a fairy tale, doesn't it?

But everybody knows that fairy tales don't last. My father went back to the cows and the chickens and the dirt, and my mother drifted away with her artwork and her magic, turning found objects into art. He hardened up, perhaps so angry over this adventure he'd taken, which he saw as his first and last lapse of judgment. I'm sure, knowing him, he was ashamed of himself for the way he turned his head from his planned path in life and fell into Tenaj, so he doesn't like to speak of her *or* those times to us.

All I know is that Hendrix and I crashed down to earth as surprises and complications, and we were left with magic flickering in our DNA and practicality knitted into our bones.

It's been a war inside us ever since. And I'm not sure either one of us has ever figured out what love really is supposed to be about.

CHAPTER ONE

2006

It's Friday night at midnight, and I'm in my bed, lying next to Mr. Swanky, my snoring little pug, trying to decide between having a good cry or taking a bubble bath when my cell phone rings.

It's Judd, of course. Time for our Dissect-A-Date debriefing.

He doesn't even say hello. He says, "Okay, Phronsie. Out with it. How'd you do?"

"Not great," I tell him. "Let me get the paper-work." I've been on my forty-third internet date, out with Mr. Cyber Security Previously Married No Kids. Judd's been out with Red-Haired Nurse Who Lives with Her Mom.

"You go first," I say. I call up the spreadsheet on my laptop. When all is said and done, I'm going to write an article about the travesty known as online dating. It will be honest, searing, and hilarious. It will be called either "How to Finally Give Up Looking for Love" or "The Successful Guide to Finding Love in New York City."

Depending on which way this ends up.

Maybe I'll quit my job as a publicist and go on talk shows and give advice. I could be known as "Phronsie the Dating Whisperer."

He lets out a big sigh. "As usual, I'd have to say *meh*. She wasn't very interesting. Doesn't know anything about football. Kept checking her phone. I ended up leaving when one of my old ladies called and wanted to know if I could come unclog her sink, and so that's how I really spent my evening. Plunging Mabel's kitchen drain."

"Ha! Is that a euphemism?"

He laughs. "If only."

It's true that Judd has old ladies, and they all have crushes on him. It's kind of a situation. He has young ladies, too, to be clear. He owns a gym downtown, and besides having muscles, he has nice brown eyes and a killer jawline, and women of all ages flock to him for their training. The ones over seventy keep proposing marriage. One of them—perhaps it's Mabel, I can't remember—says he either has to marry her or go for her forty-something daughter *or* her twenty-something granddaughter. *Somebody* in that family has to marry him, she says.

"Let's move on to the checklist," I say. "Okay. Did Red-Haired Nurse Who Lives with Her Mom look like her profile picture?"

He sighs. "Who knows? Who remembers? Write down *no*. Nobody I've met so far looks like their profile picture."

"Did she ask you any questions about yourself?"

"Not a one."

"Okay. I'll skip the rest. Overall scale of one to ten?"

"Um, one point five. It was a bust. We drank a beer, she tossed her hair, told me how immoral football is, and then my phone rang, and I ducked out. End of story." I can tell by his breathing that he's working out while we talk. Judd doesn't waste time merely talking on the phone; he's always doing lunges or squats at the same time. "Okay," he says. "Your turn."

"Awful. Black hole of despair. Bad haircut, didn't ask even one question about my life. Works for a big firm, blah blah blah, frets about cybercrime, married twice before, griped about how men can't be themselves with women anymore. More or less your typical troglodyte."

"This dating scene sucks," he says, huffing and puffing. "Let's go to the diner."

It's always about the diner for Judd.

"Luckily or unluckily," I say, "there are three other guys who want to meet me for coffee. I've said no to two of them—but one of them looks promising. A firefighter who started a fund for kids whose parents died in 9/11. I might marry him just for that."

"Nice. Now diner, diner, diner."

"No, no, no. Mr. Swanky and I are comfortable, and besides, he doesn't want me to go out, do you, Mr. Swanky G. Pug?" I lean over and pet his

15

soft little ears, and he stretches out and I swear he smiles at me.

"Mr. Swanky can't express his opinion, and even if he could, luckily for everyone concerned, he's an understanding and forgiving dog who wants you to live your best life," Judd says. "Come on. Meet me in the stairwell in five minutes. I have something important to tell you."

"You can't just tell me now?"

"I cannot."

"Oh God. Is this going to be heavy? Like, you're moving out or something?"

"I've had one of my major thinks. An epiphany."

"Always a dangerous thing. Okay. I'll meet you in seven minutes, not five. But I have to warn you I don't have any makeup on, and I'm not changing out of my leggings and T-shirt."

"And how is this different from any other night?" he says. "When have I seen you *with* makeup, is the real question. I figured you'd thrown it all out by now."

"I save it for dates. Seeing all the bottles lined up on my counter gives me hope."

"This is exactly what we need to talk about."

"The bottles on my counter?"

"No. Hope."

Judd Kovac has been my good friend for thirty-one years. We met on our first day of kindergarten back in Pemberton, New Hampshire, when the

16

teacher, Mrs. Spencer, sat me down next to him on the rug at circle time. Fifteen minutes later she separated us because we couldn't stop talking. I think he was bragging about how loudly he could burp. Turns out that was the beginning of a lifelong conversation on that topic.

It doesn't even matter at this point that we don't have all that much in common, besides the fact that we both escaped our family farms in New Hampshire and moved to Manhattan. Now that we're in our midthirties, we live two floors apart on the Upper West Side. Due to the mysteries of rent-stabilization rules in New York City, we are both in illegal, but affordable, sublets that could be reclaimed at any moment by the lawful tenants who live elsewhere. (Don't ask; it's complicated.) We've become true New Yorkers, toasting periodically (usually me) to the fact that we narrowly escaped the fate of farm life that our parents tried to foist upon us. Every now and then one of us (usually him) will get nostalgic and start idealizing the simple pastoral life we left behind, the one containing lots of cows and goats. But that's generally only when the subway is down.

And in case you're wondering—and I know you are—outside of one disastrous, experimental make-out session when we were fourteen, our relationship has never gone down the rabbit hole of romance.

We are not each other's types, that's why. He goes for women who could have appeared on *America's Next Top Model*, whereas I . . . well, I just can't make myself care enough to go to all that trouble. I barely put on mascara for work, and even then I smudge it half the time. Also, I hate wearing high heels on my off hours, and I refuse to wear any outfit that requires a special bra. (I have exactly one saggy, flesh-colored bra, and when that one loses the last of its elastic— well, that's when I'll consider going and buying another.)

As for him, he's a great guy, but he doesn't have a lot of *nuance* to him. He likes problems a person can *fix,* like weight gain. Bloat. Signing up for gym memberships. And he can't stand still— he's always doing boxing moves or bouncing up and down on his toes. Also, I hate to mention it, but he doesn't separate the whites from the darks when he does laundry, so his clothes are always a little dingy. *And* he thinks that Meryl Streep is overrated. Meryl Freaking Streep!

But I suspect we're in one of those friendships that might last for life.

I saw him through the tragic moment when his high school girlfriend, Karla Kristensen, (aka The Love of His Life) married someone else, and he comforted me with Toaster Strudel and cream puffs (big deal for a gym guy) through the demise of my short-lived marriage to Steve Hanover, even though he didn't approve of either of those foods *or* of Steve Hanover (aka The Love of *My* Life).

Also, after all these years, I appreciate that he doesn't tease me about the fact that I am terrified of heights, bees, haunted houses, thunderstorms, and the possibility of snakes coming up through the toilet bowl—and I pretend not to see that he's crying in movies that have to do with dogs dying.

Anyway.

We'd both been pretty much living the single life in New York City for years, basically hanging out together because, frankly, we were still hung up on our previous relationships . . . and then a year ago, we were at our third wedding reception in two months, when Judd suddenly turned to me and said, "You know something? I'm sick of this. What we're doing with our lives is bullshit. We need to get back out there and meet people for real."

I looked down at my patent leather Jimmy Choo Wedding Reception High Heels, bought under duress. "And by *people,* I'm assuming you're referring to—?"

He looked me in the eye. "Yeah. Our future spouses. I'm thinking this is our year to meet them. We're going to get serious about getting serious. You in?"

Well, of course I was. I'd been bumbling

around year after year since my divorce, not really finding anybody who would play the part of Husband in my fantasies about marriage. Ever since Steve Hanover took what I used to call my heart and stomped on it, I've lost a bit of my mojo. I'm mostly content to come home, strip off my glamorous work clothes, scrub off my mascara, put on leggings, and sit down at the kitchen table and make myself work on the novel that I've been writing off and on for five years now. The novel that makes me feel I'm more than simply The Person Who Attends Other People's Weddings and Then Goes Home to Listen to Her Eggs Drying Up.

But now, Judd and I were going to tackle the problem head-on. Action! We did our old Pemberton High handshake to seal the deal.

"And," he said, "I think we're going to have to do online dating. And spreadsheets. No going out with people from work either! Or blind dates. We're going to be *organized* about this! We are going to *rock this thing!* We'll have a system in place! We'll report to each other! Dissect-A-Date, we'll call it."

Judd has never found a situation in life that couldn't be improved by launching a planned attack, especially if it involves a spreadsheet.

Overnight, we turned into each other's dating concierges and post-date consolers. Dissect-A-Date provides everything from fashion advice to profile consultations and postmortems. We also give tips on getting along with the opposite sex when necessary.

"Women like to feel you really *see* them," I instructed him. "You have to listen without interrupting. And then ask questions. Also noticing her shoes will go a long way. And it should go without saying, no burping."

"Okay. And I need to tell you that men don't *love* it when women are extra picky about ordering food in a restaurant," he said to me. "Only allow yourself to badger the waiter about the origins of one ingredient per date. You do not need to see the late chicken's vision board."

Our dating experiment did not start out well. There were lots of duds.

One night, three months in, when we were at my apartment watching *Friday Night Lights* and eating popcorn, I told him that maybe, instead of finding somebody and getting married, I would just write books, take a succession of lovers, and perhaps learn to do interesting things with scarves and shawls.

"It's possible," I said, "that the short, stunted little marriage I already had was it for me in the matrimony department."

"Come on. That's ridiculous. You'll meet somebody else. You just got to put yourself out there. It's a numbers game."

"But here's the problem. I don't remember how

to fall in love," I told him. "I sit across the table from all these perfectly presentable men, and I simply can't remember what switch gets flipped to make me care about any one of them."

"Seriously? Listen to me," he said at last. "This is the writer in you, isn't it? You're always overthinking things. The way I see it: love is a decision, not a feeling. That's what you may be forgetting."

"I used to be so good at it," I told him. "Then the other day I actually found myself asking Google, 'How do you fall in love?' "

He shook his head. "Yeah? And what wisdom did the Google have to offer?"

I shrugged. "Google said you can't force it. That's why it's called falling."

The diner is hopping. Alphonse, our favorite waiter, greets us when we come in: "Phronsiejudd! At last the night can begin!" And then he rushes over with our favorite beers—me a Blue Moon and Judd a Sam Adams.

Alphonse and Judd have to take a few minutes to discuss the Jets (as usual), which are disappointing (as usual). Alphonse, jolly, gregarious, is grinning and snapping his towel as he talks, but I'm watching Judd. There's something weird about him tonight, the way he's fidgeting and smiling too hard. He keeps cracking his knuckles. As soon as another party comes in—five loud, dressed-up people, all smiling—Alphonse glides away to seat them, and I turn to him.

"So what's this great epiphany you had?" I say.

He turns to look at me, and his eyes are bright and kind of crazy. He leans forward and takes my hands. Very uncharacteristic of him, taking my hands. "Look at me. Look at my face. Do I look different to you? Because I think I might have gone two notches up on the maturity scale. I suddenly know what I want in life."

"Wait. Did this come from being on a date you hated?"

"I think maybe it did. That horrible woman with her hair tossing propelled me into maturity."

"And what *do* you want?" I release my hands from his and take a sip of my beer.

He leans even closer, and now his eyes are practically boring into mine. "I want to get married."

I study him silently, uncomprehending.

"To you," he says. "I want to marry *you*."

I laugh. It's so ridiculous. Ludicrous, even, this idea, sailing in from out of the blue. Trust me; there has been nothing—*nothing*—in the thirty-one years of our friendship that has this making any kind of sense.

"You do not want to marry me, and you know it," I tell him firmly. "I know what this is. You're having your annual going-home-for-Thanksgiving angst. This is a Tandy's crisis, plain

23

and simple. And marriage to me won't solve it."

He laughs. "No," he says. "This is way bigger than Tandy's."

Okay. Let me stop here and tell you about Tandy's. Tandy's is a bar and grill in our hometown. And every year, when Judd and I go back home to Pemberton for Thanksgiving, it's become a tradition for all our old high school friends to meet there every night, once we've gotten through with our family responsibilities and put our parents to bed, that is. Everybody shows up.

At first Tandy's nights used to be all about everybody knocking back some beers and complaining about their parents. Then the diamond rings started showing up on the fingers of the Early Marriage Adopters, as Judd calls them— and after that came a sprinkling of infants. (That was fine; we could still cope.) But now that we're all in our midthirties, not only has *every other person* in our high school class acquired a spouse, they now also have kids. Real kids. And not just babies anymore; they have middle-sized children. And mortgages! The dreaded minivans! Orthodontist bills!

And what do *we* have?

By Tandy's standards, we have zilch. (My heartbreaker of a marriage didn't even last long enough for me to show my husband off to the Tandy's crowd.)

I'm not going to lie—our trip back on the train has been known to turn into a Greek tragedy—complete with some gnashing of teeth, spilling of regrets, rending of garments, you name it. Mostly by Judd, if you want to know the truth. He's often saying he feels pathetic, which is so crazy, because Judd is doing great. Both of us are. We just don't have any spouses and kids. We're behind in that department.

What our classmates don't realize is that Judd has his own gym and was written up in the *New York Post* for the way he gets little old ladies to bench press. He has groupies! (And so what that they're senior citizens?)

As for me, nobody at home quite gets it that I'm working for a New York publisher, and that I got to meet Anne Tyler one time. And that I own ten black leggings and fourteen black turtlenecks, and I go to book launches and corporate cocktail parties. *And* that Judd and I see celebrities all the time, get takeout at three a.m., and know the ins and outs of the New York subway system, even the mystifying weekend schedule. We understand *rent stabilization,* for pity's sake.

Also, I'm writing an actual novel. I'm on page 135 of it, which is decent progress, considering I work all the time and only have evenings and Saturday mornings at Starbucks to work on it.

But no—we don't have babies and two-car garages and picket fences. And more times than

I like to admit, frankly, I'm eating dinner out of a Styrofoam takeout carton, standing over the sink, having just run in from work even though it's almost bedtime.

But I like New York life, really. I picked this. I knew early on that New Hampshire wasn't where I was supposed to be, and I escaped. I went to NYU, and then stayed. Judd came to Manhattan ten years ago—not because of me, but because in his rambling search for employment and a new start, he'd gotten a job as a personal trainer in a New York gym. I suspect he really came because the per capita number of supermodels is so much greater in New York than on the farm. (The boy appreciates beauty.)

So why do we forget all that when we're faced with our old friends and their settled-down lives? I do not know. I remember them as teenagers— the girls gossipy and funny, chewing gum, making big plans, and the boys handsome and strong, all of them smelling of Old Spice as we'd make out in their pickup trucks in the woods. I loved them then, and I love them now, even as I am so glad deep down that I didn't stay and marry one of them. The Old Spice guys are doughy and complacent now. They've somehow turned into our fathers, pontificating about the weather and the price of beans. The women are sarcastic in their discontent, hands on hips, eyes rolling. *Men!* they say. *Why can't they ever listen!*

26

But you get with a bunch of people you used to love, and see them coupled up, passing around pictures of their babies, and you can't help but notice the looks that pass between husbands and wives, and the way they finish each other's sentences, steeped in all that *intimacy* and *knowing* . . . and sometimes seeing that just kills you is all.

Even my twin brother, Hendrix, fell in love in high school and never looked back. It was as though he and Ariel Evans, his chemistry lab partner, had been destined from birth to be together. They now have three little boys, and Ariel, despite her ethereal name, manages their household like she's the CEO of a well-run corporation, making lists and schedules and barking out commands to keep all four of her males in line. And Hendrix seems just fine with that. When I once pulled him aside and asked how he adapts to all the organization his life contains—not to mention the nagging—he just shrugged and said, "So Ariel nags—so what? I love her. She's not perfect. This is what marriage looks like, Phronsie." He sounded impatient, like he was having to teach me remedial life skills or something.

And—well, now that I'm thirty-six, I have to admit that I really, really want what Hendrix has. Somebody just for me. I want a guy who has his own side of the bed next to my side of the bed, whose clothes hang next to mine in the closet, and who will take the scary spiders outside and let them loose, and who will understand the look I get on my face when I want to leave a party. Who knows that I like chocolate rum raisin ice cream best of all, but red raspberry can do in a pinch—never vanilla. And who tells me all his secrets and listens to all of mine when he's lying across the pillow from me. Who lights up when he sees me. Who has hidden places in his personality that only I know about.

And, what the hell, I want somebody to be listed as next of kin on the hospital form, should it come to that—a guy who has the legal right to visit me if I'm ever in the ICU.

And, despite my never thinking this desire would sweep over me, I want a baby. I badly want a baby. Which is a big surprise, even to myself. But I do.

But this guy across the table—the one pro-posing—well, he isn't the one for all of that. He's great. He's fun, he's nice, he's interesting. He knows the part about the chocolate rum raisin ice cream, and he's willing to carry spiders outside.

But the simple fact is: he is not in love with me, and never has been. Period.

Alphonse swoops down just then, bearing a plate of eggplant fries and hummus, and plops it down in front of Judd. The diner's idea of health food. "This is on the house, Juddie my buddy," he says. "Not to be pushy or anything, but you look like you could use some oil and salt. And thanks for helping me move my stuff the other day, man."

"Anytime. You know that," Judd says, and they do a fist bump and Alphonse glides away.

"When did you help him move?" I say.

"Oh, last week. He found a cheaper rent, and so he needed some help with the couch and a desk. I went over and helped him load up the truck."

He eats a handful of eggplant fries and looks at me. "Look. I know what you're thinking. But this isn't about Pemberton or Tandy's or anything like that," he says. "I *want* to get married, to you, and it's not about what anyone else thinks."

"But it's not really about *me* either," I say. "And you know how I know that? Because we are not in love. Case closed."

"I know, but that's the best part. Just hear me out. This is brilliant when you think about it. First premise: Nobody wants to be alone for their whole life. I don't, you don't. Second premise: We're already old friends. Unlike most of the people we know who got married because they were *madly in love, we* still actually like each other, and they don't. Third premise: *We* have what most marriages are aiming for, which is true compatibility. We put up with each other."

"Judd, I . . . forgive me, but putting up with each other is not a very high mark. That won't get us through the first six weeks."

29

"Wait. Look at this. Before we came tonight, I made a little temporary engagement ring for you out of a twist tie I had." He reaches into his sweatpants pocket and pulls out a piece of wire covered with peppermint-striped paper, all knotted up into a circle, and hands it to me. "The good thing about this kind of ring is that it's adjustable. And replaceable." He gives me a big smile. "You could get a new one from me every week."

"Wow. You are really going all out with making a compelling case."

"I know. I've put a lot of thought and effort into this."

I feel dazed. How long has he been thinking about this? Also, it's interesting that he doesn't even bother to dispute my claim that we're not in love. He's not even put out by my refusing him. I take a sip of my beer and look over at the normal people in the diner, people who are talking and laughing and who presumably know who they should marry and who they should not. Who have never had to explain to another person that being in love is an important component to married life.

"I just don't see how you can discount love like this," I say. "It's insulting to love to talk like it doesn't matter."

"No, no. It does matter. But the truth is, this *is* love. You don't recognize it. But love is all this good stuff that we already have"—he stops to

wave his arms in the air, taking in everything—
"the history we share and these diner evenings
and the times we've eaten popcorn while we
watch *Friday Night Lights*. I put butter on my
popcorn for you, Phronsie! That's what love is—
not all that moonlight and sonnets and walking
in the rain bullshit. Nobody wants to walk in
the rain! Nobody! And nobody likes suspense or
playing games."

"I don't know," I say slowly.

"Look. I made up my mind that if we both had
unsatisfactory dates tonight, I was going to ask
you. Because, Phronsie, face it: we are *not happy*
with dating. We've put a whole year into finding
spouses, and look at it this way: *maybe* we
couldn't because *we* are the spouses. You know?"

My face feels hot. I lower my voice. "Judd,
please. I want to be in love. And you do, too.
Remember that? Remember Karla Kristensen
and your year of pining away? No offense, but it
was kind of a big deal in your life."

"No offense to *you,* but how has that worked
out in either of our lives? I believe you were, as
you call it, *madly in love* when you got married
before and—"

I flap my hands at him, beseeching him to stop.
I was married to Steve Hanover for eight months,
two weeks, three days, and either ten or eleven
hours. And yes, I was in love with him beyond
all sanity. But it went badly. Maybe he was too

handsome for me—he was a 9.8, while, with excellent lighting and a new haircut and color, I can achieve an 8.2 for maybe fifteen whole minutes before I slide back down to a 7. Possibly you have to stay in your own category, looks-wise.

Anyway, I came home from work unexpectedly one day (which a person should never, ever do, by the way), and there he was in our bed with some woman underneath him. Her legs were spread out on *my* bedspread, and before I started to scream, all I could think was that sex really looks and sounds quite ridiculous when you arrive upon it without warning. When it's not you doing it.

I hit him on the butt. I also threw my purse at her little pink polished toenails. I made screeching noises and pulled at my own hair. And then I delivered the ultimatum—that she was to get *out of my apartment in two minutes* or I was calling the cops.

It took her nine whole minutes to leave. And when she did, Steve sailed out right along with her. He said something about a lawyer, and also that he wished me good luck. He looked only vaguely chagrined that he'd been caught so dramatically. He actually said maybe it had been for the best, that at last I knew the truth.

The *best?* Who was he kidding, using the word *best?*

And yet . . . and yet, when Steve Hanover proposed, he had gotten down on one knee next to the boathouse in Central Park. His eyes had been glistening with tears of joy. It felt like magic. A crowd gathered and people cheered for us. There was an actual diamond engagement ring involved. We held it up for the crowd to see.

And when he left . . . well, I hate to admit this because I want to be a strong, independent, fearless woman, still fighting and rebelling and raising hell, but the truth is that Steve killed off something in me. I stopped feeling like there was somebody out there who was going to really understand me. Who would take care of my bruised little heart.

I guess I just stopped trusting in love to be the thing that would save me.

So now the contrast is not lost on me. Here I am, getting my second marriage proposal of my lifetime, and I'm sitting in a diner, under fluorescent lights that do not bring out my best features, especially at 1:05 a.m. And the gentleman proposing is now going on and on about how nobody we know who married for love is happy over that choice. He's naming names, counting them on his fingers. This one is having an affair; this one wants separate bedrooms and separate vacations. These two don't speak. And in fact, hadn't I noticed that the whole scene at Tandy's the past few years has just been filled with married people arguing?

Judd is now leaning forward, and his eyes are lit up from within, burning into mine. "If you look around, we're the only ones who still get along, and you know why? Because being madly in love is a temporary condition of insanity, that's why. Wait until this weekend when we go see Russell and Sarah to meet the new baby. Those two are so in love that they're practically ready to kill each other."

The twist tie ring sits between us on the table, getting wet from the condensation from the beer bottle. In another hour, it will revert back to just being a piece of wire.

He stops talking for a moment. I look at his eyes, the swoop of dark hair he has falling across his forehead. He looks older than he did the last time I really took a good look at him. We're both older. God, we've been friends for so long. He knows my family history: my witchy, hippie mom in Woodstock and my algebra-teaching stepmom who worries about everything—and my grumpy old dad. He's the one who can make my dad smile. He's hung out with me and Hendrix our whole lives, slept over at our house countless times. We were the Three Musketeers.

Also, I know his parents—two sweet, baffled people from Hungary who married late and were nearly fifty when he, their only child, came barreling into their lives. They didn't even know children had to have birthday parties! And they never once went to a football game of his. Thought they weren't invited maybe.

"I gotta ask you something," I say. "Are you doing this because you're giving up? Is it because you're afraid you're not going to meet anyone you really could love?"

"What? No. *No,* Phronsie. I don't want to meet anyone else. I don't know anybody I'd rather be with than you. And I'm sick of dating. I want to be married. I want to have children. I want a regular life, like the other grown-ups. That's it. My whole case. I want to marry you."

"I'm sick of dating, too," I tell him. Forty-three men and not one of them looked like anybody I could ever love. "But," I say, "there *is* this firefighter who wants to have coffee with me . . ."

He puts both his hands down flat on the table and smiles. "Okay, so go ahead and date the firefighter. Date number forty-four. It's fine. Go see if he's your Prince Charming, but I bet you anything he isn't. Anyway, even if he is, it would take you decades to fill him in on everything about you, stuff that I already know and accept. I *accept* you, Phronsie. Just let that sink in."

My head is spinning the slightest bit. Like the way I felt one time on the roller coaster right before I threw up. I think Judd was there for that time, too.

"Also," I say. "How to put this delicately? You like women who have . . . good looks. Push-up

35

bras. Legs up to their armpits. And that's fine. For you. But I don't care about any of that. I can't make myself go beyond, shall we say, a certain level of body maintenance. I will not, for instance, ever get a bikini wax. So if you're expecting that, you are going to be—"

He is waving his arms around in front of his face. "Stop, stop, with the bikini whatever. No! No to that! God!"

"Well? It's a reasonable question. I've seen who you date."

"I don't care about any of that stuff. Seriously. You have to believe me. I want this. This. And I also happen to think we'll be terrific parents. We'll have kids and take them to the park, and ride bikes together. We're going to rock this parenthood thing."

Yes. Parenthood. He loves children; he would read them stories and let them climb on his back. I've seen him with Hendrix's kids. I've seen him making kids in the park laugh, even here in New York.

"So . . . in this plan of yours . . . what about sex?" I say.

He bugs out his eyes. "Did I not just tell you there would be children? Obviously there will be sex."

"Well, that's the part—I mean, we never have. Aren't you worried that maybe we don't have any, um, chemistry?"

"Nope. Sex is the easy part," he says. "*Of course* we'll have sex. It just won't be the *driving force*. Our friendship is."

"No offense, but I kind of like the driving force aspect. Driving force actually makes me swoon, now that I think about it."

"Well," he says. "I can manufacture driving force if that's what you need. But we are not going to have romantic suspense and agony, if that's all right with you. That I don't want."

My mind scrolls back through all the dating disasters I've endured. Years of them. All the hours and hours of waiting for the guy to call, worrying that I wasn't attractive enough or attentive enough or didn't have enough sparkling conversation to get through an evening. The fake laughter I manufactured too many times to count. The flattery and flirtations I mastered. The times I've slept with a man because of what felt like a genuine mutual attraction . . . and then afterward endured days of torment, waiting for him to call. Followed, of course, by all the meditation and soul-searching and serious talks with my girlfriends when the jerk *didn't* call.

All of it has been so demoralizing, so soul-crushing. Maybe because it's technically the middle of the night and I'm overtired, but I suddenly feel so furious at Mr. Cyber Security Previously Married No Kids for his cavalier attitude toward me. For the smirk on his face as he described how confusing it was to be a man trying to talk to women these days.

In fact, I realize, I'm angry at the whole lot of them—the whole cadre of forty-three men I've gotten myself dressed up for. Angry about the manicures and pedicures and lipstick purchases, the hair appointments, the nice underwear, the hopes rising and falling, rising and falling. The notes I take afterward. The story I'm going to write.

Furious about the number of times I've played "Love Has No Pride" by Bonnie Raitt and screamed along to the lyrics.

The only good part, I realize, has been telling Judd about these dates afterward, listening to him laugh. Hearing him tell about the vacuous women he's been seeing.

He's smiling at me. "I don't think," he says, "that I want to live in a world in which this isn't the kind of love that really matters."

I get a little shiver at that. It's really his best line.

"Okay. I have some questions. If we got married," I say, "would that mean you'd call in sick for me when I can't go to work? Because when I call, I always think it sounds like I'm faking."

"What? Well, yes, of course."

"And you'd rub my feet sometimes?"

"Okayyyy . . ."

"With no complaining about it, right? And, how about Mr. Swanky? He likes to sleep on the bed, you know."

"Phronsie, I'm not going to kick the dog off the bed."

"And . . . and . . . we'll cook together and go grocery shopping and plan meals and throw parties for our friends sometimes? And we'll sleep in the same bed, and you'll hold me while I fall asleep?"

He's smiling. He really does have a lovely smile. "Yes, all that. And I'll take care of the children with you, and we'll go on family vacations together. All of it. Marriage. Parenthood. All the good stuff."

"What about my novel?"

"What about it?"

"Will you not give me a hard time when I need to write it, even if it's in the middle of the night or when you want to do something else, but I need to write?"

He stares at me. "I don't care if you write a novel. Write it whenever you like."

"And no cheating?"

"No cheating."

"Ever, ever, ever?"

"What's with you? I *said* no cheating."

"One more thing. Will we fall in love, do you think?"

He runs his hands across his hair, hard.

"Phronsie, you may be missing the point. What we already have is love. There's no *falling* to be done. We're upright. This is what upright love looks like. Rubbing feet and going grocery shopping together—this is winning at love, as far as I'm concerned."

I drink the last of my beer and look at him. He raises his eyebrows questioningly, and I nod, so he puts the twist tie ring on my finger.

"Wait. This is not official. I might need to talk to Sarah and Talia about this," I say. "Just to run it by them."

He laughs. "No, I understand. We can't make a move without Sarah and Talia."

Sarah and Talia are my best friends; they were the first people I clicked with when I moved to New York. We were all *Sex and the City* together right after I graduated from NYU. I got to be Carrie Bradshaw because I was a writer and my hair looked like hers. We all went on dates and we drank a lot of wine, and we had fun, glamorous jobs, and we were dramatic and gloriously young with lots of good hair products and no bags under our eyes—and one by one, we met guys who became our husbands: Russell with Sarah, Talia with Dennis, me with Steve. Only *their* guys stuck around, and now they are having babies. Sarah and Russell just had one last week. They named the kid Willoughby after a street Russell lived on in Brooklyn.

When we get back to our building, I look at Judd there beside me in the brightly lit lobby, at his large moist hands, his bright eyes, the little hairs under his nose that would like to turn into a mustache except he shaved them probably sixteen hours ago. The little crinkles around his eyes are now permanent, not just when he laughs. I see the same crinkles when I look at myself in the mirror; when I don't get at least eight hours of sleep, I look like my face is collapsing in on itself. I'm a little bit stunned at how old—or rather *mature*—we've suddenly gotten overnight.

We take the stairs up to my floor in silence— Judd always thinks people have to take the stairs instead of the elevator so we'll still have muscles and bones that work when we're eighty—and when we get there, we stand in the stairwell awkwardly.

Oh God. Is he going to make a move on me? Am I ready for this?

Then he puts his arms around me like we've done casually a bunch of times before. But this time he looks at me and smiles and then puts his mouth down on mine, hard.

We don't fit together, somehow. His nose hits my nose too hard, which makes my eyes water. This kiss is somehow too wet and also it doesn't connect. Between my eyes watering and all the saliva that suddenly has sprung up between us, all I can think of is drowning. And would I be terribly awful if I mention that his nose hairs are tickling me? We move around a bit and try to make it work, but then he pulls away and laughs. He shrugs.

"Not the end of the world. We'll work on it," he says cheerfully and gives me a high five. "Also, can I borrow my ring back? My bread is going to get stale without it."

CHAPTER TWO

I wake up the next day realizing I'm as close to a panic attack as I've been since Steve Hanover walked out on me. Mr. Swanky stares at me with his head tilted to the side, as I down two pharmaceutically required cups of coffee and start pacing around the apartment.

"Am I really considering marrying *Judd?*" I ask him. "Because that's insane, right?"

He lies down with his head on his paws. I can tell he's thinking it over.

"Well, you're right. I can't be serious. There are absolutely forty-nine obvious reasons not to marry him that I didn't even begin to think of last night."

As soon as it is even a remotely decent hour, I call Talia. She's married to Dennis, a surgical resident who works about nine thousand hours a month, so she'll be able to come up with at least a few reasons why marriage might not be the best thing ever.

"Not to alarm you or anything, but I'm afraid I'm having a possible psychological emergency," I say to her as soon as she answers. "Can you meet me at Franco's?"

"Oh my God," she says. "Do *not* tell me you're moving out of the city."

"No, no."

"And it can't be that you have an incurable disease either. Please. Although if you do have an incurable disease, forget I said that insensitive thing."

"No. It's good news. I think. It might be. I mean, you'll tell me if it is. It's about marriage."

"Okay. Don't give me any more details until I see you. If this is about one of your forty-three dates suddenly proposing marriage, I'm going to need some liquid fortification."

I see her immediately upon arrival at Franco's. She's dressed in an electric-blue tunic and leggings, with her red hair up in a bun, waving her arms in the air and calling, "Yoo-hoo!" She's managed to get our favorite table over by the window.

The waiter comes over to take our order—mimosas and cranberry scones, our usual—and as soon as he's gone, I put my napkin in my lap and say, as casually as I can, "So . . . it's Judd. He proposed to me last night."

"Holy shit!" she says. "I'm going to need about four of these drinks!" She studies my face. "Hmm. Let me think. Not saying he's the candidate I would have expected, but still . . . a good guy. I like him. Dennis likes him. As much as Dennis likes anybody who's not working at the hospital. So what brought this on, if I may ask?"

I give her the rundown of Judd's proposal: friendship over romance, no jealousy or drama, partners forever, babies, security, on and on. "It actually made a little bit of sense at the time, but then I couldn't sleep all night, and now I've had two cups of coffee, and I'm hyperventilating, and I just feel . . . crazy. I asked him what about being in love, and *he* said that hadn't worked out so well for me in the past, and that life shouldn't look like a romantic comedy, and if this companionship we have isn't love, then he doesn't want to live in the world anymore. Or something. I don't know what to do." I'm so tired I just want to put my head down on the table and rest awhile. "So, that's crazy, isn't it? Nobody should get married for those reasons. Right? This is nuts."

Talia is trying to hide a smile.

"Well, for starters, he has a little bit of a point," she says. "Call it what you will—love or friendship is all semantics—but I think it's possible that this has been the path you two have been on for *years*. It's just taken some wide detours. Like the Steve Hanover detour, for instance." She leans closer. "Have you slept with him?"

"No! Judd's not—he's never acted like we were anything but pals."

"So you're saying you've *never* had sex with him. Never?"

"Never."

"Not even for boredom? Or availability? In all these years? Why not?"

"We haven't had sex because we . . . just haven't. It's not that kind of relationship."

She frowns. "Well, you're definitely going to want to make sure that part works before you sign on. He's not against it, is he? Oh my God, is he one of those guys who dates supermodels but actually he's really gay?"

"No. I know this dude. It's always been women for him."

"Okay, then. Well, you'll have sex with him, and then you'll know if you should marry him."

"It's probably going to be embarrassing. You know. Because we know each other so well . . . but haven't been attracted in that way. Last night he kissed me and all I could think of was that his nose hairs were tickling me. Is that a bad sign?"

"You just have to do a little mental adjustment. Move him out of the friend zone and into the hot boyfriend zone. It takes some imagination. Luckily, he's really handsome. And built. So it shouldn't be hard."

"Yeah. He is." I look down at my hands.

Talia sees my face and reaches over and touches my arm. "Honey. It's fine, trust me. Some love stories don't follow the usual trajectory. Also, for some people, sex isn't the main thing. Just jump his bones, and you'll see what's what."

"I guess so. I'm a little concerned, though. I

want it to be hot sex. Everybody wants a life with hot sex. What if he's not attracted to me?"

Talia says, "Of course he's attracted to you. He wouldn't be suggesting you get married if he wasn't attracted to you." She folds her napkin. "Maybe it's time for me to let you in on a little secret. I hate to break it to you, but sex is not all that hot once you've been married for a couple of years. And, also, really now, consider how little good sex you're actually getting in your life these days. You've been on *forty-three* of the craziest dates I've ever even heard of. Remember the guy who brought a rubber snake with him just to see if you were afraid of them? And the one who said he's on his tenth lifetime and that he thinks you were his naughty nursemaid back in the eighteen hundreds?"

"I know. It's been a bad run."

"Okay. So if you're asking, I think you should marry him," says Talia. "He'll be loyal to you for the rest of your life. He'll be like your own personal Saint Bernard. Unlike your stupid ex-husband, whom I would still like to go punch in the face, you can count on Judd."

We sit there in silence for a moment, me picturing all the tears I'd shed over Steve Hanover. And realizing how much I'd let that bad experience keep me from ever trusting again. Talia reaches over and takes my hand.

"I know, honey," she says. "Everything else

47

aside, Judd makes you laugh, he loves the same movies you do, and he loves your dog, *and*—I think this is huge—he won't bring rubber snakes around you or try to get you to quit your job so you can take care of his every need. You already like being with him, and that's worth everything. You're just having trouble letting your heart trust again. But Judd isn't going to break your heart, sweet pea. He wouldn't have asked you to marry him if he didn't truly want to spend his life with you. He's a grown-up, and he's dated enough that he knows what he wants, and it's not supermodels. It's *you*."

I wipe away a stray tear. "And I can have a baby," I say.

She sees my face. "And you can have a baby. Only don't move to New Jersey when you do, unless I'm going there, too."

It's a beautiful fall day, and so I walk through the park to my office. I need to pick up a file about the proposed book tour for one of my more controversial authors. But mostly I'm heading there because I love going in on Saturdays and working on my novel when it's just me. I can sit at my desk and type for hours without interruption; no Mr. Swanky to ask to go in and out, no coffee shop patrons talking out loud next to me. No people. Just me and my novel.

But then suddenly I find myself next to a

playground, which feels very auspicious, filled as it is with adorable little humans, all running and laughing and shouting.

And their parents—ah, the parents seem to me to be beautiful, stylish-looking, well-adjusted adults—both men and women—holding paper cups of coffee and talking and smiling.

I am going to belong here. I'm going to be one of those women pushing a stroller with a new baby in it, while my adorable little boy runs over to the climbing structure—he's just like his father, loves to climb. That's what I'll say to the mom next to me, as I take the baby out of her stroller, and I'll smile down at the baby as she curls her little fist around my finger and coos. And that night, Judd will give them a bath while I cook dinner, and then while he does the dishes (he loves to do dishes), I'll put the children to bed and sniff their sweet-smelling hair and nuzzle their soft little cheeks, and then I'll work on my novel, propped up on pillows on our bed, while Judd—well, I don't know what Judd is doing. Push-ups in the living room or something. Figuring out somebody's physical fitness plan.

Last year when my friend Sarah told me that she couldn't take her eyes off babies everywhere she went, I was like, "But why?" And she gave me a funny look and said, "Because they're so *cute*. And they're the future and the meaning of life, and I love the way their cheeks are so fat, and the way they have such goofy smiles, and . . ." And she went on for a lot longer than was absolutely necessary, listing every little thing about babies she could think of, even expounding about their toes and their eyelashes, until we reached the subway and I had to say good-bye to her. And when I got on the A train and settled into my seat, I felt like I'd just escaped from a very boring movie or a political rally by a not-very-galvanizing candidate.

But now. Now I get exactly what she was talking about. I really *could* get married to Judd. All I have to do is make a few minor, minor adjustments to my expectations, a few tweaks—and we could be just like these parents, right here in the park.

I watch for a few more delicious minutes, and then I tear myself away.

CHAPTER THREE

Tiller Publishing Company is located in a skyscraper-ish building overlooking the FDR Drive and the river. I work on the fourteenth floor, in an office that not only has a big window, but also came furnished with the most amazing pink brocade couch. Like a fainting couch. And bookshelves! Filled with books. There's a coffee room down the hall and a big conference room with a long walnut table and twelve chairs all lined up, where we have our weekly meetings under the watchful eye of Darla Chapman, the head of publicity.

I've been there ten years and am now second-in-command to Darla, which is why I get one of the bigger offices with a couch. As one of the more senior people there—let's face it, I'm something of a dowager here, rather like the Queen Mother—I'm assigned to mentor the younger publicists, who are always hanging around my office bringing me their questions and problems. That's who mostly sits on the fainting couch these days—people who want to know the best way to tell an author that we're probably not going to be able to send him on a thirty-city tour for a book about the life of an aquarium guppy. Publicity can be a grinding job when you're having to manage

51

authors' expectations all the time, dealing with a dwindling number of magazines and reviewers and book tours and budgets. You have to get good at smiling while you say, *I'm sorry, but that's probably not going to happen,* a lot.

As I'm walking down the hall to my office, I hear, "Oh, hey, Phronsie," from the office next to mine. My heart sinks. I won't be alone after all. It's the new guy—Adam Cunningham. He started two months ago, and he's a displaced surfer from California and has no background in marketing. He just likes to read, he told me, and somehow from that and the fact that his father is somebody important, he got an interview and talked his way into getting hired. Cutely strange-looking, with curly tangled hair that's blond on the top and various shades of dark as it gets closer to his scalp. Beach hair, he told me once. Can't do a thing to tame it.

"Hey, so what are you doing here on a Saturday?" he says, smiling. He wheels his chair back from his desk and puts his hands behind his head. He has large, white, even teeth. He's always smiling, flashing those teeth at me during staff meetings, mostly from across the conference room table. Sometimes he makes faces at me, like when I'm trying to be serious and he's trying to get me to laugh.

"Well," I say, "I've got an author who's stirring up some trouble, and I came to get the file so I can start figuring out what to do about her before Darla weighs in on the whole mess." I lean against his doorframe. "But you! You're new to the city. Aren't you required by law to be out there soaking up all the fun things?"

Go, go, go, I am thinking.

He shakes his head. "Actually," he says, clearing his throat, "I'm here because I'm trying to do extra work to suck up to Darla so she'll let me have some extra days off Thanksgiving week. My family is making a huge hairy deal of the fact that I'm missing out on my grandpa's birthday. I think he's turning one hundred and forty-two, and it's all hands on deck."

"Oh. Well, she'll probably say yes to that. She likes suck-ups."

Actually, Darla has told me she's had her doubts about whether he's going to work out, and that I should let her know if there are any red flags with him. I saw from the file that he's twenty-eight, but he seems younger than that. Maybe it's the surfer-boy persona. He's too . . . too . . . something for this job, Darla said. Too quirky maybe. "Keep an eye on him."

It's true: he is a little strange and offbeat. For instance, he has two little ceramic gnomes who sit on the windowsill like they're standing guard. Gnomeo and Juliet, he told me.

Gnomes.

And now that I look over, I see that they're not

on the windowsill anymore; they're sitting on his desk in a little platter of dirt, and Adam's holding a miniature tractor in his hand.

He sees me looking, but does he put it down and look appropriately embarrassed? He does not. He just smiles at me and shrugs. "Gnomes are creatures of the land," he says. "I found them a tractor, and so then I thought I'd bring them in some dirt to farm."

"Sure," I say.

Perhaps, as his official mentor here, I should tell him that a lot of people might not bring in their odd personal collections to the office right after being hired. Especially if they're trying to fit into the corporate culture. But why should I be the one to quash his originality? I find him kind of brave, to tell you the truth. He may even be a marketing genius, despite not having any training.

One day at a staff meeting, for instance, he made a pitch for having an author do a reading at the Stardust Diner, a New York landmark where the waiters and waitresses break into oldies songs while they serve the food. Seems the book was about rock 'n' roll, and why not have it celebrated right there, in between songs? That's what he said at the meeting. Everyone was silent, looking down at their hands, waiting to see what the correct response might be, as dictated by Darla's expression.

As I may have mentioned, I've worked there for ten years, longer than anyone, so I cleared my throat and said this sounded like a splendid, radical idea, but Darla frowned and said it wasn't "the kind of thing we do."

Yeah. So he probably won't be here long. He'll discover that we're way too boring for him, and that will lead him to remember that the Pacific Ocean really does have excellent waves, and he'll pack up his gnomes and their tractor and go back.

Right now he's smiling at me. He's got his feet propped up on his desk, like he's right at home. He's wearing brown leather sandals. "So to tell you the real truth, I'm actually hiding out here. My apartment is about the size of a hamster cage, and I have this roommate who rehearses operatic duets in the bathroom with his girl-friend. Something about tile providing the best acoustics. I don't know."

"And what? You don't think opera is more important than showers?"

"Of course. Opera is more important than *everything!* At least that's what I've learned. But every now and then a guy just wants to brush his teeth without the third act of *La Bohème* happening all around him." He laughs and picks up the gnome and says almost shyly, "Okay, so now can I tell you the real reason I'm here?"

He looks so adorably serious and vulnerable holding that silly little thing that I almost want to go over and hug him. "There's *another* real reason? Is this when you tell me you're planning a takeover of Tiller Publishing or something like that? Stealing trade secrets?"

He laughs. "Nope. The real thing is that I'm writing a novel," he says quietly, as if this is a shameful secret and he might be overheard. I know the feeling. "And there's something about the vibe here that makes it kind of a good place to work on it. I don't know, but I like working on it here."

I nod, and for some reason—though I haven't mentioned my novel to any other person there—I find myself telling him that that's why I'm there, too. Then I'm suddenly terrified he's going to suggest that we read each other's pages or form a writing group or something hideous like that, so when my cell phone rings, I'm relieved. It's Judd.

I shrug to signal to Adam that I have to take this.

"Hey, so how did Talia vote?" says Judd.

"She thinks we should do it," I tell him, walking back to my own office. I smile at Adam. "She says you'll be like a faithful Saint Bernard."

"Well," Judd says. "I'm not so sure that's *the* most flattering thing anybody's ever said about me. But does this mean what I think it means? We're a go?"

"Judd, nobody on earth uses that terminology

for marriage. You don't say 'we're a go.' And anyway, I've still got a coffee date with a firefighter tomorrow. Remember?"

"Of course I remember," Judd is saying. "The way I see it, we're just one heroic firefighter away from wrapping this up."

"'Wrapping this up'? Again, Judd, this is *not*—"

He laughs. "Okay, okay, so what do the romantic guys say?" He makes his voice go to what he considers romantic but isn't. "Let's see. I'm pining for your answer, sweet Phronsie. Your eyes are like molten pools of lava . . ."

"Stop it," I say. But I'm laughing. "So listen, I'm going to be home later. You want to come over? Have dinner? And maybe . . . ?"

"Oh. Can't," he says. "I forgot to tell you last night that I agreed to go camping overnight with Sean Johnson and his two boys. They're picking me up in a few minutes, as a matter of fact."

"Judd! Don't we have the thing with Russell and Sarah tomorrow evening?"

"We'll be back in the early afternoon. I think Sean just wants me to go so his kids won't outnumber him. And so I can fight off bears if need be."

"Oh," I say. "Well, all right. Have fun. Don't get eaten by bears. See you!"

"Enjoy your firefighter," he says. "Bye."

Enjoy your firefighter? *Enjoy your firefighter?*

I sit there, contemplating all the levels of that statement. Does he *really* mean it would be fine with him if I met someone else? He does. I think he really does. He'd be happy for me if I fell in love with someone else. He is absolutely non-possessive, non-jealous—and I'm sorry, but I hate that.

I turn on the computer and see an email Darla has written me about my problematic author. I have been in charge of Gabora Pierce-Anton for years now, one of the superstars of children's literature—only now she's written a book that is politically and racially insensitive, and it's up to me to deal with her.

We'll discuss this at the staff meeting on Monday, Darla wrote. *I have some disturbing news about her plans for a book tour.*

Great. Love disturbing news at a staff meeting! And really, really love that Darla won't tell me what it is in advance so I can prepare.

Adam shows up at my door. He's holding his backpack. "I'm taking off," he says. "See you Monday."

"Okay. Good to see you. Hope you get to enjoy the day."

But he doesn't move. Just stands there, smiling at me. "And hey—are you—I mean, did I discern from that phone call I was eavesdropping on . . . um . . . that you're getting married?"

"Am I?" I laugh, flustered. "I'm—well, I'm

thinking about it. This guy is my oldest friend from childhood, and he thinks we should get married because we're getting up there in years— haha—and sick of dating, and we didn't meet anybody else yet." I throw my hand out into the air in what is meant to be a cute, dramatic gesture of carefreeness, and instead hit it on the filing cabinet. I try to keep my expression neutral so he doesn't see that I'm in so much pain I'm seeing stars.

"Oh." Adam shifts the backpack to his other shoulder. "Is this one of those pact things? Like you get to a certain age and then if you haven't met someone else, you marry each other? Like some kind of romantic comedy thing."

"Well. No. Not really. He just sprung this on me last night. You know. The way one does. You know, the old 'let's get married because we haven't met anyone else' thing."

What is *wrong* with me? Why am I talking like this? Like none of this matters to me. When I know that if Judd wanted to cancel his camping trip and stay home and have sex with me—well, that might seal the deal right there. If it was good enough, I might even cancel the firefighter.

"Huh," he says. "Well. Congratulations? Maybe?"

"That sounds about right," I say. "Congratulations maybe."

"And hey, good luck with your novel."

"You too. Also, I guess it goes without saying that we won't talk about this, right?"

"Correct."

After he leaves, I turn on the computer and open the file with my novel and read the last chapter I wrote. It's blah. I crack my knuckles, then pack up my files having to do with my problem author, who I suspect is about to become The Bane of My Existence, and I make my way home.

I go out for coffee with the firefighter the next afternoon. I tell myself this is giving falling in love a chance to bat last. I even dress up for the occasion. My best blue silk shirt and really nice black pants with no rips in them. I straighten my hair with the flat iron, even.

I am halfway hoping he'll show up in his firefighter suit, smelling vaguely of smoke and heroism. I hope that he'll have ruddy skin and bloodshot eyes. He'll be tender and solicitous. He'll have recently saved a few children and some elderly people, and he'll be so humble about it that I'll have to drag the story out of him. I will be swept off my feet, and I'll have to explain to Judd that true love *does* exist after all, and I can't marry him.

I've written in my head a whole scenario of the dramatic life we'll have—he'll save lives and I'll quit my job and write full-time—and then when I walk into the Starbucks where we are to meet, there he is. I know him immediately. Unlike the rest of the people in there, he radiates confident heroism. It's crowded so I thread my way among the tables to get to him, a tall guy with dark brown hair, and he's reading the front section of the *Times* and looking like he could leap into action at any moment if, say, someone started choking on their latte. If the milk foamer behind the counter caught fire, he would be our man.

From his profile, I already know his name is Oliver Tansey, and although he is *not* wearing his firefighter suit, he looks like he might have just taken it off and put on civilian clothes. I start immediately wondering if I should keep my maiden name because Phronsie Tansey may just be the most absurd name ever.

When he sees me, he puts the paper down and uncrosses his legs and stands up with a slight smile on his face. He has lovely brown eyes. And one of those heroic clefts in his chin. A denim shirt. Jeans.

"Phronsie Linnelle?" he says.

"Oliver," I say. "How nice to meet you." My voice is only the slightest bit squeaky.

We shake hands, and he offers to go up to get us something to drink. "Just coffee," I say. "Venti caffè Americano with cream. No sugar. Thank you."

"Decaf?" he asks.

"Why? What have you heard?" I say. He blinks in surprise, not expecting me to be so humorous, I guess, and I say, "No. Regular. Sorry. I was joking."

"Oh," he says.

"I'll try to behave myself. But maybe ask for a double shot of espresso for my Americano. Unless you're already too frightened of me."

"No, no. Coming right up," he says. Eyes crinkle in a facsimile of a smile, but he looks a little frightened maybe. See? This is a problem I keep having. Men do not seem to appreciate my jokes. Maybe all the men with my kind of humor were snapped up long ago and aren't on dating sites.

As he makes his way to the counter, I sit down and watch him. He's slender and wiry. Nice butt. Probably excellent at leaping from burning buildings if that becomes necessary. He's probably the guy you want to hold the net while people jump. But maybe not the guy you want with you at the comedy club.

He comes back with our steaming cups and sits down across from me, smiling, and we start the business of oiling the creaky dating machinery. We both know the drill. The questions. What do you do when you have time off? Have you ever been married? Are you dating a lot these days? What's your idea of a really fun time? Mountains or seashore? Sleep late or get up early? Wine or beer? *Star Wars* or *Star Trek*?

When it's my turn to talk, I veer off script. I've been on too many dates, and so I decide not to do the usual patter anymore. I take a deep breath, lean forward, and smile, and I start expounding about my complete lack of knowledge about the *Stars*—both *Trek* and *Wars*. And telling him some vaguely adorable stories about New Hampshire farm life—the day the chicken got into the kitchen and challenged the cat to a duel, and that time that someone spiked the punch at the 4-H dance—and I'm just about to ask if he believes we're in for a zombie apocalypse sometime in the future, a fun question I just thought up, when suddenly his face changes. He puts down his cup of coffee and says to me in the voice a college admissions dean might use when he's seen your unfortunate transcript from junior year: "Okay, well. Thank you so much. It's been awfully nice to meet you."

"Um . . . yes," I say uncertainly. He's looking over my head at someone. I turn around, and sure enough, there's a woman who has just come in, and she's looking at him like she may have murder on her mind.

"You know her?" I say, swiveling back to look at his face, which has turned the color of one of the fires he's put out. "Should we be concerned?"

"Yes. No," he says. "I'm sorry. I didn't think she'd show up."

"She looks mad," I say. "Is she stalking you or something?"

"I'm sorry. I have to go," he says.

She's not making her way any closer; in fact, when I peek around, I see that she seems to have decided to lean against the window, studying him. She's wearing all black, and her blonde hair is slicked back. She looks like she might be packing heat, if you ask me.

"Why is she so angry? You're allowed to be here, aren't you?"

"Listen, I might have married her. By mistake. We went to Vegas . . . a group trip . . . I might have had too much to drink."

"You married someone by mistake?" I laugh, and then I see his face and see that it's not funny at all. He's married, and he's dating, and his wife is right here in the building with us. I make a quick executive decision to go to the restroom rather than walk past her, and when I come out, thank goodness they are both gone.

Date forty-four: Lying Cheating Firefighter. This is a first: the wife showing up. It will make a good report. I might have to lead with this when I write my story about online dating.

Chalk up another point for Judd.

CHAPTER FOUR

My stepmother calls me on the phone when I'm getting on the subway to go back home. "I'll have to call you back, Mags," I say, "I'm going underground," which sounds pleasantly ominous, I think.

I don't think she hears me because she says, "Oh, Phronsie, your father—" and then sure enough, the service goes off, and the subway is whisking me off in a subterranean rush. I turn my phone over and over in my hand, stare at the overhead ads for hair transplants, look at a woman across from me kissing a baby's head. I would like to kiss that baby's head myself.

Let's see. Your father . . . what? Your father . . . *is dead?* Your father . . . *loves you so much even though he never acts like it?* Your father . . . *is the hardest man I've ever had to deal with, and I wish he'd never left your mother and come back to me . . . ?*

Any of these feel possible.

I feel all the pricklings of dread coming over me. It's been a tough few years for him and for Maggie, worse than usual in a series of routine hard ones. This was the year they had to make the difficult decision to sell off a lot of the farmland.

Government subsidies had dried up, the price of milk had gone down, the prices for feed had skyrocketed. Add to that years of bad weather—springtime snowstorms, followed by floods and then hot, dry summers—so that when developers with money moved in closer, it was harder to say no. Friends were selling and moving away. My father clenched his jaw and said no way. He'd keep going.

And he had good reason, I suppose. The farm had been bought by his great-great-grandfather Hiram Linnelle and kept in the family for well over a century. We were all raised on the stories, told with a kind of stubborn New Hampshire pride. *We are the Linnelle family. We survive everything.* Each generation worked the land, growing corn, raising cows and chickens, facing hardships. Everybody succeeding at it, more or less, until my dad.

Yet for years, he kept plugging away at it because he had to. How would it look if *he* was the one who let it all go to hell? He invested in equipment. Added a little farm stand. He got up early in the mornings, he stayed out in the barn or in the fields until late at night; he worked alongside the field hands, planting and fertilizing and organizing. He was always tired, always sunburned, always halfway fed up, ready to explode. He had a way of taking off his hat and rubbing his hands across his hair real fast, like he had some demons in there he was trying to evict by force.

Did he ever stop and look around him and just appreciate the place? I don't know. After all, it's a beautiful piece of land, our farm, with its stately white clapboard farmhouse, and two ponds and a little stream that meanders along around the back. There are gigantic oak trees that shade the house and also hand out acorns like they're generous benefactors inviting the squirrels to a feast. And there are two barns, one of which my dad turned into a home for his mother, Bunny, after he married Maggie and needed the main house for our little family. The Bunny Barn sits next to the sunflower field, behind the main house, so for most of the year, a person can stand on tiptoes in our kitchen and see Bunny's windows and the little trellis that runs up the side of her barn, dotted with morning glories.

But life was never easy. As everyone kept explaining to me and Hendrix, this family enterprise was both our duty and our privilege. Not everyone had *land*. We were People of the Land. The lucky ones. Maggie, who was a teacher during the school year, spent her evenings doing the books and paying the bills, and her summers were devoted to selling sunflowers and corn and eggs at the farm stand. Hendrix and I worked there, too, from the time we were old enough to toddle out to people's cars with their bags of produce. Maggie and I made little dream catchers in the summer and we baked pies and fried up apple cider doughnuts in the fall. There was a field of Fraser firs that we sold at Christmas.

Hendrix and I were responsible for feeding chickens, collecting eggs, bringing cows in and out of the barn, taking care of the baby goats, and picking the flowers. Maggie cooked dinner every night, helped us with our homework, and invited our friends to come over for parties. There were hayrides and ice-skating parties, swimming in the pond, and sleeping out at night under the stars. Sort of your basic, idyllic, hardworking childhood home situation.

Or would have been—except that through it all, my father strode through our lives with a pained expression on his face, like there was some horrible secret wound festering in the center of him, something that was wrestling his soul to the ground. There was no joy in his face when he looked out at the farm, no moments when I'd be outside with him and simply feel he was taking it all in, basking in his love of the land.

He wasn't happy. My theory is that he never really wanted the farm life in the first place. Here he was, a cherished only child, a hardworking, innocent, chores-doing kid who won prizes in 4-H for the best goats, and so it was simply a given that he would take over the farm someday. No one ever asked him if that was what he wanted.

Because if he didn't take it, who else would keep it going? But then, just as that transfer was about to happen—right after he'd graduated from high school and was ready to take over a lot of the farm operations—he decided to just take a little tiny weekend off. A no-big-deal road trip with his buddy.

The two of them headed to a farmer's field outside of Woodstock, New York, for that little weekend concert, having no idea that his whole life was about to turn upside down.

He hadn't even arrived at the concert yet when—BAM!—he discovered Tenaj, followed by days of free love and freedom and music. And then, so quickly after that—another BAM! And another! Babies! Two of us!

I can just picture it. He must have been reeling from the shock of it all. Falling in love, veering off course from his intended life, and then coping with the shock of having Hendrix and me, born when he was just nineteen years old. It must have felt like he'd driven over a cliff. The country wedding, the baffled fury of his parents. All of it had to have roiled inside his good-boy soul, his stern New Hampshire upbringing.

It's tempting to believe the family myth that he spent the next few years trying to get back to the stability that had been the hallmark of his childhood. That he regretted what had happened.

But I'm the writer in the family, and I think differently.

I think he was madly in love with Tenaj. Sure, he had a girlfriend back home, but I think he loved my mom in a whole new heart-stopping way, and I think he embraced his new freedom-loving life as a hippie, playing the guitar and painting houses for a living. I can picture him coming home each day to his mystical little wife and his two conceived-in-love infants and thinking *this* was the way life should be. Free and easy, filled with music and sunshiny magic— nothing like the farm life with its demands and disappointments, its headaches and its hard work.

I'll bet he never wanted to go back.

But then, when Hendrix and I were nearly two, our grandfather died, and that's when my dad's dream world came crashing down. My grandmother needed him to come back home. Somebody had to run the farm. She wasn't one for letting it all go, selling it off to strangers, was she? No, she needed him back, and she made him return. And, just like that, it turned out the whole Woodstock thing had been a little detour after all. Like an extended vacation, the kind where you acquire a wife and a couple of kids without even meaning to.

He brought us back with him, all three of us, and according to stories I've heard, my mom lived with him and Bunny in the farmhouse and

70

worked alongside them at the little farm stand. Among the pies and the ears of corn, she offered her hippie-type artwork for sale: tie-dyed shirts, macramé, and the jewelry she made from objects she found.

Bunny has told me that Tenaj, bless her heart, tried hard to be accepted in town—but nobody was having it. Nobody liked her or made her feel welcome. She was a sweet little thing, my mama, and talented and creative, Bunny said, but they didn't want to buy her little found-object art. They didn't want to invite her to their coffee klatches. They were on the Maggie Team.

Bunny might have secretly been on the Maggie Team, too. Surely Tenaj wasn't what she had in mind for her son. Maggie was much more aligned with the values Bunny would have held. But Bunny told me once that her only concern was that her son be happy. If he had a wife and children, then she was determined to accept his choice, and look for the good in the situation. She was *not* going to risk losing her son and her grandchildren simply because he'd fallen in love with somebody who was different.

But the upstanding folks of Pemberton, New Hampshire, weren't quite as generous. The way they saw it, Maggie, as the beloved townie girlfriend, had the prior claim to Robert Linnelle—and there was no way they were going to accept this hippie girl as Robert's *wife*.

Anyway, after looking this interloper over carefully, they figured that Tenaj had clearly been a mistake. And too bad about us babies . . . such unfortunate carelessness. A nice hometown boy getting taken advantage of that way. He'd have to come to his senses, they said.

And so he capitulated, I think. It's a very old story: if I were writing the story of his life—and someday I just might—I'd say he gave up the woman he really loved as well as the dream of being free and living a life with art and music and tie-dye. Became the farmer everyone expected him to be.

No surprise, I suppose, that after a while my parents split up, and my mom took Hendrix and me back to Woodstock with her. Later, there was a big battle for him to get us back, but that's a whole other story.

Things went bad for my dad as the years went on. He developed an ulcer. A farmhand embezzled some money. Four calves mysteriously died. A flood made it impossible to plant one summer on the largest field, followed by two years of drought. The government subsidies stopped.

Then, after I'd been in New York for seven years, Bunny got sick and had to be moved to a memory care facility.

That spring a developer came up with a number that couldn't be turned away.

My father signed the papers. We all came home for that because Maggie said he needed us around him. To support him. Instead, he raged at us. Told us to go back to our "real lives." To forget where we came from. He said all kinds of things Maggie assured us he didn't mean. And since then, although he's apologized, he's grown quieter and more morose. His hands shake a little now, and he seems to be hitting the bourbon harder than I remembered.

Your father . . . your father . . .

Misses you.

Loves you.

Wishes he'd been better to you.

Wishes you'd never been born.

CHAPTER FIVE

I call Maggie back as soon as the subway comes above ground.

"Tell me," I say, all out of breath as soon as she answers. I brace myself in case hospitals are going to be involved. Or worse. "Is everything all right with Dad? What's going on?"

"Oh. Sorry. It's not such a big deal," she says. "I'm just . . . you know. Making mountains out of molehills, as your father would say." The big sigh that follows tells me everything I need to know. I get it. Nothing serious really, but just a lot of . . . stuff to worry about. There was an early morning frost a week or so ago, and my father slipped on some black ice and twisted his ankle. Nothing to be done for it, she says, just another one of those things involving my father refusing to take care of himself. He wouldn't go to the doctor, even though he can barely put any weight on that ankle. On and on. "It's the usual with him," she says. "I'm telling you so you can join with me worrying about gangrene setting in."

"Shall we schedule the fitting for the artificial limb yet?" I say, and she laughs.

I get my worrying talent from Maggie. We always joke that even though we're not genetically related, somehow I inherited her worry gene. She's the one I can call up when I have a scratchy throat and by the end of the call, we'll somehow have cheered ourselves up by imagining all the other diseases it probably *isn't*. Brain cancer, for instance.

"So, I'm hoping Thanksgiving will make your dad feel better," says Maggie now. "You know how he gets when the weather gets cold *anyway,* and he's taking it extra hard now that the construction has started. Every time they're out there pouring another damn foundation, he goes into one of his funks. But you kids will cheer him up."

Maggie knows perfectly well that I can do nothing that would cheer him up; that is, unless I had a personality transplant, time-traveled back to a past that never existed, and was a different sort of daughter, born to a different sort of mother. Didn't work in New York, hadn't ever dated the boys I dated, didn't marry the guy I could only stay married to for eight months. Had been content to sell sunflowers and milk cows and feed chickens and keep the accounts for the farm. Had married some local guy who liked to fix stuff. Had a bunch of blond-haired, trouble-free children who would call him Gramps and to whom he could teach a love of tractors.

A thought flickers in my head. If I married Judd, my father would be proud. Judd has always been somebody who could make him smile. My dad always said he was the best of the bunch of kids Hendrix and I ran around with. Strong, practical, and hardworking. Why couldn't I fall for a guy like that? That's what he wanted to know. Why did I always have to like the dangerous ones?

"Hey," I tell her. "I'm doing a little survey about love and marriage. Do you think marriage can work if the two people aren't in love but are just really, really good friends?"

"What are you even talking about with this? Are you thinking of getting married?"

"Just answer the question. I'm asking for a friend."

"I don't believe you. You're thinking about getting married again. Wait. This couldn't be *Judd,* could it?"

"I *said* I'm asking for a friend," I say.

"Did Judd propose? Oh my gosh. He did, didn't he?"

"Well, in a manner of speaking . . . yes, I guess you could call it that," I say. I've reached my apartment building by now, and I wave to Tobias, the doorman, and get in the elevator. (Judd isn't here to make me take the stairs.) "We're sort of sick of dating, and we *are* such good friends, and he said that he thinks romantic love is nothing more than a recipe for disaster, and that we'd be good parents, and we should move our lives along."

I unlock the door to my apartment, and Mr.

Swanky jumps down from the couch, where he's been snacking on my bedroom slipper. He comes over, wagging his tail, and he licks my hand, asking forgiveness. My slipper, he says, was asking for it.

"Let me get this straight. Is this just for having kids? Or do you love him?"

"Do I love him?" I say slowly. "That's the big question. I mean, we hang out together all the time. It's just not . . . what I would have expected, you know. No . . . *fireworks*. It's good. Comfortable. He says that's the best kind. So I guess my question is: Do *you* think this is the best kind?"

She takes a deep breath, and my heart clutches. We've never ventured into a discussion about the fireworks kind of love versus the comfortable kind, and I suddenly feel weird about asking her this question. I wish I could take it back. After all, poor Maggie is married to a man who broke her heart by cheating on her. Presumably he voted at one point for fireworks, with my mom, and then he had to change his mind.

And also, even *more* dangerous territory here: Maggie never got to have her own kids—a topic that I know instinctively is off-limits. I'm not sure if they ever tried and couldn't have a baby— or if Hendrix and I took up so much space in their lives that there was no room for a Robert/Maggie baby. Sometimes I wonder if she ever thinks she would have been better off if my dad had just stayed the hell in Woodstock, and then she could have found a different man and probably had her own kids, and she wouldn't have had all this heartache. It had to have occurred to her.

I feel awful bringing it all up.

She says, "Well, I'm not so sure you two *don't* love each other, to tell you the truth, and you just don't know it. Maybe you're expecting it to look different, so you don't recognize it."

"Yeah," I say. I go into the kitchen and open the refrigerator and decide finally on some tired mushrooms and peppers for dinner. "That's legit. I'm sure I've been contaminated by romantic comedies. I can't picture Judd chasing me through airports, trying to keep me from getting on a plane and flying away from him."

She laughs. "No, I suppose not. But, honey, we know he's from a good family, and we know he's not a serial killer, which was what I've been really worried about, you know. That you'd meet some New York guy that none of us had ever heard of, and that you'd fall in love before you realized his tendencies to murder people in their sleep, like what happened to a poor girl on the news—"

"Hey, I'm a better judge of character than that," I say, getting the paring knife out of the drawer. "I haven't even dated any serial killers. And I've been on forty-four dates in the last year."

"This is what keeps me up nights. Thinking of you on forty-four dates with strange men."

"You and me both," I say. I tuck the phone under my chin and cut the stems off the mushrooms. "Believe me, it wasn't all that much fun. I'm just coming home from the forty-fourth one now. With a New York City firefighter. Should have been great. But wasn't."

"And did you really think you and some anonymous firefighter were going to immediately find—what? Passion and sex? That's what you're going on these dates for?"

"Mags. Of course that's what I've been going on these dates for."

"But is that more important than a companion you feel good about? Somebody you know and trust to always have your best interests at heart? Maybe *you're* the one discounting love, did you ever think of that? Love is what you're left with when all that goes away."

"Okay, then, now we're getting somewhere," I say. "You're decidedly, then, in the category of marriage can work between friends. Yes?"

"Well, let me put it this way. I think it can work between you and Judd," she says. "I always thought he was such a nice kid. He'll take care of you, that's for sure."

"Ugh. I don't need taking care of," I say. Old argument.

"I know you don't. But you know what I mean.

79

Everyone needs taking care of. Can't you take it in that spirit instead of getting offended? He'll be your partner. He'll be there for you, as you young folks say."

And then speaking of people needing to be taken care of, I can hear my father's voice in the background. Asking her a question. She needs to get off the phone and make him some food. Or just pay him some attention.

Just like that, the call is over. My dad comes first. Always has, always will.

Before she hangs up, she whispers into the phone, "Just say yes. And bring him home for Thanksgiving. Promise me."

"Of course," I say.

As soon as I get off the phone, I call the memory care center at Hallowell House just because I miss my grandmother, and sometimes I can reach her if she's having a good day. She might be in the sunroom right now and they could take the phone over to her because she's doing fine, and why yes, the nurse on the floor will tell me, yes, she might like a call from home.

"It's your favorite granddaughter!" I always say when I get her.

And she used to say, "Ah, my darling. You aren't just my favorite granddaughter, you're my favorite human!"

But it's been months now since that has happened. Mostly, if I get her at all, she tries to talk to me and then gets frustrated that she can't make the words come out like she wants them to. There are long gaps. I don't mind the gaps; I'll wait patiently for however long it takes for her to get the words out. But it's hard on her. She was always so smart and so precise in her speech, so good at articulating her feelings, that I can't even imagine how tough it must be for her to be stuck inside her own head, with so many words already gone.

Sure enough, that's what today is like. They hand her the phone. I can hear her breathing, hear the little noises she makes.

"Bunny, I miss you!" I say. "And I have some news!" I always feel like I'm shouting when I talk to her, as if all it takes is a louder voice to reach her. "Judd and I—do you remember Judd?—he and I are going to *get married!* Isn't that wonderful?"

There's a little mewing sound. Like she's crying.

"Bunny? Are you *okay?* I'll come and see you at Thanksgiving! Like I always do! We'll have dinner in your dining room and then I'll bring you home with me to see the rest of the family! And that's when Judd and I are going to tell everyone!"

"Oh," she says. "Ohhhhh."

There's a muffled sound, the phone falling onto

81

her wheelchair perhaps. And then after a moment, someone must have come and picked it up. They hang it up again, and I'm there with only silence.

CHAPTER SIX

I was five years old the day I finally got up the nerve to ask my grandmother if my mama was dead. I whispered the question in case I wasn't allowed to know. Nobody ever mentioned my mama anymore.

But Bunny wasn't one of the people, like my daddy and Maggie, who had so many rules about stuff you could and couldn't talk about. She let me spend as much time in the Bunny Barn as I wanted to. I sat on her lap while she read me stories or put my hair in braids.

Her barn was my favorite place to be because it smelled good in there, like new sawdust and lemon Pledge and oatmeal cookies. There were shiny floors and new lights in the ceiling. Bunny had made the workmen put in a window seat, which she said was just for me, and we sewed a blue calico cushion. Hendrix was not allowed to go near the window seat, or so I told him; it was just for me and Bunny. He didn't want to anyway. Hendrix had the fields and the corncrib and the other barn. He had Daddy; I had Bunny.

In the barn, the air felt like it was soft and pink. My stomach didn't hurt when I was over there. At my house, just across the yard, the air sometimes felt all gray and cloudy, and it was hard to breathe sometimes.

When I asked her the question about Mama, she was ironing some shirts. I felt her stop and turn and look at me. She took a deep breath like something sad was stuck in her throat, and she said, "No, no, honey. Of course she's not dead. Your mama is just fine."

I said this next part very, very carefully, smoothing my dress over my knees, and not looking at her. "Then why doesn't she come and get me and Hendrix and take us home?"

"Well, sweetie, this is your real home now. With me and your daddy and Maggie."

"But she said she would come and get us."

She put the iron down on the ironing board and wiped her hands on her apron and looked at me. "The truth is that your mama and daddy both agreed you should live here with us. Your mama misses you, but she thinks this is the best place for you. And you and Hendrix will go and see her every summer when she doesn't have to work so hard and can put all her attention just on you."

I wasn't sure how far I could push this, but I took a chance and said to her, in a very low voice, so low that maybe she wouldn't hear it at all, "I heard him tell Maggie that my mama is a bad mother. He said she's a *witch*. The real kind."

"Oh," said Bunny, and the air around her head turned a different color. "Well, she's not a witch.

Your mama is a very nice person. She's just a little bit different from some other people, but that is not a bad thing, and your daddy knows that. He didn't mean that, I'm sure."

But Bunny hadn't been there the day when Daddy came to visit us at Mama's house and then made me and Hendrix go home with him. She didn't know how mad he was. He *did* mean it.

Usually when Daddy came to visit, it was kind of a nice time. He sat on the porch, and we sat on his lap, and he talked to Mama and to all her friends. Sometimes he played music with everybody. Sometimes he was having such a good time that I thought he might stay, but then he didn't. He always said he had to go back to the farm, but that he'd come again to see us.

But then one day he showed up when we were playing outside in the field next to our house, and it was the day after our birthday—we were four now!—and Hendrix and I wanted to run over to his truck to hug him. But as soon as he got out of his truck, I got scared because his face was hard and angry, and he didn't even say hello. He said, "What are you doing outside by yourselves?" in a voice that was so hot and mad it was like it burned a hole in the air.

"What's going on here?" he said. "You're filthy. And your hair is all tangled, and you're not wearing any clothes."

"I am wearing my queen dress," I said to him very sternly. "Maybe you can't see it."

He walked over in a very hard way and picked us up, and his belt buckle scratched my legs. I was squirming trying to get down, but he gripped us tighter, me in one arm and Hendrix in the other.

"You are wearing *underpants*," he said. "And it's dangerous out here by yourself!" He started walking with us toward the house. "Janet! Get out here! Damn it, Tenaj! Or whatever the hell you call yourself!"

When he got to the porch, he put us down *hard,* and he kept his hands on the tops of our heads so we couldn't run away.

We had never seen him like this. I was too shocked to move.

"What in the *world* is going on?" said my mama, and she came out on the porch. She was smiling at him, like she wasn't scared at all. "Robert, I had no idea you were coming! Come on inside and let me get you something to drink."

I had never seen her be worried about anything, and she didn't look worried then either. Everybody loved her. She wore long floaty dresses, and she was always finding things on the ground and then twisting them together or gluing them. She sold her artwork at fairs where she had a booth, and people would come up and buy them, and pet our dog, Starlight, and talk to me and Hendrix.

We were always picking up things to give to her—rocks and feathers, pieces of metal or glass, and she'd take them and study them closely, her head right next to ours, and she'd say in her soft, soft voice, "Wow! This is so far-out. Why, *thank you,* my lambs!" She had so many names for us: we were lambs and cakes and honey pies and darlings and sweet patooties. Hendrix could be Henny Penny and I was either Baby or Fwonzie because that's how Hendrix said my name. She was so very soft and calm. Her skin was warm and smooth, like she was made from sugar. Once we went to a fair and some man gave us cotton candy, and I thought, *This is what it's like to hug my mama.* She was cottony and sweet and soft, and her voice in my ear, singing us lullabies or telling us to go and play, was always like something that could make you fall asleep just from hearing it. She had all the colors around her. Like the piece of glass that hung in the front window and spun around, casting rainbows across the room, skittering across the wooden floor.

I knew she was going to make things better. She was even smiling at him so friendly-like; she would get him to be nice. "Robert? Honey? Let's all come in the house and talk."

But he was too mad. He started telling her that he had no idea she let us play outside unsupervised, and that we weren't safe here anymore, and we were dirty, and we weren't even dressed—

and she said we were perfectly happy and fine, but then, while she was talking, he put us in the truck and told us to stay there, and he went in the house with her. And Hendrix and I sat there very quietly, but the seat was hot on our bare legs, so after a while we got out of the truck and sat in the dirt instead. Hendrix was crying and he said we should run away, but I wasn't sure.

I told him Mama would make all the bad stuff go away. She had a lot of ways of making things okay, like when we were hungry or tired, or sick of having her work. She had cushions and pillows and good things to eat, and she could sit with us and comb our hair with her fingers. She was always talking to people and laughing.

"I don't like him," said Hendrix.

"Mama will fix him," I said. "He loves Mama. He was kissing Mama one time."

We watched the door. We could hear yelling voices inside, and Mama's friend who liked to make soup, Stony, came out of the house and got into his truck without even seeing us. When he backed up, Hendrix got up to go see where he was going, and then there was a loud scary sound from the truck stopping, and Stony jumped out to see if we were okay, and we were—we hadn't been anywhere near the back of the truck, but after that everything went even worse anyway. Suddenly our daddy was there waving his arms and shouting, and Mama came outside and tried to make him calm down, but nothing was going to calm my daddy. He was that mad and shouting. He said we could have been *killed*. A woman named Petal who lived next door came and took me and Hendrix to her house for a while and fed us some lunch, and then a little bit later when we were playing and drawing pictures, our daddy came over and said we were going home with him.

"Is Mama coming, too?" I asked him, and he said no.

I put my hands on my hips and I stared at him as hard as I could. "I want Mama to come!"

"You come with me and get in the truck," he said. "Now."

"Why are you taking us?" I yelled, and he said because it was best, that's why. I wanted to tell him that we were not dirty and that we loved to play outside in our underpants and that we didn't want to go with him, but he was not a man who listened. I said I wouldn't go with him until I said good-bye to our mama, but he didn't think that was a good idea either. I could tell he didn't know about good-byes being important—we even had good-bye songs we sang when somebody was leaving, even to go into town for a little while— and so I tried to tell him we had to sing the song, but he kept saying *no no no no no*. And so then I just ran around him and into the house and I hugged my mama, who was crying, and I was crying, and then he came in and said she had to get it together, so she started trying to act like everything was fine, which scared me even more because her voice was all different and didn't go with the look in her eyes at all, it was all caught up in her throat, and she said she'd see us soon, that everything was okay, and we would have lots of fun in New Hampshire. The way she said it meant that she was not happy at all and we were *not* going to have lots of fun in New Hampshire, whatever New Hampshire was. She said she was sorry about the yelling, but we had a nice daddy and a really nice grandma named Bunny, and to please tell Bunny hi. She gave me an extra-long hug and she whispered in my ear that she would come and get us, and then Daddy came over and said that was enough, and he took me out of my mama's arms and put my red shorts and purple T-shirt on me even though those two things did not go together at all, and he put Hendrix into some stupid-looking sailor suit that somebody had given him, and then he took us to the truck and put us inside once again. And we rode for a long, long time in the backseat of the truck with Daddy driving and driving and driving without even putting on the radio one time. I cried for a long time in the backseat. I was crying for so many things, but mostly for my mama sitting there in the house without me to collect rocks and sticks for her in the field and to hug her in the morning, which she needed me to do. Also, my daddy's truck smelled funny, like animals, and there were pieces of hay on the floor that stuck to our feet. It got dark, and headlights would come into the truck and ride along the ceiling and then disappear, and I stopped crying and watched them all very, very carefully and wouldn't let myself fall asleep like Hendrix did because I had to watch to see if Daddy was going to be dark green again, or if he would just be quiet brown worried Daddy, being lit up every now and then by the lights of the other cars coming toward us. Even then, I could see the muscle in his jaw working itself up and down, up and down.

And then when it seemed like we would be in the car forever, we suddenly turned and drove on something that sounded like little rocks being thrown everywhere, and I stood up on the seat so I could see, and in front of us there was a little house with the lights all on, and a porch with rocking chairs. And I saw an old woman coming out of the front door—Bunny, though I didn't remember her then—and she was shielding her eyes in the headlights until Daddy turned them off.

She came out to the truck and opened the back door just as Daddy was doing the same thing, and I heard her say, "So you got them. Are they okay?" He didn't say anything, but just handed us to her, one by one, and she hugged us and we buried our heads in her sweet-smelling neck and her fuzzy blue bathrobe, and there was pink and softness.

And that was how I met Bunny again, although she tells me that I lived there with her long ago when I was just a baby, and my mama and my daddy were both there in New Hampshire until my mama got mad and left.

"You don't remember that," she told me. "But I have loved you ever since you were just a little teeny tiny baby. Even before you were born, I loved you."

For a while after that, it was just us and Daddy and Bunny living in the farmhouse while we waited for what was going to happen next.

I thought that what we were waiting for was for my mama to come and say that she and Daddy loved each other, and that we would all live together. Or maybe she was just going to come and get us. She had *said* she would come, I told Hendrix. I said to him: we just have to wait. Daddy and Bunny seemed like they were waiting, too. We were all a houseful of sad people who weren't where we were supposed to be, and something had to happen, but nobody knew what it was going to be.

Hendrix and I had our own separate rooms during the waiting time, but every night, we made a nest of blankets on the floor in my bedroom, and we curled up together on the floor. Hendrix was a boy who cried a lot, and his nose was always running, and he jumped when there was a loud noise, and it was my job to keep reminding him that we were going to be okay and that Mama was coming.

I told him stories at night in the dark, about Mama coming back, and Daddy loving her and laughing. I said that everybody loved Mama so much, and Daddy was just upset for now, but he would remember soon and then they would be together again. And he would laugh and be regular nice Daddy again.

But then before Mama could get there, this woman Maggie started coming over, which Bunny said was such a good thing for everybody, especially Daddy because they had been boyfriend and girlfriend a long time ago, she said, and it was nice that Maggie was going to love him again.

"And you are going to love her, too, because everybody loves Maggie!" Bunny said.

I did not love Maggie at first. She talked baby talk to Hendrix and me, even though we were almost five by then. And she thought a lot of things were important—like wearing your hair in a tight high ponytail and keeping your fingernails clean. Fingernails! I couldn't believe it. Fingernails were for digging in the dirt.

But then I saw that Maggie coming over had been what we were waiting for that whole time.

Not Mama at all. And now it had happened. When Maggie came over, Daddy smiled a lot and wore his hair slicked back. Sometimes we all even danced in the living room, and Daddy acted silly and would pick us up and spin us around. I still wanted Mama, but I also thought it was kind of good the way he was when Maggie was there. He didn't look like somebody who had a bad stomachache all the time.

And then one day they sat us down and told us they were going to get married. Everybody had on big smiles, and Maggie hugged us, and Daddy said there was going to be a wedding in the garden. Maggie said we'd get to wear fancy clothes, which Hendrix did not want to wear, but I did. I said I wanted to wear a pink shiny dress with lace and a twirly skirt, like I had seen on television one time. Maggie said that would be fine, and also she would find some little white patent leather shoes if I wanted, too. Which I most certainly did.

The wedding was on a hot, sunny day, and lots of people came, and Hendrix and I did the Chicken Dance, and people laughed and clapped for us and ate a lot of food and said it was so great that now we had a new mom.

I think that's when it hit me what had just happened. One minute I was flapping around like a chicken, and then I heard the news that Maggie was now my new mom, and I started to get that funny feeling again. Like I wasn't going to get back to where I was supposed to be.

Maggie was tall and had bony elbows and knees, and there was never a spot on her lap that felt right. And she was always working, working, working, always rushing—washing clothes, hanging them out on the line, collecting the eggs, planting flowers, working at the farm stand, cooking dinner, sweeping, dusting, setting the table, washing the dishes, giving me and Hendrix baths. She had strong, hard hands and a look on her face like she meant business. Things had to be done. She hummed while she worked, a sound that reminded me of a bunch of bees. I didn't like bees.

"I like things to be clean and neat around here," she said. "We're going to spiff ourselves up."

That was what we did all the time: we spiffed ourselves up.

And even if you saw a feather on the ground, or a piece of glass, you shouldn't pick it up, because there was nobody who would say, *Wow! That's so far-out!*

Nobody to turn it into a piece of art.

Here, you didn't touch stuff on the ground because it was dirty, and it was trash.

In the fall, when Maggie took us to register for kindergarten, she told the lady at the desk that our names were Frances and Henry. "Those are better names because people *know* those names already," she explained to us. "When you're Frances and Henry, you'll fit in better here. And you want to fit in, don't you?"

She bought us little toy license plates for our bikes with those names on them, just to prove her point. "See? They don't even have your other names on the license plates in the store."

So the day I asked Bunny if my mama was dead and she said she wasn't, I said, "Well then, will you take me to see her?"

She got very quiet, like for a minute she was thinking of saying yes, but then instead of yes, she said in a bright, almost crazy voice, "I have a good idea. Do you want to make a picture about how much you love her?"

"That is not a good idea," I said. "Because how is she going to see the picture when she isn't here?" I worried that Bunny might be a little bit silly.

"Maybe you could just look at the picture yourself, and that could remind you of how much she loves you."

"No," I said patiently. I was going to have to explain everything to my grandmother. She didn't know *anything*. Finally I said, "But you know what *would* work? I could make a little magic tube that I can talk into and she'll hear me when I talk, and I can tell her stuff whenever I want."

Bunny laughed and shrugged her shoulders.

"Okay," she said. "If that's what you want to do."

So we made a tube from the toilet paper cardboard thing, and I decorated it with stick-on stars that Bunny had in her kitchen drawer, and she wrote my name and then I made her write my mama's name: "Tenaj." And then I drew hearts and purple flowers and a big yellow star.

"So I'll talk to my mama right through here where this star is, and she can hear everything I say," I explained.

"Okay," said Bunny. "I think this is a brilliant idea."

"It's magic, that's why," I said.

After that, I would get under my bed and talk to Mama. I told her everything— that Hendrix and I were fine, and that we loved her, and she should come and get us. Maybe she should come in the night and we could sneak out and see her, and then she could take us back to her house. We could bake bread again, and I could smear the butter on it, like I used to do, and she could laugh and tell me again that I was her favorite butter-spreader because I did it just right, putting on lots and lots of butter. And then we could make necklaces out of the sparkly pieces of rocks that we glued together.

I waited. But even though cars would sometimes go by in the night, and I'd hear the hum of their engines from far down the road, Mama never came back for me.

CHAPTER SEVEN

At precisely four o'clock that Sunday, Judd and I are standing on the stoop at our friends Russell and Sarah's Brooklyn brownstone, holding appetizers and a bottle of wine, and we are looking around at Brooklyn the way Manhattanites always look at Brooklyn: like we've landed where dreams go to die.

The air even seems odd here, what with trees and bushes everywhere. Not enough truck exhaust. No screeching of brakes or sirens. And the sidewalks are filled with families with strollers, with older kids zooming along next to them on scooters.

"Are we going to have to move to Brooklyn, too, once we decide to have kids?" Judd says. "I mean, I think the leaves are a nice touch—but it's a hell of a long subway ride back to Manhattan."

"I think it's the law," I tell him. "You get to be a Manhattanite up until you decide to procreate—and then you're required to move to either Brooklyn or New Jersey. But we'll resist. We have perfectly reasonable apartments, and we just have to decide which one of them we're going to live in."

"Scofflaws," he says. "I like that about us."

I'm a little nostalgic for the days when all

our friends lived in Manhattan. Before a few of them took off for New Jersey, there were eight of us, four couples, who got together at least twice a month to hang out. We went to avant-garde Broadway shows, to microbreweries in Red Hook, to the Rockaways for suntans and Mexican food on the beach. Once we took a road trip and got rooms at a funky hotel in Niagara Falls. It had been lovely—even though now that I'm really remembering it, also awkward as hell. They were all in love, having sex like rabbits, and I was there with Judd, who was just a friend. They'd go off to bed, and Judd and I would sit in the bar and nurse our martinis and watch sports.

He presses the buzzer for 3B, and says to me in a low voice, "Here's to a new baby in the world. Let's just hope Russell and Sarah haven't killed each other by now."

"It didn't sound good the last time I talked to her," I say. "He's against disposable diapers and pacifiers."

"And he says she's gone psycho on him," Judd says.

"I'm not sure Russell can be domesticated."

"We'll do this so much better," he says. He smiles, but I notice he doesn't lean over and kiss me when he says it. It's the kind of remark a person would expect to be accompanied by a kiss on the forehead at the very least.

We get buzzed in, and we go tromping up the

stairs to the third floor. Judging from the number of strollers and car seats in the hallway—as well as the noise from every apartment we pass on our way up—it's clear that the residents of this Brooklyn apartment building have very healthy reproductive lives.

"It's humbling when you see this many strollers in one place," says Judd. "Look at this one. A jogging stroller! I think we should get one of these, so we can run in the park with the baby."

"You know what I picture? We'll be in the park, and you'll take the baby for a run with the stroller while I sit on a bench and work on my novel and wait for the two of you to come back."

"Your novel?" he says. "That's what you think of?" He gives me a little sock in the arm. "Since when is that the most important thing in your life?"

"Judd, it's very important. I work on it all the time."

"Okay, okay," he says. "So you're writing it. But when are you going to be finished with it?"

"Look, I'm making progress, okay? I do have a full-time job, you know, and when I get home, I'm tired. Also, it's hard, and I don't have anybody to read it."

"Good Lord, all these excuses," he says and laughs.

I notice he doesn't offer to read it. Which is fine. I know it's not good—not yet. I'm stuck, is the truth of it. The woman in my novel comes home from work one day and finds her husband in bed with someone else, and I want it to be a funny story—even uplifting—but it just keeps drifting over into being morose. I gave this woman a great job and jokey best friends, and I even provided her a wonderful renovated kitchen, but she still just cries. The last dozen pages are her complaining to a psychiatrist that she feels like she doesn't believe in love anymore.

She and I share so many losses, all from just one man leaving. Trust me; I see what I'm doing here.

Now I look over at Judd, doing his little going-upstairs dance, jabbing at the air like he's in an imaginary boxing match.

Okay, I tell myself, so what if he never reads my pages or understands what I'm trying to achieve? He'll cheer me on in his own absent way. And the best part is that I will never be in danger of falling madly in love with him and getting hurt. I won't ever be writing a novel about *him*. It just won't happen. My heart will be so perfectly safe.

I reach over and touch him on the arm, and he turns and smiles at me.

The noise level starts to increase the closer we get to their door, which is thrown open by Russell. He's wearing a screaming baby tied to his chest and looking like an extra in *Night of the Living*

Dead, except that his hair is perfectly combed and gelled. His hair is sort of his trademark.

The apartment is a disaster zone, which is so unlike Sarah's usual way. I mean, to be honest, before Russell came along—sure, there was clutter. But it was fun clutter, *Sex and the City* kind of clutter: wineglasses on the coffee table, copies of *Cosmopolitan* magazine, high heels artlessly kicked off and landing in two different directions, some lacy laundry strewn about here and there. Even after she and Russell got married, they had sort of a modern hip/cool couples clutter thing going: their sweaters and hoodies resting adorably together on the ottoman, like the laundry itself was also in a relationship.

But *this*. Overturned baby bottles. Spilled milk. It's the smell of we're-in-over-our-heads and why-didn't-anyone-warn-us, of tears and sleeplessness. There are whiffs of recrimination and regret.

I feel slightly dizzy.

Sarah appears just then, and she has the look of a vampire who has been without blood for too long a time. Her eyes are rimmed with red. I want to reassure her that this is what life is all about, and that it will get so much better in time, but I'm afraid she'll pull a tire iron out from underneath the pile of newspapers and kill me with it.

I don't even get to admire the baby, because as soon as I get my coat off, Sarah bursts into tears and drags me into the bedroom, where she tells me that Russell is the most useless human ever to be drawing breath and that she has made a terrible mistake in marrying him. He doesn't even know how to operate the washing machine. He says he needs creative stimulation. He wonders when they'll have sex again. She sits down on the bed and says, "Why did you guys let me marry him?"

I don't think it would be a good idea to remind her that Russell is a musician and an artist, and she fell so hard in love with him that she didn't notice that he can't even tie his shoes properly. He's not a bad guy; he's just a bit clueless about regular life things except for hair gel. He is not the person who is going to turn into someone helpful just because he succeeded at a little thing like reproduction.

But I say none of that. Marriage is complex. We can't solve Russell right now. Instead, I say, "Wait a second." I hold up my hand. "Wait, wait, wait. How long since you've had any sleep?"

She stares at me.

"Sleep," I say. "S-L-E-E-P."

"I-I don't know."

"You don't even remember sleep, do you? You need to get in your bed. Right now. Get in your bed."

"I can't. I'm having a party."

"Judd and I don't qualify as a party. Take off your clothes and get in your bed, and I'm going to turn out the light, and you are going to sleep."

"The baby will get hungry."

"That's why God invented bottles."

"It's not that easy—the milk—"

"It is that easy." (I don't know what I'm talking about, of course.) "You need sleep. I'm counting to twenty and then I'm turning out the light."

She finally gets in bed, and I cover her up with the blankets.

"Stay with me," she says in a tiny little voice. "Lie down beside me."

"Okay," I say, and I kick off my shoes and get up on the bed next to her. "Your baby is really very cute," I say. Actually, I haven't gotten a good look at the baby, because she's screaming so much, and Russell is walking back and forth with her like he's in a walking road race.

"I know. I like to just stare at her."

"Maybe that's why you're so tired. You're staring at the baby instead of sleeping."

"Maybe."

We lie there for a while. There's finally silence from the living room, thank goodness. Maybe Sarah can really go to sleep.

"She's quiet," I say.

"I still hate Russell, you know."

"I know. Can I ask you one little thing before you go to sleep?"

"Yeah." Her voice is muffled in the pillow.

"Do you think I should marry Judd, even though we're just friends?"

She lifts her head up and looks at me. "Seriously? Does he want to?"

"Yeah. He thinks best friends might have an easier time with this parenting business. He thinks romantic love is a hoax."

"Hmm," she says. "I may not be psychiatrically intact enough to weigh in on this, but I say go for it. I mean, he knows how to do laundry at least."

"He doesn't separate the whites from the darks."

"Phronsie. Shut the hell up and marry that dude. He knows where the washing machine *is*, at least." Then she falls into sleep so deep it may actually be classifiable as a coma. I tiptoe out.

When I go back into the living room, Judd is wearing the baby on his chest. He looks like a natural. I admit it: there's something so sweet about a big, muscular, handsome guy all dressed up in a baby. He grins at me and points to himself. Willoughby has gone to sleep. Russell is also passed out on the couch, snoring with his mouth open and one arm flung out. His hair still looks good, I notice. I go into the kitchen and wash the dishes and wipe off the counters. I boil water for pasta and cook the lasagna Sarah was going to make, and then I fry up some ground beef and onion and add tomato sauce to it, and then I look in the fridge for mozzarella and ricotta cheese, but there isn't any, so I tell Judd I need to go out to the bodega at the corner to buy some. He points to the sleeping baby on his chest and says, "I'll go to the store. You gotta have you some of this lusciousness."

I want to protest because she's so comfortable, and also what if she looks at me and screams and then we will all know that I'd be a terrible mother, but he's already removing her and is tying her onto the front of me. She makes sweet little sounds as she's being transferred. Grunts or breathing sounds or something, and then, to my astonishment, she makes little fists and stretches and pooches out her lips as she settles against me. Who knew newborns know how to make a fist? This one probably learned it from Sarah.

As soon as he closes the front door, I am seized with a fit of terror. This little face, this weight against my chest, the slight mewing noises she makes as she sleeps. What if she stops breathing? It's like half of my whole body just wants to curl around her, and the other half wants to run after Judd and give her back to him. She likes him, after all.

The whole time he's gone, I walk around the apartment, trying to calm myself down by humming little tunes at her. And then the worst happens: she wakes and looks at me with one eye, and it hits her that she's been handed to an incompetent buffoon. She screws her little red face up, and the only way I can keep her from screaming is by walking in circles at a velocity of five miles per hour and singing "Love Has No Pride," which is the only song now that I can remember the words to.

By the time Judd gets back, she has opened her eyes and is beginning to wave her fists around in the air. When he comes over and unties her and puts her back on his chest and she goes right back to sleep, I think I *could* marry him. Obviously he was issued some genetic material for parenting, like a set of instructions, that I maybe didn't get. Maybe she likes his pheromones. A lot of ladies seem to. In our marriage, he can be in charge of calming the babies down, and I can do laundry. He can do dishes. I'll tell it bedtime stories; he can teach it calisthenics.

I watch him for the rest of the evening. He's so solicitous and kind. Funny. We sit at the table with Russell and eat the lasagna. Sarah sleeps and sleeps. Judd wears the baby all through dinner, and he looks down at her with such twinkling eyes. He actually knows how to eat lasagna without even dropping one bit of cheese on the baby's head.

I drink a glass of wine and feel bravery coursing through my veins. Russell is making a joke about birth being the most intense biology lesson imaginable, and Judd catches my eye and winks at me. A long, slow wink.

Oh my goodness, oh my goodness. I feel that wink viscerally; it actually sets off a flutter somewhere deep inside me. The first flutter caused by Judd, and I suddenly know that I really am going to do it. I am going to marry him.

I wonder if I should tell him just yet. But the truth is, it feels like it's a fun little secret that only I know. And if I tell him, and he reacts by talking about something ordinary, if he doesn't sweep me up in his arms and start kissing me, if it turns out that *he* doesn't feel the same kind of flutter—well, I can't chance it. I don't want to have to get mad at him—and then feel guilty about getting mad at him, because romance and kissing are not part of our deal and I know that. Deep down, I know that.

Walking home, I'm tense. We talk about how adorable Willoughby is, and how stunningly clueless Russell is, and how sad it is that Sarah can't get any sleep. We speculate about how long the marriage has, and whether it's more likely to end in murder or divorce.

"You know," he says, "I was thinking I could probably go over after work a couple of days a week and help them out."

See? That is just like him: coming up with a concrete way he can help. This is what is so wonderful about him: he's the first guy on the scene to help people move, debug their computers, tune their cars even. Go camping with them and their children so that bears won't eat the kids. He's kind of amazing.

"Also," I say, "you could check the premises for murder weapons."

"And that," he says and smiles.

I reach over and take his hand. "Can I tell you something kind of huge?"

"Yes."

"I think we—I mean, I want to—" I close my eyes and start flapping my hands. "Back up. I'm hyperventilating."

He stops walking, as if that's what I meant by *back up*. He's looking at me funny.

"This is hard," I say.

"It is hard, isn't it? Same thing I realized when I was about to say what I think you might be about to say."

"You know what I'm going to say?"

He puts his hands in his pockets. "You're going to say you're going to marry me, right?"

"Right."

"So . . . good," he says. He smiles. "Nice."

"I am going to pretend you said, 'Oh, my dear, oh the wonderful love of my life, please let me take you upstairs and ravish you!' "

He blinks. "Okayyy. Oh, my dear, oh the wonderful love of my life, please let me take you upstairs and ravish you!"

And this is the moment his phone rings. I shake my head no, but it's useless: he gives me a regretful look and answers the phone. It's one of those calls that I think of as his "yo, bro" kind of interchanges. There's a lot of those. This one is one of his trainers, Mercer, whom I can hear bleating into the phone, "Yo, bro, there's a situation here, you know? Down at the gym?"

Judd paces around, fielding talk of keys gone missing, and a special elite client who's training for a triathlon and . . . blah blah blah. I see the way this one is going. It's freaking Sunday night, but that's the way Judd's gym operates. They do anything for their clients. He says he'll come down and unlock the place. Of course he does.

When he clicks the phone off, he turns and looks at me.

"I gotta go," he says.

"Go," I say. "It's fine."

He looks at me incredulously. "Wait a second. Are you *mad?* You're actually mad."

"I'm not exactly *mad,* but I'm disappointed. We were having a momentous *thing* between us just now, and you had to go answer the phone, and now you're leaving."

He looks exasperated. "I've got to go unlock the gym. It's my *work.*"

"It's the *weekend,* Judd. Sunday night! The gym is closed. And it's going to take you nearly an hour to get all the way downtown with the subways on weekend schedule. And then an hour back. It's like I'm not your priority. This. Us."

He stands there, running his hands through his hair, shifting his weight from one foot to the other. "Phronz. Listen. I thought the plan was that things weren't going to change between us just because we're going to be married. The idea is that we're still going to be each other's best friends, and—call me crazy, but in *my* book, best friends support each other's business, am I right? I gotta just go do this one thing. Okay? Am I going to be in trouble now every time I need to work?"

I put my hands on my hips. We're just like any couple, arguing in the street. "Judd, don't you want to have sex with me?"

He runs his hands through his hair, rolls his eyes. "Of course I do. I'm a guy. Also, I'm going to marry you."

"Then why doesn't it happen?"

He looks up at the sky beseechingly. "Phronsie? Seriously? Come on," he says. "Let me go help out this guy. We'll get to this sex stuff, you know we will, and it will be amazing. I promise you amazingness. I'll fall at your feet. I'll bring you red roses. Whatever you think you need."

"Just . . . go," I say. "Go. Do it."

"Oh!" he says. "I almost forgot. I have something for you."

He digs in his pocket and pulls out a bright green twist tie.

"I bought a new loaf of bread, so I have a

brand-new ring for you. Wove it into a circle and everything. Here." He grins, bounces up on his toes. Does a few boxing moves.

Oh my God. He's so impossible. Or maybe it's me. Maybe what I'm signing on for *isn't* going to look like love. Why do I even expect that he'll suddenly change and want to be romantic?

"Could our lives *not* be a comedy routine?" I say. "Could we just pretend to be normal?"

"This is normal. This is the *real* way love should be!" He blows me a kiss and turns and walks back down the street, back to the subway. He calls me later to say he's stuck at the gym fixing a plumbing issue, and now he's going out for a much-needed beer with Mercer.

"You're not still ticked off at me, are you?" he says, and I sigh and say no. Because there's no point being mad. He's my best friend. And if it was unthinkable that I would have been mad at him last week for going out for a beer after work, then I shouldn't be mad at him now just because of a little thing like we're going to get married.

Mr. Swanky thinks that if I want romance, maybe I should watch *Sleepless in Seattle* for the millionth time, and so that's what I do. Just in case Judd comes over after having a beer with Mercer, though, I take a nice bubble bath and get myself cleaned up a bit.

Just in case it's going to be our first time.

CHAPTER EIGHT

The year after my dad and Maggie got married, when I was six years old, our cat, Mama Kitty, died. She was just a barn cat—not particularly friendly or anything, didn't even have a real name so she was definitely not a pet—but I came upon her dead body one summer afternoon out by the barn, next to a raspberry bush, and when I saw her there, so still and quiet for the first time ever, with the green-headed flies buzzing around her matted fur, I just sat down on the hard dirt and stared.

The flowers were all in bloom, and it was a yellow-green afternoon, with the breeze blowing my hair. I felt like I could hear everything that the whole sky was saying. Birds were making a big racket, and I heard Maggie call me in for lunch. There was the sound of the tractor down by the cornfield, and an airplane flew overhead, leaving a long, lazy white trail.

But I just sat there.

The sky said, *Your mama is dead, too, little child. You know she is.*

"Bunny said my mama is not dead," I said out loud.

A fly landed on Mama Kitty's belly and walked up to her mouth. The fly said, *Bunny doesn't*

know. If your mama was alive, why didn't she ever come see you?

The white trail from the airplane whispered as it was fading from view, turning back into the blue, *You know she would have called you if she was alive. You know she would have. She said she was going to come get you back.*

I sat there for a very, very long time. Maggie stopped calling my name after a while, and then started back up again. I lay down in the grass next to Mama Kitty, and I told Mama Kitty that I wished she hadn't always run away whenever I would try to pet her, and also that I had loved her kittens, and pretty soon I started to cry.

And that's what was going on when Bunny came and found me.

"Here you are!" she said. "You should get out of the dirt. Maggie's been looking for you for lunch, you know. Didn't you hear her calling?" And then she said, "Ohhhh. Are you *crying?* What's the matter, child?"

I couldn't say what was the real trouble, so I said I was sad about Mama Kitty, and Bunny said she understood about that. She hugged me and we walked back to the house, and later we all had a little funeral and buried Mama Kitty in the yard, and Bunny said nice things about her, and so did I and so did Maggie. But that night, after we lowered her into the hole in the ground, my stomach started hurting, and it just kept on

rumbling and hurting and keeping me awake at night.

It was the kind of stomachache that a little girl would get when her mother was dead, I thought.

Everything was terrible for days. I got in a fight with Hendrix and got sent to my room. I dumped out four puzzles onto the floor and got sent to my room. I said I wouldn't go get eggs from the henhouse and got sent to my room. Every night I had to eat dinner up there all by myself as a punishment, and instead of eating, I threw my dinner out of the window and watched as it landed on the grass and the dogs ate it.

Finally, Bunny said I should come and stay with her for a little bit.

"What's going on with you?" she said.

And so I told her. "My mama is dead, and that's why she doesn't come to see me."

To my surprise, she didn't try to tell me that Mama was perfectly fine and alive somewhere like she did the year before. Instead, she said, "We are going to fix this, little one," and she clamped down her mouth and narrowed her eyes the way she did sometimes when she was having a big think.

And then the very next week, Bunny told the rest of the family that she and I were going to visit her sister Alfreda, who lived in Pennsylvania, and who needed company in the nursing home. Hendrix couldn't go, she told them, because only one child at a time was allowed to visit patients there, and she had no one to watch him when I was visiting, and no one to watch me when it was his turn.

That next Saturday, which was a very hot day in July, we got in the car, and we drove for a long time, and then when we were miles away from home, Bunny said to me, "We're not going to go see my sister, you know. We're going to Woodstock, and we're going to look for your mama. And this is going to be just our secret, and we aren't going to tell anybody else what we did."

I thought the top of my head was going to come right off. I grabbed on to Bunny's arm, which made the car swerve all over the road. And I was laughing and kicking my legs against the dashboard, and I wanted to jump out of the car and run around in a circle I was so excited.

We had a map that was spread out on the front seat, which Bunny would pull over to look at from time to time. I was nearly out of my mind with excitement and questions, bouncing up and down on the seat and singing all the songs I knew, until Bunny said maybe I should try to take a rest. I looked out the window at all the fields flying past, then at the mountains as we turned onto the state highways. Then I sang more songs.

When we stopped for lunch and ice cream, Bunny cleared her throat and said my mother might not be like I remembered her. It had been a long time, and she hadn't been able to reach her to tell her we were coming.

"Things are going to be fine," I said and wiped my sticky hands on my shirt. And then I got up and spun around and around, mostly because I didn't want to see Bunny's face anymore. She had started out on this trip so happy, and it seemed like the closer we got to my mom, the more worried she looked.

My mama was going to be so happy to see me. I said that over and over again so Bunny wouldn't be scared.

When we pulled up to the old house, I jumped out of the car and ran up the steps to the front porch, even though Bunny and I had discussed this. How we would go carefully and easily up to the door. We didn't know for sure who lived there, she said, so we would knock politely on the door and wait to see who came.

But it was Mama who came to the door. Mama! I started to cry the minute I saw her. I felt like a balloon that had just lost all its air. She was standing at the old white screen door with the torn screen, and she opened it, and her face was lit up like the moon. All the colors dancing all around her. She was wearing a shirt that was soft and blue and filmy with little shiny things on it and her old blue-jean shorts, the ones she was always sewing stuff on. And she didn't say a word; she just picked me up and held me close to her, and we stood that way until I could hardly breathe anymore. She smelled just the way she used to smell, like something sweet. Like the earth and soap.

There was music playing inside the house and people talking, and Mama was saying my name over and over.

"Tenaj," Bunny said from behind us. "Honey, it is so good to see you!" And Mama let me go then, but I kept both my arms around her waist, and the two of us moved over to be hugged by Bunny, too. Bunny had set down a big bag that she'd brought, and the three of us just stood there together like we were one person with six legs and six arms all mashed in together.

"Look at my baby!" Mama said. "Oh my goodness! Look at you! You're six years old, and you're so grown up now!" Her face changed suddenly, and she looked at Bunny, like she was scared. "But where is my Hendrix?"

"He's at home, honey. He's fine," said Bunny. "I just brought Phronsie this time. She's been wanting to see you so much, and I thought she and I could get away with a little secret visit."

"Hendrix would tell *everything* to *everybody,*" I explained. "He's a big blabbermouth."

"Is he?" said Mama. She was smiling and wiping away tears. "Oh, come in, come in. I can't believe you're here. You're really here!"

Then we went inside, and I remembered the place like it was part of my bones. It was like my brain kept going *click, click, click* as it saw things it recognized. The colors! The way Mama had a color for everything. Each wall had its own feeling—orange and yellow and some kind of shade of blue—and the couch was purple, and there was a red wooden table, and a rug that had big round circles of different kinds of green. It was like you were in a big box of crayons, in Mama's house—so different from my daddy and Maggie's house, which had big brown chests of drawers and tables and bookshelves, crowded in against every wall and so heavy and dark they looked like they ate all the light in the room and might come and eat you, too.

It made my heart beat faster, just to see it all, like it was from a dream. And that guy, Stony, was there looking just the way he looked before, and the woman, Petal, from next door was visiting, and everybody hugged me and said I was so big, and some of them remembered Bunny, too. Mama made us some tea that tasted like leaves and grasses, and we sat in the living room on the big paisley pillows, and then we walked outside and picked up little flowers and pieces of fluff for Mama's art, and we just talked and talked. I told her about the farm and Bunny's barn, and how Hendrix liked to play with the baby goats and that I wanted a puppy because our old dog was so old and wouldn't climb the stairs anymore to sleep in my room, like he used to.

Bunny was smiling now, and Mama made her laugh a couple of times, and Bunny put her hand to her throat and said, "Oh my!" when Stony teased her about looking too young to have a granddaughter my age.

Bunny and Mama started talking about things that had happened before I got born, when she and my daddy had a wedding right out there in the field, and how fun it had all been.

"We stood right over there," Mama said. She pointed to a place in the field where there was a little tree standing all by itself. "And your daddy wore a shirt that I'd made for him—and it had puffy sleeves and all kinds of embroidery on it. Remember that, Bunny?"

"Well," said Bunny. She turned away, like she'd seen ghosts out there in that field. "Yes, it was *quite* a shirt. It was that." And Mama laughed, too, and said it might have been a little over the top, that shirt, but she had been proud of it—and the two of them smiled at each other. Then Bunny said *well* again and looked over at the house and moved her handbag over to the other shoulder.

I got a little shiver, and then all of a sudden, I started to get that sad kind of stomachache again. Because I could see this wasn't going to last. Soon it was going to be time to go get back in the car, and Mama would still live here, and I would still live in New Hampshire and be Maggie's girl—and when I was Maggie's girl, I was not Phronsie because I was Frances—and little by little, I would forget about being the girl who twirled around in the field finding pieces of feathers and wearing sparkly clothes like my mama did.

And then Bunny cleared her throat and put her hand on my arm and said we should all go into town and get something to eat at the diner, so we did. Mama sat next to me in the big orange booth and she told Bunny that she was making a little bit of money now from her art. She said she was getting by and that there was a whole bunch of people who were doing art with her, and they had a co-op thing going on. There was magic in the art, she said. I started playing with her hair, which was long and curly and yellow, like mine, except Maggie always had me wear mine in a tight high ponytail to keep it out of my face. But Mama took the ponytail holder out, and she combed her fingers through my hair and said how pretty it looked. She said my eyes looked just like hers.

"You look just like pictures of me when I was a little girl," she said in kind of a dreamy voice. "As my mama would have said, you're my *spittin' image.*"

That's when I felt brave enough to say the thing I had wanted to say since we got there, but which

I didn't know until right then that I could ever say.

"Do you ever miss me?" I said.

"I miss you every single second," she told me. Her eyes got shiny, so I took her fingers and played with all of them, one by one, sliding her rings on and off. She had rings with beads on them.

"Well then," I said, "how come you don't ever come and see us? Why are you so far away?" I swallowed hard. "I thought you died."

She and Bunny looked at each other. I saw Bunny nod.

"He doesn't tell them I call?" Mama said.

I looked from one of them to the other. Bunny cleared her throat again. "You call? On the phone?"

"I call every week. I beg to talk to them. He always says they're busy or they're taking a nap or they've gone to the store. Once he finally said it would be too upsetting."

Bunny banged her hand on the table, and she looked away with a mad look on her face. She shook her head, and she said this was something that had to get fixed.

"I tried a few times to come see them. Stony said he'd drive me, but Robert said he wasn't going to allow me to see them even if I did get there. He said—he said it's not good for them." She started tearing up the paper napkin in front of her. "Does he even give them the presents I send? For their birthday? For Christmas?"

Bunny shook her head. "Nothing. He's never mentioned anything."

"Maybe it was the magic that scared him," Mama said, and Bunny said, "Hush with that kind of talk. It's him. This is all on him."

"And the divorce decree said there'd be visitation," Mama said. "But that doesn't happen, and I can't afford an attorney."

"No," said Bunny, and I had never seen her look so mad. "This is the end of that, though. You don't worry about this for one more second, you hear me? I'm taking care of things from now on. There's going to be visitation."

On the way home, Bunny said that it wasn't going to be a secret after all that we went to see Mama. That she was going to march in the front door, and she was going to make sure that my daddy did what the court said he had to do.

The next day there was a big fight and lots of yelling. Hendrix and I were supposed to be upstairs in our room, but I could hear Bunny telling my daddy that he had to do what the court said, and my daddy said the court didn't know everything that was right.

"Children need to see their mother," she said. "*That* is what is right."

He yelled a whole bunch of things, how our

mother wasn't good. He said Woodstock was a bad place, and he told Bunny that Mama had let us run wild. He was also mad that Bunny took me up there without telling him. That was lying.

I tried not to listen, but I couldn't help it. The yelling was all over the whole house. It bounced against the walls and filled up all the spaces, even where Hendrix and I were hiding behind the door.

Then Bunny told him that *he* was the wrong one here. She kept saying, "She is *their mother.* And Phronsie thought she *died,* Robert. This child has been suffering because of you and your stupid pride."

After that, the grown-ups found out we were listening, and even though there was more of a fight to come, Hendrix and I got taken by Maggie over to Bunny's barn, where we slept for a few nights, and when we came back to our regular house, everybody was acting like nothing had happened at all, except the air still felt thick with something bad.

Every summer for the next four years, Maggie would drive me and Hendrix to the little ice cream place in Massachusetts, where Mama would be waiting in Stony's old pickup truck, and we would eat an ice cream cone, and then Mama would take us back to her house. Hendrix and I would spend a couple of weeks with her and her friends, and we would swim at the swimming hole and we'd listen to the music that her friends made, and we'd help Mama with her art collection, and we'd sleep outside some nights in the tent with her and see the fireflies and we'd help her pick the strawberries and the tomatoes. She and I would make bread, and she would tease me about how much butter I liked, and then she would bring out the jar of honey, and we would load up the pieces with butter and honey until they were just completely perfect. That's what Mama would say: "This is just completely perfect."

She was witchy and magic and knew how to harness the moon energy and how to make people fall in love with her. I thought she was everything. Hendrix, though, was a little bit homesick. I could always tell what he was thinking because he and I had been together even before we were born, and I knew he liked things to be all normal and regular. I could see in his eyes that he felt scared when Mama would talk about magic and moonlight. So I tried to keep him happy when we were there, telling him stories at night, letting him sit in the front seat in the truck when we went places, giving him the biggest piece of bread with the most butter and honey. Just so he would smile and be happy there.

And things didn't get weird for a very long time.

CHAPTER NINE

News flash: Judd did not come over to my apartment after having a beer with Mercer on Sunday night, and therefore, we did *not* make love for the first time ever.

Surprise, surprise.

I wake up on Monday morning, feeling grumpy and unsettled. What does it say about us that he didn't even *want* to stop by? Doesn't he want to have sex with me? Then, while I'm in the shower, mulling over the question of whether I have the right to be disappointed, Mr. Swanky eats all the leftover popcorn from last night's movie marathon and throws up on the carpet, and after I clean that up, I discover I'm out of coffee beans, and so I miss the 8:06 subway because I have to stop to get takeout coffee in order to live, and the line is ridiculously long. Well? I have to stand in it, fidgeting and fuming. I need coffee. Life without caffeine is unthinkable.

Then, when I get to work, there's Darla beginning the staff meeting by saying, "We have a very difficult situation here with Phronsie's author."

Some context here: Darla Chapman has been the head of publicity for Tiller Publishing for two years, and as far as I can tell, nothing has ever derailed her. She's known in the business as a firecracker, even a firebrand, with plenty of ideas for how to get our authors front and center in the vast, loud world of publishing, where it seems as though every third person you meet has a new book out and needs it reviewed by someone.

She also has social relationships with bookstore owners, magazine editors, other publishers, and media experts. And not only that, but she also has four children, a banker husband, a live-in nanny, a cook, four dogs, two cats, a Komodo dragon, three cell phones, and a pager—and yet somehow she always seems preternaturally calm. Maybe it's because she's about seven feet tall and has a deep, contralto voice that commands attention. I think she terrifies most problems into submission, to tell you the truth.

When she says there's a very difficult situation, I think most of us in the conference room start to imagine that it may be time to take cover under our desks. Adam, sitting across the conference table from me, gives me a look meant to approximate a silent scream and then quietly adjusts his shirt so that a little gnome head comes peeking out of his pocket. He shifts his gaze down when Darla shoots a look in his direction.

Then she fixes her stare on me. "Phronsie," she says, "you're the resident expert here, so would you like to fill the rest of the group in on the Gabora situation as it now stands?"

So I explain.

Gabora Pierce-Anton is a positively ancient, sweet-faced, beloved children's book author who years ago was one of the backbones of Tiller Publishing. However, she writes books that depict life from a simpler time. She tells the story of the adventures of Peter and Eleanor, two wealthy children who are able to disappear through a little door and go back and forth in time. Sometimes they just zip back to visit their great-grandmothers' childhoods where they learn to roll hoops and knit scarves and cultivate family values, but they have also gone to other continents and, over the years, have visited nearly every epoch you can think of, from dinosaurs to space travel. Parents and grandparents have flocked for years to buy these sweet, charming little books.

"But her latest," I say, "coming out after a five-year hiatus, is about Thanksgiving, and— well, the plot is that little Eleanor and Peter zipped back in time and befriended some little Pilgrim children and 'helped out' the Native Americans by teaching them how to prepare the Thanksgiving feast. Eleanor even showed them how to set a proper English table, and the Native Americans were so, so grateful."

There are groans around the table.

Adam says, "How in the world did this ever make it through our editing process?"

Darla steps in. "We're dealing with that now," she says and gives Adam a fierce look.

What I suspect is that we've just always given Gabora a free pass on anything, because her books sell so well. *And* she did agree, grudgingly, to abandon the word *Indians* and go with *Native Americans* instead.

"Early reviews have been devastating and rightly so," I say. "*Publishers Weekly* and other publications had some harsh words about the cultural insensitivity and irresponsibility of allowing such a view to escape into the world. There have been protests, and we were asked by several Native American rights groups to pull the book."

Darla interrupts me. "Which would be unheard of. So, after several high-level meetings, we decided our response would be to simply forego the usual widespread publicity tour that Gabora is accustomed to. The book would be out, but we would be silent about it. No publicity. Maybe the whole thing would just . . . go away. A few diehard fans might buy it, grandmothers who weren't politically inclined, and that would be that."

"We salute you, Gabora Pierce-Anton, at the end of a brilliant career," says one of the other publicists, and everyone chuckles a little.

Darla taps on the table with a long pink fingernail. "But now the bad news is that Gabora has contacted lawyers, with encouragement from her two grown daughters. And she is insisting on going ahead with bookstore appearances that were previously scheduled by us, back in the summer when we assumed we'd be proceeding as we always have with her books. Her attorney says she wants to go FULL SPEED AHEAD, all caps," Darla says. "She wants to confront her critics, and she has contacted bookstores on her own—or her daughters have, more likely—and they have bookstore appearances lined up."

"But do bookstores want this kind of attention?" Adam asks.

"Don't misjudge her appeal," says Darla. "The fact is, bookstore owners are rallying around her. There are now readings scheduled the week of Thanksgiving, in South Carolina, ending on Wednesday night itself. And with predictions of protesters, we can't just leave our frail little author out to fend for herself. The optics are very bad for that."

She looks at me. "I'm afraid we're going to have to ask you to postpone your Thanksgiving travel plans," she says. "You need to be with her. You've traveled with her before, and you know how to keep her in line. Rumor has it she's been known to get a little tipsy at times."

Ah yes. Once she *tipsied* herself into an endcap of books and gave herself a concussion. Another time she fell out of the backseat of the car when her driver opened the door she was leaning upon.

"But wait," Adam is saying. "This seems insane. Are people seriously going to go to a bookstore reading for a children's author when they're supposed to be making their turkey dinner? I bet we could talk those bookstores into canceling. There's hardly anybody who's going to show up for this."

Darla looks at him and narrows her eyes. "Adam, would you like to rethink what you just said, in light of what our responsibility is to our authors?" she says.

He looks down; he probably would rather not.

"You know what?" she says in her deepest no-nonsense voice. "Phronsic is going to need your help with the tour. I'll need you *both* to escort Gabora to her events and keep her out of trouble and see that she's protected."

I look over at Adam, who has settled back in his seat and is tapping a pen against his thumb. So much for extra days off for him.

And for me, too. Even if by some miracle, I'm able to leave for New Hampshire after her reading on Wednesday night, I'll still miss my favorite part of our family Thanksgiving celebration, which takes place in the few days beforehand. In the ideal, perfect world of family traditions, Judd and I usually take the train home on Monday and then go to Hallowell House, where Bunny lives, and then I bring her home with me.

Hendrix and his family come up, and we usually spend Tuesday and Wednesday working on the Thanksgiving dinner, doing chores, polishing the silver, playing games, and visiting. Hendrix and his kids drive the tractors—or at least they have in past years. There's not much land left to drive tractors upon these days.

But Gabora takes precedence. I know this.

After the meeting, I go into full-throttle mode. Call the bookstores where she's scheduled, hoping they've rethought things. But nope. They're not backing down. They have people signed up to come see her. They want to show their love.

"Are there going to be protests, though?" I ask.

"Oh, who knows?" says one bookstore owner. "We're just thrilled to have Gabora Pierce-Anton coming to our little indie bookstore. We can handle the rest."

So that's that. I call Judd and tell him the news that I probably won't make it to New Hampshire until Thanksgiving Day. He is crunching an apple while we talk, and he doesn't seem all that concerned.

"At least we can still get together at Tandy's on Friday with all the peeps," he says. "Oh, and guess what. I talked to a guy who comes into the gym, and he has a little wholesale jewelry business, so I'm meeting him there tomorrow night. I'm getting you a real ring. A metal one. I want you to have something to show everybody."

"Well," I say. "Huh. That's nice of you."

He laughs. "I just want you to have a pretty ring so that even though you're marrying a guy out of friendship, you don't have to suffer when the other ladies want to see your ring."

"Oh God," I say. "You are so crazy."

"But wonderful crazy," he says.

"Well," I say. "That's one way to look at it."

Late in the afternoon, I call Maggie on the speaker phone and tell her about my work situation and how sad I am not to be there early in Thanksgiving week.

Maggie says, "Well, but will Judd still come ahead of time?"

"He's planning on it. He said he's buying me a ring so I can show it off to the other women."

"A ring! That's great. Are you happy?"

"I think I am. There are still a couple of little personal details to be worked out between him and me. You know."

"The fireworks?"

I laugh. "Exactly. The fireworks, yes."

"Look, he's a good, healthy, red-blooded man, so you'll figure it out. And as I may have mentioned, I'm just so relieved that now we don't have to worry about you dating serial killers."

"What is it with you and these serial killers? Trust me. Whenever a serial killer asks me out, I always say no."

"Serial killers make themselves look very normal and very attractive to young women," she says. "You *could* meet a psychopath and not realize what you were dealing with. That's what can happen if you think you're running out of time."

"Okay, Mags, that's it. I gotta go."

I turn my chair back around and my stomach drops. Adam is standing at my door leaning against the doorjamb with his arms folded. He's smirking at me. I swear, the guy is smirking. And I have no idea how long he's been there or how much he's heard. Damn that speaker phone.

I hang up and bark, *"What?"*

He's not thrown a bit. He saunters in and sits down in the chair across from my desk. He's still got that slightly smiling expression on his face. Let me be clear about something: Adam doesn't so much as sit in a chair as he inhabits it. He slouches down, stretches out his legs. If his feet could reach my desk, I swear he'd put his feet up on it. He also still has that little gnome sticking out of his shirt pocket. Juliet this time.

This guy is impossible.

"So break it to me gently. This Gabora . . . is she really a nutjob? Like how bad is it really going to be? Is she, like, senile? I read the book after the meeting, and I can't believe we're publishing it. What were they *thinking?*"

"Close the door, please," I say. While he's

doing that, I try to control myself. My face feels like it's still blazing from a mixture of embarrassment, fury, and a whole host of other emotions that haven't yet introduced themselves by their full titles. When he turns and looks at me, I say in the coldest voice I can muster, "Listen to me. Gabora Pierce-Anton is a respected children's author, and she's partially responsible for our jobs even existing here. She may not be to your taste, and she may not even be up with the current line of thinking about anything you care about, but she is an author who belongs to our company, and I want you to go into this tour with the attitude that you are going to contribute in such a way as to protect her, to make sure she's all right and comfortable, and to show the utmost respect for her and for Tiller wherever you go. You are representing this publisher, and I am not going to tolerate all this joking about her."

I might as well set the tone for this tour right this minute. That's what I'm thinking.

He has not taken his eyes off me the whole time I'm scolding him. He's looking right at me, right into my eyes, and then he sits up a little straighter and salutes me when I'm all finished. "Yes, *ma'am*," he says. Like it's all a big joke.

"Do *not*," I say.

"Do not?"

"Do *not* even . . ." I can't think of what I was

135

going to say. "Do not even try to make light of this conversation," I finish lamely.

"Absolutely not," he says. "This is a very serious conversation. High seriousity." But he looks like he just might start laughing, and I know that if he does, then I will start laughing, too, because, let's face it, I am never good at this kind of thing. Scolding. Which is why I will probably make a lot of mistakes as a mom, and disciplining the children is yet another thing that will have to fall to Judd, and Adam is looking at me in such a way that I want both to smack him and, for some reason, to kiss him at the same time.

I stand up to shift the energy in this room. "That's enough. I have some calls to make. You need to leave."

He stands up and prepares to go. But then he stops at the door and turns and looks at me. It's hard to describe the exact way he looks at me; his blue eyes are directly staring into mine, and his mouth is a hard line, like he's trying hard not to smile.

"So," he says, "just for the record, with all due respect, I don't happen to think you're running out of time."

CHAPTER TEN

Every year when Maggie would drive Hendrix and me to meet up with Mama at the ice cream place halfway between New Hampshire and Woodstock, my heart beat so hard that the blood pounded in my ears like a drum. It was because the best time of my year was about to begin, but first we had to get through the very worst time.

Maggie called out to us in the backseat as she drove, saying all these things she was worrying about as we got closer. Things like, "Don't go swimming if there's not a grown-up watching you," and "Be sure to take your vitamins every day and make sure you eat plenty of fruit and drink milk, because you don't want to get sick while you're there." She said, "If anybody is smoking something, and it smells funny to you, I want you to promise me that you will go outside and get away from it."

I poked Hendrix when Maggie said that, just to make him laugh.

The switch from Maggie to Mama at the ice cream stand was always a bad moment. Everybody was all fake nice about it, but I could feel the tension. Maggie didn't like to take us to the place to hand us over, and she certainly didn't like to see Mama, but I heard her telling Daddy one time that as much as she hated it, *she* was always the one who was going to do the switch because she didn't trust him to see Mama again.

"What do you think I'm gonna *do,* Maggie?" he yelled.

And she said, "How about the mistake you made with her that *other* time?" And then she laughed like she was joking, except she wasn't, you could tell from her eyes. "I've gotta keep my eye on you, mister."

I thought about that for a long time. I knew by then that my daddy and mama had met at Woodstock, and that he got married to her there and made me and Hendrix, so was *that* the mistake? Were me and Hendrix the mistake?

But how could *we* be a mistake? People can't be mistakes.

Everything changed as soon as Maggie pulled her station wagon out of the parking lot to head back home. That's when Mama stopped acting like she was a calm grown-up lady, and she did this little dance with her arms in the air that she said a person should always perform when seeing somebody after a long time. It was a silly dance, really, shimmying and clapping and then a full-body hug, spinning around, and then a dip. It made her laugh every time. I was always willing to join right in, but Hendrix was a little shy and had to be coaxed. She'd go over and take him by the hands and jiggle him around until he was laughing.

She was fabulous, our mama. That was my new word the summer I was seven. I used the word *fabulous* over and over because that was the word my mama liked, too, and also everything about her was fabulous: the floaty clothes she wore, her long yellow hair cascading down her back, messy and tangled up, like a nest of something. It felt like she could do anything. Life was like one big party time, with people coming to sleep over without even having to call first. Music was always playing, either on the record player or from somebody sitting on the floor playing a guitar. One guy who came over a lot had a harmonica that he played nearly nonstop. My mama was always singing "You Are My Sunshine." It ran through my head all the time, that song.

Also, there was a big firepit in the center of the yard, with stacks of wood around it, where we'd sit at night and sing songs. The house was next to a big, open field, which was dotted with flowers—white and pink and yellow, like someone had thrown little bits of paint here and there, just for fun.

When I wasn't out running around with Hendrix, Mama and I sat on the porch and she taught me to sew things.

She also told me stuff she believed, like how

you were supposed to have as much fun as you could. You had to find work that was like play, and then you could be having fun all the time. *Some* people didn't know that life wasn't supposed to be hard.

"Which is fine for them," she said. "If people want to think that life is hard for them, then they are welcome to that idea, believe me. But you don't *have* to see it that way. You can look for good things instead."

Look for good things.

Nobody at my New Hampshire house ever talked like that; there was always some big problem going on, and even if we'd been outside at night, Daddy or Maggie would never have stopped walking and said, "Look! Just *look* at those millions of stars!" And yet Mama said that nearly every night.

Mama was always looking for signs. Seeing a cardinal meant that somebody we loved was thinking of us. If we saw a snakeskin, that meant that we were going to have big changes. If your right palm itched, you were going to get some money—and if your left palm itched, that meant you were going to have company. Or maybe I have it backward.

She also had a lot of beliefs. She said, "Things always work out for the best."

She said, "We were put on this earth to be happy and free."

She said, "Everybody just wants to be loved. And if you close your eyes and think really hard, you can picture love flowing to every single person out there in the world. And they will feel it because all love is energy."

She said, "When you miss somebody really, really bad, all you have to do is think of them, and if you think hard enough, they'll feel it and they'll start thinking about you, too. Like if you sing them a song, your voice will travel up into space and find their voice singing it right back to you."

One day, just she and I were sitting on the porch, and I was sewing a big red heart on one of the dish towels, and she said, "Watch this. I'm going to flow some love to Hendrix right now, and he's going to come out of the house and find me, because he felt all that love swirling around the house looking for him."

She closed her eyes and scrunched up her face, and sure enough, in a few minutes Hendrix came drifting out of the house and sat down next to her. She and I both laughed.

"What?" he said. "Why are you laughing at me?"

"We're not laughing at you," Mama said. "I sent you some love in the air, and you felt it. And you came out."

"Well, *Frances* was laughing at me," he said.

"My name is not Frances here," I hissed at him,

141

and I looked at Mama quickly to make sure she hadn't heard. I didn't want her to know about my Maggie name.

But Mama was humming a little song, and she didn't seem to notice what Hendrix had said, or maybe she just didn't like to get into discussions about what our life in New Hampshire was like.

Instead, she jumped up and said, "Let's go swim in the river, and we'll look for rocks and feathers, and then tonight—tonight we'll catch us some fireflies."

"Will we keep them in a jar?" Hendrix wanted to know.

"No, no, heavens," she said. "They would die in a jar. They've gotta go see the other fireflies, just like we have to see all the people."

"We could poke holes in the top," said Hendrix, and she picked him up and swung him around and told him he could keep a firefly in the jar for ten minutes, but then he'd have to say good-bye and let it fly back home.

I was a different girl there, and Hendrix was a different boy. The grown-ups treated us like we were part of the whole scene, and they said bad words around us without saying, "Ooh, pardon my French," and they told funny stories, and they fell down on the pillows sometimes, kissing and hugging. That was where I learned the startling fact that everybody has a butt.

Mama also let me turn on the oven when we

made bread, and I could sit on the counter while she cut up vegetables because I had my own little knife. Hendrix and I picked blueberries, and Mama taught us to roll out the crust and push it down into the pie plate.

One day, when we were eight, everybody in the house had a cartwheel contest outside in the field, and Mama could do the most. Then we played Pile Up, and everybody got on top of everybody else and we were all laughing and pushing and yelling, and I think it was the most fun I ever had. I nearly peed my pants I was laughing so hard. Only Hendrix wouldn't play. He sat down on the ground just watching us, with his head resting on his hands.

Then that night, in the dark, he said to me, "Do you think it's okay that Mama does cartwheels and plays Pile Up?"

"Why wouldn't it be?"

"Because . . . because it's not like she's a real mom, you know?" he said. "No other moms do that stuff."

"Are you crazy? That's the good part of her," I told him. "It's because she knows how to have fun and have adventures. She doesn't always get so worried about every little thing!"

"I think she should worry a little more," he said quietly. "I had a splinter in my foot, and she said it would just go away."

"And did it?"

"No," he said. "I took a knife and pushed it out myself."

"That's good, Hendrix. That's a good skill to have."

"Phronsie, I am eight years old. I shouldn't have to take out my own splinters with a knife. It's like we don't even have a mom when we're here!"

You see? Already it was turning out that there was a Maggie Team and a Mama Team. If the two teams had different dugouts, like with the Little League, you could see that Hendrix would go to the Maggie dugout and I'd be across the field in Mama's dugout, making clover necklaces and waving to him from far away.

When we'd get back to New Hampshire after our two weeks with Mama, there were always a lot of questions. "What did you do? Who lives in the house with your mom? What kinds of food did you eat? Was somebody watching you the whole time? The whole time? Was your mother well, or did she do kind of nutty things?"

I made Hendrix promise he wouldn't tell the part about how he ate the brownie with the dope in it. I had to pay him fifty cents and do his job of collecting the eggs from the henhouse for a whole month, but it was worth it. He didn't mention it.

And then, a funny thing: After my daddy and Maggie asked us those few questions, there was never anything else they wanted to say. Mama didn't get mentioned for the whole rest of the year.

She'd send a box at Christmas and on our birthday, and it would be filled with odd little things: pieces of ribbon, a ukulele song book, feathers, buttons, torn-up pages from a calendar, and some loose squares of old jeans. Maggie would shake her head and throw the whole thing away because, she said, the box smelled like that hippie smell, patchouli.

"Robert, I tell you, she's getting worse," I heard her say one time. "Why even bother to send a box if it's not going to have anything in there a kid could play with? Broken glass! They could have gotten hurt."

But I didn't think so. I knew that everything my mama sent to me meant something wonderful to her. They were messages, all meant to be reminders of things we'd done together: the stuff we'd collected, the songs we'd played on the ukulele, the jeans we'd embroidered. I knew she was sending me some love, the best way she knew how. And I'd sneak out to the trash can and get the stuff Maggie threw away and put it all under my bed. And at night, I'd sit on the floor and bury my face in it, just breathing in the scent of my mom.

I didn't talk to her on the toilet paper roll anymore because I knew by then that was stupid, but I did write her letters. I told her how I kept everything she ever sent and that I made a collage in art class with the buttons and feathers. And then I folded my letters away because I didn't know her address, and I knew my father would never mail them for me.

I'd get in my bed at night and sing "You Are My Sunshine" and pretend that she was singing it right then, too, and that our two voices were meeting somewhere up in space.

CHAPTER ELEVEN

I'm exhausted by the time I get home from work, but I call Hendrix to tell him about the Thanksgiving plan. Over the years, despite our different dugouts, he and I have done pretty well at divvying up the responsibilities of being the children of the Robert and Tenaj and Maggie Triumvirate, as we call it.

We have staked out our territory, family-wise.

Hendrix has always been the perfect child when it comes to being loyal to the whole farming, life-in-New-Hampshire thing. He stuck it out with farming, year after year, wearing his maroon down vest in the winter and his ratty old T-shirts in the summer, working side by side with our dad, planning, planting, pruning, growing, harvesting, hiring field hands, driving the tractors, tallying up the figures—both he and my father committed one hundred percent until it became clear that the farm's situation was so dire that it could no longer support Hendrix and his family. At which point—and with the permission of our father, who gave it wholeheartedly—Hendrix and Ariel took their three little boys and moved to Massachusetts, where he got a job managing a tractor store, and she started working as a school secretary.

But I'm the perfect child when it comes to

staying in touch with everyone; I'm the one who makes the phone calls and arranges the visits. I ask about everyone's health and what they're having for dinner, and who they've talked to recently, and I know my parents' aches and pains, the bitterness they don't want to talk about, their fears, their silences, their quiet evenings, their deep well of sadness that can never be erased and never be spoken of.

And furthermore, what I know is this: that deep down in the dark recesses of their three o'clock in the morning thoughts, Hendrix and I are the flesh-and-blood reminders of an affair that shouldn't have taken place.

Getting Hendrix to settle down on the phone is a feat in itself. He's always got about five things going at one time. In the background, I can hear Ariel banging pots and pans and talking to the children about homework and washing hands and, "What's that on the floor? No, pick it up. No, *now. I said pick it up now.*"

"Can you talk for a second?" I say to him. "I just need to tell you—"

"Wait a second. Ariel, it's Phronsie. Phronsie. *Yes,* on the *phone.* Kids, can you please just pick up whatever that thing is and be quiet for like one tenth of a minute?" A beat of silence from him, with protests roaring in the background. "You can't? Are you quite sure? Try it anyway, how

148

would that be?" He comes back to the phone. "Hello, sister of mine! I'm so sorry about all this commotion. How are you? It's been way too long!"

"I'm good," I say. "You sound . . . busy. Kids doing okay?"

He says everybody's fine. Work, school events, house stuff. You know. The whole nine yards. He has that tired but satisfied tone you hear so often in married couples with kids.

"Good. Well, I just wanted to tell you that I can't come early for Thanksgiving. A work thing has come up—"

"Oh no! That's our favorite time together!"

"I know," I say. And then I tell him the short version about Gabora and the Pilgrims. Maybe he could pick up Bunny from the nursing home on Monday night? He says he'd be happy to.

Somebody in the background is yelling about whose turn it is to feed the dog.

"So, if you have another one tenth of a second," I say, talking quickly now, "did you know that Judd asked me to marry him?"

There's a silence. Then he laughs. "What?" he says. "Wow. I did not see that coming. I thought you guys were strictly pals."

"Yeah, that's what I thought, too," I say, "but it seems that I've said yes. A new direction in my life!"

There's another beat of silence and then I hear

him say, "Guys, I'm going to take the phone outside now. I gotta talk to Phronsie."

"Uh-oh, this sounds like a serious talk," I say.

"Well, I worry about you," he says. I can hear him breathing hard as he walks. "Don't get me wrong. Judd's the nicest guy in the whole world. But he's . . . ordinary compared to you. Don't take this the wrong way, but you've got a lot of our mom in you—"

"Thanks," I say sarcastically.

"No, I mean all the best parts of her—all the fun and creative stuff," he says. He pauses. "Phronsie, you know I adore you. You're the most adventurous person I know, and when you had that marriage to Steve Whoever, and I watched you get so hurt, I just hoped there was somebody out there who could appreciate all the great parts about you."

"And you don't think it could be Judd. Is that it?"

He laughs. "Well, marriage is freaking hard sometimes. And I've studied you my whole life. Before I even knew I *was* alive. Even in the womb, I think you were redesigning the place and making sure it wasn't too boring. I just wonder if you're going to be as happy with all the conventional life stuff Judd's attached to. That's all."

I laugh. "Well, womb-mate, I appreciate your concern for me. But I really do think Juddie and

I are going to be fine together. I'm not as much like Mom as you think, maybe. I want kids and a real life with a man who's not going to cheat on me. I'm ready for this."

"Well," says Hendrix. "If you're happy, then I'm happy. And now I've got to tell you that Ariel is just practically leaping at me, trying to get the phone away. She has somehow surmised exactly what's going on, and she has to weigh in. So I'll say good-bye. See you whenever you get to Thanksgiving."

And then there's Ariel in my ear: "Phronsie! Omigod! Congratulations to you! Welcome to the married-people club."

"She was in it before," yells Hendrix from a distance. "She left the club. Whose turn is it to feed the dog because whoever it is better get to it!"

"Well, welcome *back* to the club," says Ariel. "New, improved partner. Am I right?"

I squeeze my eyes closed. "Thank you," I say. "Yeah. He's an improvement."

"So—we won't see you before Thanksgiving? Is that what I'm hearing? Boys, would *one* of you for God's sake just get out of this kitchen so I can get this soup made? *Why* are you all underfoot? Scram!"

"Dad said I had to feed the dog!"

"I'll be there—just not until after the dinner itself."

151

"Oh. Well, good, then," she says. Her voice is the distracted voice of someone who's dealing with a roomful of chimpanzees. "Anyway, honey, I couldn't be more thrilled for you and Judd. And you know what I'm thinking? Maybe we can all go on vacation together sometime. The boys just love Judd!"

"Sure," I say. That's a comforting and strange thought. I try to visualize us all camping out somewhere in the woods, or even at a resort somewhere, lounging by a pool. I have to say that no mental images come to mind.

She laughs. Maybe she can't picture it either. But it doesn't matter: in another minute, she's hung up, gone back to her life, where her whole existence depends upon taming wild chimpanzees and holding tight to her very loving husband.

I sit there for a moment in the silence. How is it that some lucky people avoid all the pitfalls of love—the cheating husband who blindsides you, then the indignities of "putting yourself out there again," waiting for someone to click on your profile, the retelling again and again of your life story to a random, bored stranger, and then the slow realization that time may be running out and that you need to figure out how to settle for a life that is so far from what you imagined? How, indeed, do they get that lucky?

CHAPTER TWELVE

The summer I was ten, I asked Mama why she never married anybody else after my daddy.

I was expecting her to say, *Because I still love your daddy, and someday we're going to get back together again!* And then *I* would say I thought she had a good chance of getting him away from Maggie, who wasn't nearly as nice as Mama was. She was sewing a butterfly onto Stony's jeans. She stared down at the jeans like the whole secret of life was contained there and said, "Umm . . . because . . . I didn't want to."

I decided to help her along. "Because you still love Daddy," I said. "I bet that's why."

"Well . . . no." She sighed. "I don't want to be married to him. Or to anybody for that matter."

I looked out at the fields and thought about this. It seemed she should be married to *somebody.* "What about Stony?" I asked her. "Because he sleeps in your bed with you, and I think he likes you a whole lot. And I bet he would want to marry you if you told him."

"Nope," she said. "I just don't like being married, I guess. I like being free."

I almost laughed out loud at the ridiculousness of this. I had never heard of such a thing. Everybody got married! And if they weren't already married, then they were waiting to get married. Or hoping to get married, like my fourth-grade teacher, Miss Stepkins, who was waiting for her boyfriend to get out of the army and come and marry her.

I draped myself across the back of her chair and started playing with her hair, twirling it around my finger. "Well, why don't you like it?"

"Because marriage isn't so great for women, Phronsie. We can do just fine in life without a husband." She broke off the thread and tied a knot in it, and then held out the jeans to look at her work. "Look at me, for instance. How happy I am. Do you think I'd be this happy if I had some *husband* telling me what to do?"

"You could tell him not to tell you what to do!"

"Oh, but once you marry somebody, sweetheart, then all bets are off. He's your partner, and he thinks he gets to tell you what you're supposed to look like and act like, and even though you might not want to, you find you're putting every-thing *you* want aside. Like if you want to do art, and he wants you to start a business with him? Or you want to do art, and he thinks you should be in there making dinner? No, thank you. It's not a good deal if you like being free and doing what you want in your life. Trust me."

"My teacher *wants* to get married."

"Fine," she said. "I wish her every happiness."

"Also Maggie and my dad are married. Did you

154

know that?" I slid my eyes carefully over to her face when I said the name Maggie, just so I could see if I'd hurt her feelings. I didn't know quite where the pain might lie.

"Yes," she said. "I did know that."

Her voice seemed so easy and calm, so I ventured a little further. "Did that make you mad when they got married after he was married to you?"

"Nope. I understood it perfectly."

I left her chair and went and hung on the railing to the steps. "Well, what if you wanted to have another baby? What about that? You'd have to get married then, wouldn't you?"

"Another baby!" she said and laughed. "I am so done with all that. But just so you know, even if I did want a baby, I could just have one. I wouldn't have to get married for that." She stood up and stretched her arms overhead and did a couple of deep knee bends. The sparkly things on her shirt caught the sunlight and flashed at me.

I walked my two fingers up and down on the porch railing banister, pretending they were people needing to jump over the places where the blue paint was chipping off. "But I thought you couldn't make babies if you weren't married."

"Some people want you to believe that, but it's not really true. Like, I had already started making you and Hendrix long *before* your daddy and I got married."

155

"You did? How did you do that?"

She looked at me. "Has anybody ever thought to tell you about sex?"

I shook my head and stubbed my toe on the riser to the step as hard as I could. "I mean, I *know* a lot about it."

"What do you know about it?"

"Well, I know that you have to be in a bed. And that when you do it with somebody, it makes babies. And you have to be married."

She pursed her lips. "Good God. You're ten years old, and you—well, never mind. It's time you knew the real story. I'll tell you all about it."

"Hendrix doesn't know about it either. I know way more than he does. Like, get this! Last year, we went to a wedding with Daddy and Maggie, and when the bride and groom kissed at the end, Hendrix leaned over and said to me, 'I think they're doing sex and they're making a baby now.' And I had to tell him that it's not sex when you're standing up. *He* said sex was kissing for a long time, and *I* said you also need a bed. So sex is kissing in the bed, isn't it? When you're married."

She was smiling and shaking her head. "Oh, sweetie. You don't have to be in a bed. It's just comfortable there."

I looked at her for a long time, feeling a little bit shy. "Well. If you don't *have* to be married to have babies, then why did you marry my daddy?"

156

"I'll tell you the truth. When I got pregnant, *Bunny* said we needed to get married. So we did."

"But I don't get it. Why would she want you to get married if marriage isn't good for women?"

"Well, some people don't think women should have babies by themselves. They think women need men to hang around and take care of them. Which would probably be great, if men didn't think they got to be the boss of us."

I could feel myself blinking very fast. "Is that why you and my daddy didn't stay together? Because he wanted to be the boss of you?"

I could actually picture that. I remembered the day he came and picked us up, and the way he was so mad at her. And how at home, he was the one who always got to say what was going to happen. He *was* the boss of everybody.

"Oh, honey, it's so complicated. Who knows? We just didn't work out, that's all. We weren't so good at regular life together. We wanted different things. That's all. You can probably tell how different we are from each other."

"Yes," I said quietly.

And then she laughed. "He loves the Woman with the Organized Hair," she said. "That's the kind of woman for him. Somebody who has all her hairs trained to obey her commands, to all lie down going the same way."

I laughed, too.

"I wonder if I'll get married," I said.

"If you want to, you should. But if you don't want to, don't listen to anybody tell you that you have to, okay? You'll be just fine either way." She flexed her bicep. "Strong women, remember? Strong, free women!"

That day, after lunch, she took Hendrix and me to the river, and we sat on the sand and she told us the whole story of sex and love and how people decide who to love and how it's all magic and mysterious and it's a force in the world that's very powerful, and when it takes over your life, you think you've discovered the whole world because you're so happy and proud, and that's called being in love and it's worth everything. Everything. Because you're all lit up from the inside. Something has happened to every single one of your cells, she said—scientists have proven that.

We nodded. Hendrix and I were mesmerized by the whole story—except when she got to describing the mechanics of everything, the penises and vaginas part of the situation. We covered our eyes, and she laughed and said, "Okay. You think this way now, but this is going to be a very, very fun part of your life, and it's all about love and being close to somebody you love. But you shouldn't do it for a very, very long time. Not until you're grown up and completely ready and you really, *really* love somebody." And she hugged us both, one on each side.

"I am never doing it," said Hendrix. "I know that for a fact."

Well, she said, he shouldn't say that for sure. She thought love might change his mind. Love was *everything*. It ran the whole universe. "Just always remember that love will get you through anything."

I had told Hendrix my theory about how our family was split up into two teams, and later that summer, he asked me, "Are you on the Maggie Team or the Tenaj Team?"

I knew already he was on the Maggie Team, because of how worried he always was when we were with Mama. And bad things happened to him, just coincidences, although Tenaj said there were no such things as coincidences. He stepped on a piece of glass in the field and had to get stitches. He would have headaches and stomachaches. The smell of the marijuana smoke made him sick. He got burned one Fourth of July by a sparkler. He cut his thumb on the can opener. He had nightmares because of the bats that flew around in the trees. He was homesick.

"It's only two weeks, Henny," I would say to him. "Can't you *try* to have fun?"

"This isn't fun," he said. "It's highly *dangerous*."

I said there was nothing dangerous, that he

159

needed to learn to have fun, to be brave and adventurous.

I said he should even try being like me. I danced and stayed up late and wore cast-off clothes that were like costumes and learned to play the ukulele. I wore a tie-dyed shirt and embroidered jeans and kept my long hair in braids, and people said I looked just like a hippie chick.

"Try to enjoy things for a change," I told him.

And then one day everything went sideways.

It started out as any ordinary hot day. We'd lain around all morning, listlessly. I played the ukulele, Mama finished designing some cards, and Stony and some other friends were milling around drinking beers and working on the trucks. Hendrix was whiny. Why couldn't we go *do* something? At last we packed everything up. It took a huge effort to get that many people to actually get moving.

But we did it. We went down to the river— Mama and Stony and a whole bunch of other people. We took a picnic basket with egg salad sandwiches and potato wedges and carrot sticks and beer. There was iced tea and lemonade and apple slices. Some pears and raisins. Some more beer.

We spread out on towels and blankets on the sand and the rocks. I watched as Hendrix, who was usually not all that brave, waded into the water. And then I saw his face change when he was staring at the big rock that sometimes people jumped from. I saw him decide to do it, too. He looked around, licked his lips nervously, did a couple of boxing punches into the air. He was a skinny, pearly-white kid with no fat on him whatsoever. His hair was shorter than anyone else's. He breathed with his mouth open. But now he was going to be brave. I saw Hendrix think that, just like there was a thought balloon that came out of his head.

It wasn't all that reckless a thing to do, to be honest. But he was Hendrix, and he was always getting hurt. And this time, after he climbed to the top of the rock and stood there for a moment, holding his arms close to his side and closing his eyes, I saw him almost come back down. But he didn't.

With a suddenness that was almost breath-taking, he jumped. He flailed in midair, waved his arms around, kicked out his legs. I held my breath, seeing him soaring there before gravity grabbed hold of him. Then I stood up. He hadn't jumped far enough out, and there was an awful moment when I realized he had hit the edge of the rock. I threw down the egg salad sandwich I was eating and ran. He hadn't come up. I was screaming and screaming, but I didn't even know if the sound was getting out, because people just kept talking and laughing on the rocks.

"Hendrix! Hendrix!" I kept shouting his name

and running into the water, and as if in slow motion, other people started yelling and coming after me, too. There was red in the water where he had jumped, and he still had not surfaced.

The men dived down and brought him to the surface. They carried him to the shore, and he was lying in their arms. I was shaking on the shore next to them, wet and shivering, holding my hands up to my face, not quite able to make myself look. My teeth were chattering so hard I thought they might break off in my mouth.

An ambulance came. The sirens, the white look of Hendrix's face, the gash on his head. His eyes were open. He looked at me, and he was so *not* in his head that I could barely stand it. I touched his hand. I said, "You'll be okay," which I did not for one second believe, but it seemed like something that might help him.

Mama went with him in the ambulance. She was clutching her skirt and a string necklace she always wore that had stones on it. Lucky stones, she'd told me once. She was white and quiet, and I wondered if she thought he was going to die, like I did. Her face was hidden by her sheet of hair, and I couldn't see her eyes. I wanted to see her eyes, to know if she was as scared as I was. I needed to know if this had been my fault for telling him to be brave.

But then they went away.

Like that, they were gone, the siren shrieking

down the road, the sound getting smaller and smaller until you couldn't hear it at all.

The day they left behind was a ruined, horrible gray thing that settled over all of us who were left on the shore. Petal helped pack up the food, and Stony carried me to the truck and tucked me in with a blanket because I was shaking so hard. The other people stood around describing to themselves what had happened, what they'd seen, when they first noticed the trouble. Then they all got in their cars and trucks and left. Went back to their houses in town.

We went home, it got dark, I sat on the porch by myself watching the day fade away. Watched the night as it crept across the sky. Too scared to move. I made deals with the universe. *If I can sit here and count to one thousand, then Hendrix will be okay. If I can just not blink for the rest of the night, then Hendrix will come wake me up, and it will be morning and I will have been in my bed this whole time, and the whole thing will all have been a bad dream.*

Finally, there was a sweep of headlights, the sound of tires on gravel, a car swinging into the driveway. Someone was coming.

Mama was home, coming back for me. She got out of her friend Eric's car, and I waited to see if she picked up Hendrix from the backseat, but she didn't. I ran to meet her, and she put her arms around me, and then Eric waved and backed up and drove away slowly. I heard him call out, "I'll come back for you later to take you back to the hospital if you need me to," and she said, "No, I think I'll be here with Phronsie." The headlights brushed the porch as he went. Mama said to me, "He's okay. I just wanted to come and see you before you go."

"Before I *go?*"

We sat on the porch steps, her and me, and she took my hand and told me that Maggie and my daddy had driven there, and they were at the hospital with Hendrix. They were waiting until the doctors said it was okay for Hendrix to leave, and then they were coming to pick me up, too, and take us back to New Hampshire.

"I don't want to go back there."

"I'm sorry, but that's just the way it has to be."

"Are they mad?"

I saw her face change as she tried to figure out what to say to me.

"Tell me!" I said. "They think it was your fault, don't they? But it was my fault he jumped off the rock! I said he should try to be brave." I started to cry.

"Sssh," she said. "It was just an accident. These things happen. You didn't make it happen."

I leaned against her, and she put her arm around me. Then, from out of the darkness, after a long time, she said, "You know what I was thinking about tonight? I saved your life one time."

"You did?" I said.

"When you were born. You and Hendrix were born at home, in the back bedroom of our little house. And your daddy was there, and my friend Annie Louise, who was the midwife. It took a very long time for the two of you to decide to come out, I think. And first Hendrix came out, and then you came out after him. A few minutes later. You weren't breathing so well. You were a little gray thing, and Annie Louise looked worried, and then I sat up in the bed and I said, 'Give her to me.' And Annie Louise handed you to me, and I put you up next to my breast, and I stroked your cheek and your forehead, and I looked into your face, and I said, 'I am your mama, and I am going to take care of you always always always, and I want you to breathe because you *can do it*. I want you to stay here. Stay here, stay!' And you know what happened? You made this little noise, and then you started to breathe and cry, and you turned pink and you looked at me with those wide eyes, and you calmed right down."

"I decided to stay," I said slowly. The shaking was beginning to go away.

"Yes. You decided to stay."

I loved her so much, loved the world that I was seeing through her eyes, loved all the colors she had around her and the way she always said that anybody could be her friend and how she knew that love ruled the world. Also, I had been there, and I knew it wasn't her fault, what Hendrix did. And I would explain it to everyone in the whole wide world if I had to. She *was* watching us and paying attention. It had all happened too fast, was all. I held her hand and looked up into her eyes and smiled. I beamed over love love love love love to her like she had taught me to do.

And we sat together and waited for the storm that was on its way to us.

My daddy and Maggie showed up an hour later, furious and silent. As soon as they got out of the car, I could see my daddy's jaw working itself in and out, in and out, and Maggie's lips were in a thin, hard line.

"Where's Hendrix?" I said, and my daddy's eyes swiveled over to me like he was noticing me there for the first time.

"He's in the car. Get your things," he said to me. Mama went to the car to sit with Hendrix, and Maggie and my daddy followed me into the house. They stood there like statues, but I heard Maggie suck in her breath. Just the way they looked around at the house, at the cars in the front yard that needed work, at Mama's little glass trinkets hanging in the windows, at the sagging porch and the furniture that was mostly just pillows. Nothing in the whole house had any structure to it—the beds were simply mattresses

166

tossed on the floor, and even the tables were wobbly and scarred. The dining room table was an old door held up by cinderblocks. There was artwork piled around, and plates left over dirty from last night's feast. There was Stony's pipe left out, next to a pan of half-eaten suspicious brownies. Suddenly I could see the whole thing through Maggie's eyes, and I was embarrassed for my mother: the torn tie-dyed curtains, the wet towels on the floor, and the bare mattress that had been dragged by somebody into the living room.

"Get your things," said my daddy. "And get Hendrix's stuff, too."

"Robert, this can't go on," said Maggie. "Look at this place! That's a marijuana pipe over there! And all this mess! I can't believe people live like this. Around *children!*"

"I know," he said in a hard, tight voice. Then he looked at me again. "Are *you* all right?"

"Yes."

"Then go get your things. Now," he said. But his voice was gentler than I expected it might be. He had gotten scared for Hendrix, and that fear had made him softer.

I did what he said. I picked up all our clothes that were scattered all over the place, and I took a rock that Mama had said we were going to paint on, and a little dove carved out of ivory that she wore sometimes around her neck. Just because I knew from the looks on their faces that there would be no more *visitation*. No more switches at the ice cream place in Massachusetts. They were done with letting us come up here.

I saw it all through Maggie's eyes, and I felt sick inside.

But as awful and terrifying as that day was, it wasn't even the worst day. The worst day was when I turned on my mama myself.

CHAPTER THIRTEEN

After I get off the phone with Hendrix and Ariel, I go into the kitchen and open the refrigerator and stare into it. Mr. Swanky saunters in with me to look. He sighs.

There are three blueberry yogurts, a half bottle of wine with the cork floating in it, a moldy lemon, a bag of string cheese, and a jar of pickles. There is really only one impressive thing: an eggplant the size of Texas. What was I thinking when I bought it? That I was going to have a dinner party for eighteen?

I rummage through my purse for my phone, and I call up Judd.

"Hey, want to come over for dinner?" I say brightly when he answers. "I'm making an eggplant parmesan that's the size of a football field."

But he can't. He is helping someone; of course he is. Helping a guy at work set up a training schedule to run a marathon in the spring. And then—well, he's going over to set up a stereo system for a guy named Bernie. He's always got somebody else who needs his help.

"Okay," I say. "You could come after."

He hesitates. "Really it's probably not the right night. This guy's apparently got a complicated setup with woofers and tweeters, and it'll be late, so I'm probably just going to want to shuffle on home and crawl into bed. I've got a seven a.m. appointment tomorrow with a senior women's group. That's a lot of strenuous ladies to deal with first thing in the morning."

"Okay," I say. I look through the kitchen window at the fire escape next door. Lights are coming on in all the apartments.

There's a beat of silence. Then he says, "So what's up with the eggplant parm thing?"

"Nothing. I just thought it would be nice. We could eat together. You know, since we're engaged and all."

He laughs.

"Laugh if you want to, but I've heard that often people who are engaged eat dinner together every night. And sometimes they even sleep in the same bed."

"I've heard that, too," he says. "And I would come, honest, if it weren't that I have these other plans."

"All right. It's fine. Forget it."

"So what else?" he says. "Uh-oh. I know that tone. You're ruminating."

"I just—well, tonight I talked to Hendrix and Ariel, and I realized that I want to get married because I'm lonely. It's not just that I'm sick of dating. I want normal life. Like us, spending time together, sitting on the couch, talking about our plans and our day, and to be *partners*. A couple."

"I know," he says. "And we are like that sometimes. But we also have work and responsibilities."

"But if we were *really* a couple, then you'd
have already told me you were staying late, and
then when you got done with work, you'd come
home to bed at our place, and I'd be waiting up
for you, and it wouldn't matter if you had to get
up early in the morning. Because this is where
you'd live. And . . . and we'd figure out things
together. That's what partners do. We haven't
even talked about where we're going to live
once we get married. Whose apartment we'll go
to."

"You decide," he says. "I'll move to yours if
you want. It's bigger, right?"

"Yes, it's bigger, but the point is, we should
talk about it."

"We will talk about it. We're going to talk
about all the things we need to get to before we
get married," he says. "We have some time, you
know."

I don't answer. I say I should go, I've got to
salt the eggplant. I don't want to be on the phone
when he tells me he has to hang up because the
guy is there right now. I don't want to be shut
down. I will do the shutting down, thank you
very much.

"Okay, bye," I say. "Eggplant parm tomorrow.
Bring your appetite."

Later, I take Mr. Swanky out for two walks because he demands it. And after staring at my novel and deciding the scene with the woman talking to her psychiatrist needs to be cut in half, I fall asleep on the couch, reading, with the light on—drop in my tracks is more like it—and I wake up later with my neck hurting. I'm still wearing my shoes, for heaven's sake, from the last time I went out.

I stagger into the bedroom and put on my sleep stuff, which consists of leggings and my long-sleeved T-shirt, heavy socks (don't judge me—it's fall, okay?), and I get myself underneath the quilt and turn off the light. Outside, I can hear sirens far away, and the sound of cars on the street four floors below. In the hallway, a woman is laughing, and a man says, "Ssh. It's two thirty in the morning."

And I am nowhere near sleep. I lie there on my back, and I think about Maggie and my father, and what my mother would say about my getting married to Judd. Did she even believe all that stuff she once told me, how marriage is bad for women? Are her words like a little curse I carry around in my heart?

Every time I hear myself saying that I'm getting married—I felt this when I was telling Hendrix and Ariel even—I believe it for exactly that instant. And then later, like the way a necklace can get itself all tangled up in a drawer, without

172

anyone interfering, I find myself asking again: *Am I marrying him? No, really, am I really doing this? Is this the right thing?*

I flop over onto my stomach and let out a big sigh. And then onto my back again. Damn it, he could try to be in love, couldn't he? He could make this so much easier. But maybe he can't. Maybe that's not even what's wrong here. Maybe I'm the one who can't try to be in love.

Oh, I don't know, I don't know, I don't know.

And just like that, I suddenly find myself getting out of bed, throwing on my ratty old blue bathrobe over my leggings and shirt, and I get my keys and go into the elevator and go up to the sixth floor. Judd's apartment is 6145, and I go and knock on the door. I'm only knocking for politeness's sake. I have the key to his place, and he has the key to mine, so we can feed each other's plants or save the other person from a possible lockout.

He doesn't answer the knock, and so I go inside. It's dark, but I can see the dim night-light in his room, and I can hear him breathing—a nice, even sleep breath.

I go stand at the door to his room. "Judd," I whisper. "Judd, it's me."

Nothing. He's just a big breathing mound under the covers. Judd keeps such a neat apartment; he would never let clothes take over the bedroom, as happens at my place. His rooms even smell nice, like lemon Pledge. I think it's possible that he *dusts*.

"Judd, I need to ask you a question."

I wait for what seems like forever, and then I go over to his bed and stand over him. He turns over. He must be in the deepest level of sleep possible. Honestly, I feel like I wake up if the curtains so much as move in my room. Does the man not ever worry about break-ins? Who in America today can sleep this soundly, life being what it is and all? So I sit down on the edge of the bed, and stare at him, and finally he opens his eyes and looks at me. I can barely make out his features—just the shine of his eyes from the streetlight coming through the curtains.

"What?" he says from sleep, and then he looks happy. "Oh, you brought the pastrami. I was hoping you'd do that."

"What pastrami?"

"You know what pastrami."

"I didn't bring any pastrami. You're having a dream."

"Oh," he says. He closes his eyes again.

"Judd, I need to talk to you."

"I'm on the subway," he says.

"No, you're not, Judd. You're in your bed, and I need to ask you a very important question. You don't even have to open your eyes. Just answer my question."

"What is it?"

"Do you love me?"

"Yeah," he says after a while.

"Yeah?"

"Yeah."

"All right, I have one more question for you in that case. Do you think you're *in love* with me?"

"What?"

"You're not, are you? I keep expecting that you're going to change and want to be in love with me," I say. "But you don't. And I don't think—I mean, I know. I *know* I don't want to go through life this way, with someone who doesn't think I'm really special. You don't *want* me the way I need to be wanted." And to my own mortification, I start to cry. "You—you just treat me so ordinary. All the time, like I'm just one of your guy friends or something."

"Wait a second," he says. He's awake now. He sits up in the bed and looks at me. He turns on a lamp next to the bed, and it makes a nice, soft puddle of light all around his bedside table. He has a water glass, an alarm clock, a jump rope, and a *Men's Health* magazine on his table. A *jump rope?* It's just as well I'm calling this off before I have to sleep with a man who jumps rope before sleep every night.

His face is creased with sleep. "You say I don't want you?"

I am crying too hard to speak. I just nod at him. He sits there in the bed, looking at me like maybe this is all a bad dream. And then he says, "Wait. What's really going on? What's the matter? Is it the pastrami?"

"Judd! You are not awake, and there is no pastrami. We are talking about you and me! And love! The love you don't feel! *Wake up!*"

He rubs his eyes and looks at me. "There's no pastrami?"

"No."

"And you're crying. Because you think I don't want you. What the hell time is it?"

"I don't know. It's probably three a.m."

He sighs. Rubs his eyes. Yawns. Then he says, "Come closer, will you?"

"I don't want to."

"Then I'll come there," he says, and he sits up and moves over closer to me on the bed and puts my head on his shoulder. "Nothing good has ever happened at three in the morning. It's the hour of terrible thoughts."

"I suppose so, but I've been having these thoughts for days."

"I've made such a mistake," he says after a minute.

"Asking me to marry you."

"No. Not showing you how much I want you to be with me. I do love you, Phronsie. I really, really do. I couldn't go through life without this—what we have. You know that." His voice is fully awake now.

176

"But you don't feel—"

"Oh, stop with that telling me about what I don't feel," he says. And he puts his finger on my chin and tips my head up, and he puts his mouth on mine and kisses me, like, for real. A kiss a person could remember. Then he pulls away and looks at me.

"Here. I think you should lie down next to me," he says, and I do.

"Are we going to sleep together?" I say.

He laughs. "That's what I had in mind. Is that okay?" He's leaning over me, propped on one elbow. I realize this is what I have wanted—his body, the way his body would feel, the heft of it leaning over me, reaching for the light switch. Something so routine as that kind of wanting.

"Yeah. We should."

"We totally should. Should have long ago, probably."

"Well, at least sometime in the last few days. After we—you know, decided. Only I suddenly can't remember how you start."

"I think we should just close our eyes and start touching, and it will all come back to us."

"Okay," I say. He holds on to me. And then he tentatively kisses the top of my head, and he does that for a long time, and then he kisses my forehead and the tip of my nose, which may be slightly damp and probably even gross, and then he kisses my cheeks and moves down

to my lips, and then Judd is kissing me for real.

He kisses me. Like, really kisses me.

Judd and I are lying in bed kissing.

The next thing that happens is that his hands are warm underneath my T-shirt, and when he takes off his T-shirt, I close my eyes and make up my mind that this is going to be perfectly normal, having his skin next to mine. It is not going to be embarrassing even though he likes women who have much better bodies than I have. I am going to put out of my head that this is Judd, my friend, the one who burps on command for fun, and whom I've seen naked from the time we were little, except lately, of course, when it might count for something.

All the systems take over. It's Judd, and he is here on top of me, and he's both familiar and exotic at the same time, which could be a wonderful combination. And will be, just as soon as I shut the hell up in my mind and stop overthinking things.

He sits up and, without looking at me, takes the rest of our clothes off of us, throws them off the bed, and then runs his hands over the length of my body. I try not to think of what he's thinking as he looks at all of me.

"Is this . . . okay?" I say softly.

He closes his eyes. He says, "It is. It's everything."

Which—well, okay. I'm glad he thinks that. It

is not everything, however. It is not, for instance, the moon and the stars, and it's not the firecracker or the sudden blinding flash of light.

It is a first effort. Embarrassing in only the tiniest sense. Putting the condom on, for instance. When he makes love, it turns out that he closes his eyes very tightly. Who does that? Also, he sighs a lot. My arm gets caught underneath us, and I have to shift him over a little bit. There's a moment when I think I'll be smothered from his mouth on mine.

It's a little bit like watching someone else doing it, from afar.

But the parts all work.

When we are done, he looks at me, relieved. "That was fun!" he says.

Fun, he says.

And I say, "Yes."

And a few minutes later, he is so relieved that he falls asleep.

I stare at his face, which is so soft and unprotected in sleep. His cheekbones and his excellent jawline. His eyelashes, peaked nose, and some little lines forming, heading down to his mouth now like they'd been drawn in with a pencil. Stubble where whiskers are growing even as we lie here.

He is my destiny, I think. I try that thought out again. I am going to make up my mind once and for all. He is my destiny, and I am going to stop asking myself the question every couple of hours: Am I going to marry this dude? Because I am. True, he is not cuddly. He is not romantic. He doesn't stare into my eyes. He doesn't make things flutter inside me, except for that once. But on the plus side, he makes me laugh, he bounces on his toes, which is entertaining, and he walks backward down the street when he's telling a story just so he can see my face. He's kind to old ladies. He washes dishes, he never yells, and he folds up the paper bags very nicely when we come in from the store. Babies like him.

That could be love right there, if you add it all up.

On the minus side, sex might not ever mean as much as I want it to. It might always be just this, an exercise that we have to schedule. He may never stare into my eyes and send shivers all the way down my body. But maybe that's not important.

And . . . well, big on the plus side—I have seen him successfully carry a baby on his chest.

I lie there in the dark, adding up the pluses and minuses, and realize I'm not going to get any sleep at all. And then, right on schedule, Steve Hanover comes roaring into my thoughts, as he so often does after I've made love with somebody else. I married him out of that obsessive, can't-live-without-seeing-him-for-one-more-second kind of love. He made me feel—electrified, like

I was seeing the world in technicolor, like I could do anything.

But now I see it true. I was always off balance, insecure around him. Always with a stomachache that he'd see the real me and it would be over.

This stops now, I say to myself. *No more stupid suffering.*

I'm going to join the ranks of married people—Sarah and Russell with their fights, Hendrix with his admission that marriage is sometimes freaking hard, Talia who says the hotness just dissipates into thin air. I'm going to be one of the grown-ups, the people who know that love is sometimes simply a matter of having someone there to show up and battle back the loneliness with you. Someone to sleep next to, to cook eggplant parm for, to watch a movie with.

I turn and look at his sleeping face, at the shadows the streetlight is casting across his cheekbones, at his rather majestic nose. This familiar, dear face of my friend—I don't think I've ever really studied him so closely, all these years. He's just been a fixture in my life.

But now. Now he's taken on another shape in my head. The shape of *husband.* He is going to be my husband. Replacing the husband who failed me.

I reach over and touch his cheek, softly. I can do this. I can have a plausible, successful marriage with this guy. It doesn't have to be fireworks.

In the darkness, it almost seems as if he's shifting before my eyes, turning into the man I'll see across the pillow for the rest of my life. We'll have children and we'll bring them up in New York, and people will forget that we weren't always a couple because we'll fit together when we walk down the street. We'll be like Hendrix and Ariel, marching forward into the uncertainty, not even acknowledging that it's a risky road we're walking.

I finally fall asleep with my head on his shoulder, and it feels like the most natural thing in the world.

CHAPTER FOURTEEN

It went just the way I thought it would go after Hendrix's accident: we couldn't go see Mama anymore. Oh, I argued with Maggie and my dad plenty. I said it wasn't Mama's fault that Hendrix had gotten hurt. I said it could have happened anywhere. I said we *needed* to see her.

But they were resolute. "It's not safe there. She and her friends take drugs. It's not a place for children. If your mother wants to see you, she can come here and stay in a hotel and have proper visitation with a chaperone."

"Like that would ever happen," I said. I couldn't picture my mother ever coming back to New Hampshire, where they despised her. And stay in a hotel, and be *chaperoned?* Never, never, never.

"You're being mean," I said to my father.

"I know you love her, but she's not a responsible person," he said calmly. "She can't be trusted because she's impulsive and she's flighty, and she holds her stupid art above everything else in her life. Even her children's safety. And that is not what grown-up people do."

So I wrote her long letters that I never sent. I wrote stories about her that I kept in a notebook under my bed. I let my hair grow long like hers, and I embroidered hearts on my jeans.

One day I was snooping in my father's desk drawer, and I came across the carbon copy of a letter he'd had his attorney send to her. I couldn't make out everything it meant, but it said that she shouldn't try to get Hendrix and me back again or else there would be legal action taken. The police would be informed that she lived in a house where there were drugs.

There was another thing shoved into that envelope. A little piece of paper, folded up. I opened it, and there, in my dad's scrawly, loopy handwriting, was my mama's phone number, written with a blue ballpoint pen so hard that it perforated the page. He'd written the number and then "Tenaj" right under it. He even wrote "Janet" in parentheses, like he still couldn't get over the fact that she changed the letters around. I put it in my pocket, because someday I might want to call her up. It had been two years since I'd heard her voice.

It was just that I didn't know what I'd say to her. I kept the piece of paper in my underwear drawer, just in case.

And then one day everything changed. I got my first period.

The day it happened I was at school wearing a pair of white jeans. These were statement jeans that I'd wheedled out of my parents for my thirteenth birthday. Maggie, of course, would have preferred for me to wear dresses to school, but I wasn't having it. It was 1983—girls were wearing tight jeans and ruffles, lots of eye makeup and big hair. I had longed for a maroon and emerald-green jacket with padded shoulders, but Maggie had reached her limit with the white jeans.

And now they were ruined.

It was not all that unexpected, this period. I *was* thirteen and a half. I'd had a box of Kotex in my closet for two years just in case. All my friends got theirs ages ago. Missy Franklin got it in fifth grade and lorded it over everybody else, swanning around the locker room each month moaning about The Curse. But now it was my turn, and the first thing I thought was that this was the most shocking thing in the whole world. Women put up with this? If this kind of thing happened to boys, I knew for sure that Hendrix would *just die* of it.

I was in the stall in the girls' bathroom upstairs, and Jen Abernathy was talking to me out by the sink, and I knew she was reapplying her eyeliner, and she was telling me she wanted to ditch Spanish and would I go with her to sneak out of school, and I just said, "Jen. Oh my God, Jen. I just got it." And she thought I meant I just got it why Spanish was worth ditching, so I ended up having to explain. No, IT. I just got IT, Jen, you dope.

She came over and knocked on the stall door

and said, "Seriously? You just right now got your first period?"

"YES!" I said. "You don't have to tell the whole world about it. Do you have any pads?"

But she did not. And the stupid pad machine in the girls' room was always empty, so Jen wadded up some paper towels and stuck them underneath the stall door, and she said, "Just put these in your underpants until you get home."

This did not seem like a foolproof plan. But I did it anyway, and then we both nearly fell down laughing at the way I looked when I tried to walk with that big, bulky, scratchy wad of paper towels stuck between my legs.

I could hardly think of anything else for the rest of the day. And when the school bus dropped Hendrix and me off at our road, he wanted to race me to the front gate, and when I said no, he said, "God, you're being such a weirdo," and I said to him, "Listen to me. I am a woman now. I am officially now in my reproductive years, and you need to stop calling me names. Women deserve respect."

I started telling him about the period thing for his educational awareness, but he said I was grossing him out, so I hit him in the arm as hard as I could, and he said he was going to tell Maggie on me, and I said I'd do even worse to him next time if he did, and then when we got in the house, I started to cry for no good reason, and then I walked upstairs and got rid of that huge wad of sandpaper I was wearing and put on a proper pad from my closet, and all of a sudden, all I wanted in the whole world was to talk to my mom.

I dragged the upstairs extension from the hall into my bedroom and dialed her number. Downstairs, I could hear Hendrix and Maggie talking. She got home from school every day just before we did so we couldn't get into any trouble, she said, and she usually had cookies and milk for us, and she wanted us to tell her about our day and what homework we had. Like we were five years old or something. It was as though she'd taken a course called "How to Be a Real Mother," and she wanted to get a good grade by the end of her life. Whatever.

The phone rang about five times and then I heard this soft voice saying *hello*. Only she said it like one syllable: *'low*. Her voice was sleepy, like she just woke up, which is probably exactly what was going on. She slept ridiculously late sometimes.

For a minute I couldn't even talk because the tears got all jammed up in my throat. Finally she said, in a cheerful voice, "Is this a crank call? Are you about to ask me if my refrigerator is running?"

And that made me start laughing. And then I said, "Mama, it's me." And she said, "Oh my God. Phronsie?"

"I got my period today," I said. "I wanted to tell you." All of a sudden I felt stupid, like this wasn't a good reason to call her for the first time ever.

But she was cool with it. "Oh, honey! You did? Your *first* period?" she said.

"Yes."

There was a silence. Then she said, "Wow! Well, this is a very heavy moment in your life. Let me put my teacup down and study about this. And you know what? It's a full moon, which is very auspicious." I heard a bunch of muffled sounds, some strains of music in the background. I could picture her in her little studio, the paisley curtains blowing behind her in the window, the candles all around her, the wooden door propped up on cinderblocks that she used as a table. Then her voice again, dry and soft: "Tell me this: When you discovered it, were there any wild animals around you?"

"Mom, I was at school. In the girls' bathroom. I *hope* there were no wild animals in there. Because if there were, they would be rats."

"Well," she said. "That's a good point."

Her next question was, did I notice any signs when I was walking home later—feathers, or little rocks shaped like hearts? How did the clouds look?

"There's snow on the ground, so I couldn't see many rocks or feathers," I said. We always looked for signs, me and her, when we were together. Her windowsills were filled with stones she'd bring home with her, and each one gave her a different energy.

"Did you see any tracks in the snow?" she wanted to know. I didn't, so she got out her book of spells, which is exactly what I wanted her to do, and she said she was making me a concoction of raspberry leaves and some echinacea and a red ribbon and a cardinal's feather she had lying around. She was going to call for a prayer circle for me at the full moon ceremony she was going to have that night with her friends.

Then she said that I was now in a long chain of women—women who had bled and brought forth life on earth. It was a sacred trust, being a woman. I must learn to pay attention to outward signs, she said. I would probably start to feel very intuitive, in tune with the moon. Her voice was soothing and sweet.

"Just think—the chain of womanhood is being handed down from me to you. You are a citizen of the greatest tribe of humans there could be. Woman power, my sweetest! You're an agent of your own destiny. And you must get those around you to celebrate your entry into womanhood with a menstruation ceremony."

"That's not very likely," I said and laughed at the idea of me, Maggie, my dad, and Hendrix even *talking* about menstruation, much less conducting a ceremony for me.

"Come on," she said. "Tell the Woman with the Organized Hair that she should do something special for you."

I laughed a little bit, just to show that I was in on the joke. "I haven't even told her yet," I said. "I wanted to call you first."

I knew that would make her happy, and I think it did. Because next she said, "Well, if you want to call me again, I'd like that." She paused, and then said: "Hey, I have an idea. What if you went to the store and bought a phone card, and then we could talk anytime? Because I think your dad will blow a gasket if he sees my number on the phone bill."

"Okay," I whispered.

"Do you think you could get a phone card?"

"Yeah," I said.

"Good. I'm glad you called me for this. It's a blessing to talk to you," she said.

"Okay, good-bye," I whispered. I was looking at my bedroom door, listening for sounds. Was Maggie going to come up to see what I was doing?

After I hung up the phone, I went downstairs for a snack. Maggie was in the kitchen unloading the dishwasher, which was usually my job, and she said to me, "So, Frances, Henry said you have something important to tell me."

"Yeah," I said. "Whatever. I got my period."

And she nodded and pursed her lips, all businesslike. "Funny that Henry had to be the one to tell me," she said. I said that I would have told her, but I had had to run upstairs to get some supplies because the school didn't have any, and she asked me if I had everything I needed. Then she wanted to know if I had cramps. When I said I did, she had some boring medical thing to say about cramps—like how they're caused by the fluid buildup. And you have to be sure to drink a lot of water and get plenty of sleep when you're having your period.

Then she stood there looking at me and wiped her eyes.

"You're growing up so fast," she said.

"Yeah," I said.

I knew she would want to manage the whole thing. That's why I hadn't wanted to tell her first. Because there had already been too many times when Maggie stepped in to manage everything about me. She knew when I should go to bed and when I should wake up, and how many vegetables I ate each day, and how many pieces of fruit. She knew all my teachers' names and who my friends were, and when I needed vaccinations and dental cleanings, and what kinds of things were under my bed and what television shows I watched, and how my digestive system was working, and how often I should take a bath—and I was sick of it.

Sick to death of being under the Maggie microscope.

Maggie put her arm around me when I went to the fridge to get a drink of water, and for a moment, we stood like that, and I tried to make her happy by putting my head next to her shoulder, and I could hear her heart beating and smell the laundered scent of her blouse, but as soon as I could, I moved away. I couldn't stand to be touched, and the smell of the laundry soap was making me feel sick. It was like my skin was alive or something.

She stared at me for a long, long time, and then she sighed and said maybe we'd have hamburgers for dinner, to give me some iron. She said, "You know, you have to not use your period as an excuse to be in a bad mood."

"I'm not," I said. "I just have a headache and cramps, and I'm tired, is all."

"Okay," she said. Then she said, "It's an exciting thing, your first period. You could have a baby now, you know." She smiled at me and added, "But *don't*."

"I *know*," I said. I got an apple and walked out of the kitchen. All I could think of was that tonight, up in Woodstock, New York, some women were going to gather to do a moon ceremony for me with a talking stick and some feathers, and here was Maggie making sure I knew how dangerous periods were.

When I got to the stairs, I called back, "By the way, I think I want to go back to being called Phronsie. That *is* my real name, after all."

Boom. The silence from the kitchen was thick, like a bomb had gone off.

I felt pretty good about that.

Having Mama back in my life after the period call was a little bit like having a huge, delicious secret. I bought a phone card like she suggested, and a few times a week, I'd go call her from a pay phone located out behind Dinah's Dress Shoppe, which had closed down the year before. The phone booth was way in the back of the parking lot, hardly ever used, and it was cramped and filled with papers and broken glass, but over time I came to think of it like another home, and I fixed it up. I cleaned out all the trash and brought a little plastic stool from home and left it there so I'd have someplace to sit. While I talked to Mama, I would draw pictures, and I propped the pictures I did against the walls of the phone booth, and so it was like my own personal little art gallery.

On the days when I called her, I would get off the school bus in town instead of going home. I told Maggie that I liked to go to the pet shop and pet the puppies and play with the kittens. I wanted to be a vet, I said, and this was going to give me some good experience.

I think Maggie was just relieved not to have me brooding and underfoot, so she ignored the fact that I had never once thought I would become a vet. She said, "Just don't talk to strangers." As if there *were* any strangers in our little town. It was a whole town of non-strangers.

But, there's this: if she'd known how magical and weird the conversations were that I was having, she might have preferred I was talking to strangers.

Mama wasn't like anybody in Pemberton, that's for sure. Or maybe anyone in the whole state of New Hampshire. She talked to me about everything. She believed in goddesses, of which she was one, and apparently so was I. She was also a witch and she had a group of women she called "the women who run with the wolves," and she told me they spoke of their vaginas like they were personal friends of theirs, not simply parts of their bodies.

We roared with laughter over that.

"Of course my vagina speaks to me as well," she said, "but it's mostly my stomach I hear from."

Just her voice—her throaty, low voice coming to me through the receiver—moved me beyond words.

I told her all my problems. All of them. And I asked her all the questions I couldn't ask anybody else. Was it worth it to take science when all I wanted was to be a writer? Should I wear eyeliner only on the bottom edge of my eye or draw the line up near my top lid? Should I stay mad at Hendrix for telling Billy David that I had a crush on him? What was the best thing to do to get to be friends with catty girls? How often should I shave my legs? Should I buy my own bras because the ones Maggie bought for me were horrible?

Her advice was never anything I expected to hear. "Yes, take science. You never know what you'll need in your life as a writer. Eyeliner: everywhere you want! Look how you want to feel inside! Don't stay mad at anybody. Maybe Billy David needs to know you have a crush on him; that kind of information could change a person's life. As for the catty girls . . . who needs 'em? Ignore them until they behave. Leg shaving: a barbaric ritual sold to women by the patriarchy. Bras: same thing. But if you wanted a nice lacy one, and Maggie doesn't want you to have it, go find one yourself."

There are signs everywhere you look, she said. Messages coming to you. You just have to watch for them.

There were other things, too, random things. Back when she was a teenager, she'd ironed her hair every single morning before school. She had wanted to be a ballerina and a concert pianist and a witch. In ninth grade, she was voted homecoming queen in a tie vote, and she won in a runoff, but she let the other girl wear the crown and she wore the sash because she really didn't care and the other girl did. Now she wished she'd let her wear the sash, too. She'd had eleven boyfriends before she met my father.

She'd had such an interesting life, and here I had practically nothing. I had—what? A farm-house and a stepmother who was uptight and a father who scowled all the time, and a brother who never wanted to talk about anything real. Besides all that, I had homework and good grades and a job on the school newspaper.

"No, no, no," she would say to me. "Stop with that kind of talk. You're at the beginning. You're creating your reality, and the words you tell yourself, the story you believe about yourself, is the way things are going to turn out for you. You have to fill your heart with love for yourself, Phronsie. That is the first and most important thing you have to do. Everything you want will follow from that."

"Okay," I'd say quietly.

Sometimes she was talking to me from work, from the gallery, and she had to stop to wait on customers. She always made fun of the city people, people who came up from New York City, wanting only to gawk at the hippies and buy paintings that would match their couches, she said. Once I heard her order a customer to leave the premises immediately for asking if she could repaint something a more orangey color. "Grief is not orange," she said. "And this is a painting about my grief."

"Wait a minute. What is your grief?" I asked her when she came back to the phone.

"You," she said. Then when I was silent, she said, "No, no! That sounds horrible. You could never be my grief. My grief is that I don't have you here with me. That's always my grief. But it's little. Just a little manageable-sized grief. I keep it in my back pocket and it only comes out when I let it, when I'm painting. I just want you to know that I'm someday coming back for you."

After that, we talked all the time about the extravagant measure of our sadness for each other.

"Today I missed you one thousand elephants."

"Yesterday I took the grief out of my pocket when it was the size of a Chiclet, and five minutes later, it blew up to be the size of an aircraft carrier. But I shrank it by telling it to go away. I filled up the grief with love, and it slinked off."

"I took my grief out to the cornfield and buried it," I told her once. "But it beat me back to the house. It was sitting next to Maggie when I went inside for dinner."

Tenaj never did come back for me, and from that I figured out that grief is something you can get

197

used to. You shrink it down, put it in your pocket, like a phone number scrawled on a piece of paper, and maybe after a while, you just leave it in your drawer and don't carry it with you at all.

CHAPTER FIFTEEN

"Wow!" Judd springs awake like he's just been catapulted back into the room—sitting up fast in the bed, rubbing his eyes. Then he looks at me and pretends to do a double take. "Whoa! Wot's dis?? Is there a *laaaady* in my bed?"

"I'm no lady, I'm your fiancée," I say.

"So you are, so you are," he says. "Say, that was kind of a nice sneak attack in the middle of the night. Highly, highly unexpected." He reaches over and pats my hip over the blankets. "A rather brilliant maneuver actually. I owe you a debt of gratitude."

"Well," I say. "You're welcome."

I stretch my arms over my head and sit up. It's still barely light in his room, but I can see his pants folded nicely on the armchair in the corner. Silver picture frames lined up on the dresser. The deep pile carpet. It hits me that I am way messier than he is. I wonder if *that's* going to be an issue when we're living together.

"Holy shit, it's nearly six o'clock," he says. "I've gotta get out of here. I have my ladies coming to bench press at seven." He jumps out of bed, flinging the covers back. And there we are, naked. In the daylight. I want to scrunch up my eyes. He reaches for his boxer shorts superfast, and I rummage through the covers for my under-wear and leggings.

"So this part might be a little weird, isn't it?" he says. "I don't think I've seen you naked since you were five."

"Well. Yeah."

"You look different." He laughs and runs his hands through his hair, looks a bit sheepish.

"So do you."

"But it was okay for you, right? Last night?" My heart contracts, seeing how worried and hopeful he looks. "We're good together, right?"

I say, "It was great."

He seems relieved. "So I guess you still want to get married?"

"I do. I am officially throwing in my lot with you. Yes."

"Well, that's great," he says. He hesitates for a moment, looking just a little bit shy. "I gotta run, get in the shower. You pushing off? Normally, I'd make some coffee and a formal breakfast, but . . ."

"No. No. Of course. You weren't expecting company," I tell him. "Go take your shower, and I'll get up and let myself out. I've got a busy day, too."

He goes padding off down the little hallway, and then he calls back to me, "Oh! By the way, look in my pants pocket. I got you the ring."

"Well, but don't you want to present it?"

There's a silence, and then he says, "Nah. Just take it out of my pocket and see if you like it. If you don't like it, I'll give it back to Eddie."

"Listen. I can wait for you to give it to me."

"No! Phronsie, just take it, all right? See if it's what you like."

So I go over and feel around in the pocket of his sweatpants, and sure enough there's a sweet little white box with a silver ring inside, nestled in a black velvet groove. It has a smooth little diamond, nothing ostentatious, which is good. It fits me. And he'd somehow discerned my size, which pleases me. Denotes effort on his part. Or maybe just amazing luck.

The shower turns on, along with the ceiling fan.

"You like it?" he hollers.

"Yeah! I do! It's nice!"

"And it fits?"

"It fits."

"Fabulous!"

"Okay then. So. Well, I'm leaving now. Have a good day for yourself."

"Are you wearing the ring?"

"Well, not yet." I go and stand at the bathroom door.

"Why not? You don't like it?"

"Judd," I say. "No offense, but I think—I think I needed you to want to put the ring on my finger. So I'm not going to take it now. I'll wait."

"What? Okay. Whatever."

201

"See? This is one of those things. It's kind of symbolic. The ring. Putting it on the woman's finger. You know?"

"Uh-oh!" he says. "We're having an RCM."

"What's an RCM?"

"It's a romantic comedy moment."

The water running is loud. After a moment, he turns it off and opens the shower curtain and looks at me through the clouds of steam that are filling the room. "Will you hand me my towel?"

"The green one?"

"The brown one."

I give it to him. "I don't know what you're talking about."

"It's one of those moments where you *could* look at me with the eyes you used when we were just good friends—when you thought I was just fine because I was your friend—*or* we could compare me to every single romantic comedy out there, in which case I'd come off looking like some kind of moron."

"Just put the ring on my finger. I do not think that's too much to ask," I say.

"Fine. I will."

"Fine."

"Give it to me."

He's standing there with his towel around his waist. I hand him the ring, and he looks at it, and says, "Give me your hand."

So I do. And he puts the ring on my left ring finger. We stand there, and then he says, "So we're good?"

I roll my eyes. "Yes."

"RCM survived," he says cheerfully. "We've had sex and an RCM, and it's not even seven o'clock in the morning on day one of our official engagement. I think we're off to a good start. A momentous day."

I laugh because I can't help myself.

"Oooh, and now I've made you laugh. See? I think this is a trifecta. We're off to an auspicious start to our entire plan here. Where you're adorable and I'm adorable, and we do a whole bunch of things that make the other one crazy, but because we are such wonderful, forgiving pals—it all works beautifully. Ta-*da!*"

He swoops down and gives me a kiss on the cheek and then pulls back and studies my face. "Right?"

"Right," I say.

Because he is.

As I let myself out, Marguerite Hubbard from 6185 comes out of her apartment with her three corgis. We call her the Queen because she's stately and British, plus she's always on about her dogs, which are so well-behaved that she can maneuver to take them for a walk, all three at one time.

"Hello," she says, and in my imagination, I think she raises her eyebrows at the sight of me in my bathrobe and slippers coming out of Judd's apartment.

Yes, Queen, I spent the night with Judd. And yes, in another stunning development, we're getting married. Here is my ring!

I say nothing of the sort. I say hello in an overly friendly voice, and then I wish her a nice day and go to the stairs and head down to my little apartment, where Mr. Swanky is waiting and wagging his tail.

"Guess what. News flash: Judd and I are getting married, boy," I say.

He cocks his head to the side, like he's trying to figure it out. I know the feeling well. "Don't worry," I tell him. "You too. You're getting married, too."

He wags, but he's got that worried pug look going on. I think he lacks confidence in the future.

"Don't take it so hard. It's what all the adult humans do," I tell him. "We have to match up with other people, you see. It's like a rule or something. It's because we didn't get neutered or spayed. I'm sorry to bring that up if it's difficult for you to hear about that chapter of your past, but there's the truth of it."

Mr. Swanky goes over to the door. He'd just as soon go pee than hear any more about this matter.

204

I call Maggie as soon as I get off the subway.

"Well, it's set in stone!" I say when she answers the phone. "I have a ring!"

"Well, praise the Lord," she says. "That's wonderful. I knew it was going to happen." Then she says to my dad, "Robert, Robert! Pay attention to me for just one second, will you? Put the paper down and look at me. They're going through with it! We're getting a new son-in-law . . . *yes, it's Judd! Of course it's Judd. Oh, stop it!"

This is the way they talk to each other these days. I try to remember if they ever acted like they were in love with each other. Maybe this is what married love is supposed to look like. As has been pointed out a lot lately, I'm a victim of sitcoms and romcoms, so I don't even know.

I hear him saying something in the background, but he doesn't ask for the phone.

"Hey, could you put Dad on?" I say, and she does.

"So I hear congratulations are in order," he says gruffly. "Or is it still true that one doesn't congratulate the bride, but says 'best wishes'? We don't want anybody to think you deserve congratulations for trapping him, you know."

"You can say congratulations if you want to."

"I'll just leave it at saying he's a good man."

"Yes. He is."

"So do you think the two of you will find your

way back to living in New Hampshire?" he says. "Or have you converted him to being a New Yorker?"

I close my eyes. Why does everything my dad says to me sound like an accusation?

"Robert!" says Maggie. "Don't hit her with all of that right now. We've got a wedding to plan. Here, give me the phone."

He mumbles something to her, and then she says into my ear, "Okay, honey. What do you think about a summer wedding at our Cape house? That way we don't have to worry about getting a reservation for a venue on such late notice. What about a destination wedding—we'll put some people up at the house, and I'm sure we can get hotel rooms for the others, and we can have the ceremony in town at the church in Wellfleet."

"I'll have to get back to you," I say.

"Well, hurry up," she says. "This is the only real wedding I'm ever going to get to plan in my whole life, so I've got a lot of pent-up thoughts."

It's true. She and my dad had kind of a hurry-up thing out in the orchard when Hendrix and I were five. And Steve and I eloped, because we thought that was romantic and exciting. Although to even call it an elopement would be to give it some degree of romance and panache. Really, we went to some government municipal building, stood together and said our vows with two witnesses—

one of them Judd—and then we went and had brunch at a French restaurant and then went home to bed to make mad, passionate, newlywed love.

Thinking of that day, I briefly lose my train of thought. But Maggie doesn't notice; she's gone on talking about how fun it's all going to be to plan something. And just like that, from out of nowhere, a little dark cloud flits across my mind and then settles there. Steve—whom I had just hours ago decided I would never think of again—is now figuring rather prominently. It hits me that he didn't want to marry me in front of witnesses and family because he didn't really, really love me; and now Judd doesn't want to even *pretend* we're in love. Even my father doesn't act like he loves anyone. And Tenaj . . . gone from my life.

No one, *no one,* loves me the way I want to be loved. No one loves the whole me.

That news sailing in on the November wind hits me so hard that I almost can't breathe for a moment. I have to stop walking. I don't think I know exactly what prayer is, but I would gladly fall down on my knees on Tenth Avenue right between this nail salon and the Indian restaurant if I could feel really, really loved.

After that, it's rather a headache of a day. I have somehow gotten scheduled for two face-to-face meetings, the worst kind, with authors who have come into the city to discuss the plans for their tours. I have to watch the disappointment on their faces when they hoped for so much more. Then I have to call a third author and tell her that all the major reviewing periodicals are passing on reviewing her picture book, a history of worms. Worms who have personalities. And then there's the Gabora Situation.

That's what I'm discussing in Darla's office when my cell phone rings. I glance down at it as I am turning it off.

The name *Tenaj* flashes across the screen on the caller ID. Now maybe it's because I didn't have any breakfast, or that I didn't get much sleep, or that I have slight cramps and a headache—but I feel myself almost falling backward. I feel like black squares are filling in all the spaces in the air.

I hear from my mom only very sporadically—the way you'd perhaps catch up with an old acquaintance after years of silence. And each time she calls, it's to drop some random piece of information that just crossed her mind and perhaps tripped the wire that made the "Phronsie" bell ding in her head. The last time, about a year ago, she called to tell me that she was dyeing her hair black because when you're bleaching it blonde, the color is so rarely just right. It's often brassy or gold, or even too white. Didn't I agree?

That time I tried to keep her on the phone, plying her with questions about her life. That's when she told me, laughing, that she was getting divorce number three.

"Wait! Wait!" I said, in the same merry voice she seemed to be insisting on. "You've been married *three times?* Weren't you the one who once told me that marriage was so terrible for women that you weren't ever going to get married again?"

She laughed. "Honey, what can I say? With this last one, I fell in love with a rich New Yorker who bought two of my paintings and was the benefactor to lots of artists I knew, and he loved my work the best, so when he asked me to marry him, what could I say? But it was a big mistake. Big, big mistake. I will not go into the details. Perpetuates the negativity, you know. Muddies up your aura if you're not careful."

We never did get to the explanation of divorce number two.

Darla keeps talking, something about airports at Thanksgiving. After a moment, my phone pings. Voice message. Despite everything, all the years of silence, which I am so used to by now, my heart can't seem to stop pounding. Darla says, "Are you all right? Do you need to go take that call?"

"No, no, I'm fine," I say.

Which is a lie. Fifteen minutes later, as soon as I can get away, I go into my office and close the door and lean against it. When I can calm my

"You know what it is," she says. "It's probably not the coffee."

I look out the window at the office building across the street, at all the people in the windows having a routine, ordinary day. Who aren't right now—and probably never will be—getting messages from the universe, courtesy of their mother.

Mothers who didn't leave and then forget to come back for them.

She's different now from the way she was when I knew her. I know that. I've seen her. For too many nights than is probably mentally healthy, I've been known to get up out of bed and find my way to the computer where I type her name into the Google search engine.

What I've learned is that she's somewhat successful now in the art world. She's known for her "whimsical jewelry made from polished stones and glass and wire." She has a little company called Spells and Blessings, and she produces bracelets and necklaces that give healing messages and bring world peace and love. There are pictures of her out in the world, wearing her long boho-style dresses and dangling earrings and necklaces. She has bright eyes and long crinkly hair, and usually she's holding glasses of wine and smiling. Clearly she's no longer shackled to whatever customers happen to come into her gallery in Woodstock.

In fact, the *Times* profiled her once in their Home section, and showed her standing in a futuristic, all-glass kitchen with modern appliances. She was smiling into the camera and stirring a big pot of a famous love potion she'd made, which turned out to involve turmeric and ginger and other secret herbs that would bring long life and vitality, she claimed.

The caption read: "Tenaj DeFontaine, artist, cook, and psychic explorer, knows the secrets of love don't always reveal themselves without a little help from the unseen world."

The article said that Mrs. DeFontaine considers herself a free spirit and has had several marriages.

"Mrs. DeFontaine says that love is out there for everyone. It just may not show up in the form we're expecting."

CHAPTER SIXTEEN

My mom was my lifeline in those clandestine phone calls when I was in middle school and high school. Girls at school being mean? Who cares? The important thing was to love yourself. And to laugh at anything that might take you away from all that love. The other important thing, she said, was to always be yourself, even if that person you were was weird and quirky and didn't know anything about getting along in life.

"You may not know who you are, but remember that nobody else knows who they are either. Those people who seem like they've got it all together? They don't. You can always love everybody and everything," she said. "Flow it to anybody you think you might hate. Flow it to that David Billy—"

"Billy David."

"Yes, him, and to whoever else needs it. Hendrix needs a lot of it, my poor lamb. No, no, I'm not going to think of him as my 'poor lamb.' That handicaps him. I'm going to picture him in the bloom of safety and love and health. Everything happens for a reason, you know. Even his accident. We are all where we were meant to be."

I said that accident meant that I couldn't have

visitation anymore. It meant that I was adrift.

"No, no," she said. "It didn't. It meant that you and I found this much more deeply personal way to connect. We'll always have our secret, Phronsie. I love secrets."

One day I said as lightly as I could, "So, hey. I need you to tell me about you and my father and Woodstock. I want to know the whole, whole thing."

"Oh God," she said and laughed. "Oh, man! That. It's got a lot of parts you might not want to hear," she said. "Things that might not be considered *appropriate*."

I was fifteen by then. We talked about things that weren't appropriate all the time. It was sort of our *thing*.

"It's your love story," I said. "Nothing wrong with a love story. And it's my origin story, so I have a right to know it, don't I?"

I was hungry for stories of love, because I was in love with Billy David, and I'd even gotten grounded for making out with him in his truck parked in our driveway in broad daylight. And then, in the most romantic gesture I'd ever even heard of, Billy David sneaked over to see me two nights in a row when everyone was asleep. I sat at my window and he stood on the packed-down snow and we did sign language to each other. *I love you.*

"Nothing you can tell me about Woodstock would shock me," I said.

I scooched down on the floor of the phone booth for this one, sitting there in the cramped space, in the dirt, next to the candy wrappers and an old penny that somebody had dropped so long ago that it was fused into the concrete floor.

"Well," she said, and I held my breath. "First, a little background. I was twenty-three when Woodstock happened, five years older than your father. And very worldly! Ohhh, I was worldly. I went there because I had me a plan to meet the musicians who were performing. Not to be a groupie or anything. I wanted to design album covers for them. So I figured I'd meet a bunch of musicians and start doing portraits of them, you see? And that way I'd get to be a famous artist. So my best friend, Cissy, went with me, and we took along this other guy we both liked. What was his name? Oh! Gary Stephenson, that's right. He was cute in a kind of artistic, I-don't-have-time-for-talking kind of way. Very, very sexy. He talked with his eyes closed. And he had a beard. We loved his beard, and also the way he wore his jeans. Way low on his hips. And he didn't wear any underwear. Said he liked going commando." She laughed.

I stayed silent just in case she'd remember I was her kid and would start censoring any juicy details. But she didn't.

"So we drove there in Louis the Lizard, which was the name of my old 1965 VW Beetle. Ha! You should have seen that car. He was some kind of faded horrible lizard green—well, I thought he was beautiful, but no one else did. He was the first car I owned, and he had a window that was about four inches wide and four inches tall, and it was so smoky from all the dope that got smoked in him that you could barely see out the back. Everybody got a contact high just from riding in him. With me so far?"

"Yeah, yeah."

Her voice got all dreamy. "We got on the road coming from Albany, and there were just cars everywhere. The traffic was unbelievable. We didn't live that far away, just an hour or so, but we couldn't really even get close. Cars were stopped on the highway, and everybody was heading to Max Yasgur's farm, where the festival was taking place. Only as we got closer, the road was impassable, so we all got out of our cars and were standing around talking to each other and smoking joints and passing them around. Some people just left their cars altogether and were walking five or six miles with their sleeping bags. And the people! Oh my God. Everybody was like the most fun person you ever met! We were all so high, and we were singing at the top of our lungs. I was singing Joni Mitchell, and—"

I hated to interrupt, but she was showing signs

of going off on a long, unnecessary tangent. "So, how did you meet Daddy?" I said.

"Well, your daddy. Let's see. He came in a truck with one of his friends, a guy named Tom, and they happened to be parked near us on the highway. It was all random—if you *believe* in random, which I don't. Everything is for a reason. Anyway, they'd just happened to stop there, and they were outside, leaning against the truck, and Robert had a beer, and we were all just talking, and it was like everybody who came along was like my instant best friend and we'd just all been invited to the same groovy party. I kept thinking, *Wow! I've never seen so many people who are exactly like me!* We had a couple of joints, and so we started sharing them, and Robert offered us a beer. I hadn't ever had beer before, because I thought that was just for 'juicers.' In those days you were a juicer, or you were a stoner. And I was definitely in the stoner category, but he said I should try it. Right away, he was looking at me—and Phronsie, he was so—well, he was so gawky and shy." She laughed. "Okay, I have to try to recreate for you what your father was like. He hadn't grown into his body yet. You know the type? He reminded me of a big puppy who is falling all over himself because he hasn't gotten used to his own size yet. Long, skinny legs, big feet and big hands. And this neck that was totally white even when his face was so red. Oh, and he kept blushing! I had on a long patchwork skirt and a halter top, and things kept slipping out of place, and I'd see him looking at my tits and then he'd have to turn away because he was so embarrassed for looking. I'd been with guys for a long, long time by then, and none of them were like that. Everybody was jaded by that time. Nothing was new anymore. And Robert just kinda stood out. He was so *fresh*. Like, he hadn't ever smoked any dope, hadn't ever seen so much love and sex and mud and hippies. His jeans were worn way too high on his waist, and his hair was so short, like a haircut Richard Nixon would have thought was cool, and he had on a plaid shirt, and everybody but me was just sort of ignoring him. Oh, and he had these sun-burned ears that stuck out, so big it was like they didn't really belong to him. I love me an under-dog, so I went over and put some of my beads on your father like a necklace, and he turned almost bright purple. My fingers touched his cheek when I did that, and man oh man, it was like we'd both had an electric shock or something. I could feel it going all through my whole body, that current."

"Did you have any idea at all that you were going to marry him and that he was going to be the father of your children?"

She laughed. "No. Oh, God no. I wasn't any-where near thinking that way. About him or about children or anything. I was just there to have a good time and get myself famous."

It was dark, she said, by the time they got into the concert, and even then, they didn't make it to the front gate; they broke through a hole in the fence.

"By that time, everybody was just piling into the festival. It was a free concert. Music was playing, people were dancing and talking, and I heard a girl saying, 'I feel like I've found all my true brothers and sisters right here!' And then Robert and I found a spot and put our sleeping bags down and we walked around, looking at everybody and everything. And laughing. We couldn't stop laughing. There were tents where you could buy food and water pipes and posters and beads, stuff like that. I told Robert I did glasswork art and crocheted necklaces. We sat down on the ground and shared a hamburger, and a little girl about five years old came over and sat down with us, and Robert gave her his half of the burger. I loved that he did that! And when I looked at him, I thought he looked like somebody who was all lit up from the inside. Maybe I was stoned, but he just had all this love in his eyes. Rockets of love."

Her voice ran down.

"And?" I said.

She took a deep breath. "Then Richie Havens— he was the first act—he started to play, and the music just kind of swept over us," she said. Her voice got a little husky. "Robert—there was something about him that was so touching and sweet. His eyes were just wide with amazement at everything he was seeing and experiencing. He was so *open* to absolutely everything! When I told him I was going to go up to the stage to talk to the musicians, he came with me, just in case, he said, any of the rock stars wanted to kidnap me and have me live in their trailer with them, can you imagine? So funny! And along the way he told me about his life in New Hampshire— the farm and everything. I couldn't imagine that kind of life actually. He told me that because he was the only son, his job was to run the farm alongside his dad. And he said he was going to get married to his high school girlfriend. They'd gone to *prom* together. He said that like it was the biggest deal in the whole world, going to prom. He even knew what color dress she'd worn—can you believe it? He'd had a cummerbund the same color, lavender, he said. The word *cummerbund* just sounded so weird and hilarious, and I started laughing at it. For the rest of the day I called him Cummerbund. And it would make him blush. But . . . well, it was also just so sweet and also so foreign to me—the idea of this all-American, short-haired guy with the stick-out ears, who had pretty much just come right from the prom! I kind of dug that about him, that this kind of life existed somewhere. And here he was, looking around at everything like he was Dorothy in Oz: 'Toto, I don't think we're in Kansas anymore.'

"By the time we got back to our spot, Gary and Cissy had kind of become a duo. And Tom, your dad's friend, had lost interest in all of us and was wandering around. He'd met this band camping near us, and he was spending most of his time with them. I could see I was going to have Cummerbund to tend to, and here he was, talking on and on to me about his completely normal, American life on a farm in New Hampshire. He could do a whole riff on how dumb chickens are! He was hilarious on the subject of chickens. After a while, he asked me about my life, like he expected that I was going to have the same kinds of stories he did. I half expected him to think I was going to talk about what color *my* prom dress had been. But oh, Phronsie, my life was so different from that. My parents had both died already—my dad had cancer and died when I was twelve, and my mom had drunk herself to death after that. I pretty much raised myself, 'cause I lived with an aunt who didn't have much time for me because she already had five kids. So there I was, working as a waitress but determined to make it with my art, living in a little cottage on the outskirts of Albany, and when I started talking to Robert and he was the nicest, most solid human being I'd met in a really long time, he made me laugh about how crazy everything was. He didn't know any hippies, he didn't know anybody who was cool, really, and he just looked at everything with this wonder in his eyes. I loved it. I kept falling over laughing at the things he'd say. And—well, he'd just look at me like he had the moon in his eyes or something. He'd say, 'You're so *beautiful.*'

"So over the next few days, what happened between Robert and me was just inevitable. It was magic at work. It was transformative. Like serendipity. Meant to be." She was quiet for a moment. And then she whispered, "It changed my life completely, those days."

"Because you fell in love?"

"Yes, sure, but not just with him. Because I fell in love with the whole world. Every blade of grass, every molecule of mud, the notes of the music, the smell of the people there and the dope they were smoking. All of it was just surreal. That night, we climbed up a hill and looked down on the whole scene, and it—well, it knocked me out. There were campfires everywhere and lanterns and candles. Little dots of light all over the field. Sooo many people, and all of us were listening to the same music all at one time, and I couldn't get over it. We were—I don't know—so *connected.* By those songs. Even Robert, who lived a life so different from mine, even *he* knew all those songs. They were our common language. We sat there on that hillside in the dark, looking down at almost half a million people all listening to the same songs—and you just couldn't help but fall in love with all of life. All of humanity."

She stopped for a moment. I could hear her take in a ragged breath. And I waited. Then she said, "I knew he had a girlfriend back home. Maggie. He was very clear about that. But we wanted each other just the same. He hadn't had much experience in sex stuff, and we were joking around about how he needed to rectify that situation *immediately,* and then we were just fooling around in the little tent he brought, and we were in the sleeping bag, kissing and stuff, and then—well, he kind of went wild on me. He said he loved me, and I said, 'No, you're just loving everybody in the world right now!' But I thought, *Well, what if this is the real deal with this guy, and I turn it away because of being afraid? What if this guy is the love of my life? And the girlfriend back at home* isn't *really the one for him, but just the only one he's ever known?* So we just let go. Fell into the whole experience. Let it happen. And well, we kept doing it all through the three days. We went skinny-dipping with about a hundred people in the river, and looking at all those bodies—all shapes and sizes and conditions—well, *damn,* it felt like the way life was supposed to be. You know? This was going to be the new world order after this."

She let out a big sigh. "We'd wake up in the morning and there would be this fog all over everything, and people around you waking up, too, and getting food, with music playing. All these groups playing the most amazing songs. Sly, Country Joe, the Grateful Dead, Jefferson Airplane—really amazing music from everybody you ever wanted to hear. Groups I'm sure you never even heard of.

"And then the rain started. Oh my God, the rain! A big storm came in, and everybody just got drenched, and the place got so muddy. We were playing in the mud, sliding in it like toddlers, soaked through and laughing so hard, like we were little kids again.

"We couldn't keep our hands off each other. Cissy took me aside and said, 'What are you *doing?* This guy is not your type at all!' But it felt like none of that mattered. I had never laughed so much.

"And he was the same. He walked around through that whole three days with a hard-on. We were living in this euphoria, like a time out of time kind of, and—oh yeah, then I got sick. Maybe it was the mud and the lack of sleep and all the people around me, but I got really, really sick. Ran a fever and everything, and he took care of me. He was so gentle and helpful, like the way he probably was around the farm with the animals. He took me to the medical tent, and he stayed there with me while they gave me fluids and food. He'd been planning to leave; Tom wanted to get back, to be home by Sunday night, but Robert said he wouldn't go. Not while I was sick. Isn't that the sweetest thing? So Tom and Robert had an argument, and finally Robert told him he'd find another way home. We all figured he could hitch a ride; lots of people were probably going to New Hampshire, and so Tom left. I was feeling a little better by then, but I let Robert carry me back to our tent. By then, it was *our* tent. We were a couple. Nobody knew for how long— maybe for only another hour. Or a day.

"And then this is the part I'll never forget. Coming out of our little tent on Monday morning and standing there in the fog, wrapped up in the sleeping bag, and there was Jimi Hendrix on stage, playing 'The Star-Spangled Banner.' He played it with such crazy discordant notes, like he was creating a whole new anthem for us. A lot of people had gone by then, and all around us it looked like a war zone, like Gettysburg, maybe, there was so much trash and garbage everywhere—but there was Jimi Goddamned Hendrix, and this just seemed like the new America, what we were all going to come to, a land of love and music, and everything was going to be all right. The war was raging on, and everything that had felt so messed up before was now going to be fixed. It sounds stupid to say now, and naive, but it was like mankind had moved in a whole new direction, like the war was going to end, and everybody was going to connect to everybody else and everything in the universe. I started to cry it was so beautiful. And I was standing there next to Robert, and he felt it, too, and later we just got into my car, with Cissy and Gary, and we drove back to my little house, and he stayed with me. Every day he'd say he was going to go back home. Every day we'd look up the bus schedules and then he'd decide to hitch a ride back, and every day we were having the most amazing sex, and then he started helping some guy fix his car, and the guy said he'd start paying him and giving him work. Your dad was always good at machines and stuff like that, and—I don't know—I think we both just kept expecting it to end, and then it kept not ending.

"And then . . ." She let out a big breath. "I found out I was pregnant."

"Ohhh," I said softly. "Us."

"Yeah, you little rascals!" She laughed. "So much for plans, huh? You had other plans for me and your dad. It was a shocker. When I told Robert I was pregnant, I was scared what he'd think, but he got the biggest smile on his face, and then he and I started dancing around the house. This was a baby that was conceived in the new world, he said. A baby of huge, intense, great magic and change for the whole world. A Woodstock child from the music and the love. That was it, then. We took it as a sign that he wasn't supposed to go back to the farm. He was going to stay with me, and we decided we'd move back down to Woodstock, because it was our lucky place, and we rented that little cottage—the one I still live in—and everything felt so perfect and right."

I cleared my throat. "What did his family say? Were they so mad at him?"

"Well . . . yes." She laughed drily. "He had conversations on the phone with his mom and dad, and I think he called Maggie and told her, too. He didn't really want to talk about that part with me, because it didn't have anything to do with me, he said. Maggie was his problem, was how he put it.

"But then Bunny and Gordon drove up to meet me, and we all had lunch together in a little diner near the house where Robert and I were staying. And I'll never forget how Robert was brave, even though I could tell that seeing his parents there really was hard for him. And Bunny was sweet to me. She asked how I was feeling, and she brought me a present, some farm ointment that helped with dry skin and stretch marks, I think. And also a plant. A peace lily. She hugged me before they left, and she said, 'I rather think that you and Robert need to get married. You're a family now.' And so we did."

"And then we were born?"

"Yes. Then you were born in the back room of our little cottage. Two of you! *That* was kind of a shocker, let me tell you. I hadn't been so much keeping up with the prenatal care, and we thought you were just one giant baby—and then after Hendrix was born, it was like you said, *Yoo-hoo! Don't forget about me!* Oh my God. We were so sweaty and tired, and both you and Hendrix were these wide-eyed babies, looking all around, and snuggling up to nurse. And Robert—" Her voice catches. "Robert got up in the bed next to me and next to you and Hendrix, and he said to me, 'Tenaj, you're a sorceress. You took three days of music and magic and turned it into two babies.' "

We were quiet for a long moment. I couldn't believe my dad said that. I thought of how he certainly wouldn't have said that anymore. But it was amazing to think of how he wanted us. At the time. That he was glad. Something fluttered inside my own heart. He wanted us.

She let out a long sigh. "So that's how it happened. That's your story, baby."

"Wow," I said.

"So you came from love," she said. "You were conceived during the most incredible display of peace and love on the planet—half a million people gathering in the mud and the rain for music and love. No matter how it turned out, you

228

came from love. Sent here special delivery by the universe."

That May, Hendrix and I turned sixteen. He was fully involved with Ariel by then and also working with our dad on the farm. For me, I was still writing poetry and working on the school newspaper and writing short stories about unrequited love. I stopped seeing Billy David with his clumsy hands and his childishly obscene way of sitting on his bike seat, and I started going out with a guy who called himself Steppenwolf for some reason, and he was dangerous and wicked and also a poet, and we sneaked out and ran the streets at night when the good people of Pemberton, New Hampshire, were sleeping. My parents detested him, although I was sure Tenaj would have liked him if only I could manage to get him and me up to Woodstock to meet her.

We'd go on long hikes in the woods by ourselves, and I'd tell him about my hippie mother and the stories about Woodstock, and he'd tell me about his plan to move up there someday himself and his wonderful ambition, which was to set up a card table in the downtown area, and write five-minute poems for people who came by on the street. He would charge five dollars per poem, and he'd get famous and probably rich.

The day he told me that, we made love in the

woods, using his black leather jacket as a blanket underneath my hips.

It was my first time, and I lay there afterward, with my vagina stinging and burning, and twigs digging into my back, and possibly a rock pressing against my head. I had tears in my eyes, thinking that this was the most romantic thing that could ever happen to a person. And if I was pregnant from it, then so be it. This would be a child of the woods and the leaves and the poetry and the dream of Woodstock. I looked over at Steppenwolf, who right then was the most beautiful human being I'd ever seen in my whole life, lying on his back, his eyes glistening in the sunlight, his hand flung over his forehead, his gorgeous body exposed there in the daylight.

If I was pregnant, it would be karma, and I would have a reason to call Tenaj and tell her of this celebration of the amazing ongoingness of life, of her legacy. She would be so stunned and amazed. We'd have moon ceremonies and we'd light candles and I'd travel up to see her and dance with her at the full moon, and oh, there would be all kinds of things we'd do, to welcome this child. To welcome *me* into motherhood.

For some reason, she and I had stopped talking every week. Maybe once a month I'd call her, but she seemed busy and distracted. I'd try to talk to her about Woodstock again, to hear her talk once more about how loved Hendrix and I had been.

But she was focused on the gallery, and her voice felt far away. She said she was tired. She was busy, and I was busy.

We were connected somehow . . . We weren't talking much, but it was fine. I made up my mind I'd probably move up there and live with her if I was pregnant. Steppenwolf could come, too. We could be hippies up there with my mom.

But then I wasn't pregnant, and I forgot all about calling her. One day, months later, when I went back to try, I discovered that the phone booth had been removed. There was nothing there but that little penny, still stuck to the concrete.

CHAPTER SEVENTEEN

"You know that I think of you as a daughter, don't you?" says Gabora. She smiles at me, activating her sweet old-lady dimples. But I am not fooled. Gabora, bless her heart, is not harmless. I've worked with her since my first day on the job at Tiller, when I was still a "baby publicist," as she called me. She tells people she had to break me in—which always makes me sound like a racehorse or something. But it's probably true; she was my first big test of strength.

"Why, thank you so much," I say. "You're sweet to say—"

She interrupts me. "Which is why I feel perfectly justified in asking you why in the world you're wearing those shoes! Who would even *try on* those shoes in the store?" She laughs and shakes her head.

I am wearing clogs, ladies and gentlemen. So sue me. They're comfortable. Also I've been on an airplane. I have had to remove shoes in the security line. Clogs come off and go on very easily. This was ideal when I was not only managing my own items in that line, but also the items of a certain ungrateful old lady, for whom I am responsible for the next three days.

I sigh. We have survived the TSA checkpoint,

as well as the endless wait at the gate (during which I was sent off to procure bottled water, a *People* magazine, sugarless gum, a neck pillow, and a sleep mask), and the flight itself, during which she needed help with her seat belt and the itinerary, and *then* we landed and were staggering through the terminal, searching for the location of our driver who was hired to meet us but was late . . . aaaaand the drive to the Charleston Pines Inn & Conference Center.

And now we are in the lobby, resting Gabora's bunions while Adam checks us in.

"Never mind," she says and leans over and pats my knee. "I can see I still have some work to do with you. It makes me happy. Gladdens my heart to be working with you again. Remember the blue suit?" She winks and pats her huge blonde bouffant hairdo—a wig, the kind Dolly Parton might appreciate—and smiles at me with her Kiss Me Pink lips, circa 1954.

Ah, yes, the blue suit. I knew it might come up. One day ten years ago, as we rode in a cab to one of her many readings, she was delivering me a pointed lecture about *fashion* and *professionalism* and the need to *dress for the job you intend to do*. And then suddenly she leaned forward and tapped the driver on the shoulder and instructed him to pull over, right that second. Then she marched me into a high-end clothing store called Gina Louise's that had seemed to materialize right out of thin air at her insistence, and she bought me a royal-blue linen jacket and skirt and a white chiffon-type blouse to wear underneath it. I tried it on under duress. It made me look like a member of the 1950 Junior League, and I didn't even want to come out of the dressing room to model it. But she made me. And then she declared it perfect. She said, "There. You look nice. We are going to bring you some *class* if it kills us," she said.

"I don't suppose you still have it," she says now.

"I do. I have it. It doesn't fit so well anymore . . ." Which is a lie. I have no idea if it fits or not, because it is in the back of my closet. The only reason it hasn't been given to Goodwill is that it reminds me of that day, and the truth is, I have a little soft spot for Gabora Pierce-Anton. It was so nice of her, even in her pushy way, to care what I looked like. I had been pretty much emerging from my Poor College Girl Slouchy-Style days, which had been preceded by my New Hampshire Farm Girl days, with a smattering of hippie boho thrown in, in honor of my mother. Far, far from Junior League.

And now here we are. I think I look pretty nice in my black slacks and an oatmeal-colored silk tunic, with a little twist of silver hanging from a cord. And my clogs. No matter what she says.

She's looking me up and down. I cast a longing

glance over to the check-in counter, where Adam seems to be next in line. He looks over and shrugs.

"I have just one big issue with you," Gabora says. "You know, in the past, you would have gotten *People* to do a story about my new book. What happened here with your team? I got nothing." Her eyes narrow.

I want to say that the fates smiled down on us by not having *People* write about her book, since every story that has run anywhere has been filled with criticism of the implicit racism of her book. But I manage to shrug. "Well, magazines do what they do," I say. "We sent in the press release, but they were tight for space this week, I think."

"Well," she says, sniffing, and folds her hands over the pocketbook on her lap. "I suppose they think an old woman like me doesn't care anyway. *They* no doubt think I've had all the attention I'm entitled to. Getting old is not for the faint-hearted, believe me. Maybe my next book will be about Eleanor and Peter losing their grandmother to some kind of mercy killing. See how *People* magazine likes *that.*"

She bares her teeth at me, which is meant to be a smile.

It's been five years since her last book, five years since we've gone out on tour together. Back then, we only went to major bookstores, where throngs of children, parents, and grandparents showed up and waited in line to get their books signed. Sometimes they'd bring stacks of Peter and Eleanor books from the series, and the little girls would wear pigtails just like Eleanor does. A few times, children even brought along little stuffed white mice, like Lancaster, the pet that Peter and Eleanor take along on their adventures.

And then . . . well, Gabora stopped writing books. There were a few little health issues once she reached eighty. She and I kept in touch sporadically; she said she was thinking of traveling the world, just as soon as she felt strong again. Her daughters, Lois and Tillie—known to me as Cinderella's wicked stepsisters—were looking after her, she said.

And then suddenly—there was another book! I would not have put it past Lois and Tillie to have forced her to write it, for reasons of their own. Perhaps the family coffers were getting dry; maybe it would be great to have one last bestselling infusion of cash to see all the grand-children through college.

At any rate, Gabora now seems much, much older and tireder. Whereas she used to boss me around pretty severely, now she's adopted a little-girl tone of voice.

She is looking now at Adam. "*He's* certainly no snappy dresser. Not a competent woman alive would want *that* in her bed. What has happened to men, anyway? Those short jackets they wear, the five o'clock shadow all day long! And their hair—they just let it do anything! Anything at all. Who do they think wants to see anything like that?"

Adam is now one-handedly staring at his BlackBerry. *Au contraire*, I think. He does look a little tousled, but the truth is he is sporting a delightful bedhead mess of beach hair. With his sleepy eyes, he looks like a guy who maybe just fell out of bed after having hours of divine sex. Gabora probably doesn't remember what that's like. The bigger question is why did her generation of women want men with oily, slicked-back hair anyway? What was so great about that?

I smile at her and say nothing. That's the difference now, five years later; I've learned the power of silence.

She's looking at me sharply. "Wait, you're married, aren't you? Now I remember; you have a husband. What's his name?"

"His name was Steve, and no, we're not married anymore." *We divorced years ago; you knew this.*

"You divorced him?"

"I did."

"I'm obviously behind the times. What was the reason, if I may ask?"

"He found someone else."

She looks me over. I can see she's thinking he probably left due to my clogs. Or my hair. Or the fact that I didn't wear the blue linen suit enough times.

Instead she says, "The same thing happened to my Tillie. Men today are just not fit for being husbands. Not like my Jerome, that's for sure. In those days, you married a man, and even if things were hard sometimes, you stuck it out. You knew he would stand by you."

"Yes," I say.

"You'll find someone else," she says and pats my knee.

"Actually," I say, brightly, "I have found someone else. I'm getting married this summer." I hold out my left hand, where my new ring is sparkling on my finger.

"Huh! Sorry, but I thought that was just costume jewelry," she says, peering at it. "See? You've learned a thing or two now, and no doubt you've picked someone who'll make it work. Am I right?"

"I do believe so."

My cell phone rings just then, and I take it out of my pocket. *Tenaj*.

I hold up a finger to Gabora, indicating that this is an important call. "Yes?" I say.

"Did you figure out what my message meant?" Tenaj says. "And did you stop whatever it is you were doing?"

"I'm at work," I say. "I'm afraid I can't really talk now."

"Of course," she says. "Call me when you have time."

I click off and let out an involuntary sigh.

Gabora is staring at me with narrowed eyes. "So this is your life then? You have to travel around with authors and put your own life on hold. You poor, poor thing." She leans forward and says in a low voice, "You know, I don't really need you now, so if you want to go live your own life, that's fine by me. They just want to make sure I don't say things that are politically incorrect, and I am not having it. I'm going to say what I please. So, go home. I'm fine."

"No, I like being with you," I say. "I'm happy to be here with you on the tour."

"No one would be *happy* about this. It's Thanksgiving week, for God's sake. You should be home with whatever family you have, that new fiancé, and we both know it." She turns around to look at Adam. "What's taking that boy so long? Oh, here he comes. A person could die here waiting for a chance to get into a room around this place. And look at that rain outside! How are we going to get to the reading without getting soaked?"

Adam lopes over to where we're sitting. I try not to notice that he has sort of a sexy walk. "We're all set," he says and offers her his arm to help her get up, and after a moment of considering what the ramifications of accepting help would be, balanced by the realization that he is

239

really quite charming and handsome, she simpers and takes his arm.

"I'm really not all that old," she says. "And just so you know, you probably have time for a haircut and shave before the reading tonight."

He lifts his eyebrows and smiles. "Why, Ms. Pierce-Anton, you'd be shocked to know that I just got a haircut last week. I'm afraid that this is as good as it gets with my problem hair."

"It's all . . . tousled," she says. "Like you just got out of bed or something."

"Well," he says and winks, "I've been going through our old files and I came across some old pictures of you and your husband. Old Jerome looked like he had some hair tousling a time or two."

To my surprise, she laughs. Then I take one of her bags, and he takes the other, and we make our way to the bank of elevators. Once we get her settled in her room, she tells us she plans to rest until it's time to go to the reading. "You can come and get me then," she says. "I'll be ready at six. And make sure this hotel provides us some umbrellas. I've never seen such rain in my life!"

I frown. "Perhaps we should make sure you get some dinner first," I say. "Do you want me to call room service for you, or would you like to meet downstairs for a bite before we get in the cab?"

"I'm perfectly capable of managing that on my own," she says. "I don't like to eat before a reading, as you very well know." And then, as we're leaving, I see that she's opened her massive suitcase and has taken out her silver flask. Ah, yes. It all comes back to me now: Gabora's famous liquid dinner.

"Well, I don't know about you, but *I'm* starving," says Adam as soon as we get in the elevator. Two grandmotherly type ladies in flowered dresses scoot to the back to make room for us.

"After we put our stuff away," he says, "do you want to grab a bite at the bar? I need to recover from being bossed around for the last five hours."

"This is her on her good behavior," I say. "Trust me, things are going to get worse."

"So this is like the pre-apocalypse? Is that what you're trying to say?"

He is leaning against the wall of the elevator, studying me.

"I'm just saying there are some disturbing signs."

"She's going to drink before the reading, isn't she?"

"She will drink before the reading, yes. An amount that you probably wouldn't think wise."

He winks at me. "Ah, we're so in for an adventure."

"Did you actually just wink at me?"

"Did I? I don't remember."

The elevator door opens, and two businessmen

get in. There's some awkward sorting out we have to do with our bags because my backpack strap gets tangled with the wheel of Adam's roller bag. It requires some adjusting, and my Nalgene water bottle falls out and rolls across the elevator floor. Adam stops it with his shoe and leans down to fetch it.

As he hands it back to me, he says, "So it looks like I'm the only one in this trio who didn't bring a flask along."

"This, I'll have you know, is a water bottle."

"So you say. I'm feeling quite outmaneuvered here, like maybe I should go shopping."

I stare at the numbers. The elevator is stopping on every floor for some reason. The other passengers have stopped talking.

"Okay then," he says. "Let's get something to eat. Because I'm sensing that the end-of-the-world zombies really might show up. We have to be able to outrun them."

"Excuse me, but zombies are slow. They're dead."

"What? Which zombies exactly are you referring to?"

"You know. The movie zombies. *Night of the Living Dead*. They get out of the graves and come at you very, very slowly. Also, I'm not hungry."

"Nope, nope, nope. Today's zombies are in a rush. They run in and start killing everyone right away. You're going to need some serious calories to help you get away from them. Also, if I may say so, I think you're going to need some serious calories just to handle the Gabora Apocalypse, especially if that flask is going to be involved."

"Ssh," I say and look nervously at the ladies. For all I know, they could be Gabora fans, here with their little granddaughters to attend the reading tonight. But they seem to take the whole conversation with equanimity; one smiles at me and gives a slight tilt of her head toward Adam, because he really is awfully cute and energetic. She seems like she's congratulating me on landing such a catch. If only she knew.

The elevator door opens on our floor just as my phone rings. I glance down at it and see that it's Judd. I let it go to voice mail.

"You know," I say to Adam, once we're in the hall in front of our rooms, "I think I'm just going to unpack and have a bit of rest. Maybe we can get a bite later or something."

"That's the fiancé, isn't it?" he says. "On the phone."

"Yeah. So I'm going to have to take this. I'll catch up with you later."

"Sure, of course," he says.

Once I'm in the hotel room, though, I'm restless. I try to call Judd back, but don't reach him. It feels like the whole world is settling in for its turkey-making plans, except for me. I'm stuck here in a driving rain with an author who is right now guzzling her weight in whiskey. I want to be on my way to New Hampshire with Judd.

I stand and look out the hotel window. Below me, the highway traffic is backed up as far as the eye can see. People going home. Red brake lights snaking along through the pouring rain. The sky is black with clouds. I'm feeling luxuriously sorry for myself when my phone rings. It's Judd, calling back.

He's full of news. He got in about an hour ago, and he and Hendrix are going to hit the town tonight and check out who's come home for the holiday already. Also, Maggie has called him and said she'd like to have his family over for a post-Thanksgiving dessert and begin planning the upcoming nuptials. She is completely set on a Cape Cod wedding in the summer. Already looking at hotel rooms to reserve for the over-flow because we'd have to reserve those way in advance. Judd thinks that would be just fine. What do I think?

I close my eyes. They will all be there in our cozy dining room, with the damask tablecloth and the good silver and the candlesticks—and oh gosh, the gravy boat. I love when the gravy boat comes out for its annual venture to the table! There will be company and laughter. And Judd's parents! I can't imagine. They are really quite elderly by now, but they always seemed old and sweetly stunned that a son had landed in their lives when they were already past time for "that nonsense." Santa Claus didn't even know to come to their house. He'd probably given up on their ever having a child to bring presents for.

Judd always shrugged off their reticence: "They just weren't into me. What are you gonna do?" But he spent a lot of time at my house just the same. Where people knew what kids were for.

"What do you think?" he's saying. "Summer sound good to you?"

"Sure," I say. "The summer sounds great. So are you going to be telling everybody that we're getting married?"

"Well . . . yeah. I mean, I *want* to. That's okay with you, isn't it?"

"Sure. I just want to know what you're going to tell everyone about *why* we're getting married."

"What do you mean? Nobody asks *why* anybody's getting married."

"Well, I think in our case, people might wonder why we just came up with this plan after all these years."

He laughs. "Phronsie. What are you actually saying?"

"I don't know. Just don't make us sound like losers, okay? Like this was the best we could do. I don't like being the consolation prize."

"Phronsie, Phronsie. How often do we have to go over this? *They* are the losers! They probably all have their divorce attorneys on speed dial because love ran out on them long ago. Hendrix was telling me in the car that *three guys* from his work are having affairs. Three guys. Doesn't that seem a bit much? It's rampant, this discontent."

"Okay . . . okay, I know," I say.

"Chin up," he says. "Believe me. We're the wave of the future. After us, everybody is going to want to give up romantic comedies and just get married to the person they happen to get along with."

My phone makes a little buzz; another call is coming in. I look down. Of course it's Tenaj.

"I gotta go," I tell him. "We'll talk later. Tell everyone hello."

When I click over, there's my mother's breathy voice. "Oh! I thought I was going to be sent right to voice mail prison," she says. "But it's the real you, isn't it?"

"It's the real me."

"Can you talk for a minute?"

"Okay. But only a minute."

"What are you doing? Where are you?"

"I'm in Charleston, South Carolina, in a hotel room, and I'm unpacking before I have to accompany an author to a reading tonight."

"Wow," she says. "This is more information than you've given me about anything in a long time."

"Yeah, well, I'm throwing caution to the wind. Why are you calling me?"

"Why am I *calling* you? I wanted to tell you the most hilarious thing. I've joined a cabaret group, and I'm singing tonight in Brooklyn."

"Brooklyn! Brooklyn, New York?"

"Yes. Is there another Brooklyn? Seriously, I do go to the big city, you know. And I thought if you were around and were free . . . you might want to meet."

"Well . . . I'm not there."

There's a long silence. *I am on the Maggie Team now,* I want to tell her. *I am not going to fall for you anymore.*

"Look," she says, as if she could hear me. "If you'll just let me tell you a couple of things. The first is that I'm into radical forgiveness. I realized the other day that you and I are so deeply connected that we can never lose each other. And that made me so happy. I know I let you down, but I miss you. And also, that message I got for you the other day—the one that says you're making a big mistake—I hope that didn't upset you, darling, but I felt I needed to tell you."

"Tenaj."

She takes a deep breath. "Let's be in each other's lives again. I've made mistakes, but, honey, I love you."

"Listen," I say. "I'm sorry, but . . . I can't . . . just now. I only have an hour or so until I've got to be ready to go to a reading with this author I'm here with. And I need my head clear so I can do my job. I think I need to get off the phone and rest."

She's silent for a moment. "Okay," she says. "No, this is good. You have to be you, my sweet."

"So . . . well, good-bye," I say.

"Just . . . hold on to magic, Phronsie. Remember our days together. Remember that you will always have me in your corner. For whatever that means to you. You came from the magic and the music, remember that. You are a love child of the universe."

I click the phone off. Then for good measure, I throw it across the room.

CHAPTER EIGHTEEN

The morning my father told me that I couldn't go to college in New York, I didn't do my usual thing with him—the thing where I made myself go numb. Instead, I decided to try to reason with him.

Being numb was the way I'd coped before, like when I was told, at age ten, that I couldn't go see my mama anymore, or when Maggie was overpowering me with rules, or when my dad gave me the look like I was a big disappointment. When he'd take Hendrix with him into town but wouldn't take me. When he said I didn't do my chores quickly enough. When he dismissed my writing as something not even to be noticed. When he wouldn't come to back-to-school nights. When he wouldn't look at the school newspaper I edited, and supposedly "by mistake" used it to start the fire. When he said that I should try to be more practical. Take accounting classes instead of writing. When he said I was just like my mother.

That was the worst insult he thought he could hurl at me: being like my mother.

But I hated going numb. It was like flipping a switch somewhere in my brain, and at first it would feel good, all that nothingness, the silence filling up my head, blocking out the words and feelings. But then being numb became something I had no control over. It was hard to *stop* being numb.

There was something different this time, though. It was breakfast time, a Saturday, October of senior year, and I was making pancakes, and Hendrix was setting the table, and my father was hunched over at the table already, drinking his coffee and rustling the newspaper. He'd come in from mucking out the stalls, which was Hendrix's job, but for some reason Hendrix hadn't done it to his satisfaction, so there was already a current of tension in the house. Like a wire was sparking somewhere and no one quite knew where it was or what to do about it to keep it from setting the whole place ablaze.

I knew my dad was in one of his moods, and normally that would have been enough to make me keep quiet. But that morning, with him kind of mad at Hendrix—aka The Golden Child, the one who helped out on the farm, the one who didn't argue—I decided maybe I could say something that might make him feel a little bit proud of me. Maybe I could cheer him up, I thought.

So I said, "Hey, Dad. Guess what? Mrs. Spezziale told me that nobody else in the senior class has a perfect four point oh, and she thinks that I should apply to a university."

Silly me.

There was a silence. I debated whether to tell him the rest, that Mrs. Spezziale and I had already filled out the application for NYU, and that every day we met in the guidance office and decided on which other schools I should apply to. I wanted to live in New York and be a famous writer. "Dream big," she'd said. Those were the words written on a poster on the mint-green wall of her office. I had straight As and almost a perfect PSAT score, and I was scheduled to take the SATs in another two weeks. I was a guidance counselor's dream, she told me. We sat at her desk in the back room and discussed the advantages of small versus big, fine arts programs versus general studies, New York versus California, like it could all really happen. My English teacher had said she'd write a recommendation letter for me that would "pop people's eyes out." I was a writer, she said. I would be great.

I had sat there so happy in that guidance office, dreaming big, and it never once occurred to me that this wasn't in the cards. Everything seemed possible when I was talking with Mrs. Spezziale in her office with the posters. I was a different girl, the editor of the school paper, a creative writer, a success, when I was in that room. I was going to have a life hanging out with other writers, talking about our stories, going to readings. I wanted to live in a tiny walk-up in the

Village and write all day and go to clubs at night. I had put up posters of the New York skyline in my bedroom, and I ached to walk through those streets, to get out of this stupid farm town.

My father rattled his newspaper and said in a quiet, low voice, "You're not going to a university in New York."

"But why not?" I said.

"Because you're not, that's why."

"Is it the money? Because she thinks I could get a scholarship . . ."

He put his paper down. The way he was looking at me was already causing something to curdle inside me. His eyes were saying STOP IT RIGHT NOW.

"Because you can get any education you want around here, that's why." He got up out of his chair and folded up the newspaper. He was tall and big, his dark hair cut sharp against his head, and he had steely blue eyes that looked like beads, and although he mostly was kind of mild-mannered and unhappy, he knew how to look menacing when he wanted to. It was how he argued, pulling himself up to his full height and towering over people. I'd seen him do this with the field hands for years.

"But if I get a scholarship, what's the difference to you?" That's what I said. I flipped the pancakes over in the pan, and when I turned back to look at him, his eyes had gone dark with trouble.

Hendrix, sitting at the table, tried to signal me to stop. But I shook my head.

"I can't believe I even have to explain this to you," my father said. "You have a perfectly good life here. You have a farm. This is *your* farm, *your* land. This farm is our family's livelihood, and it is your birthright, and you have a duty to protect it. Your ancestors sweated and sacrificed for this land."

"I know, but—"

"No *buts!* What? You think these rocks put *themselves* in that wall out there? Let me give you some news. They did not. Your ancestors *hauled* these rocks and built these walls and plowed these fields and planted and suffered and put up with droughts and floods, and they got up at three in the morning and worried over the barn catching on fire, and delivered the foals and the calves. And it's yours to protect. Do you know what I'm talking about? I'm talking about *loyalty* and *pride.* They don't teach that at NYU."

I waited a respectful amount of time, during which I put two pancakes on the plate and walked them over to his place at the table.

"So could I just say something?" I said in my most reasonable voice. I even smiled a little bit. "I know you, and I know that neither you nor I think it helps anyone to expect people to live their whole lives doing things they don't want to. You know yourself that's not how the world should be."

I was talking to the boy he had been, the one who went to Woodstock, the boy that Tenaj had told me stood on the hill and thought the whole world would change because of that three-day rock concert. I said these words even though his eyes were coldly staring me down and even though the numbness was already coming upon me like a slow dose of Novocain. In a moment, I knew, the fight would be gone out of me. He would retaliate, and I would sink back. But I said the words anyway. I said them with a smile, with as much bravery as I could muster, with an optimism born out of hearing from his ex-wife about the wonderful, idealistic young man he had once been. I thought there was at least a shot that I could reach that guy.

But he was beyond that. He'd gone reptilian on me. I should have known.

"I am *not* arguing this point with you!" he roared. "And I am *not* going to stand by and watch you throw all this away just because you have some damn fool idea that you have to go to New York to be a writer. Art, young lady, is for when there's not a crop to bring in or washing to do or a fox in the chicken coop. You're staying here, and that's final. We owe our loyalty to this farm. You can go to the community college and study writing all you want on the side. But you're staying here."

I started to open my mouth.

"Case closed," he said. "You're just like your mother. I bring her here, I show her this whole wonderful life she could have here—and what does she do? She rejects all of it."

And then he looked at me, with the muscle in his jaw pulsating back and forth, and then he left the house. In a moment, his truck started up and backfired in the driveway, like a gunshot, and then he was gone.

It got worse after that. He didn't want me to take the SATs. He said he wouldn't pay the money for the test, and then it turned out he wouldn't even let me take the car to go to the test. He said the community college didn't require SAT scores, and that's where I was going to go to school—so why was I even bothering?

I stopped speaking to him. The house became a silent, seething horror show. Like something was alive and dangerous in there and could spring out at any time and bring the whole place down.

Maggie said, "Why do you have to cross him?"

Hendrix said, "You've gotta give in on this one. You know him. He's not going to change his mind."

Judd said, "Your dad is a tough guy, but he's got your best interests at heart."

"No, he doesn't," I said.

Mrs. Spezziale said, "I've dealt with fathers like this before. This is the 1980s, not the 1950s. He'll come around."

She and I worked on my essay in the guidance office, just as if nothing had happened, as if I were going to college. She paid the fee herself, and we mailed in four applications. She said again and again, "He'll come around."

But he didn't.

I told Bunny about it during one of my lazy days with her. We used to sit and knit together, and we were making Christmas presents for everybody. Socks and scarves and hats.

She sighed and said, "Your father can be a very stubborn man." Then she put down her knitting and rubbed her eyes. "This feels like something that should never have happened, and I feel partially to blame."

"How are you to blame? That can't even be possible."

She stared out the window. "Your dad never wanted this farm. He had other aptitudes, and yet he got saddled with it after his dad, your grandfather, died. I asked him to come home and run things, when what I really should have done was let him be free. I should have sold off the land right then and cashed out and gone traveling or something. But I didn't because I selfishly couldn't bear to let it all go. But I should have.

I knew almost immediately that it had been a mistake, calling him back. Maybe his marriage with your mother would have worked if they hadn't come back here. I don't know. We can't know, can we? But now I feel like he's taking it out on you."

She did not say that she would go and fight him just the way she'd done when he wouldn't allow us to have visitation with Tenaj. The fight had gone out of Bunny. Even I could see that. But she said I could sleep at the Bunny Barn. She said I should remember that I was strong and that I had my own life to lead. She said she was sorry that she had any part to play in this drama.

And I said she was blameless. It was him.

My SAT scores came back. I had gotten my friend Jen to drive me to the test, and I had done well.

And then on April first of senior year, I got my acceptance letter from NYU.

My father brought it in the house. It was big and fat, too big to fit in the mailbox, so the postman had seen my father outside and handed it to him. Walked it over to him, said, "Wow, looks like one of your kids is headin' to college!"

I'd never seen my father so mad when he came in the house and held it up.

"So you did it anyway," he said to me in a voice that might have come from James Earl Jones playing the Voice of Doom. "Applied to New York University."

His face was red and sweaty. His hair was plastered to the sides of his head, and his eyes now looked like they were capable of shooting sparks. He threw the envelope on the floor and went to the sink and started washing his hands.

I stood and watched him, my arms folded.

"I just wanted to see," I told him.

"See what? See if I would find out? See if I would change my mind? What exactly *did* you think was going to happen here?"

I looked down at the envelope, which was big and thick with promise. If you were rejected, Mrs. Spezziale said, they'd send you a dinky little one-page note telling you that there were so many qualified candidates, blah blah blah. But if you're *in* . . . that envelope holds lots of pieces of paper, all the promises for your future. Her eyes were shining when she told me that.

I was in. I so wanted to pick up the envelope and take it off and read what they said. I wanted to know the offer for financial aid. I was greedy for the news of my new life. Because I knew that whatever he was saying wasn't going to move me one bit. I had to leave. I was going.

"Oh, you want to see this, do you?" he said, following my eyes. "Go ahead and look at it, if you want. But you're still not going. New York City is a dangerous place for a young person. We are farm people. We are New Hampshire people. Maybe I didn't make that clear enough before. We are not the kind of people who go live in New York City. Get over it. We have a *farm*."

"Maggie has a college education," I pointed out. "While you were living in Woodstock— having me and Hendrix—Maggie was in Boston getting an education."

He looked at me so hard his eyes bugged out. That jaw muscle was so tense I thought it might leap right out of his face. "You!" he said. "You have no business talking about stuff you don't know anything about! Go to your room."

"It's just because you wanted out of here yourself," I said. "Bunny said you didn't want to stay on the farm either and that you were mad when you had to come back here. You wanted to be a musician, she said. And now you're taking it out on me. Trying to crush *my* dreams."

He came toward me, and I actually thought I might get hit for the first time ever.

But he stopped. Looked at me. And then he smiled, a lip-curling smile that didn't reach his eyes. His jaw muscle was twitching hard. "I am not going to have this conversation, do you understand that? You're not going to New York University, you're staying here, you're helping out on the farm, and you can go to the community college. Period."

I held my chin up and looked him in the eye.

Little bits of his spit had landed on my cheeks and chin, and I had flinched, but I was still standing.

Shocked, but standing. I felt myself sink into the numb zone. Everything moved in slow motion.

Now his voice dropped. His eyes had turned opaque, and he was jabbing his finger in the air. "*And* you are furthermore grounded until the end of the school year. No prom, no school play, no yearbook, no parties. This is what you get for being sneaky and going behind my back. You *will* learn that there are consequences."

I heard Maggie, from the doorway, say, "Robert—" but he held up his hand to shush her without even looking in her direction. He stared me down like a cobra staring at a mongoose.

But you know something? I was the mongoose, and at least in the movies I'd seen, the mongoose wins, so I was not as afraid as I thought I would be. Even in the moment of greatest danger, I was formulating a plan. I knew deep down what I had to do, as though I'd been heading this way for years. As though I knew it was someday going to come to this. I snapped out of going numb. I felt fortified.

And when the standoff was over, when he stomped off and went out and chopped wood or tore down a fence, or kicked the stones in the barn, whatever the hell he did, I went upstairs and packed my things. I put everything I loved in a little blue overnight bag and I hid it under my bed. And then I dragged the phone into the closet, and I called up Judd and told him everything. I asked him to drive me to Manchester, to the bus station. From there, I'd take the bus to Woodstock, and I would live with my mom for the rest of the school year.

She would help me go to NYU.

"Jeez, this doesn't sound like your dad," he said.

"Well, it *was* him," I whispered. "This is how he gets when somebody makes him mad."

"But . . . Maybe I could come over, and we all could sit down together at the kitchen table and talk it through. We might be able to work something out."

"I don't think he'll listen to anybody. Even you."

He was silent for a moment. Then he said, "But I'm going to miss you!"

"I'll miss you, too," I said. "But I have to do this."

I told Hendrix that night when we went outside to do the last chores of the day. When I told him that I was going to Mama's, I made him promise not to tell; he turned pale there in the barn. I could feel his body going stiff.

He looked down at his shoes, which were

covered in muck. His face looked worried in the dimness of the one yellow light bulb over the door. "You know how it is at her house," he said in a low voice. "What if this doesn't work? What if Dad sends the police? What are you going to do then?"

"I don't care if he sends in the whole damn Marine Corps. Don't you see this is what I've got to do? You might have to have this fight one day, too, you know, unless you just want to stay here your whole life slopping hogs and mucking out the stalls." I touched his arm. He was seven minutes older than me, but he always seemed like my younger brother. "It's okay, Hendrix. It's going to work out. You're sweet to worry about me, but you don't need to. Just keep my secret until I'm gone. And then you can tell them, or you can pretend you didn't know. Whichever way you want it to be. By all means, make it easy on yourself."

He hugged me, and when I pulled away and really looked at him, he was smiling. "You're kind of awesomely brave," he said.

I said, "I know."

The next morning, I woke up at three thirty, before the first rooster had started up, before my father had risen from his bed and gone out to do the early chores. There was no one stirring, but I knew I didn't have long. I dressed silently in the dark, grabbed the suitcase, and slipped out of the house. I walked down the driveway and down the lane, walking softly so the gravel didn't even crunch, going all the way out to the main road so they wouldn't see the car that was coming for me. I stood, shivering in the early morning cold and watching until I saw headlights sweeping across the road, and then there was Judd. He slowed down and reached over and opened the door for me.

"So you're really going to do this?" he said. "I kinda hoped you wouldn't be out here, if you wanna know the truth."

"Yeah, well, I am."

"Does your mom know you're coming?"

"Nope. It's all a surprise."

"Huh," he said.

So for the rest of the ride, he told jokes because he could see I was nervous, even though I was pretending not to be. He said that at first he felt sorry for me not getting to do all the end of the year school stuff, but now he said he was envious. This had been my brilliant plan all along, he said, to keep from having to do all the boring things coming up.

"Let me guess. You didn't want to buy a prom dress, am I right?"

"My dad wasn't going to let me go anyway," I told him. I leaned against the window. "I've been grounded from everything."

"Oh, he would have changed his mind. You

didn't let me try to talk to him." He leaned over and tapped my knee. "If you end up going to the prom in Woodstock with some anonymous hippie guy, I'm going to be very, very jealous."

"You've got Karla Kristensen. You'll be too busy to miss me."

"So. What shall I tell people?" he said. "You know, when they ask?"

"You don't have to worry. I'm going to write them all a letter when I get there, telling them where I am. I already left a note for Bunny under her doormat just so she won't worry. It's completely legal what I'm doing. And anyway, in a month, I'm going to be eighteen, and I can do what I please."

"Okay," he said. "Well, if you need me to come get you, I will. You know that, right?"

He walked me to the bus when it arrived, and I got on, lugging my suitcase. The sun was just barely showing itself as the bus pulled away and headed out on its thirteen-hour journey to Woodstock. It looked like a butterscotch candy coming up through the trees. I gazed back at Judd, still standing next to his car, his hands shoved into his pockets, rocking back and forth on his heels.

The bus stopped at practically every mailbox and convenience store along the way. I read and slept and looked out the window and worried. My seatmate was a woman who was going to see her sister, and we talked about farm life and sisters who had gotten away and how sad that was for everyone. I didn't tell her my situation, but my story was like something clogged in my throat, and after we stopped for lunch, when we got back on the bus, I pretended to sleep for the rest of the way.

When we finally pulled into the Woodstock station, it was eight thirty at night. I tried to call Tenaj from the bus station, but her phone number was disconnected. I got a recording. I hadn't figured on that. I stood outside the bus station in the cold, windy night, looking down the darkened streets and wondering what to do. Why hadn't I thought to call her earlier? Oh yeah. Because my phone booth was gone, and I certainly wasn't going to make the call from my house. Also, I had been grounded.

The thing was, I was perfectly calm. I knew that I was going to find her. Woodstock had a population of about four thousand people—you ran into the same people every day—and I was sure she was still there. Sure, we hadn't talked in a long time, but she would have written to me if she was moving somewhere else.

I was picturing a lovely reunion—Stony and Petal and all the other people so glad to see me, and I could hardly wait to light a fire outside and sit around it and tell stories, like before. They'd all be sympathetic when they heard about my dad. They'd know that I was a Woodstock girl, one of them, and they'd help me.

I had a little bit of money in my pocket—twenty-two dollars after I'd paid the bus fare—but I knew I wouldn't need much once I got to her house, so I called for a cab and gave the cab driver her address. The driver was a hippie guy with long hair with streaks of silver in it, and when he drove me up the hill, I saw the old cottage lit up just like in the old days, and my heart felt this flutter of relief. I got out of the cab with my suitcase and gave the guy a five. He said, "I think I'll wait for you here, just in case. You never know."

"She'll be here," I said. "This is where she's always lived."

But then, walking up to the door, I felt just a pang of something bad. The porch was all swept clean, and painted gray now, not the bright purple that Tenaj had painted it. And the yard was kind of a manicured lawn now. There weren't any trucks parked on it.

My hand shook just a little as I knocked.

A woman wearing her hair in a chignon opened the door and looked at me blankly. No, no, she said when I asked, she hadn't heard of Tenaj. Or Stony. Petal? Nope, never heard of anybody by that name. She'd lived here for over a year, she said, and she didn't know where the previous tenants might be. "They left this place an unholy mess, that's all I know," she said with a laugh.

I went back to the cab, grateful now that he'd waited. It was nearly ten, and the driveway stones crunched under my feet. A wind had come up, and I shivered.

We sat in the cab trying to figure out where I should go. The blackness was pressing against the windows. *This is freedom,* I thought. *I am the bravest I have ever been in my whole life.*

"Don't worry about me. I guess I'll just spend the night in the bus station and look for her in the morning," I told him.

"Nah, I can't let you do that," he said. His eyes, looking at me in the rearview mirror, were kind. "Listen. Let me call my wife to see if she's still up. I can take you to our house. We have a spare bedroom. I'm sure she wouldn't mind, a young girl like you. By the way, my name's Bill."

"I'm Phronsie," I said.

"Phronsie, huh?"

"Yeah. I was named for a character in a book that my mom liked."

We stopped at a pay phone, and I waited in the car while he got out and made the call. When he got back in the cab, he said it was fine with his wife. "She said I gotta stop doing this to her, though, bringing folks home with no notice." He laughed and started the car again. "But you know, that's what the sixties was about, huh? Hell, none of us were strangers."

"My mom and dad met at Woodstock," I told him.

"Is that right? I was there. That was a powerful experience," he said. "Lotta people don't think about those days anymore; it's like it never happened. But Hendrix, man. That performance alone. Changed my whole life."

"They named my twin brother Hendrix because of that."

"No kidding. Wow! And your mom's still living up here."

"Yeah, she's an artist. Tenaj is her name."

"Your mom is *Tenaj?* Holy shit." He banged on the steering wheel. "I know Tenaj. Wow! Small world. She does all kinds of amazing things with glass. I love her new gallery. She's good people, that Tenaj. She and Jesse."

"She has a gallery? Of her own?" *And a Jesse?*

"Yeah. You didn't know? The Magic of Found Objects. And I gotta say—I love the way she just carries that baby everywhere with her, wherever she goes. Jesse doesn't have a chance with that kid. Chloe's a mama's girl for sure."

The breath slowly curled out of my body, like a trail of smoke. I stared out the window, feeling my throat closing up. It was starting to rain, and little rivulets of water were streaking down the pane. He was talking on now, about this and that. I couldn't pay attention.

"I take it you don't get to see your mom very much," he said.

I cleared my throat. "No. I live in New Hampshire with my dad." Then, striving for a casual tone, I said, "So how old is the baby now, would you say?"

"I want to say she must be about two now. Always at the gallery with Tenaj, riding around on her hip, like I told you. A real butterball, that one. Cute as a button."

Two years old, I thought. So that child would have been born around the time that Tenaj and I stopped having our weekly conversations. Was that why we'd stopped talking? I remember that I'd stopped calling her. I was too busy dating Steppenwolf and writing bad poetry and running the school newspaper and plotting my escape to New York. And I suddenly didn't have time to go to my old phone booth.

It was my fault. Totally. I had stopped calling her. But damn it, we had a long-lasting bond; we were kindred spirits, weren't we? But by not calling her, I'd missed out on the news that she'd started a whole new life. And—there was another nagging thought rattling around in my head, too—why hadn't *she* thought to get in touch with *me?* I wouldn't have expected her to call me at my dad's house, of course, but couldn't she have written me a letter? Couldn't she have called Bunny?

My head started to hurt.

"You know," I said, "maybe this isn't such a good idea after all. If you would just take me back to the bus station, I'll take a bus back home. I-I don't think I want to see her."

"What?" he said. "No way. You can't do that."

"I-I want to. I don't think I can go see her after all."

He suddenly jerked the steering wheel and pulled the car over and turned to look at me. His eyes looked alarmed and sad. "Oh, my. You're in a lot of pain, aren't you? I read faces, with this job. And I knew when you got in my cab that you were in some kind of trouble. And here you are, looking for your mom, and then I have to go sound off with my big mouth, tell you all about her new life now. I am so, so sorry."

"It's okay," I said. "It's not you. She isn't going to want to see me. I want to go home."

"No, no, no. Lemme just tell you one thing. Ain't no mama alive that wouldn't want to see her child that took a long bus ride just to find her. She'd be so crushed if she found out you were here, and then you went back." He looked out the front windshield and then back at me. "I don't know what's gone on in your life that made this breach happen—"

"I was a mistake, that's what happened," I said.

I started to cry. "She got pregnant from my father at Woodstock, and they didn't know each other, and they split up, and now nobody knows what to do with us. A big, big mistake."

"You are not a mistake," he said. "You are *not* a mistake. God, don't think that. Nothing that came from that festival could be a mistake. That's just impossible, right there." He looked at me for a long time. "You came from a moment that was magic in the world. Something that had never existed before. There was music and love and all this connection going on—people laughing and loving each other and being generous and sharing this experience like nothing anybody had ever seen. And you came into being right then. *You* were called to earth by all that love and joy. Think of that, will you? The spirit that is you was answering the spirit that was that time!"

He started up the car. "So here's what we're going to do, Woodstock Baby. I'm going to take you home to my house, and my Janie will fix us some dinner. You probably didn't get much to eat today, did you? And then you'll get a good night's sleep in our spare room, and tomorrow morning we'll go over and see the gallery and find your mom, and she'll take one look at you, and she'll remember the magic. And seeing you will remind her of all that love. And if she doesn't remember it, I'll be right there to tell her."

• • •

Tenaj's gallery was small and tucked on a little side street off the main drag, next door to a coffee shop. There were trees and a cracked sidewalk, and the smell of bacon and eggs wafted out through the open doors, and I could see customers clustered around the counter inside, laughing and talking. My stomach growled. Janie had offered me oatmeal and toast, but I'd been too agitated to sit still and eat more than one tiny bite. I hadn't had much sleep at all, and now it was like every cell in my body was rigid with wanting—and fear.

I made Bill drop me off and leave, promising him I'd be fine.

"I am the bravest right now that I have ever been in my whole life," I said, despite feeling sick with fear. Tenaj had once told me about affirmations—how you could chant something to yourself, and your subconscious mind would make it be true. Or something.

There was a wooden sign outside the window that said THE MAGIC OF FOUND OBJECTS in a flowing script in lavender, with little blue curlicues. I stood there staring in the window, feeling like my head was overrun with bees. A chime sounded when I opened the door. Inside the gallery, it was all a riot of art and color: bright red, turquoise, yellow. The stucco walls were loaded with glassworks, mosaics, and knitted scarves hanging down the wall like animal tails. Glass jars of colored beads were arranged along the side wall, and there were animal-print armchairs and bright-colored pillows and rugs scattered everywhere. A turquoise table with a cash register (painted red) was near the front.

Nobody was in the main space. I could hear a baby talking from the back, and Tenaj's voice saying, "Oooh, I think somebody came in. Shall we go see who it is? You readdddddyyyy?"

And then there she was.

My mom.

I hadn't seen her since I was ten, and here she was. Baby on her hip, and wearing a long, patchwork gypsy skirt. Her blonde hair was browner than I remembered, and it was tied back and looped up in a bun on top of her head, and she was smiling her public smile, impersonal but warm. And as I watched, her face went white with shock.

"Phronsie!" she said. "Phronsie? Oh my goodness. Look at you! You're all grown up!"

I could only imagine what she was seeing when she looked at me, grown up now. We looked alike—the same long blonde ringleted hair and blue eyes. I was tall now and wearing jeans and a leather jacket and my cowboy boots. Looking as boho as I could, as if that could remind her who I was to her. Stake my claim as her daughter.

The baby on her hip was staring at me wit

an open mouth. She had curly blonde hair and fat, red, chapped cheeks. She was wearing what you'd think a hippie baby on display might wear: a tie-dyed romper and red tennis shoes. At the sight of me, she took two plump hands out of her mouth and placed them on either side of my mother's face and turned her head, forcibly.

"Yook at meeeee, Mama!" she said. "Yook at meee!"

"Baby, I am looking at you. But look who's here! This is *Phronsie,* sweetie cakes! We love Phronsie."

At that, she crossed the room over to me, and tried to gather me in a hug. For some reason, I stepped back. Maybe I was tired from not getting much sleep, maybe I was reacting to the gooey presence of Chloe, whose hands were wet with a mangled-up cracker. Tenaj had traces of cracker on her face. Her smile faded. I saw her look at the suitcase I was holding as she stepped back.

"Are you all right?" she said. "How did—why are—what's happening? How did you get here?"

She was wearing dozens of beaded bracelets and rings on every finger. I took it all in—the jewelry, the hippie clothing—the look of her that didn't quite jibe anymore with what I remembered. She seemed a little false, like someone who wanted to appear hip, an actress maybe who had studied the look. She used to wear rags most of the time, artlessly flung over her shoulders—embroidered jeans, T-shirts, but now she looked like a hippie in a Hollywood movie instead. The All-American Hippie Artist, all fresh-faced and natural, ready for her close-up. But I could see the lines around her eyes, and oh my God, she was wearing eyeliner. She was trying too hard, and it was sickening.

She was—how old? I stopped to figure it out. She had been twenty-three when I was born—no, twenty-four, because she was a Scorpio, she had told me, so her birthday was in late October—and I was seventeen, so she was forty-one. Forty one. Too old for this charade. Obviously.

"I came on the bus," I said. I was fighting back tears. "I came to see you. I didn't know when I left home that you had—" All I could seem to do was wave my arm, to take in the whole scene—the gallery, the child, the jewelry in cases, even the eyeliner. My nose started to run, and I set down my little suitcase on the wooden floor. It fell over, and I had to lean down to set it upright again.

When I looked back up at her, everything was blurry, and she seemed like somebody who'd been turned to stone. Like she didn't know *what* she was supposed to do. There was grief in her face. She was upset that I was there; she didn't want me and whatever complications I was bringing along.

"Well," she said at last. "It's great to see you. And this little one here is Chloe."

"Hi, Chloe," I said.

"She's going to be two next month," she said. She was smiling at Chloe like she'd never seen her before, like Chloe was the embodiment of all that is heavenly and holy on earth, and that if she could just concentrate on her, then maybe I would vaporize myself and not exist at all.

"Nice," I said. "She's cute."

"Two!" yelled Chloe.

"Yes," I said. "You're a very cute person of two."

I felt like I'd been hit in the stomach. Looking at those fat little hands, the blonde curls that had been like mine, those reddened cheeks, and the proprietary way that Chloe rode on Tenaj's hip, maneuvering her face around whenever she pleased, made me feel nauseated. The way Chloe touched her. Owned her. The way I surely had when I was a baby.

"So my life has taken, ahhh, several unexpected turns," Tenaj said. "For one thing—ta-da!—I got married. Can you believe it?"

But you said . . . you SAID . . . marriage was bad for women. You were a free spirit!

"To Stony?" My voice sounded all croaky.

"Stony? No! Oh my goodness, no. That was— that was never in the cards."

Chloe again: "I *two,* Mama! *Two! Two! Two!*"

"Yes, Chloe, you're *two*. I married a guy named Jesse. He's a musician. Sort of new to the area scene here. A really good guy. He's—haha—calming me down. I'm channeling some of his vibrational energy now, for success. You know? Like how it's not a crime to be successful at things?" She smiled and shrugged. "A whole new way of looking at things."

"That's great," I said in the dullest voice I'd ever heard come out of my mouth. It was like there was cotton batting on my tongue. "I'm so happy for you. I didn't know you ever thought it was a crime to be successful at things."

She started to talk about herself then, but she seemed all fluttery. She said she thought she'd been "keeping herself small" out of a misguided idea that artists needed to suffer. I could tell I was making her nervous, and I hated the way I had this stone-cold resentment sitting right at the center of me. What I could see, though, was that she wasn't mine in the least. She was saying things about life and success and the universe and dreams that came true, and the miracle of found objects. Transformation. Transformation as it related to jewelry. Blah blah blah. Transformation as it related to the sky and to babies, to light. But there was nothing about me in there. I might as well have been just another customer showing up in the gallery, examining her life choices along with her jewelry.

"Do you like the gallery?" she said. "Isn't this just a marvelous space?"

"I do," I said. "It's beautiful."

"So much light," she said. "It grounds a person, this kind of light. Grounds me, and also seems to give me wings. You know? It's perfect, like a sacred space in here. A sacred space of art."

"Yes."

"Jesse found it for me. And you're not going to believe this, but I have employees! Can you believe that? Me, a boss, hiring people?"

"Well, sure," I said.

"The universe certainly comes up with some surprises," she said. "I met the love of my life, and now I have a baby . . . well, *obviously.*" Maybe she saw my face then or felt how much time had passed, because she trailed off, and then she said, "Look. I'm sorry if I've been out of touch. It's just so hard to know whether I should, you know, *intrude.* You have your whole other life."

"Well," I said stiffly. "You've had a lot going on." *Never mind that you are a big liar and a hypocrite who has gone back on every single thing you ever said. You said we'd be together sometime. You said that you'd never get married again. You said women have to live for themselves, for their art. You said . . . you said . . .*

"We both have had a lot going on," she said.

She went silent, fiddled with Chloe's shoe, which had a speck of something on it.

"This is the part when you might want to ask me why I'm here," I said.

She laughed. "I'm sort of scared to, to tell you the truth."

"Well," I said, taking a deep breath. "I ran away from home."

"I was afraid of that when I saw the suitcase. Tell me this: Does your father know you're here?"

"Well, he might know by now. I left a note with Bunny. I caught the bus from Manchester yesterday morning."

"Yesterday morning," she said slowly. She didn't say, *But where have you been since then? Where did you spend the night? How are you doing? Oh, my poor lamb, are you okay?*

Chloe said, "Milkies, Mama, milkies," and started pulling at Tenaj's tank top, and in a gesture that was almost balletic, my mother sank to the floor in a cross-legged pose and pulled up her shirt so that Chloe could latch on to her breast. A brown nipple came into view, then disappeared into Chloe's wide, wet mouth.

I wasn't shocked exactly, just a little taken aback with the suddenness, and my mother's unquestioning compliance. I had never known her to do anything upon request.

"I'm pretty much a snack bar to her," she said,

laughing. "This is how we spend our days. She rides around on my hip, and then periodically we do this. I'm not even able to do art anymore most of the time with only one hand available. So *this* is what we're doing. My new life."

"Milkies," I said.

"Yes."

We were silent for a moment. I tried to take a deep breath, to look at the beam of light shining through the front windows, look at the rainbows dancing across the stucco walls. I followed the light; they came from dagger-shaped prisms in the window. Chloe was smacking loudly, and my mother was staring down at her face.

I sat down next to her on the hard, wooden floor, and I told her all the things she should know, all the things that a good mother should have asked about. I pointedly said that I didn't have her new phone number, so I couldn't alert her that I was coming. I told her I couldn't tolerate my dad's authoritarianism anymore, that he wouldn't even let me go to New York City to college. Then I told her about the bus ride, and the leaving home early in the morning. I told her how I left a note for Bunny, and that I was planning to mail a letter to the rest of them telling them I was safe. I told her about meeting Bill, the cab driver, and then Janie, and being allowed to sleep at their house, and how he dropped me off that morning at the gallery.

"Let me ask you something," she said. She had to drag her eyes away from looking down at Chloe. "What are you expecting me to do?"

"Well," I said. I swallowed. I had still been hoping for a few expressions of sympathy, actually. One or two expressions along the line of *oh, you poor sweet baby* would have been nice. "I'm actually hoping to finish high school up here. There are only a few months left of the school year, and *then* I was hoping that you could maybe help me a little bit with the tuition, or help me find work in New York. You know a whole lot of creative people, and I thought I could stay with you while I work on . . . you know . . ."

"Hmm," she said.

"I'm a writer," I told her grandly. "I know that about myself. I'm the editor of the school newspaper, and all my English teachers agree that I've got real talent, and I did great on the verbals of the SATs, and I got into such a great, great school . . . and now Daddy won't let me go! He didn't even want me to apply. I had to do it all in secret. He says I have to stay on the farm, and you and I both know it's only because that's what *he* had to do. He's taking his disappointment in life out on me, and I can't stand it. I *won't* stand it."

She listened, frowning. "Wow. This seems very hard," she said.

I stared at her. "Yes! That's what I'm trying to

tell you. It is very hard. It's impossible. I can't live like this, being on the farm for my whole life. I want to be a writer, I want to be a creative person. I'm like you, Mama. You weren't able to live there, so I know you know what I'm talking about. I can't do it."

We waited, Chloe and I, to see what she would say. Chloe, still nursing, stuck her fingers in Tenaj's mouth.

"Listen," I said. "I can help you in the gallery, I can babysit Chloe. I'll be one of your employees, doing whatever. I just need to be away from home. And he's grounded me from *everything*. He's being totally unreasonable. I even got some scholarship money, but he won't contribute. He's been terrible all year long, and now I can't. I just can't stay." My eyes were filling up with tears.

"Honey, I don't—I can't . . ."

"Mama, please. You can't what? You can't be my mom anymore? You can't help me? Look at you! You're doing fine. You have this gallery, *you've* made it. And all I'm asking is to live with you and make some money until I go off to college. For heaven's sake, Mama!"

"Phronsie, I don't have room for you. Honey, I live in a really small house, and I—"

"I could sleep on the couch."

"Nooo," she said. "That wouldn't really work. Baby, I—"

"But there were always people sleeping on your

couch! That was the whole point of the sixties, right? People helping each other—"

"It's not like that anymore," she said quietly. "It's the eighties. I have a new marriage and a kid . . ."

"Wow. You don't *want* to have room for me," I said. "You know something? You don't really care about me, do you? It's like I'm not even connected to you, like *I'm* not your kid. Just in case you don't remember, you actually have *three* kids, not just this one."

"Honey, you will always be my kid . . ."

"No," I said. It was like I was putting all this together for the first time. All the absences, all the silences, all the lack of effort. "No, that's not really true. You threw me away. You let my dad come and pick up Hendrix and me when we were four years old and take us off to New Hampshire, and you didn't even do anything to keep us. You just let us go. I remember that day. You just said good-bye and that was that. How *could* you? How did you do that? We were your *babies*. And you told me we'd be together as soon as you could manage it. And look at you! Look at us! You *abandoned* me."

Chloe stopped nursing and stared at me.

My mother took a little bit of time to answer, and then she said in a low voice, "I don't expect you to understand everything that went on. It didn't ever seem like my fighting him was

283

going to do any good. Also, I knew you'd have a good life. It *was* hard saying good-bye to you. It was the most awful thing I'd ever had to do. But I knew Bunny would take care of you and love you, and I knew you'd have stability on the farm with your father. You'd have a community that wasn't just people smoking pot and taking drugs and hardly making any money. It wasn't as idyllic as it looked here, and I didn't know if I'd be able to take care of you. Don't you see that? And, Phronsie, really. A family farm—what's more family-oriented than that? And your dad is a good, hardworking man, and he's strong and he's earnest, and I knew he would raise you. And—take it however you want to, Phronsie, but I wasn't sure that I could."

I sat back on my heels and shook my head. I felt honestly like I might pass out. Like air was blowing through my brain cavity or something.

"But didn't you even miss us? Who *are* you? You didn't even fight for visitation. I had to make that happen. When I was six years old, *I* was the one who made sure we could come and see you and have the court-ordered visitation. Do you remember that, even?"

She pursed her lips and looked down at Chloe, settled her back against her breast. "I know," she said. "And I was grateful to you and to Bunny. You don't realize what I was up against. I didn't have any money. I wasn't going to take him to court for visitation. It would have just made things worse."

"So you say." I tried to think how long I'd been angry with her without even knowing it. I hated her. In science class one time the teacher passed around a piece of petrified wood; it looked like an ordinary piece of wood, he pointed out, but it had turned to stone. I had a petrified heart. I could feel it turning to stone right as I sat there.

There was a long silence. Then she said, "I love you, Phronsie, whether or not it feels like that to you. This is what love is sometimes: letting the other person go have the life they're supposed to have. And I want to tell you something. Sure, you got a raw deal. Who didn't? You didn't get to grow up with both parents together in a perfect little family. Get over it, okay? Hardly anybody on the planet grows up without some huge lack in their life. Don't run away from home over this stupid little bump in the road. Your father doesn't want you to go away to college? So go to college right there. You want to write? So write! What's stopping you? Do you think I waited for someone to come along and bestow upon me the title of artist? No! I didn't have any money for supplies, so I made jewelry out of stuff I found along the side of the road. And I worked at it, for years, getting better little by little, and the whole time telling myself that I was going to succeed. And that's what you'll have to do, too. You're going to need to make up your stories out of the raw materials of your life. Suffering won't kill you. Writing and rewriting and figuring things out as you go along won't kill you. Not going to NYU won't even kill you."

Chloe pulled away from Tenaj's breast just then and touched her chin, like she could understand. My mother looked down and smiled at her and then nuzzled her baby's face with her own.

"I baby," said Chloe, and Tenaj smiled and said, "Yes. You're the baby."

No, I wanted to say. *I'm the baby!*

The bell dinged above the door, and a cluster of customers came in. Tenaj turned to them with a wide smile. "Hi, welcome! Feel free to look around and come to me if you have any questions."

I got up then, in a sweeping motion. There was no one—no one—to count on but myself. This airiness, this lack of substance, was suddenly exhilarating. It was like the top of my head had a huge opening, and air was circulating all through me. I didn't even feel sorry for myself. I just felt like my eyes had been opened to a truth that maybe everyone else had known about for a long time, that Tenaj was not to be trusted. She was a fake. I had wanted to be her, I had wanted her to acknowledge me, to be proud of me, to tell me stories, to do artwork with me again, to include me in her world. I wanted her to see that I looked like her, which was something my father always held against me.

"We saw the story about you in *Yankee Magazine*," said a woman with gray hair.

"Oh, did you?" Tenaj's smile grew larger. She was even simpering at the woman. It was disgusting. She got up and put Chloe back on her hip, adjusted her shirt back to normal. "Yes, that was quite a day I spent with that reporter. I loved the photographs. Did you just love the photographs? He really *got* my work, the transformative power of the objects."

"Miraculous," said the woman's companion, a man in a tweed suit.

And oh, they went on—the photographs, the beads, the light. Always back to the light. This fucking *light*. So big deal—there was sunshine through the windows, and white stucco walls. And glass. What did they expect?

I pushed past them. Went outside with my suitcase. I stood on the sidewalk looking up and down the street, thinking what to do next. Feeling the air on my skin, in my eyes.

What do you want to do? That was what the voice in my head said.

I'm hungry. I think I want to eat.

I went next door to the little restaurant where the tourists now seemed to be gathering for lunch. I went in and sat at a table by the window and ordered an egg salad sandwich and a bag of potato chips and stared out at the street. I had no idea what I was going to do next.

When I was halfway finished with my sandwich, Tenaj burst into the place and plopped herself down in front of me. She didn't have Chloe with her. She reached out and touched my hand. "Baby," she said. "I have a couple of things to tell you."

Maybe, I thought, she's changed her mind. She's realized what I could be to her.

"Just hear me out," she said. "I may not be the mother you would have chosen, but hardly anybody gets who they want," she said. "I can't offer you daily life and cookies after school—"

"Or even a place to live, apparently."

"—yes, or even a place to live. But besides all the wonderful artistic genes I passed onto you"—and here she smiled—"I also can tell you that you're on the right path. But you need to go home. I can read energy, and I can see your life, and you're not meant to be here. Your life is waiting for you elsewhere, and you're going to be great, Phronsie. You're going to find success and love, but it's not always going to be easy. Do you believe in the unseen realm?"

"No. Absolutely not." I rolled my eyes.

She smiled. "Well, I do. It's real, baby. Magic is real."

"I don't know why I should listen to you. You said marriage was bad for women, and that the only way women could be happy was to be independent. And now look at you! Married to some random guy who shows up, and with a baby who won't let you go for one second. You said yourself you can't even do your *art*. You told me art was the most important thing. That's what you said!"

You said . . . you said . . .

She smiled at me and shrugged. "I know. I changed my mind. And I don't blame you for being angry," she said. "You're furious with me for having another child. But I fell in love, Phronsie, and I couldn't say no to this. You'll find out someday what this is like, honey. Just one caution: don't settle for what you don't want. I mean, I know you want to go to NYU and maybe you can't do that just yet. But you'll figure out what that desire *really* is all about. And you're going to succeed. I know that."

I pushed my plate away, filled with fury. I got some money out of my pocket and slammed it on the table, and I grabbed my suitcase. When I got to the door, I turned and said, "And you didn't even ask about Hendrix. What kind of mother are you, anyway? You should take a good hard look at yourself."

I didn't have any idea what I was going to do next, but I felt free and unfettered, fueled by my anger. I wandered around the town and thought how fakey-fake the whole place seemed. Filled with tourists all walking around looking in the shops, not appreciating that it was once supposed to be a real haven for artists, and not even knowing that the artists had sold out and were just pandering to everybody's idea of what art was. It was all commercial and stupid.

Later that afternoon, I called Judd and told him I now officially hated my mom. He listened to me complain about everything, and he did not once say that I was an idiot for going there. He just said, "Man, your mom is kind of lost, isn't she? Do you want me to come and get you?"

"No," I said. That was the last thing I wanted: to come slinking home like a failure. "I'm going to stick around and figure some things out." Actually, I had no idea what I was going to do: beg for a job somewhere? Enroll in the high school? Maybe, I told him, this is when I could become a writer. This was the kind of experience that might define my life, give me a reason to write.

Then I called Hendrix and told him he'd been right about Tenaj the whole time.

"Let's not even call her Tenaj," I said. "From now on, she's Janet to me."

He laughed. "Does this mean you're going to be Frances?" he said.

"Of course not. Phronsie is a beautiful name." Then I swallowed. "Was everybody really mad when they found out I'd gone?"

"Well, yes," he said. "Maggie and Dad had a fight about it."

"So I'm in trouble?"

"I dunno. When are you coming back?"

"I don't know. I have a notebook, and I think I'm going to start writing a memoir about how awful everything in life is, and how you can't make a life for yourself until you're willing to be lonely and bereft."

"Jesus, Phronsie," he said. "Does it have to be that bad for you? Can't you just conform for now, and do what you want later on?"

"No," I said. "And neither should you."

Later, when it was almost getting dark, I was sitting in the park, scribbling away, when a car drove up and stopped at the curb. The driver honked the horn, and I looked up in annoyance. I had just gotten to page five, where I was describing the agony of being the rejected daughter of a farmer and a witch.

It was Maggie, of all people. She rolled down the window and leaned out. I tried not to look at her.

"Hey! Would you like to get in?" she said. She didn't sound mad, just neutral, like this was the most normal thing in the world to happen.

"What are you doing here?" I said after a moment, but I noticed that I had gathered up all my things and I was walking over to the car as

I said it. I stood there for a bit, and then I slid into the front seat next to her. There was a funny feeling in my chest—something like relief mixed in with sorrow at my defeat. Heartbroken, and yet strong. I would have to figure out how to get these emotions down on the page, I realized.

Maggie had both hands on the steering wheel, and she turned to me. She didn't smile, she didn't make a big deal, she just looked at me.

"I don't know. I was just passing through, and I thought maybe you might be ready to see somebody from home," she said.

I stared at her. "You were not just passing through."

"No," she said. "That part isn't true, but the other part is."

We sat there in the car, and she said this was a cute little town, but it gave her the creeps, all this peace and love shit, when it didn't add up to anything concrete in the world. It was the first time I'd ever heard her say the word *shit*. She said that practicality and duty were what built character, not this "airy fairy" stuff. Character came from paying your bills and working your way toward the thing you really wanted in your life. Character was who you were when all the rest was stripped away. It was the you that people could recognize and count on.

Then she told me she was sorry about the way my father had been to me. She said he wasn't always fair. But she had talked to him, and she'd gotten him to agree that I could go to NYU. But they wanted me to stay home and go to the community college for the first two years. That would allow me to save money, and to grow up a little before leaving home, she said. I could tell she really thought I'd change my mind about New York, but I knew that I wouldn't.

"Anyway, that's the deal. Take it or leave it. We'll contribute a little money toward tuition. You'll have to work, of course, but who doesn't work their way through college? It's character-building," she said. "So, what do you think? Want to come back home?"

I nodded and leaned my head against the window.

She started the engine and turned on her turn indicator.

"You're going to be fine," she said, and she reached over and patted my knee. "You just need to stop reacting out of drama, you know? Life is what you make it. See yourself as a victim, and that's how it will always be."

Outside the car, under the darkening sky, farms unrolled like green velvet paintings, interspersed with pine forests.

A hundred miles later, when we were on the highway, she said, "When I married your father—when I forgave him for what he did to me, to *us*—it was because I knew that I loved him and

I was always going to love him. So I took him back. It's not perfect. But nothing is perfect. It takes character to live with the imperfect facts of your life and to change the things you can change, and to be willing to live with the things you can't do anything about. I've had to finally realize that I wouldn't change anything about your father—or you, or Hendrix, even if I could."

I stared at the road ahead lit up by the headlights, and it hit me for the first time that I might have been wrong about Maggie. Here she had driven five hours to come and rescue me, and she wasn't talking to me like I was five years old. Or a juvenile delinquent.

"Listen," she said, after a long time had gone by. She turned and smiled at me, her thin little smile. "You're a bright young woman, Phronsie, and I'm so proud of you. I shouldn't tell you this, but even your making this trip, to see your mother—well, that showed character. That's what I told your dad. You were taking care of yourself. Taking care of your dream, and I like that in a person. And—well, I promise to help you. I'm on your side, you know. I should have probably told you that before now."

"Thank you," I said.

She'd called me Phronsie for the first time. It was suddenly like I'd been drowning in misery, and Maggie was my lifeboat.

CHAPTER NINETEEN

The bookstore reading doesn't *start* as a disaster. It starts with a miracle—or if not an actual miracle, at least a hopeful sign.

That is that Gabora is dressed and ready when I go to her room to fetch her. There she is, opening the door, her blonde wig combed and sprayed and installed in the right place on her head, and she's wearing her Author Lady costume—a bright-red pencil skirt and a white blouse with a little mouse medallion. She always wears that. Children like mice, she insists, as proven from her years writing about Peter and Eleanor, who always traveled with their pet mouse, Lancaster.

But then my heart sinks as I see how she wobbles when she walks, and how she grabs for Adam's hand as we go down the hall. Her eyes are a little glazed over, and when I look more closely, I can see that the slash of red lipstick didn't quite make it onto her lips the way all of us might have hoped.

Adam, however, is the picture of a young, cool professional, dressed in khaki pants and a light blue button-down shirt and a sports jacket. His hair, which can't be tamed, is curly and unruly and magnificent. I have to look away.

The lights in the lobby are flickering when we

come out of the elevator, and outside, the wind seems to have picked up a bit. The bell captain, a large Black man with a big smile, herds us over. He says our cab is just arriving now.

"Y'all be safe out there now, y'hear?" he says. "It's a big one comin'."

"A big what?" asks Gabora, but we're already outside, under the awning, and a driver has hopped out of his yellow cab and is tipping his cap as he hurries over to us, bending against the wind. The decorative palm trees in pots look like they're trying to touch the sidewalk.

"To the Magnolia Bookstore?" he says, and half of his words seem to get carried off. He helps steer Gabora to the car, and I tuck her in and close the door and then go around to the side and scoot in to the middle of the backseat. Adam jumps in and closes the door.

"Yes, sir. Magnolia," Adam says.

"I didn't know there was going to be a storm," Gabora says. "Sometimes readers don't like to bring children out if the weather isn't good." She leans forward and tells the driver about how she's an *authoress*—a term I've never been able to convince her out of—and that she's here to meet her young fans from the South. "Do you have any children, young man?"

He says indeed he does, two boys and a girl.

"Well, then, here, honey, I have an extra book in my bag. I'll sign it to you!"

"Why, thank you, ma'am, and don't you be worryin' about this storm," says the driver. "It's those summer storms we have to worry about here." He says *here* as though it ends in an *ah*. Our eyes meet in the rearview mirror and he smiles. "You folks from New York?"

"Right," says Adam.

"Well, welcome to Charleston. Hope you get you some of our Southern hospitality while you're in town."

"I'm counting on it," says Gabora, and she struggles with her bag so she can get a book out, and I hold it while she signs the title page. Or tries to sign it. The moving car and the darkness don't make it easy.

"And here we are!" the driver says. "You let me help you out, miss." He jumps out in front of a sweet little bookstore on a leafy street, with lights twinkling in the window. MAGNOLIA BOOKS, says a sign that's flapping over the door, held up by a wrought iron hanger.

There is a smattering of people going into the store, leaning against the wind as they walk.

"My fans!" Gabora says. "So nice of them to come to see an old lady authoress!"

But I am not sure. Upon a closer look, I can see that some of the people going inside have signs that say STOP RACISM.

Gabora doesn't see those, thank goodness, and as soon as we get out of the car, the bookstore manager, a woman named Cindy Reynolds, rushes over and smothers us all in hugs and kindness. She is so thrilled to see Gabora, and oooh, could she just take a moment to say that she's admired her since she was a little child (which looks like it might have been sometime in the last six months), and then she quickly ushers us all inside, guiding us through the center of the store, and into a back room that's filled with boxes of books, a worn corduroy couch, and a quaint little writing desk. There's a pot of tea waiting and a stack of books for Gabora to sign.

"I felt like Peter and Eleanor were my best friends growing up!" Cindy Reynolds exclaims, and I see Gabora smiling and squinting, like she's trying hard to focus. She allows herself to be hugged and petted and to have her coat hung up. Adam flashes me an oh-no look as she sinks down into the fluffy sofa cushions to start signing the stock copies before the reading starts. She seems competent at operating the pen, although a couple of her autographs look like they have more loops than the name Pierce-Anton might, in fact, contain. Maybe thirty excess loops.

I watch as she surreptitiously reaches into her bag and grabs her flask and takes a big gulp from it. Adam catches my eye and makes googly eyes.

My phone rings just then, and I take it to the back of the room, away from everyone. It's Judd telling me that he's heard there's crazy weather headed into South Carolina. "You should maybe leave now," he says. "And I'm not even kidding."

"As much as I'd like to, I am kind of at an event," I tell him. "What kind of weather are we talking about?"

"Snow!" he says. "Hurricane-force winds. Rain. Ice. The whole bit. Seriously, it's much nicer up here. Tell them you have a policy against snow hurricanes. They're unnatural."

I see Gabora reaching for the flask in her purse one more time.

"I've gotta go," I say to Judd. "It's almost showtime here. Wish me luck."

"I'm wishing you snow boots," he says, "and deicing for the plane wings when you do leave."

"I have snow boots," I tell him, and I can barely hide the irritation I feel. "I'm coming to New Hampshire afterward, remember?"

"You won't need them here. It's sixty degrees. The world has turned upside down."

And then he hangs up. No mushy good-bye, no *I love you,* no *I miss you so much my heart is just pounding in anticipation for when we see each other again.* Because: Why would he? We're best friends who happen to be getting married, and I've got to get that through my thick, grouchy skull.

Adam is looking at me. "It's time to go in," he whispers. "Also, I went out for a little stroll through the store, and from the looks of things, it's a restless crowd."

"Restless, in that they can barely wait for her to finish signing the books and get out there?"

"More like they can hardly wait to explain to her that she's a racist author, and that they want her to suffer for all her bad views."

"Oh God."

"I'd say the metaphorical knives are sharpened. I wonder if there's a way to have her *not* appear."

"Are you kidding? She has to go. Also she'll never agree to that."

"Of course not," he says. "Well, we'll just have to stand guard."

We both help Gabora to her feet. "But I didn't finish shining the books," she says, looking from one of us to the other. "All my fans are going to want to have the books."

"You can shine them later," says Adam. He winks at me again. Something flutters inside me.

The bookstore is buzzing. There are people sitting in all the twenty-five folding chairs as well as a cluster of angry-looking young people in sweatshirts leaning against the shelves, holding signs. Sprinkled here and there are a few sweet little grandmothers—wearing long skirts and cardigans, just like Peter and Eleanor's grandmother did in Book #37, the book about the suffragettes. They hold their purses on their laps, looking a wee bit nervous, while their pigtailed little granddaughters (just like Eleanor) lean against them, straining for a look at Gabora Pierce-Anton.

I bite my lip as Cindy Reynolds brings Gabora to a podium at the front of the crowd. She does an excited and warm introduction, but I can't pay any attention to it at all because I'm looking from Gabora to the cluster of young people, who have now started shifting restlessly from one foot to the other. A young woman is typing something on her cell phone, while the guy next to her, wearing a gray sweatshirt, faded jeans, and a navy-blue watch cap, is beating his hand against his thigh.

"Thank you for coming," Gabora says. "You are all sho very, very, verra nice." In the silence that follows, she opens her little book and starts to read from page one in a quavering voice.

The crowd isn't paying attention. People are talking, putting their heads together, looking at the guy in the blue cap. He seems to be weaving back and forth, about to say something, and then not saying it. The girl next to him shakes her head, and says, "Don't, Micah," and he says, out loud, "Stop it, Lucy! I'm warning you!"

Gabora clears her throat and puts her book down and looks out at everyone with a polite, quizzical smile that breaks my heart. "I am eighty-five years old," she says, "and I can't—I can't . . . make my voice heard if people are going to be talking. If you are not interested in hearing my shtory about Peter and Eleanor, maybe you could go to . . . maybe you could go to . . . um, another part of the shtore."

"Your book is a gross misrepresentation of Native Americans," says the guy named Micah. "And I don't think we need to hear any more of this kind of racist misinformation."

She swings her head in his direction, and I can see her try to focus her eyes on him. One beat goes by, then another. "Young man," she says, "you should be ashamed of yourshelf. This is a book for *children*."

"But it's wrong to teach children these lies about our native populations!" says a woman in a sweatshirt.

Gabora stares at her, blinking in shock.

"It's all a big lie, this Pilgrims and Indians bullshit," says a man. "And you're perpetuating the idea that the English had a right to this land, had a right to just come in and plunder—"

Cindy Reynolds says from the side, "I am going to have to ask you all to be polite."

And then, as if some signal was given, pandemonium breaks out, with people yelling out things. A couple of people stand up. I see one man yelling at the protesters to sit down, that this isn't the time or the place. Another guy says, "There's *never* a time or a place, have you noticed? We're all just supposed to let this crap be perpetuated! Is that your answer?"

Adam and I have been standing at the back of the crowd, but now he looks over at me, and without a word, we start heading to the front of the room. Gabora sees us and holds up her hand, wanting us to stop.

She smiles at the crowd, appealingly. "Listen, listen. Don't worry. Thish book is just fiction. It's not something that really happened! It's okay! I know it didn't really happen. That's how fiction works."

"Don't you see that that doesn't make it any better?" a woman in a black dress yells. "This book never should have been published!"

Gabora squints into the crowd and for a moment I think she might cry. But then she gets it that she's in enemy territory and that it's time to fight. I see her swallow and look up at the ceiling for a moment, gathering her thoughts. She's a tough old woman after all. She's used to being adored, but she has a core of steel to her, too. I've seen it.

"Excuuuuse me, but I am the author of—I wrote sheventy-sheven books about children—and I get letters from all over the world, thanking me for teaching children about . . . shtuff . . . and I will *not* have anyone say I shouldn't publish my books! I wrote a book about Peter and Eleanor going to see the . . . uh . . . dinosaurs during the . . . the dinosaur times, and no one came yelling at me that it wasn't true dinosauruses!"

"Lady, you need to go back to the dinosaurs,"

yells Micah. "Write about something you know firsthand."

People start barking things, and I'm readying myself to take action, if only I could think of what to do, when Adam says in a low voice in my ear, "Okay, that's it, I'm stopping this."

He makes his way to the front of the room, holding up his hand to quiet everyone, and he says the reading is over, and Ms. Pierce-Anton will be happy to sign books if anyone wishes. Books make lovely gifts, he says.

He has never looked more commanding. He's going to clear this room. You would never know this guy hangs out with gnomes.

"Hey, who are you to say she doesn't get to read? I want to hear how she thinks the Pilgrims were so damned smart, all right?" Micah threads his way through the crowd, picking up speed. I realize that he's actually furious now, and also probably drunk—and that he's going to reach Gabora's podium in about ten seconds. "Listen here, old lady!" he yells. "Tell us again how smart the Pilgrim children are!" His eyes are narrowed and his mouth is twisted in rage. I feel myself drawing back, my heart pounding.

"Language, please," says Cindy Reynolds. She's clutching her necklace.

"You're going to need to leave, sir," says Adam, stepping in front of Gabora. "Ms. Pierce-Anton will not be reading tonight."

304

But of course Micah keeps coming forward, and then—quickly as can be, Adam goes over to him and does some kind of martial arts move, a classic wax on/wax off move from *The Karate Kid*, is what it looks like to me. And as Micah reaches up to hit Adam, I stifle a scream, but Adam calmly pins the guy's arms behind him, stopping him mid-step. I can barely breathe. Cindy Reynolds and a man from the audience take Gabora by the arm to the back room, just as a security guard shows up and escorts Micah off the premises.

The rest of the people seem to be stunned into silence.

Adam smiles at them. "For those of you who want a signed book," he says, straightening his tie as Cindy rejoins him at the podium, "you may pick one up from this lady right here, Cindy Reynolds. And we want to thank you all for coming. Good night. Travel safe in all this weather out there."

Then he goes over and picks up a chair that fell in the scuffle, and props it upright again, and heads to the back room. Three or four people come up to select a book, mostly the grand-motherly types, while the rest of the people are grumbling, but they go out into the night without more trouble. I go to the back room, too, where Adam is squatting down next to Gabora, who' on the couch fanning herself.

"Why didn't you let me read?" she's saying in a whiny voice.

"Because we weren't going to put you through any more of that," Adam says. "Let's get you out of here and back to your hotel."

"Usually I get to read to the children," she says. "That's what I like to do. My public expects it."

"I know," I say. "This was unusual. But you're okay."

Cindy Reynolds is back from ringing up the books, and she looks at us all with such big, sad eyes. "I really didn't have any idea this was going to be this way, or I would never have put you in harm's way, Ms. Pierce-Anton." She hands Adam the cardboard poster of the event from the front of the store. "Here, take this with you. And also the cookies I had made for the refreshment time. And—oh, I wish I could do more. I am so very sorry."

"It's okay, dear. I just hope they understand now," says Gabora. "Some people don't know what fiction *means*." Adam helps her to her feet, and I see her melt against his shoulder, and he puts his arm around her.

"I'll call our driver," I say.

Outside, the wind is blowing everything sideways. The wooden sign announcing Gabora's visit is skittering down the street, and Adam goes and gets it and sets it inside the store, while I help

306

Gabora into the car. Fortunately, the protesters all seem to have vanished.

Gabora settles down in the cab, first glaring out the window at all the palmetto trees bending low, and she's leaning against Adam's shoulder. And then, to my surprise, she falls asleep, mouth open and actually snoring. He looks at me over her head and makes his mouth go into a round, shocked O.

"I can't believe we published that book," he says.

"I know."

It takes both of us to get her out of the cab and walk her to her hotel room after that. Once we're in her room, he waits in the sitting area, while I follow her into the bedroom. She needs help getting out of her red skirt and the white blouse and the jacket with the mouse pin. She stands there mutely, as I unzip and tug everything off of her, looking tired. Her body looks pink and dimply, sagging in places, as though it might have been constructed from those foam pieces you make pillows with. A body that has worked hard and given birth and done years of work. It reminds me of my years of helping Bunny, who never made a big deal of naked bodies needing to be hidden. I feel my eyes stinging as I help her on with her long white nightgown, thinking of not being able to be with Bunny.

"Well, I'll leave you to it," I say once we've

gotten her gown on. She looks like a snow queen standing there. "Your toiletries are all on the counter in the bathroom. Do you need anything else? I could get you a glass of water . . ."

"Oh, dear," she says. "Oh, honey. No, no. Please—I'm going to need some help."

And she does. I'm to put her wig on the wig stand and then comb out her short, wiry gray hair. I put toothpaste on her purple toothbrush and stand there while she cleans her teeth. She's weaving slightly, and for a moment I think I may need to take over the tooth scrubbing, too. But then, thank goodness, she's done. There are fake eyelashes to be removed, and some product to take off her eyeliner. I shift from one foot to the other, keep myself smiling. Actually, I am fascinated at all this . . . effort.

"Done?" I say at last, when the eyelashes—looking like scary spiders—are vanquished to their plastic container.

"Moishturishze," she says. And, oh dear God, that turns out to mean that she has miniature jars and jars of creams to be applied—serums and oils and night cream and eye cream and throat cream, and we apply all of those, in an order that seems as complicated as solving an algebraic trinomial equation. At one point she smacks my hand when I try to apply an oil before a serum.

But then, praise heaven, we're done, and I walk her back to the bedroom and tuck her in under the sheet in her enormous king-sized bed.

"Well," I say. "Good night. Hope you have sweet dreams." I go over to the door, and she squeals, "Oh! My pills! I need my sleeping pill and my vitamins."

"Of course." I go get them out of the suitcase and get a glass of water and take them over to her.

"Phronsie? I never was treated that way," she says in a sad, little-girl voice after she swallows them and settles back on her pillow. "I *love* Thanksgiving," she says. "I . . . thought it would be good. Pilgrimsh. Everybody loves the Pilgrimsh. I wish they would have let me read it to them, then they would have *seen*."

"You should get some sleep now."

Adam is sitting on the couch looking at a magazine about things to do in Charleston when I come out of the room. His eyes meet mine.

"Is she okay?"

"Yeah." I fall down onto the couch, clutching my chest. "I may not be okay. I may never recover."

"You will. I have just the thing for you. If you don't mind a brief run through the rain and wind, there's a club about two blocks away we could get to. And they have a DJ and a dance floor, unlike the bar here, which has only stuffed-shirt businessmen."

"Have you seen that wind? What if we lose power?"

He has his arm propped along the back of the couch, and he's smiling at me.

"Yeah, so if we lose power, where would you rather be?" he says. "In an unfamiliar dark hotel room crawling around on the floor looking for your toothbrush, or sitting in a bar where there are plenty of candles and people? Come on. We'll have fun. We need some fun after that career-ending monstrosity."

"Yep. It's a sad finale to a successful career," I say.

He stands up and holds out his hands for me to grab on to. "Actually, I was talking about me," he says. "Fighting in bookstores was *not* mentioned in the job description."

I allow myself to be pulled up. The idea of complete blackout darkness in a hotel doesn't sound all that appealing. "Maybe we do need to decompress. Debrief and all that. Figure out a strategy for the next two readings. And, of course, drink."

My phone rings just then. I take it out of my purse. It's Judd.

Adam sighs. "Go ahead. Talk to him," he says. "Want me to wait in the hall?"

I shake my head at him. "Hey, Judd," I say. "How's it going?"

He tells me that it's all great there. He and Hendrix have fetched Bunny. Maggie's tucking her into bed, and Hendrix's kids are playing

Monopoly with Hendrix and my father and yelling about Park Place and Broadway. I try to picture my father succumbing to something as frivolous as a game of Monopoly—and then I hear him shouting in the background about a hotel on the wrong space, and I realize that nothing is ever frivolous to my father. He's playing it with the same half-angry consternation that he brings to his whole life.

"Sounds like everybody's having a wonderful time," I say.

"Yeah, it's still like the freaking Waltons around here," says Judd happily. He talks so loudly on the phone that I'm sure Adam can hear him. "Fire in the fireplace, ladies making the appetizers in the kitchen, Frank Sinatra on your dad's stereo. And hey, I'm legit for the first time! I'm one of the family! The kids are even calling me Uncle Judd, and your dad gave me one of his signature back-slappings—the kind that threatens to put your back out for six months, but I knew it was coming so I bobbed and weaved and managed to stay upright."

"Smart," I say. I bite my lip. "Tell my family hello for me, why don't you?"

"Sure," he says. "Phronsie says hey, everybody!"

There's a chorus of hellos. "They'd come and talk to you themselves, but there's a fight shaping up over a deal for the railroads. And I gotta go play the part of John-Boy Walton. Do you think I can be John-Boy? Have I earned that, or would that be Hendrix?"

"Definitely Hendrix. You still have to apply, you know."

"That's where you're wrong. I'm in. I think your family would sooner expel *you* from the cast before they did me."

And then there's a screech in the background, something about the Reading Railroad, followed by a mild ruckus, and he tells me good-bye, and we hang up.

That's when I realize I want nothing more than to go running to a bar two blocks away and drink a cocktail. Maybe three. Or twenty.

Whatever it takes to dissolve the lump that has formed in my throat.

The rain is coming down sideways in icy needles—it's given up on being just ordinary raindrops—and we're cold and wet and wind-blown by the time we get to the bar. It's nice and warm and cave-like in there, and also there's a DJ playing loud music—which is perfect. Best of all, it's filled with lots of people who don't seem to be aware at all of the erroneous, racist Thanksgiving story told by a little old lady *authoress*. In fact, they don't even seem to be worrying that the oncoming storm is going to be the end of the world. Or maybe they've decided that if the end of the world is coming, they might as well be dancing when it happens. If that is the case, then I salute them.

I can feel myself actually starting to breathe normally again. Adam steers us to a booth in the back that some people are right then vacating, and we sit down. A waitress dressed all in black except for a sparkly tiara riding on top of a red ponytail comes over and wipes off the table.

"Quite a night out there," she says in a Southern accent. "Thanks to the forecast, the bartender has invented the Snow Hurricane special. You interested?"

"Wait. There's a drink called the Snow Hurricane?" I say, as Adam says, "What's in it?"

The waitress smiles at him. "Well, it's got some sloe gin and grenadine and maybe a lime to be the hurricane, and I think a little bit of shaved ice—that's the snow part," she says. "It's good. Everybody's having it."

"Sure," I say. And Adam says, "Two of those, please."

I watch her walk over to the bar and give the order to the bartender, a swarthy, bearded guy in a white shirt. And then I turn back to Adam, who is regarding me steadily, half smiling.

"What?" I say.

"Nothing. I was just thinking about Gabora. Wondering if she's ever going to recover from this. You could almost see her going backward in

313

time, until she was like the child she used to be. So innocent and trusting."

"Yeah," I say, "but trust me. This is just for tonight. She's resilient. You watch—she's going to come out guns blazing for the next two readings. *She'll* be the one yelling at the audience tomorrow night and fighting them off with karate moves."

"Oh God. Do we really have to go through this again? I'm ashamed to be associated with this book, to tell you the truth."

"Well, yeah, me too," I say. "All in all, I'd say that reading was saved only by the fact that you'd watched *The Karate Kid*." I do the wax on/wax off movement. "Maybe this could be your sub-specialty. You know? Put it on your business card. 'Adam Cunningham: Public Relations and Personal Karate Person.' Wait! What *is* a karate person called? A dojo?"

He rolls his eyes and laughs. "A dojo is the place. A sensei is the expert."

"Okay. How about 'Adam Cunningham: Public Relations Sensei'? And underneath that, it could say, 'Will Protect Authors from the Furious Hordes.' Or: 'You Offend, I'll Defend.'"

He laughs, and I feel a slight appreciative shiver. Of all my forty-four dates—and this is *not* a date, I remind myself—hardly any man laughed at my jokes.

The waitress comes back with our drinks and

314

sets them down. They're a startling but lively shade of red. Just what the evening calls for, a drink that looks like blood.

"Well, here we are," I say as brightly as I can muster. We clink our glasses in a toast. It tastes sweet and . . . well, red. "So . . . here's to living through reading number one! Mostly."

We drink up.

"So, I didn't get an answer to my question." I put my glass down. "Does this drink mean that this isn't just an ordinary windy, rainy night in South Carolina? We're in a . . . snow hurricane?"

"That is correct."

"In *Charleston, South Carolina?*"

"Also correct," he says.

"Are we in the apocalypse then? First bookstore patrons have gone mad and now there's going to be snow *and* a hurricane?"

"These could be early signs, sure."

"You sound cheerful about it."

"Well, yeah. I've been preparing for this for most of my life. All the dystopian books from my childhood. Also I know karate, so when the zombies come . . ." He does some martial arts moves.

"That's right. You can outrun them or wax them on and off," I say. "So *you're* set. Not sure that my skill set is going to come in handy."

"Well, but you're with me," he says. "I'll totally protect you."

Then he just keeps looking at me, like he's memorizing my face or something. I feel embarrassed suddenly. I wish he'd look somewhere else.

He clears his throat. "I take it your fiancé is already celebrating Thanksgiving with your family," he says. When I don't say anything, he says, "Sorry. Couldn't help overhearing. Also, it was fascinating to hear that your clan is the actual Waltons."

"Please," I say.

"I thought it was a charming call. From a fiancé. Who wants to be John-Boy. Which, of course, he can't be. Anyone would know an outsider can't be John-Boy. I was thinking for a minute there that I might have to take the phone and inform him of that."

I take another sip of my drink and give him my most steady stare. "So . . . besides the gnome situation, do you have any other craziness?"

He laughs. "Are you by chance referring to my *gnome village?*"

"I believe I am."

"I will thank you, Ms. Linnelle, not to use *gnomes* and *craziness* in the same sentence. The gnomes are doing their part for a better world. I don't know if you've noticed how they stand in the window and look outward, ready to detect any emergencies that may come up."

"I have noticed that, yes." I clear my throat.

"Too bad they couldn't have been on hand tonight."

"They don't travel," he says flatly. "Everyone knows that."

"Huh," I say. "Fascinating. And, um, if I may ask, how did you come to be in charge of a gnome village, or are you at liberty to discuss this?"

He eyes me carefully. "My first gnome showed up, uninvited and unasked for, I might add, arriving in a box from my sister for my birthday one year. That was it: just an unassuming little gnome who got put on the shelf and forgotten. I didn't much relate to him. Seemed like one of her weirder presents. But then she came to visit and brought a girl gnome to keep him company. And apparently girl gnomes are kind of rare, so my sister said he was a lucky fellow, indeed, to have a partner. And—well, my sister's visit was a little longer than I would have liked, and so rather than argue with each other as we tend to do, we started spending our evenings building a house for them. I made a little dining room table and bed out of balsa wood, and she created a couch and a blanket for them. And then, after she went back home, I got them a rug and a desk. Later . . . a lamp and a full-length mirror for their bedroom. And then other gnomes started showing up. More houses needed. More lamps and couches. Then I moved them to my fire escape because they required more space.

Gnomeo and Juliet, of course, come to work."

"Of course," I said. "And obviously they needed a tractor."

"Yeah. They'll be coming in soon, now that winter's on the way. Time for these guys to hibernate."

"Hibernate!"

"They go into my closet in a box until spring. Say, this is probably weird, but do you want to dance?"

"I'm not sure I can dance with anyone who puts gnomes in boxes and calls it hibernation."

"They actually like it. It's like a long nap for them. Come on. Let's move."

Michael Jackson's "Billie Jean" is playing. I love this song. Hendrix and I used to dance to it when we were supposed to be doing the dishes when we were kids, and Maggie would come in and watch us and shake her head and then get us to hurry up and finish. When I go to stand up, I realize the Snow Hurricane special seems to have already found a nice little place in my brain and is settling in like a soft puppy.

Adam dances just like I would have expected— all loose and goofy and as though his joints have ball bearings in them. There may even be some Karate Kid moves in there. His blondish surfer hair keeps falling into his eyes, and at one point he unexpectedly takes my hand and spins me around.

By the time we make it back to our table, I'm a little out of breath. And I can't seem to stop smiling. It's been ages since I've danced. I think the last time was at Sarah and Russell's wedding, where I danced with Judd, who is one of those showboat-type dancers. People always clap for him because he's so athletic.

"Also," Adam says, once we're sitting down, as though only ten seconds have gone by, "what would *you* have me do with them? I can't leave them on the fire escape to freeze, and I don't have room for them in my apartment."

"Are we back to the gnomes?"

"*Yes,* gnomes."

"You know, you really are kind of goofy," I tell him. "Everyone knows that gnomes should go to a warm climate for the winter. They need to go to Florida. Or to Europe—how about Gnome, Italy?"

"Hey. Don't call me goofy just because you don't have any crazy relatives who start you on a lifetime of gnome care . . . You're in the Walton family. Wholesome farm people. Actual chickens and goats, I'll bet."

"You think I don't have crazy relatives? I'll have you know that I've got a mom who's on speed dial with the entities who are running the universe."

He looks impressed by this news. "Do you now?"

"She is also the Queen of Mayhem, my mom. She calls herself *Tenaj,* T-E-N-A-J, which is Janet spelled backward, in case you didn't realize. And she does magic and spells and is kind of an artist-slash-guru-slash-free-spirit type who makes things out of objects she finds on the ground. And she loves causing trouble wherever she goes."

"And despite all this, I'm guessing she's still in your life?"

"Off and on. Currently very on. She's been calling me for days, in fact, wanting to give me messages she's gotten for me . . . from the universe."

"Well, sure. That would only be the polite thing to do, I suppose, pass them on. But—why can't the universe give *you* the messages? Why is she the middleman?"

"She has connections."

The waitress comes by, and Adam lifts his eyebrows to me. "Another?" he says, and I nod. "Two more," he tells her.

"They're good, aren't they?" she says. "And highly effective, if you know what I mean."

We both nod.

"They are highly, *redly* effective," I say.

"Very redly," says Adam. He's smiling at me. "So, I can't let this go," he says. "What is the universe trying to get you to know?"

"Well," I say. "It's hard to tell specifically."

"Why? Does it talk in symbols? Hieroglyphics?"

"Haha. No. Not when my mom is delivering the messages at least. It sort of yells."

"Well, what was the latest one, for instance? A yelling one."

"Oh, Adam. Well, if you really want to know, the latest one was right after I'd told Judd I would marry him, and then an hour later my mom calls for the first time in a year and says the universe is telling me WHATEVER YOU'RE DOING, YOU'RE MAKING A BIG MISTAKE, STOP IT."

He bugs his eyes out and pretends to rub them in amazement. "Wow! Just like that? From out of the blue?"

"You see what I'm dealing with?" I take a sip of my drink, which really is going down so easily. I feel like I just want to laugh with him. The world is so crazy, my *family* is so crazy—this whole place. And it's so *fun,* because no one ever wants to talk about this stuff.

He curls his hand around his glass. He has really nice hands. Big and wide, nice roundly clipped nails. You can tell a man anything if he keeps gnomes. That's what I want to tell him.

He's looking at me. "I think, if you don't mind, we need to back up and unpack this story a little bit more. I need some more information. This could take four or five Snow Hurricane specials."

I laugh.

"So your mom, communicator with the universe, is the one who gave you the name Phronsie, I take it? And how did she come up with that? Do we know if the universe was naming children the year you were born?"

"Oh, it was a character in a book she liked. *Five Little Peppers and How They Grew*. I am officially named Phronsie Pepper."

"And your father—what was his take on this highly unusual naming situation? Or does he communicate with the universe, too?"

"No, no. God, no. Straight as they come."

"God, this is fascinating stuff." He rubs his hands together. "The origins of Phronsie Pepper Linnelle. I never would have been able to get to this in the office. That's for sure."

"It's not so fascinating."

"I'll be the judge of that. First question—you don't mind questions, do you?—how did your parents meet? Pa Walton and the Communication Director of the Universe."

"You've heard of Woodstock, right?"

"A time or two," he says drily.

I laugh. "Sorry! Well, that's where they met. At the festival." And I tell him the story—side of the road, innocent farm lad runs into dazzling hippie fabulousness in the weed-smoking, road-dancing, high-fiving personage of my mom. "It was just out of the blue, just like that, a totally random event—unless you believe my mom, who thinks *nothing* ever happens out of the blue and that everything happens for a reason, all dictated by those entities or forces who are spinning the universe—"

"Of course she does," he says.

"Yes. And so one thing led to another—the music, the mud, the stars, what have you, yada yada yada, and Hendrix and I got conceived right there. At Woodstock. Under a blanket, in a tent."

"Hendrix is . . . ah . . . your twin?"

"Yep."

"And he's named Hendrix because . . . *no!*"

"Exactly. Because Jimi Hendrix was playing 'The Star-Spangled Banner' right then."

His eyes shine. "Get outta town! You got conceived during Hendrix's rendition of 'The Star-Spangled Banner'? Like, for real?"

I laugh. "Well, I wasn't there, so I can't say for sure. But that's what I've been told."

"Oh, you were there, Phronsie. The little spark that was you was absolutely there." He sits back and rubs his eyes. "Wow. This is a heavy, heavy story."

"I'm glad you appreciate it. That's the end of the good part, because after that, it all got screwed up. My dad, it turned out, was sort of engaged to someone else when he left for Woodstock. Or at least his girlfriend thought they were. And his parents and all the people in their town agreed with her."

"Ah. And so then—what does a guy like that do? Does he stay there with your mom, or does he go back home?"

"He stays. Doesn't come back to help his dad out on the farm, like he was supposed to do. Abandons the aggrieved girlfriend. Stays in Woodstock, marries my mom in a little hippie ceremony, and has us."

"Does he stay because he's a dad now and has a duty to perform? Or because he's madly in love?"

"Well, now that's the question. That may be the question I've been grappling with my whole life. My theory has always been that he really was madly in love with my mom, who was like nobody he ever met before, and that he really took to the whole Woodstock lifestyle he was living. But—who knows? Anyway, it doesn't matter because when Hendrix and I were two years old, my grandfather died, and my dad had to go back to take over the farm. And so that's what he did. Gave up. Settled down." I put my hands flat on the table. "So that's the story. Aaaand . . . we don't have to keep talking about it."

Adam is watching my face. "No, I want to. And I happen to remember there's a stepmom in this story. So *I'm* thinking . . ."

"Correct. He brings my hippie mom to the farm, they break up soon after, and then later he gets married to—"

"Please, please tell me it's the old girlfriend."

I laugh. "Yes!"

He claps his hands. "Wow! She forgave him? How did he manage that?"

"Well, who knows, really? I was four when it happened. I suspect a lot of groveling was involved."

"And what happened to your mom? She went on to work for the universe as a message-deliverer?"

"Yeah," I say slowly. "That's right. She went back to Woodstock, became an artist who picks up stuff off the ground and makes art out of it, and she does spells and runs spiritual meetings, and gets married to people that she has no business marrying, and that's pretty much it." I look down at my hands.

"Hey," he says. "You just went dark on me. What happened?"

"I-I don't know. She's just . . . she's just never been all that dependable. She's all about fun and magic and art and stories, which would be great, but she left us and didn't come back. And my father and stepmother did all the day-to-day raising of Hendrix and me. But they're—I don't know. Old before their time, maybe? They seem fixated on all the hard parts of life. While my mom just flits around, having fun with whatever life throws her, and no matter who gets hurt by her. And I don't really belong to either camp, is the truth of it."

"Well, are they happy together—your father and stepmother?"

I shrug. "What does happy look like?"

"I'll tell you one thing happy looks like, and that is dancing. Because 'I Heard It Through the Grapevine' is playing, and I used to play that in a band, and if I don't dance, I might start playing air guitar and singing."

"Oh, please do that."

"You wouldn't say that if you'd heard me sing."

We go out on the dance floor, and this time he takes my hand like it's just a perfectly natural thing to do, the most normal thing in the world. People are pouring out onto the dance floor, and I let myself be swept into the music, which is loud and Motown. Familiar as my own name. Words everyone knows. Everyone's smiling and some people are singing along. Rock music is the great equalizer. Like Woodstock was, maybe. Bringing people together who had no idea there were so many of them out there who were all part of the same culture. I wonder if something like that could ever happen again.

It hits me as I'm shimmying and twirling and smiling that Judd has never once wanted to talk about my family life. I've always assumed that's because he was there living it with me for a lot of the time. Being my best friend and all. But there's a way he just shuts down whenever the subject of my mom comes up. He believes the worst about her and thinks I should just get over it.

Not your most introspective person, Judd Kovac.

Adam pulls me to him, and I feel his breath in my hair and move my body just slightly away from his. There are warning signs flashing in my head. *You are making too many mistakes here! Telling an attractive, already-a-bit-flirtatious coworker about your family, and then slow dancing with him in a bar!*

Also drinking. Drunk!

Also looking at his eyes.

Also the karate-admiration thing.

And the gnome-flirtation thing.

And now comparing him to Judd. Favorably, I might add.

By the time we make our way back to the table, he's telling me how he grew up in Orange County, California, and was always sure he'd turn out to be a professional surfer. "When you had the beach at the end of the street, it was pretty much the goal of everybody I knew to spend their lives surfing and getting paid for it," he says. "It never occurred to me that I was going to have to work on dry land. Until I was about eighteen and wasn't getting all that much money from surfing."

"How much *were* you getting?"

"Zero. But, not to worry, because I made ten bucks every now and then for my guitar playing. Kids' birthday parties mainly."

"Brilliant."

"So my father had a little talk with me, and we came up with the plan that I'd better go to college."

"And what did you major in?"

"Philosophy." He shrugs. "Yeah. I have a super instinct for careers that have pretty much no chance of any income."

"Until now. Darla Chapman *is* paying you, I hope."

"Mostly." Then he shrugs. "So I have a question, now that we're two drinks in and I'm about to order another one for both of us."

"Is the question whether or not I want another drink, because if it is, I do."

"I kind of suspected you might." He holds up two fingers, and the tiara-wearing waitress knows what that means and brings them over. When I look up at him, he is looking right at me.

"Sooooo . . . if I may ask, and it's clearly none of my business—but just out of curiosity—what is it about you and this guy you're marrying?" he says. Dead serious.

"What?" I say. "What kind of question is that?"

"I dunno. Just interested. I mean, with all due respect, I don't get the idea that this is the love match of the decade, no offense. And apparently the universe is in agreement with that. It sent you a yelling message, I believe you said."

"Yeah, but, no offense, what the hell does the universe know about anything?"

"True. When did it ever get things right? All those oceans and mountains and stars and stuff . . . that was pretty much a fluke. Lucky accidents."

He keeps looking at me. Right into my eyes.

After a moment, I mop up some of the condensation that has come off our glasses. I watch a couple at the next table, who are deep in conversation, heads together. The woman is upset, and she's hissing something at the guy, and her mouth is all distorted, and the guy is nodding, looking gloomy, and then she says something to him, and he protests, and then she hauls off and slaps him on the hand. He draws back, looks at her in shock.

"Wow," whispers Adam. "I did *not* see that whack coming."

"No, I didn't either. And evidently neither did he."

"You know what's going on?" Adam says in a low voice. "Okay. I think I've got it figured out. This is their third date. She's mad because he's clueless. He probably hasn't even kissed her. And so she's yelling at him trying to get him to react to something, *anything*. And all he does is just look forlorn. Like a big wuss. So—she had no choice but to clobber him."

"Yup, trying to get feelings from a stone. Been there," I say. "But, alternatively, it could be that *he's* the one pushing things too fast. Maaaaybe with his other hand—which we cannot see— he's taking some pretty bold liberties, and she's warned him, but he's hard of hearing so he didn't know she was upset—"

He gives me an admiring look. "Hard of hearing, is he? Now that's a plot twist. I can see why you're a novelist."

"—and then, *pow,* he gets hit. And now he's stunned. He thought things were going so well."

"That could be the theme of tonight," Adam says. "I Thought Things Were Going So Well: The Gabora Pierce-Anton Story."

"I Thought Things Were Going So Well: The Weather Channel Story."

He gives me another long look. "I Thought Things Were Going So Well: The Friendly, Non-judgmental Discussion Among Colleagues of the Engagement of Phronsie Pepper Linnelle."

Somehow, we don't seem to be able to move off the subject of me and my love life.

I find myself telling him about the forty-four dates and the piece I'm going to write, and how sick I am of first dates and men who talk to me like they're reading off their résumés or employment histories. How my mother said marriage isn't any good for women, but then she did it *three times*. And then I'm babbling about Judd and his gym and how he carefully removes spiders from my apartment, and the fact that he washes the dishes and takes the dog out, and he's so good with children. Wears babies on his chest just like a pro.

He listens. God, this guy listens. He smiles, he tilts his head, his eyebrows lift, he mops his brow. And he never takes his eyes off mine.

"So what are you thinking while you're staring at me like that?" I say when I wind down. Because I am drunk. I'm leaning on my elbow. My third Snow Hurricane has been demolished. And it occurs to me that if I'm not careful, I'll soon be telling him about my marriage to Steve Hanover, and *then* I'll find myself telling him the plot of my novel, and offering to read his pages, too. And then—oh God, things will get so out of hand. I need to get control of this.

"I have some questions," he says. "First of all, why did you go on forty-four dates when you already had a person you were attached to?"

"What kind of question is that? Because he's a good friend, is why. I-I didn't expect that he was going to want to get married."

"Well, but did you miss him when you were out with other people?"

"Adam! It's not like that. It wasn't like I was

331

pining for him. He was dating, too. We both were—and then he said something like, 'This sucks, and we should marry each other.' And so I thought about it and then I said yes, because he's been my friend since we were five, and besides that . . . I mean, I *know* him through and through, and he's really responsible and fun and steady, and my family loves him, and there's a shorthand when you know somebody so well. And also—getting married means no more first dates!" I give him a grin when I deliver that last triumphant part, but I can feel my mouth wobbling.

"Huh," he says. "Then I think you totally should do it, because that makes perfect sense to me. It's a brilliant, brilliant plan, marrying somebody just so you don't have to date anymore. And what do you say to going back on the dance floor? While we're still young and before you get yourself married off."

"Sure," I say.

We go back on the dance floor, and wouldn't you know, they switch immediately to a slow dance. I hesitate, but he takes my hand and pulls me close to him.

He says in my ear while we're dancing, "I just think—well, just an observation here. I notice that when you're talking about your mom, your face kind of lights up. And when you're talking about the Walton kind of life—well, you look a little bit pained."

I pull away and look at him. "What are you talking about?"

"I guess I just know what you look like when you love something. You have this face that shows all your emotions. Your eyes get big. But when you talk about this fiancé of yours, there's none of that. I just feel I should report that news to you, as a public service. You don't look happy when you talk about him. Or getting married. Just saying."

I stop dancing. "Look. I don't know what you're seeing in my face, but I do love him. And what's more, I *trust* him, and I know everything there is to know about him, and he's part of my family. It's easy to be with him, and we get along well, and I tell him everything, and that's love. And as for my mother—my mother . . ."

"What?"

"I spent years wanting to be like her, but I don't want that anymore. The way she goes about just letting life take care of itself, falling into one thing and then another, thinking that creativity is all that matters. Hearing from the *universe*. I don't want to be like that. I want a life where you don't have to constantly worry that you're about to get left. And I want *real* life, not pretend. I picked Judd for a reason."

"Okay. Sounds absolutely, insanely perfect." He takes my hand and spins me around. "But I'm just saying—if I loved somebody, and she went

333

out on a date with someone else—never mind forty-four someone elses, because *that* would not happen—*I'd* want to make my feelings for her clear. I'd do what I could to make her happy, and part of that would be wanting her with me laughing and eating dinner and going to clubs. Making love. I don't think I could stand it by the time we got to—oh, I don't know—date number *two,* let's say. That's just me."

The song ends, and we walk back to the table. I'm having only a little trouble walking, and I feel something turn over in my gut. The Snow Hurricanes?

"Well," I say, "while we're talking, what's your situation? Are you in love with somebody right now? Why don't we dissect *your* love life for a while?"

"Dissecting my love life would take about five seconds. I dated a girl through college, and then we broke up when she found somebody else. And I spent some time traveling in Europe by myself, and then I moved to New York for this job, and I've gone out with a few people, but basically I spend all my time at work."

"Maybe *you* should go on Match.com."

"Yeah. Sounds like a real fun time."

We stay until the bar closes, until the DJ starts packing up and some sadistic person turns on the overhead lights, and we're left blinking and shuddering in the sudden cruel light of reality.

Good, I think to myself. *Now that the lights are on, I can snap myself out of saying way too much about my personal life. And how I'm getting all shook up, and everything is so confusing.*

In the staggering light of the bar, I look down at my phone, which has blown up with messages. A million of them—or at least ten. I had forgotten to turn my phone on after the reading. Oh God. One after another, ten messages, all from Darla Chapman. My heart stops right there in the fluorescent light horribleness, knowing there's going to be some other, even worse, horribleness to come. I feel like someone has just poured ice-cold water over my head.

"What is it?" says Adam.

"Just a minute," I tell him. "Something . . . Darla's been trying to reach me."

"Did she say why?"

I scroll through, rapidly. "Mostly they just say variations of *Call me when you get a chance,* but—uh-oh. This one. *Gabora's daughters have driven to the hotel, and they've taken Gabora home with them. She was so upset about the way the reading went and then there's the weather,* and then all in caps she wrote: *WHERE THE HELL ARE YOU? WHAT IS GOING ON? WHAT HAPPENED AT THE READING? The hotel says you're not answering your room phone. Call me when you get this!!!!* And in Darla fashion, she has included four exclamation points, and we all know what that means." I look at him, feeling the blood draining from my face.

"What the actual hell—*Gabora's daughters* came and got her? If they were so nearby, why couldn't *they* have taken her to the reading in the first place?"

"Yeah. I think they live in Georgia. So not that far away."

My head hurts a little, a preview of the headache I'm going to have tomorrow perhaps—and all through next week when Darla fires me for reasons I can't quite discern just now but which are certainly sure to be legitimate.

"I wonder if Darla means I should call her now, when it's nearly two in the morning. Do you think 'call me when you get this' includes now? Do you think she's still up?"

"Absolutely not," he says. "Are you nuts? That's why God invented tomorrows, so we could do all the things we didn't get to in the current day."

I keep staring at the phone, as if it's going to have answers. "This is just unthinkable! Why didn't Gabora call us?"

"I don't know. It doesn't matter. But would we have gotten it, even if she had?" There are a few stragglers still getting themselves together. The DJ is gone. The bartender, wiping down the counter, calls out as we walk to the door, "Good night. Be careful out there. It's kind of crazy."

And that's when I see that it's snowing. Like,

blizzard kind of snow. It's coming down sideways, and the night has turned bright white. New Hampshire–style.

"Oh my God," I say. And I laugh. "Would you just look at this!"

It's so fantastical, so stunning in its whiteness—like the world has been taken over by forces beyond anything we could imagine. *This* is a Snow Hurricane! I feel something in me just give way—all the tension about Gabora and Darla's calls. Like nothing is what it seems anymore. I can't seem to stop laughing. I turn to Adam, and he's laughing, too. His eyes are saucers.

"Hang on!" he says and takes my hand. "Let's make a run for it! I just want to play in this stuff!"

And so we do—it's amazing, and for a moment, we're running and laughing and slipping and sliding in the blowing snow under the streetlights, as it piles up in doorways and on palm trees, on flowerpots.

People have come outside their apartment buildings and hotels to look at it, and who cares that it's the middle of the night? It's like winter wonderland stuff; you almost think that Santa Claus will show up, and Adam and I ice-skate on the sidewalk all the way to the hotel.

And when we arrive, the desk clerk is shaking his head at us. "I think the world has gone crazy," he says.

In the elevator, Adam reaches over and brushes the snow off my hair. He bites his lip.

"You have snow on your eyelashes," I say, and I raise my hand and touch his face. The snow is really ice crystals. It's stuck in the curls of his beach hair. "This is nothing that your surfer hair could ever imagine, I bet."

"My hair is ready to call 9-1-1," he says softly. He puts his hand up to my cheeks. "Your eyelashes, too . . ."

It is a romantic gesture that I know well from my New Hampshire life. That kind of touching of the face, the need to brush snow off ostensibly, but really a need to touch. Touching and gazing at the same time.

The elevator rumbles to a stop, and the bell dings, and the doors slide open. We walk down the hall, our wet shoes tromping along on the carpet roses, in the hush of the sleeping hotel.

Our rooms are not far away.

I make myself say good night. I say I will see him in the morning.

He says, "You know what? Being as how the universe—Tenaj's universe—is seemingly out of control, and we're now pretty much in free fall, I think there's more fun to be had. What do you say we get our hats and boots and go outside and slide around in the snow some more?"

I want to say yes.

"Come on," he says, seeing that in my face.

He sees everything. He knows it all. "It's a once-in-a-lifetime event, snow in Charleston before Thanksgiving! It's like magic out there, a magic world—snow in the palm trees. Snow in the mimosas. And how often are we going to be this tipsy?"

He actually says the word *tipsy,* which is such an old-lady word, I tell him. It's like what Gabora would say about herself after some time with her flask. And what's with Gabora anyway? She was going to sleep! And *then* she got upset—after I left? So upset that her wicked daughters had to come and fetch her?

"Forget Gabora," he says. "Let's go have fun. This is like apocalyptic stuff out there. I think, as young people, it's our solemn duty to have all the fun possible right now."

He leans against the wall next to my hotel room door, smiling and looking down into my eyes. He looks lit from within, that's what. He looks like there's a fire burning inside him; the light from it shines out from his eyes.

There's a moment—I feel all my resolve slipping away. But I know what would happen, and there are forty-seven reasons why it would be a bad idea. He's too young for me. And he's a coworker. And I have already allowed him to say too much to me. And I have told him too much about myself.

And I am engaged.

Those are only the starter, surface reasons. The rest lie just beneath the surface, reasons I will contemplate later, in shame.

But I am hesitating, and his face comes closer, questioning. And I must give off some signal, because all of me is yearning toward him, and then his lips are on mine, and we're suddenly kissing, pushed against my door, and it's so perfect, sudden-but-not-sudden, so soft and full and perfect, and I am dizzy.

That's it. All there is to it.

Say yes, says the universe.

But there's this other voice, more strident. Did you not just tell Judd Kovac that you were going to marry him? And is he not now celebrating with your family while they wait for you to show up and celebrate, too?

It takes everything I have to stop, but I do. I do because if I don't, it really will be the apocalypse. I say no, and I pull away. I am not going to be the kind of person who goes back on her word, who changes her mind, who gives in to a moment like this.

I am not my mother.

I make myself look tired and disinterested. He knows I am not, but I yawn and stretch. I see the way his eyes are locked onto me, the way he's tilted toward me, outstretched, like our bodies are having the real conversation. But then I break free of the spell. I have this desperate need to get away from him, but the key card is stuck in my purse and I can't find it right away, so I'm standing there, fumbling and trying not to look at him. When I finally find it, I say good night and leave him there and go into my room and close the door hard, and then I am so overcome with emotion and passion and confusion and yes, maybe tipsiness, that I slide down onto the floor and sit there against the door, my legs stretched straight out in front of me, and I take deep breaths, deeeeeccceep breaths, one after another.

This is not love. This is not what love looks like.

I can give a little speech in the morning—too many Snow Hurricanes to drink, too much *snow. Whew!* I will say. *All that dancing, and fun talk. We need to pretend this never happened. Go back to the way things were.*

Sorry if I misled you.

Sorry if we got to talking about love too much.

Things got out of hand.

Sorry.

And, to myself: love is a decision, not a feeling.

But what I want—what I really, really want to do—is to go to his room, kiss him again, look into those eyes, and then . . . well, I want to rip his clothes off. Lick him. Make love to him. Then curl up in his arms and laugh and sleep. That's all. Just that.

At one point, I even get up and start to turn the handle to get out of my room, but then I make myself stop.

Don't make things worse, I tell myself.

I finally fall asleep around three thirty, only to be awakened when a text message comes blaring in around four a.m. I bolt awake, thinking it might be even more disasters.

It's Tenaj. A particular kind of disaster, to be sure.

Whether you know it or not, she writes, *your life has just taken off in an amazing direction. I know this because my life is doing the same thing. Also I don't know if you've ever really thought about this, but the more fun you have, the better you are at life.*

At five o'clock, she writes, *I doubt if those Puritans who have raised you have let you in on a little secret: The whole universe is your playground. You were meant to be happy.*

I stare blearily at the phone. I have exactly one dot left of power, and then the screen goes dark.

CHAPTER TWENTY

After I left Woodstock with Maggie and went back to the farm, I stayed mad at Tenaj for a long time. I settled into life on the farm. My father was somewhat contrite. When I came into the house after Maggie collected me, I expected him to yell, but he didn't. He hugged me, technically speaking, although if there were ever a way to hug somebody without truly *hugging* her, that would be Robert Linnelle hugging his daughter, Phronsie.

He said he was glad I was back. He said he was sorry that things got so out of hand. He said I could go to the prom and to graduation. He wasn't exactly *loving,* but he looked at me with a bit more grudging respect. I knew that Maggie had made it all possible, and I was grateful for that. I was also worn out from fighting, and I was madder at Tenaj than I could ever have imagined being.

At graduation, I was the valedictorian. I scrapped the "we are the future" speech that the administration had okayed, and instead went all out on how people shouldn't let their dreams get stifled. I believe I might have said, "Don't stay in a small town if you want to go big, and don't simply accept the life that got handed to you because you're too scared to do what's calling you! Live for yourself because tradition is just another way of saying, stay in your place! Dare to hope for more." At the end of the speech, I said—and I do remember this part, "I'll tell you one thing. After two years at the community college, I'm getting the hell out of here and going to New York! You can come and visit me there if you want to!"

My classmates—all seventy-four of them—stood and yelled and threw their caps in the air. There were some boos. But mostly from drunk people who didn't have aspirations to leave New Hampshire. They mostly wanted to drink a lot, drive fast in their cars, and have lots of sex with each other.

My father sat across from me at the graduation dinner and made a toast—"To my son, who knows the art of compromise and duty, and to my daughter, who won't rest until she's created a ruckus wherever she goes!"

I raised my glass and looked him in the eye and said, "Thank you! That's the nicest thing you could have ever said. I believe that the summer after high school, when you were my age, you might have started a few ruckuses yourself, if you recall! Named those ruckuses Phronsie and Hendrix."

My father sat back down in his chair, and Hendrix buried his head. I looked over at

Maggie, who pursed her lips. Only Bunny looked directly back at me, and the look on her face was unreadable.

I was known now as a Dangerous Force, a role I kind of liked. I was struttingly proud of the way I'd handled things, turning myself into someone who was not going to be contained. Unlike Maggie, unlike Hendrix, unlike my father—all sheep, as far as I was concerned. Even my father, after his oh-so-brief period of teenage rebelliousness, had turned into a slave to what people thought he should do. They, all of them, let themselves be dictated by *duty*. People asleep at the helm of their lives.

That summer I worked at the farm stand selling sunflowers and corn and dream catchers and went out at night with my friends. I thought about Tenaj only rarely. I put away all the rocks and letters I'd written to her. I stopped dressing like her, and even took down a Woodstock poster I'd hung up years before, just to torment my father.

My family stayed out of my way. I bought notebooks and wrote all the time, whenever I wasn't doing anything else—ostentatious writing, I now see—making a big point of doing it at the breakfast table, during the slow times when I was overseeing the farm stand, and in the evenings when my father liked us all to congregate in the living room. I'd whip out my notebook and pen, and sit there, forehead creased, staring into the distance and then scrawling furiously as though some muse had landed in my head right at that moment and could not be turned back.

Looking back, I am embarrassed by how I acted. Conceited, strong-willed. Obnoxious.

And then one day everything changed. I was at the Bunny Barn, the only place where I could let my guard down and not act like I was the eighth wonder of the world.

I was in my usual spot, lying on my back in the window seat, and she was doing *her* usual thing, ironing. My God, that woman loved to iron. She ironed pillowcases and underwear and dish towels. She said there was something about the back and forth motion, and the heat rising up from the sweet-smelling, just laundered fabric, that made her feel safe and in control.

"There's so much we can't control in our lives, so many mistakes and problems, but when I'm ironing, I'm smoothing all the bad, hurtful things away," she told me once. "We control what we can."

That day I was instructing her about how important it was to put thoughts down on paper before they slipped away. I said that in my opinion, solving problems didn't come about through smoothing out wrinkles, although that was very nice if *she* wanted to do it, but solutions truly came only when a person wrote them down.

"I write everything down," I said proudly.

"I'm documenting my life now, for the books I'll write."

She made a little murmuring noise, which I took to be encouragement.

"I've had some setbacks," I continued, "and not being allowed to go to New York was a big disappointment, and I'm not going to sugarcoat that, but I feel I can get to the soul of myself this way. Find out what makes me tick."

"Phronsie," she said.

"I know," I said. I went on then, about what it was like being the black sheep of the family, slightly misunderstood, when all I wanted was to be free. I was in love with my own words. I told her I now wished I'd bothered to act in the school drama productions because it was clear that acting in plays gave a person a sense of story, of inhabiting a character.

"I want to *inhabit* characters," I said. I had just thought of that line, and I took out my notebook to write it down.

"Phronsie."

I felt the crash almost before I heard it. The iron had fallen to the floor, and Bunny was leaning on the ironing board with her head in her hands, and the whole wobbly board itself looked like it was going to go down. I jumped up and ran and yanked the cord out of the wall, and then I put my arms around her.

She was so slight. When had that happened?

Bunny used to be all soft and upholstered, and now she was like a rag doll that had lost half of its stuffing. Her face was white, and I walked her over to the window seat and sat her down and knelt in front of her. She was weaving a bit, and her eyes seemed wide and scared against her paleness.

My heart was thundering, horse hooves in my chest. I supported her head. I wanted to get her a drink of water, I wanted to call an ambulance, I wanted to beg her not to die right here, not now, not ever, and certainly not right in front of me. But I didn't dare let go of her, or she'd fall down. I rested her head on my shoulder. I drank in the fragrance of her: the smell of her lavender/rose bath powder (she had a whole canister of it on her vanity table; she called it her one nod toward her past happy life as Gordon's wife—this loose box of powder that every morning she'd puff out into the air while she sprinkled it all over her pink, just-showered body), and she smelled like ironing and laundry, and some muffins she'd baked earlier in the day, because she knew I was coming over.

Then I just held on to her with all my might and listened to her breath gain its traction once again while I prayed she'd be okay.

After a few minutes, she pulled away from me. Her face looked damp. It had been a spell, she said. That was it, just a spell. One of those things.

"These happen to me sometimes," she said. Never when there was anybody here, until now. She got over them after a few minutes, she told me. Nothing to worry about.

She wanted to go back to ironing—to get control—but I said no. I said I needed her to come in the living room and sit with me on the couch. Besides, I told her, the iron was looking a little beat up after having flung itself to the floor.

She laughed a little bit at that, at the idea of the iron doing its own flinging. And to my surprise, she agreed to let herself be led into the living room. We sat there on her big, wide blue plaid couch, and we held hands. Her hands were dry and crinkly and still so strong. I looked at them in the long silence, at their liver spots and their tendons, at the short, clipped, perfectly clean nails, at the ring she wore, the one that had been given to her by her mother. It was the ring she'd always told me would be mine someday.

She saw me looking at it and wrestled it off her finger.

"Here, help me take this off," she said. "It's yours. I promised myself I'd give it to you when you graduated from high school—which is when my mother gave it to me. About two hundred years ago now, I'd say." She smiled. "But—I guess I forgot. Here. You take it now. It's yours."

I hesitated. It seemed wrong to take even one thing from her. "Thank you," I said.

I slipped it on my index finger. It had a large blue stone and a gold band. I'd always loved seeing it on Bunny's finger, but now I loved seeing it on my own hand even more.

Except for the feeling of guilt in the pit of my stomach.

"But I don't want to take it from you . . ."

"No, no, it's yours," she said wearily. "It's always been waiting for you. I didn't give it to you on graduation night because . . . things were a little tough then, as you might recall." She stopped talking and took a deep breath. "That was a heedless, headstrong girl at the celebration that night."

I started to cry.

She didn't try to make me stop. She didn't say anything comforting or soothing. She just sat there with me, and after a moment, she put her hand on mine, like she was looking into my heart and could see all the grief and guilt built up there in the caves inside me. Could see what I hadn't found my way toward in my writing.

"Phronsie," she whispered after a while. "I think I know how you must feel. How difficult it is for you here. And how you're pulled out of our world into another one. But, my darling, I would urge you to remember that we've all done the best we could here. Even Robert. He might be a little clumsy at it, he's not perfect, but none of us have done it perfectly, have we? Not even you. You can leave us if you want to, but think about whether you might do it kindly. There's a beauty and a completeness to our lives that you might not be able to see right now. I don't think you have to set fire to what's behind you in order to go. Don't hurt your father's feelings—or Maggie's. Or mine."

I clutched her hand.

She whispered, "Just take your place in the world with as much grace and gratitude as you can muster and try to see the best in us."

After that, things changed, not all at once but bit by bit. I settled myself down, stopped trying to prove who I was to the rest of them. I worked at the farm, helped Maggie with cooking, spent time listening to Bunny's stories. I'd seen her disappointment in me for the first time, and I felt chastened. Like something inside me had been scorched clean.

In the fall, I started at the junior college as a commuter student. I took writing and Western civilization and chemistry and history and French. I learned about playwriting and psychology. Everything electrified me.

The farm stayed the same—always on the brink of some disaster with weather or insects or tired soil. Hendrix joined my dad in working full-time, taking some classes in accounting and business management for the day when he was going to inherit the whole mess. My father's face had hardened into a kind of calcified disappointment, but I tried to be kind to him. Poor man, still possibly in love with someone he'd never again have, tied to this land that threatened him with ruination day after day after day. He couldn't be saved, but I didn't hate him anymore, or fear him. My new feeling was pity, and I didn't see at the time how that might have been just as unfairly destructive.

At the end of my first year in college, Tenaj wrote to me that she'd left Jesse. She hoped I was doing well. She and Chloe had moved into a house with a lot of interesting people. She said she'd been right all along, that marriage was bad for women. But she was glad for it just the same: after all, she'd gotten a gallery and a daughter from the deal.

A precious, precious daughter.

At first, I felt the old rage and disappointment coming back, and I didn't want to answer her, but then I remembered how Bunny had urged me to react with kindness. People were incompetent and clueless, but I was, too—and we were all just doing our best.

I wrote a little note back. I said, "I'm sorry that your life has changed and that your marriage didn't work out. But I know you are finding your way. You always do."

That was it.

She didn't write back, and before I knew it, between doing my school work and helping Maggie and Bunny, and going out on the weekends with Judd and Hendrix and Ariel, my sophomore year at the community college had passed.

That May, two big things happened in our family. Hendrix married Ariel. They got married in our barn with crepe paper streamers over the bales of hay and candles set out on rented folding tables. There was a big dance afterward with just about everybody in town, and I had a great time, shimmying and jitterbugging with all the former Old Spice guys.

Was there a moment in the dancing, drinking, and swooning that I thought of staying there forever? That I looked at Hendrix and Ariel and felt envy? I don't think so. Judd was happily slow dancing with Karla Kristensen, whom he'd had a crush on since tenth grade when she'd suddenly burst forth with enormous breasts and an ability to lead all the cheerleaders in pyramid formations. He winked at me across the barn and gave me the high sign. They were going to be an item. I gave him a wink right back.

A week later, I graduated from junior college, and at the end of the summer, I packed up and moved to New York City so I could attend NYU and get to be a writer.

And in my pocket, I had a check to NYU from

Bunny for the first year's tuition. She had given it to me, she said, because she believed in me. She knew I was a writer. She and I had spent so many hours together, me reading her my stories. She made suggestions—gentle ones, kind ones.

She had once wanted to be a writer herself, she said.

Maybe I would go to college for both of us. And maybe someday I'd bring her to New York, and we could walk down Fifth Avenue, see Tiffany's window, maybe go up to the Empire State Building, and get a White Castle hamburger. She'd heard of those.

"Live your life," she said. "And do it for both of us."

CHAPTER TWENTY-ONE

By the time the baffled, outplayed South Carolina sun struggles to come up, the world is blanketed in snow. I know it from the moment my eyes fly open. I so recognize that feeling of living in a muffled, snowbound world. There are no traffic noises outside—no cars whooshing by, no sirens in the distance. Nothing.

I turn, bleary-eyed, to look at the bedside digital clock. The numbers are dark, and as a special treat, my head is throbbing.

Shit. Is the power out? Why is it dark?

Yes. The power is out.

And I'm hungover.

And I'm in trouble at work.

Aaannnd . . . my crazy mother was on a texting tear through the night, and thanks to that, my phone is dead.

I stumble out of bed and go over to the window and push aside the blinds. There is nothing but whiteness, so bright it makes me squint. It's still snowing. The stuff is heaped up on the roofs of the parked cars. The awning of the building across the street. Looks like about eight inches. Maybe.

There's a knock on my door. It feels like someone might be knocking from inside my head, using a ball-peen hammer.

"Phronsie? It's Adam."

Go away, I want to say. *I'm not fit for human companionship this morning.*

"Have you talked to Darla?" he asks. "Because I have."

My heart starts doing its calisthenics. Have I already missed calls from her this morning? I grab my phone and then remember it's dead. That's right; you have to plug these things in, especially if you have a mother who wants to discuss the universe with you all night.

"No. My phone died. What time is it?" I say, leaning against the door. I look at him through the peephole, and there is his big eye right at the hole, staring in at me. I jump back.

"Nine forty-five."

Oh dear God.

"All right. I'm letting you in, but I'm warning you. I haven't brushed my teeth or combed my hair . . . or anything. You can come in, but you are not to look in my direction. And if you do look in my direction, you are to forget what you saw."

"Agreed," he says, and I slide the chain-link lock open. He comes in, looking around. Smiling. All dressed. Carrying a bottle of orange juice, which he thrusts in my direction. "Sustenance," he says.

"Thank you. I have some questions."

"Shoot."

"First: Are we fired?"

"We do not seem to be fired as of this morning."

"Okay, at least there's that. Now—"

"She does, however, want to talk to you."

"Of course. We'll get back to that conversation with her in a moment. The next *huge* question is: Is the power really out, or am I just in a particularly defective room?"

"Power is out."

"And so does this mean there isn't any coffee?"

"Correct," he says. "Only orange juice."

"Orange juice is not going to get the job done," I say.

"It helps though. Vitamin C, hydration, sugar, pleasing color." He squints at me. "Just how bad are you feeling?"

Maybe this is when I should mention to him that we will never again be kissing. But I can't seem to think of the proper segue. And anyway, I am surely not someone who would be desirable to kiss. In my present state, I am in no danger.

"There are elves in my head who have hammers." Having said that, I go back and sit on the bed because it's too painful to be standing upright. Also, another advantage to being on the bed is that I can put the blankets back over me. Less of me to look at. I'm wearing my usual sleep outfit, which consists of black leggings and a black long-sleeved T-shirt, so I'm decent, but I don't like it that he's looking at me after

I specifically said he shouldn't. He is, in fact, standing there staring at me—or gazing or whatever. His hands are in his pockets and he's rocking on his heels, smiling.

He is fairly adorable this morning. Despite the haze through which I am seeing him.

Tell him you're sorry about the mistake of kissing him. Now.

"So, what's the news from Darla?" I say. I take a sip of the orange juice. It's much too zingy for my current state—not comforting, not coffee, and it is probably not going to help.

"She just wanted to know what the hell had gone wrong. So I told her the truth, that Gabora took out her crack pipe and starting bashing people over the head when they complained about her book, and that you and I had to fight off the bookstore people using only our fists, and then the cops came and took Gabora away, and we spent all last night dancing for tips in a club so we could bail her out of jail."

I fix him with my most imposing stare. "God. You're actually happy this morning, aren't you?"

"Yep. I'm not in the office, and I'm not on my way to California for Thanksgiving, and I suspect that all flights are canceled anyway, so I think you and I are pretty much stranded here for a bit. And we don't have to go to any more bookstores and fight for Gabora's honor. And all that makes me happy."

"What did you really tell Darla?"

"I gave her the rundown pretty much. People were rude, there were protesters, the reading got cut short—wait a second. Are you worried?"

"Well, of course I'm worried! You're not? I mean, we had the job of protecting our author—and then while we were out *carousing,* she got so upset that she called her stupid daughters to come and get her, and we didn't even know about it."

"You know, these days you hardly ever hear the word *carousing*. Which is a shame, really—"

"And Darla left me like fifteen messages last night that I didn't even get!"

"Riiiiiight . . . you didn't get them . . . and so . . . you didn't answer them. Perfectly defensible." He goes over and gazes out the window at the white world below. Then he sits down in the armchair by the window. "This is all going to be fine. We know Darla. She's not going to freak out about something like this."

"No, she will. Because I should have probably let her know what was happening when it happened."

"Excuse me, but you didn't *know* it was happening! You were out dancing and drinking in a club."

"Exactly! Dancing and drinking! That's not a great defense."

"What were you supposed to be doing? Standing guard outside Gabora's hotel room?

Sleeping next to her? If you ask me, you went way beyond the call of duty, frankly, when you actually took off her clothes for her and put her in her pajamas and practically brushed her teeth for her. I mean, come on, Linnelle. *That* is combat duty, as far as I'm concerned. And now it's another day, and she's gone, and we're still here, and there's nothing to be done about it."

"But I was unavailable."

"What? You're not supposed to have any fun? Were we supposed to be on duty twenty-four seven? I didn't get the memo on that. Sheesh. Between that and the expectation of being combat-ready, I might not have agreed to come."

I rub my head. "I don't know, I don't know. It just is . . . unseemly, us being out. Somehow. Hard to defend. Did she sound mad?"

"She sounded . . . Darla-ish. You know her. Brisk, no-nonsense, in command. Where were we? What happened? Why didn't we take her calls last night? Demanding answers. It was Professional Darla."

"Oh God."

"Oh God, what? There's no 'oh God' to this."

"Demanding answers? I should call her now and explain the whole thing. And I should call Gabora and see if she's okay. And then see about a flight out of here. Let's see, it's Tuesday morning—I also need to call the bookstore and tell them we're canceling, which is not a good look for Tiller. Our author bailing—"

"See? That's the very best part: this whole city is shut down! Nothing is taking place anymore. Nada. Zilch. Power outages, snow piled up in the streets—and these poor sun-loving Southerners don't have the equipment to remove it." He gets up and goes over to the window again. "Come. Look down here—you'll see that nothing is going on. Nothing. The stoplights aren't even working."

"I'll call her. Where's my—oh God. I forgot. It's dead, and I can't charge it. Wait. Where's yours? Give me your phone."

"Nope. Mine's dead, too."

"But what are we going to *do?*"

"I think," he says, upping the wattage on his dazzling smile, "that once we calm down a little, we are going to have the time of our lives. I suspect we're going to leave this horrible hotel and go in search of caffeine, swanning down the street like celebrities who know how to walk in the snow—the Southerners will be stunned at our prowess—and they'll beg us for lessons, but we won't have time, because after we find coffee, we're going to take the Gabora poster that the bookstore gave us and turn it into a snow saucer and ride down the hills in the park. And after that, who knows? Snowball fights? Snowman building? Hot cocoa, if we play our cards right.

And later, I do believe there are some alcoholic beverages in our future, and possibly more dancing, although who can say for sure? Lots of talking, that's for sure. I need to hear more about Tenaj, for starters."

I look at him.

"About the kissing last night," I say.

"I know, I know. No more of that stuff. We're coworkers. You're engaged to John-Boy Walton. Totally inappropriate."

"It was the alcohol talking. And the dancing."

"Of course it was. But now we have a day off," he says. "There's nothing we can really do about anything. So why not enjoy it?"

He's right. Or he might be right.

I hear my father's voice admonishing me that I really stepped away from my post. Even Maggie is there in my head saying that I should take action now, do something to make things right with my boss. Make sure everyone's okay, all fine, and that all people concerned realize that I didn't do anything wrong.

I am terrified of doing anything wrong.

But you know what? I say to the Maggie in my head. *I don't want to just be good all the time. I have to have fun. The Maggie in my head isn't convinced.*

"Think of it this way," Adam says. "This is like time out of time. We're away from all our responsibilities. Our last responsibility got in a car driven by her daughters and went away from here, not even bothering to leave a message for us. The airport is closed, the hotel is out of power, we can't even call our boss. So—what the hell? Let's go see how much fun we can pack into one day."

I look at his face, at how he's still unshaven. His cheekbones. The light in his eyes. Maybe he's right. Maybe I don't have to be the most responsible human in the world right now. No fretting, no worrying.

Luckily I have my down vest, my boots, my heavy coat with me, because I was planning to go straight to New Hampshire from Charleston.

I'm going to get that Gabora poster and look for a hill to slide down.

With Adam.

Just this once.

There's an agenda for Time Out of Time Day, Adam tells me a half hour later, after I've met him downstairs in the lobby, dressed in warm clothes and more or less willing to give fun a try.

First, he says, we have serious needs: coffee and food, for starters. Ibuprofen will be important. It's snowing so ridiculously hard, and we walk, laughing, in it until we find the street where the power company has somehow been able to restore electricity—oh merciful zappings of life. That was Adam's line.

There's a coffee shop, with grits and ham steak and runny eggs and buttered biscuits, and I'm so hungry that I'm afraid I'll fall on the food and devour it in one go. Adam has snow in his eyebrows and on his eyelashes. The waitress there blesses our hearts and keeps bringing coffee refills. She is only eighteen, she tells us, and she's never seen snow before, she said, except on television. She didn't know, for instance, how wet and cold it really was, and so when she came outside this morning, the first thing she did was to throw herself down in the middle of it and roll around.

"And—well, I learned my lesson real fast!" she says. "That shit is frozen water!"

That became the motto of the day: "That shit is frozen water."

The snow falls steadily all day long, piling up in windows and doorways, and all the Southerners are confused, but we walk throughout the city, ostentatiously sliding and jumping. We have a snowball fight in the park. We ride down a tiny hill on our Gabora poster over and over until it rips apart. And then we scrounge for cardboard in liquor stores, and make two sleds and ride down the hill together. For some reason, my cardboard sled always seems to turn me going backward, and I'm shrieking with craziness. I have to roll off to save my own life. And then I lie there on my back, no smarter than the waitress, letting the cold seep into my bones.

Two kids come over and want to be shown how to sled, and so we give makeshift lessons, pushing them off from the top of the hill and making sure they don't land in the pond that's also covered in snow.

Later, the power comes back on over the city, and Adam says, "What would be fun now?"

Making love, I think. *Making love would be the most fun thing.*

Because all day, every moment, it seems I'm aware of sex. I may have mentioned that I'm in my prime. I'm a childless woman in her midthirties. We have raging hormones, we thirty-somethings. And I am so much in my prime on this very day that it's like all the hormones have gathered together and are having a circus. I am weak from these thoughts.

And it's been so long, I think.

Except that then I realize it hasn't been so long really.

A week. Since Judd and I . . .

Oh God, oh God, oh God.

We're freezing, so we find a brewpub and we go inside. It's cavernous and there are television sets all around, and basically the whole place is just about beers and production of beers and drinking and testing of beers. I like exactly one kind of beer, and they don't have that, so I choose something in a blueberry IPA, whatever that means, because what the hell. Then it tastes so awful that I nearly spit it out on the table.

Adam is staring at me, his face all contorted with trying not to laugh. "No good?" he whispers.

"It's like cough medicine!" I say. "Who would put blueberries in beer, anyway? What kind of a scam are they pulling here?"

He gets up and takes my glass to the bar, and I hear him tell the bartender that I need something in a wimp flavor—"beers for amateurs," he calls it—although what he should have said is that they should leave the Robitussin out of the brewing process. The bartender looks over at me, and I smile and wave, and then he and Adam decide I'd like something in a light amber. He brings it back over to me, and he and I both taste it, and it's okay.

Way better, I say. I can drink this. But what I am thinking is that both our lips have been on the glass, and I have got to stop thinking about that. He gives me a high five, and his hand is warm.

I cannot seem to stop looking at him. He leans over and whispers, "Phronsie, tell me what your novel is about."

"I-I can't," I say.

He nods. "I get it. Not a good idea to talk about novels before they're ripe."

There's no music to dance to, just sports talking heads with the volume turned down. So we play rock-paper-scissors until I beat him fifty games. Not in a row, but still. Enough.

He drinks the last of his beer and looks at me. His eyes flicker just a little. His hands circle his beer mug. "So . . . let me ask you this: When you went out on forty-four dates, what did you talk about with the guys?"

"Oh, I had a set of questions I asked."

"Oooh. Ask *me* the questions."

"Why?"

"I just want to be prepared for when I might go on Match.com. What women will say. You said last night that I might want to consider it."

"Okay," I say. I lick my lips. "First, I always ask, how was your day?"

"My day was excellent. One of the top ten days in life."

I swallow. "And then—um, where do you like to go on vacation?"

He wrinkles his nose. "Anywhere I haven't already been. Australia. Hawaii. Italy. Surfing if possible."

"Are you a dog person, a cat person, or neither?"

"Seriously?" He hides a smile. "*These* are the questions you ask?"

"Yes! And I ask what they would consider a perfect date. And . . . whether they have been married before, and where they grew up . . . and . . . what are their pet peeves, and well, like that. Why, Mr. Smarty? What would *you* ask?"

"Oh, I don't know. Maybe: How soon after sitting down at the movie theater do you think it's okay to finish off all the popcorn—first preview? Second? During the commercial for the theater's snack bar? And . . . let's see . . . when was the last time you woke up at two a.m. and ate an entire box of instant pudding powder before you realized what you were doing? And this is very important—how many friends do you currently have who would drive the getaway car for you if you needed it? And, um, what do you think the penalty should be for trying to pass off raisins as chocolate chips in a cookie? And when's the last time you tried to move an object with your mind just to see if you really could?"

He stops and gives me a long look.

"Well," I say.

"See, it's no wonder you didn't find somebody when you weren't asking the right questions." He is smiling. "You probably don't even know what anyone you dated thought about which condiment is the most controversial."

"Well, if *I'm* answering that question, I'd say it's unquestionably mayonnaise."

"Correct."

"But anyway, you're discounting a very important point. And that is that I did find someone, and so it all worked out."

"Yes, but you merely imported someone from

your childhood, so that hardly seems like it counts. Kind of a technicality, actually. An asterisk."

"Whatever. But it's still love."

"The debate rages on about that point."

"I don't see why it matters so much to you. It's not your life."

"You don't? You don't see why?" He keeps smiling at me, but his face looks pained.

"No."

"Because I'm beginning to think you don't recognize what love really is, and *that* is an unmitigated tragedy, if you ask me."

"What do you mean, I don't recognize it?"

"Who hurt you, Phronsie? Who turned you into such a love cynic?" His eyes are kind, turning from blue to green now. I never saw eyes that could change color.

"What are you *talking* about? I am the last person to be a love cynic, as you say." And then, like that, the words just line up. It's as though I've been living in one room of my mind while there was another, secret room, where everything real was happening, and in has come this other *person,* bumping his way in, turning on the lights, sitting down on the sofa I never let anybody sit on.

"Tell me who he was."

Really, I'm just going to tell him this part—this one part—and then I'm going to be quiet, and never speak of this again to him or anyone.

Although I can't imagine how it will be when we're back in the office or sitting at a staff meeting being all normal.

Maybe Darla will do us a favor and fire both of us, and then I can tell Judd we should get married immediately and move back to New Hampshire, which is where I bet he really wants to be anyway. Maybe this is where all this is leading. Full circle: right back home.

I lift my eyes up to Adam, and I hear myself say, "Okay, so I was married before."

I tell him about Steve Hanover, how we met and fell in love. And how he was such a good man— wore his heart on his sleeve, my grandmother Bunny said—she'd never seen a man so loving and warm and giving. I said how I'd loved him so hard and so good. And that the best, best part had been that he loved me back. That he said nobody had made him feel this way. Except that when he slept with someone else and then left me, I saw all our good times again in my head, and this time I saw the times for what they really were. His acting ability. The way he was really always holding back a part of himself, how his smile seemed rehearsed—how swept away I had been, and how duped I felt when I stopped and really remembered it.

"So that's what it was," Adam says softly. "A good old heart bruising." He leans forward. "I so get what you're talking about."

"I thought he really loved me," I say, and he nods. "I thought that was all there was to love. You just got it, and then you had it. You got to keep it, as long as you tended it every now and then, touched it up. You ate dinner together, had regular sex, did things for the other person. And I did all that—I loved being his wife—and then one day there was someone else, and she was in our bed with him, and I couldn't believe it. I wanted to say, *What did I do? What did I miss?*" I run my hand along the surface of the table, feel its smoothness. And then it hits me with a little ping of shock: I am going to tell him the thing I've just realized.

"When—when you're raised by people who got love all wrong, you just want to do it better. I had *studied* them. I knew their mistakes. I wasn't going to muck things up like my mom did, and I wasn't going to walk out on somebody I loved because of *duty* like my dad did—and yet there were no signs. Not one sign that I'd hooked myself up with a bad guy. Nothing. So after something like that . . . well, you don't trust yourself anymore. Maybe."

He's smiling at me. "Maybe. Yes. The same kind of thing happened to me, too. I got left also, blindsided. And you feel so stupid. Like there must have been all these alarm bells and red flags, and you didn't see a thing."

"And . . . well, that was the thing I said to Judd

371

when I decided to marry him. I said there would be *no cheating!* No cheating ever, and he agreed. And he means it. He isn't the type who cheats."

"Safe," he murmurs.

"Yes. I want to be safe."

He is looking at me and *looking at me,* and I get a shiver. He would be so goddamned good in bed. It's almost ridiculous how good sex with him would be.

I'd start kissing on his face and work my way around. Those earlobes, his neck. I would like to kiss his clavicle. And all the rest.

"I'm writing about this," I say in a low voice. "My novel. It's about a woman getting left by her husband."

"And the heart bruising." He nods.

"But it doesn't work. I can't get it to be the way I want it to be. I want it to be a funny story, but it just keeps drifting over into being morose. This woman can't move on, even though I gave her a great job and some jokey best friends. But she still feels like a failure."

He's silent for a moment, fiddling with his glass of beer and the condensation on the table. Then he says, "Sometimes when you can't get a book to do what you want, it's because you might be telling the wrong story. Like, what if this woman who can't stop crying is instead someone like you, someone who is hilarious and has this spark about her that she isn't going to let anybody

372

crush. Write about how she doesn't need this stupid man. Maybe that's the story, how she gets revenge on him. Maybe her mother is magic . . ."

"Yeah, right."

"You should let me read it. I'll help you see what's funny and real about her."

"I don't know," I say. "Nobody has read it."

"Not even John-Boy Walton?"

I let out a guffaw. Involuntarily. "He would never."

"Well," he says in a light voice, "if you ever want a reader, I could be the one. I like novels about imperfect people who do stupid things like fall in love with the wrong people but keep their sense of humor. And then they have friends who help them see who they are."

I should ask him what his novel is about. That's what I should do. But I don't. Because my eye drifts over to the window, and I see that it's getting dark, and I suddenly spin into a panic. Like a switch has flipped. Daydream over, credits start rolling. Time Out of Time Day is drawing to a close. All my worries have caught up with me, marching back into my head with their relentless reminders of doom and gloom ahead.

"I have to go," I say and stand up. "It's nearly five o'clock, and we should get back to the hotel. And oh my God, I never called Darla to let her know what's happening. And also, I'm worried about Gabora. It just occurred to me—what if her daughters *didn't* go and pick her up? What if it was one of those protesters from last night, and they followed us and then kidnapped her out of her room? And then they found her cell phone and made her tell them somebody they should call, and so they told Darla it was the girls."

"Whoa, whoa, whoa!" He shakes his head, so hard it's like a dog after a bath. "Wow, woman, this is quite a one-eighty you're pulling here. Where is this coming from? None of that is even slightly true."

"I-I just think—I just have been away too long from my life, that's all, and there are all these things I haven't done. I want to call home, and I've got to call Darla before she leaves for the day. She must be worried sick. Not hearing from us."

"Our phones were dead because we lost power," he reminds me.

"But she doesn't know that. And anyway, don't you see that's no excuse now? The power's back on. The phones are probably charged. Let's go back." My feet are wet, and my hair is dirty, and I'm tired of walking through snow and tired of being cold. Tired of Time Out of Time. I want to face whatever Darla's going to say to me, hear what I've done to the company through my negligence. I'm not a person who takes whole days off and kisses men that I shouldn't kiss and then recounts the time she got left by the man she really loved. What have I been thinking? And now I've even told him about my novel! Good God in heaven, what was I thinking?

He stands up. "You know what this really is, don't you? What you're doing just now? My mom's a therapist, and she says when people are getting really close to a big emotional breakthrough, they kind of freak out a little. Try to run back."

"Emotional *breakthrough?* I'm not having an emotional breakthrough." My voice might be a little shrill. "I'm seized with responsibility is all, and I've got to do my job."

"Yeah, well, I'm having a breakthrough." He reaches over and tries to take my hand, and our fingers graze each other before I reach for my coat. "I won't speak for you. I'll tell you about me instead. I'm having . . . feelings for you."

"Feelings?" I keep putting my coat on, coaxing my hands through the sleeves, which are wet and tangled up. "Don't. Please don't do this. I can't—"

"Yes, you can. You can stand to hear about feelings."

"But I don't think you're right about them."

"But you don't know, do you? Instead of trying to find out, it's easier to run away right now and then go get married to some guy who won't cheat but who's just not really in love with you.

Because it's safe and it puts a stop to you having to believe in love."

"I believe in love!"

"Then listen to me, Phronsie. Because I'm going to tell you what I see. I could love you. I could so easily fall in love with you right now, and nothing would ever be the same for either of us."

It's too hard to look at his eyes, all intense and smoky, so I stare down at my shoes, wet still, in a puddle on the cement floor. "Could you . . . not?" I say.

There's a beat of silence. "Yeah," he says. "Yeah, I could not. I definitely could not. But I'm not going to *not*. Because I've been feeling this way for a long time, and this is a true thing. In fact, I'm going to tell you something you maybe didn't think about. And that is that this John-Boy Walton guy—he doesn't need anyone who doesn't wholeheartedly love him either. He may think this is fine, but it isn't. He doesn't do it for you. I see it in your eyes, I hear it in your voice, it's written all over your face whenever you talk about him. You know something? I think I'm on Tenaj's side, with all those messages she's getting from the so-called universe or whatever the hell she's talking about. I bet I would love your mom! I bet she would agree with me that when you're drawn to someone, they also feel the same way about you because it's the spark in you talking to the spark in them. And I believe that nothing ever really is an accident. And I believe in love at first sight and that love is a way of seeing the world, and that nobody is safe from it, because it just takes over; if there's any little crack of light, it can work its way in. And I believe that we're put on this earth to trust all joy. And today I got a new insight, thanks to the waitress this morning, and that's that snow isn't some kind of lovely illusion or metaphor for coldness or even a beautiful backdrop for winter sports. That shit is frozen water."

I look down at my hands because I can't stand to look at his face. "No," I say quietly. "No, I'm sorry, but you're not right. You don't really know me. And we're coworkers. And this is just because we're at the end of an adventure. That's what this is."

He looks at me for such a long, hard time that I can't stand it. "Okay then." He puts on his coat. "And now," he says, "let's go back to the hotel, so you can take whatever punishment you're expecting Darla Chapman to decide to dish out to you. Because heaven knows the quota of fun has been had for today. Maybe for life."

And he turns and walks out. He's walking slowly and I could easily catch up with him.

But I don't.

CHAPTER TWENTY-TWO

The Wednesday evening crowd in Tandy's seems extra-large this year. When I enter with Judd at my side, a shout goes up, and people rush over to us. *"The fiancée!"* someone yells. And, "She's here!" Somebody else calls out, "She escaped from snowy South Carolina!" and "Yes, back to the basking warmth of New Hampshire!" and "Congratulations!"

I stand there blinking in the dim light of the bar, startled. I try to remember how it is that one activates the response called Happy Smiling Reunion Face.

But it's hard. I am not feeling totally like my regular self. I only arrived in Pemberton about two hours ago. And the hours leading up to that were not easy ones. Darla was just as furious as I expected she'd be, blah blah blah, and when she said she doubted that Adam had done enough to keep Gabora from being upset—well, I'm afraid I just stayed silent. I know, it was awful of me. I'll have to straighten everything out when we're back in the office on Monday. Also, in an attempt to smooth things over with Gabora, I called her on the phone and sweet-talked her. She seemed more confused than ever. She didn't want to talk about calling her daughters or her trip with them to Georgia. No! Amazingly, all she wanted to talk about was my upcoming wedding. She just kept weeping and begging to be invited.

But here's the part I feel the worst, worst, *worst* about: I simply texted Adam and told him I was leaving on a flight the next morning. When he texted back to ask if we could see each other that night, I didn't even answer. That's how bad a person I am. I don't even know why. Except I do, sort of. I didn't want to face him.

The Tandy's evening has all the elements of a surprise party. Once my eyes adjust to the darkness, I see that it's all exactly as it's always been, as though it had been preserved in amber—the dark paneling, the long bar running along the side, the little candles on the table that look like miniature colonial lamps. The neon beer logo signs hanging on the walls, always crooked. Even the smell is the same: hamburger grease and spilled beer. The stained and crusty brown carpet, worn down to nothing in spots near the bar, is the same as always.

And . . . the faces of our old friends.

They're all there, and I feel myself getting verklempt with a feeling that has to be nostalgia. This is what I forget every single year—that I get overcome with a wave of tenderness, seeing it all again: the Old Spice guys, the cheerleading squad, the mean girls, Judd's football teammates, everybody looking older and tireder, but still standing. Even old Mr. Tandy, who's now about a thousand years old, is sitting at the bar, watching us all while his son tends bar. I want to hug him. The television set on the wall, filmy with grease, is showing a commercial about baby products. And the piped-in music is playing the Carpenters.

The Carpenters! Like it's 1970. The year we were all born.

I get hugged and patted, and somebody puts a drink in my hand. Judd is next to me, telling some story about the drive from the airport, traffic, the route he took. All the guys nod and clap him on the back. Route talk! Always a crowd-pleaser.

The women are all talking at once—wedding plans, babies, manicures, leggings. My fabulous black leggings are mentioned, I'm pleased to report, and also the fact that my hair now has some really good streaks of blonde intertwined in the curls. Little *episodes* of blonde, says Missy Franklin, who does hair and somehow feels entitled to touch my hair and examine the underlayers. She approves, and I want to hug her, too.

Judd heads to the back, where the pool table is, with the football guys—he was the captain for a year, the year they won the championship, and I hear them telling each other the story again, of how poor Lincoln Barton intercepted a catch and then started running the wrong way on the field, and almost lost the final game for them.

It's a story that always has to be told again. They probably told it last night when they all got together, too.

Okay. To be honest, I had wanted to be at home instead of here. Not New York home, but *home* home, with Bunny and Maggie and Dad, and Hendrix's kids. Mostly Bunny. I got to see her for an hour at dinner, after Judd picked me up from the airport. She seemed alarmingly frail and thin, but when she saw me, her face broke out in such a big smile, and we sat next to each other on the couch while Maggie and Ariel got dinner together beanies and weenies—and it was enough, just sitting there, inhaling the scent of her powder, and patting her hands. We didn't even have to talk; we just listened to the others and breathed at each other, and every now and then she would squeeze my hand and then put her head on my shoulder.

Then she leaned over and whispered, "Remember when you washed my hair?"

Ohhh. That's what I always do when I pick her up at Hallowell. It was always our thing anyway, hair washing in her sink in the Bunny Barn. She did mine and I did hers, even from the time I was a little girl and had to stand on her kitchen chair. I'd look out the window while I massaged the foamy shampoo into her hair. The smell of the shampoo—we used No More Tears, and it had a sweet, almost baby smell to it that I loved.

381

My heart contracted and grew again.

But anyway—after everything was cleaned up and Bunny said she was tired, I took her upstairs and helped her into bed. Hendrix's family is sleeping in the Bunny Barn, because that makes the most sense, and so she and I are sharing my old room. I was nervous, not at all sure that she would actually be okay up there all alone, but then Ariel said she was putting the baby monitor in there, so that Maggie and my father would hear if she needed anything. I stacked pillows on the floor along the side of the bed in case she falls.

And then I took a deep breath and came. And now I'm glad I'm here. Everyone smiling at me, all happy that the last two waifs and strays have come home again, and with news. It's as if we've finally agreed to join the Family of Man. Buying at last into the social norm.

Jen Abernathy-now-Homer, who had been with me the day my first period started, comes over and slams me in a body hug.

"Look at you, girl, marrying a hometown boy after all!" she says. Then she points at her giant belly. "Yep. Number four. But I think we're closing in on what's causing them, and so we're taking steps."

Sally Fernando, who used to be the head cheerleader and now has a dress shop downtown, says in a singsong voice, "Okay, girls, now we've got to get the real scoop on this engagement. How did he pro*pose?* What did he *say?* Did he get down on one *knee?* What did *you* say? Where's the *ring?*"

I take a deep breath and go through the details, just as Judd and I rehearsed them in the car when he picked me up from the airport. Here's the story as it will now forever after be told:

We got engaged in a diner at midnight. It was spontaneous! Wonderful! Neither of us could be more surprised!

We both realized that, as best friends for, like, practically *forever,* we must have been always meant to be together. We can't believe we missed all the signs, such as our mutual feeling that romance isn't real and that friendship is all anyone needs. (That was his contribution; I said no one would ever believe that.)

No, he did not get down on one knee because— well, it was the diner! You don't kneel down on the floor of a diner unless you've lost your contact lens. Am I right?

And oh yes—the ring? Here it is, gleaming on my finger. And funny thing: when he proposed, he just *happened* to have a twist tie in his pocket, and so he fashioned it into a little ring. Then, Judd being Judd, he had to take it back so his bread wouldn't get stale!

"Awww," they say in unison.

And the proposal itself? A very romantic-for-

Judd proposal, the best he could do really as he laid out his case that . . .

"We're sick of dating," I hear myself say, veering off script.

No sooner have I said it than Judd materializes beside me. "And we want children," he says. He's on his way back to the bar for a refill and now has flung his arm over my shoulder and is smiling at the group of women. "That's the God's honest," he says. "We want kids, we've always been the best of friends, and frankly, my dears, I think we're going to be smashing at this whole marriage/parenthood thing."

"You both look so—New York," says Lisa Peterson coolly. "So cosmopolitan. Do you think you'll stay there?"

I blink. "Well, yeah—I mean, I think so. We both have jobs there, after all."

He shrugs. "Ah, who knows what's in the future? After the knockout surprise of Phronsie here agreeing to take me out of the friend zone and actually *marry* me, I can't pretend to predict anything that'll ever happen again in the world."

"I've always thought you were the cutest couple," says Karla Kristensen.

Judd's old crush. I turn and smile at her. I hadn't seen her come in, but here she is, still luscious (those boobs have aged well) and now smiling at him over the top of a martini glass. It's the smile of someone who knows she has broken his heart about five ways from Sunday, twisting it out of his body, stomping on it, and then picking it up only to fling it against the wall a time or two. And now she's clearly picking up the knife for one last dramatic twist.

I may still hate her.

But Judd—he's looking at her like he doesn't hate her at all. I elbow him in the ribs so he can remember to close his mouth.

I go back to the farmhouse early, pleading exhaustion. There is only so much of a good time at Tandy's that I can take—my father had a saying that fits right in here: "I've enjoyed about as much of this as I can stand." Judd is spending the night at his parents' house, but he walks me out to the car, running his hands through his hair as we walk, smiling and telling me again and again how much fun it is to be here.

"They're all so happy for our news!" he says. "Did you notice that?"

He's a little drunk.

"Yes," I say. We stand there in the parking lot. Tandy's neon sign has a *T* missing. ANDY'S BAR AND GRILL. There's the sound of a train whistle in the distance. And the wind stirring the pine trees lining the parking lot. I make a little mound in the gravel with my toe. It's balmy here, compared to Charleston.

"Well," I say. "This was fun."

"And tomorrow—my parents are coming over to your folks' house for dessert," he says. "Maggie says we'll nail down a bunch of stuff about the wedding."

I stand on tiptoe and give him a kiss. He kisses me back and then pulls back and laughs.

"Look at us here, acting all like an engaged pair of humans," he says.

"Yep. That's us," I say. "Engaged as hell."

"Engaged as all get-out," he says. "Remember when we talked like that?"

He kisses me again, and then finishes off with a peck on each cheek. Closure kisses.

"I'm going back in for a while," he says. "Sure you don't want to stay?"

"No. I'm tired. And I want to check on Bunny."

"Okay, then, have a good night," he says.

"Good night to you," I say.

When he opens the big oak door to the bar, for a moment—just a moment—I see the inside of the bar, hear the strains of music tumbling out at me (the Bee Gees now singing "How Deep Is Your Love") and a woman is laughing. I catch a glimpse of blonde hair, jeans, hear a guy saying, "And *that* was the day I got the ticket!" and then Judd slips inside, gets swallowed up, the door closes, and I stand there in the parking lot in the silence.

And what I'm wondering is where Adam might be right now.

• • •

All night I'm aware that Bunny, like some precious cargo, is beside me in my old double bed. The curtains are open, and the moon is shining in the window. For a long time, I lie there on the pillow next to hers just watching her. She's so beautiful and frail, with her lined face so peaceful in sleep, and her white hair like a cloud on the pillow. Her breathing is soft and even, but every now and then she does an extra little breath that sounds like a gasp. Like she's about to say something.

At one point she opens her eyes and stares at me. "You," she says in a foggy voice.

"No, *you*. I'm glad you're here with me."

She closes her eyes, drifts back to her dream landscape. I watch her for a while longer, see how the patch of moonlight marches across the sheet, bringing the shadows of branches along with it.

She was so strong, and she spent so many years watching over me and protecting me, and now it's my moment to do that for her.

I reach over and put my hand on top of hers, and when I wake up in the morning, it's still there.

CHAPTER TWENTY-THREE

I have several long-time jobs on Thanksgiving morning: making the cream cheese pumpkin pie, peeling the potatoes, and making the dinner rolls. But my main responsibility is to rescue the gravy boat from its cabinet above the refrigerator. Every year I go looking for this gravy boat. Every year it's shoved into a different part of that cabinet above the refrigerator, the one no one can reach.

There's an annual conversation that goes along with this official rescue, too.

Me: "I'll get the gravy boat now." I love gravy. I think one of the reasons I love Thanksgiving so much is for the turkey gravy—and for that, you have to have a special boat.

And then Maggie says it's so much trouble to get it, and why don't we just use one of the bowls instead this time, and anyway, there are too many things piled on top of the refrigerator, blah blah blah. And I always laugh and insist on getting it, and things nearly fall over, and Maggie has an exasperated look on her face, but I rescue it. And when it comes down from its shelf, I wash it so carefully because it may have a little chip and some dust, and she says, "Oh, that old thing—why do we even keep it around for once a year?"

This year, Judd—who has watched this ritual time and time again—listens to Maggie's insistence on not having it and says *he's* the one who'll get it.

He winks at me as he hands it to me. "Thanksgiving is saved," he says. "*This* is what John-Boy would do."

We traditionally eat at one thirty, so by noon, the kitchen is a mishmash of everyone doing their own particular thing, a situation that would have made Maggie lose her mind years ago, but now I can tell she sort of welcomes all the commotion. Maybe being alone with my father has brought her to a new realization. I see her at one point, juggling all these things at once: handing Ariel a peeler for the pumpkin, instructing Hendrix on where in the attic he can find the electric knife to carve the turkey, and directing the little boys to the closet where the cloth napkins are kept, so they can set the table. And she's glowing, Maggie is. Like she was made for this.

I smile at her, and then I have this moment that's so sharp it might qualify as an epiphany. I was so judgmental about how hard she tried to reach me when I was a kid. I get it now. She just wanted to be a good mother. It wasn't enough to be a good stepmother, whatever that would look like—she actually had hoped to replace our mother in our hearts. And of course that could never be, but I was so mean about it. Everything she tried, I resisted.

She catches my eye and gives me a wink. Maybe she's on drugs, I think. Some special potion that lends her an ability to see the grace in the family dynamics, the magic beneath the mess.

Because it *is* magic—and I'm buoyed by it, too, swept along in its clockwork-style predictability. I can hear a recording of the Macy's Day Parade on the television set in the den, hear the children shrieking at a video game, and my father instructing them to for God's sake put down that game and *look* at the floats. Which they couldn't care less about. Ariel looks at me and smiles. "They are never, ever going to care about balloon floats on television, are they?"

"No, and my father is never, ever going to stop being disappointed that they don't. It's as though he personally produced this parade. And none of us have ever cared all that much."

"Turkey time in ten!" yells Maggie.

I sit there at the table, among them all, seeing their bright, flushed faces, their strenuous attempts to stay nice to each other, their willingness to come together each year for this, the greatest of family rituals, and I pass the mashed potatoes when I'm asked to.

And I'm fine.

It's just that every now and then, when I close

my eyes, or turn suddenly, to pass the gravy, to say the blessing, to get up to clear the table, it's as though I see Adam standing somewhere nearby. Standing in the doorway, arms folded. Smiling. Feel him, is more like it.

Go away. Get out of my head. You don't belong here.

Because I am here now. I've made the transition back to where I belonged all along. I am going to be Judd's wife.

Judd brings his parents—Daisy and Rudolph Kovac— to our house around five o'clock for dessert. They are the same as I remember—sweetly daffy with slight, bemused frowns, as if they are trying to work out what the hell wrong turn they took to find themselves on this planet. Much less the parents of a human man.

Yet now, here they are, having been delivered to Maggie's rambunctious table, where my three nephews are tossing a dinner roll back and forth, where my father is sighing and scowling, and Maggie and Ariel and I are rushing around, ferrying pots of coffee and plates of pie to the table.

Somehow we make it through pie eating and coffee drinking, and then, as if on a secret signal, the menfolk retire to the living room, and we women clear the table and turn to the female business of planning a wedding.

"But wait," I say. "Maybe Judd would like some say in this, too."

"He doesn't," says his mother.

"But *I* would like him to be involved," I say.

"But *would* you?" says Ariel. "Really?"

I think it over. No. She's right. No, actually, I wouldn't.

"Smart decision," she says in a low voice. "You have now entered Traditional Wedding Mode, New Hampshire–Style. You have to just sit back and let the industrial wedding complex take over. These women have been training since birth for this."

Maggie gives me a triumphant smile. I see Mrs. Kovac sit up straighter.

"Now, Maggie," Daisy Kovac says, "I know the rules here. The mother of the bride picks dress color. My job is to show up and wear beige."

Maggie and I share an astonished glance. Daisy knows *this?* How is that even possible? Maggie reaches over and touches her hand. "Oh, Daisy. You can wear whatever color you'd like! This isn't going to be that kind of thing at all." Then she smiles. "But beige will be fine. I myself am thinking of something in a royal blue."

"Of course," says Mrs. Kovac. "That's the mother of the bride color."

They know so many things, it turns out. June seventh is selected as the date, and from there it seems a quick jump over to the fact that the napkins will be yellow, the flowers will be tulips and daisies, there will be three bridesmaids and three groomsmen—and who thinks the ceremony should be on the beach?

That last one is my question.

They all turn and look at me.

"The *beach?*" says Maggie.

"You mean, where sand is?" says Mrs. Kovac.

"Well, sure," I say. "I've been to a beach wedding, and since it's going to be on the Cape, in Wellfleet, why not invite the waves and the sand to the ceremony? I mean, why else have a wedding on the Cape if you're not going to make use of the beach?"

There's a silence.

"Maybe the beach after the ceremony," says Maggie.

They move on to more important matters. Centerpieces.

"I really don't care that much about center-pieces," I say.

Ariel pokes me in the side. "It's not up to you," she whispers.

Maggie says, "I think tea lights and perhaps a spray of daisies."

Mrs. Kovac agrees. "Yes, and some ribbon tying daisies."

"And some seashells?" I offer.

Maggie smiles at me. Ariel pokes me in the side once again.

Band or DJ?

"DJ," says Maggie. She sees my face. "All these are just suggestions, you know. It's your wedding."

"It's not," whispers Ariel.

Invitations?

"Judd and I can pick them out—"

Maggie wrinkles her nose. "Honey, please. Remember this is the only wedding I'll ever get to plan in my whole life. You got married before and didn't let anybody know in advance. And, Ariel, bless you, your mother got to do all the planning. And goodness knows when I got married to Robert—well," she says. "We just won't go into *that* except to say there wasn't much to plan. Certainly it didn't get to the level of centerpieces and DJs."

For just a moment, I see it—that old flicker of sadness in her eyes.

But then we're onto the guest list, and Ariel and I slip away, out to the back porch where—to my surprise—she wants to smoke a joint. "It's the way I keep myself sane," she says. "Do you want some?"

"No," I say. "Yes."

"Exactly," she says. "I know the feeling."

We stand outside in the cold, staring at the barn. In the distance, I know, are the bulldozers and earth-moving equipment. Tomorrow they'll roar to life, Maggie has told me. The noise will be excruciating.

Ariel shivers.

"Do you ever look at all this and see it practically dying right in front of you?" she says. "A whole lifestyle. Just gone."

Maggie and I go up to the attic on Friday afternoon to put away the Thanksgiving things, like we always do. I like to help her bring down a few of the Christmas decorations. They'll be going up next week.

"Out with the garlands of autumn leaves and in with the evergreens and holly!" she says, like she always does. And then we get busy. I'm stacking up the bins that hold Thanksgiving stuff and putting them in the corner of the shelf, and she's pulling down the boxes with the Santa Claus figurines, the Styrofoam balls decorated with sequins and toothpicks that she likes to hang from the beams in the living room ceiling. There's a life-size sleigh and reindeer set that Hendrix will put on the roof.

New Hampshire Christmas coming right up.

For a moment, we're working side by side. "You want these bowls up here? Look at these wreaths! And the snowmen collection. I always love when the snowmen come out."

Then she says, "It's nice having you and Judd here together. Being engaged really agrees with you, I think. You look . . . different."

"Like different how?"

"I don't know." She straightens up and studies me, tilting her head. "I think you're in love."

I go quiet, look away. Then when I can speak again, I say, "Am I? Yeah, I guess I am." I get busy with a bag of ribbons. Maggie has saved every ribbon that has ever entered the house.

I kissed a guy in Charleston. What about *that?* Is that what she's seeing?

"Funny how things can change between two people after so many years, isn't it?" Then she's quiet. "Listen to me, like I'm any kind of expert. You know what? It's just so good to have something nice to think about. You know, after everything with your father." She gets busy dusting off one of the boxes with her sleeve. Then she laughs. "You want to know something kind of crazy? I've never told you this, but I sometimes have this little fantasy that I'm your real mother. That I was *supposed* to be. You know?"

I set down the bag of ribbons. "You mean like maybe there was a mix-up in the paperwork?"

"Exactly! I mean, had the world gone the way it was supposed to, with Robert and me staying together and getting married, I should have really technically *been* your mother," she says and laughs. "Can you imagine how different things would have been?" She straightens up, pushes back a lock of her faded brown hair that's escaped from her bun, and gives me a sheepish look. "Well. It's just something I think about from time to time. Maybe I should have been a little more irresponsible, you know? If I'd gotten pregnant before he took that little trip to Woodstock . . . well, he wouldn't have gone."

"Sure," I say, swallowing.

"I overheard Hendrix saying one time that there was a Maggie Team and a Tenaj Team." She leans back, stretching out her spine. "And there wouldn't have been any need for that sort of thing. You would have both *had* to be on the Maggie Team, because I would have been the only team in town."

I am so ashamed then.

"I'm sorry," I say. "We must have been so hard on you."

She shrugs. "Being a stepmother is never what you think it's going to be. You have it in your mind that you're the *rescuer,* and that even though fairy tales are full of wicked stepmothers, that everyone will see that *you* are different, because you mean well. And then one day you hear yourself screaming, and everyone's looking at you with hatred and fear in their eyes, and you realize that you never can afford to get even one thing wrong. You're not the real mom, and nobody gives you the benefit of the doubt."

"Oh, Mags, you tried so hard. And we were terrible. *I* was terrible."

"Yeah," she says with a short, harsh laugh. "You were. Though I wasn't all that wonderful at it. But, hey, look at us now. Together. We made it through. And the funny thing is—I've gotten over all that feeling of being mad about how I had to do all the hard parts of raising you guys, and she got to float around through space, being perfect because she wasn't there. So . . . there's progress. I was the one who got to watch you grow up, front-row seat. She missed out on that."

"Totally," I say faintly.

I look over and really see Maggie, true and plain right there in front of me. Her face is actually lined with pain, and her eyes look sad. She's wearing baggy blue jeans that are just a little too short for her and beat-up sneakers and a gray cardigan. She looks so very tired. In fact, everything in this attic suddenly seems so wavy and sad, like it could all disappear—and I feel a kind of gentleness settle over me.

"And then that day came when *she* let you down. When you went to Woodstock. It was her for once, and not me. I feel like that was the day you became mine." She lets out a little laugh.

I'm quiet, but the blood is beating in my ears.

"*You* don't *still* hear from her, do you? After what she did?"

I don't say anything right away. Then I say, "Well . . ."

I feel her shift next to me. Then I see that my silence has told her the answer, and it has shocked her.

"Oh," she says and moves farther away from me, gets busy with another box. She's embarrassed. "Well. I wouldn't have thought, after everything that happened, that you—"

"You know how she is," I say. "She just pops up from time to time, unexpectedly. Calls me sometimes. Still flaky!" I laugh a little bit to show how very little it means to me, but she is not fooled.

"Ah, well. It doesn't matter anyway. Water under the dam," she says briskly. And then, in her crisp Maggie voice, she says: "You know what? My therapist would say it's good you have some kind of relationship with her. I'm really glad for you, Phronsie, that it wasn't a total loss for you. This is probably healthy."

"Wait. You have a therapist? You never told me."

She sits down on one of the cardboard boxes. "I didn't want to talk about it, but yeah. For about a year now. I wasn't into it at first, but now I see that it's helping me. Sort things out. You know."

"There's a lot here to sort," I say carefully. I'm holding the turkey platter, but I sit down on another box and stay quiet, hoping she'll say more. The air between us, filled with dust motes, feels so fragile and tentative.

"There's something else," she says and looks down at her shoes. "I'm going to talk to your father about going to a therapist, too. It's time he got some help."

"Wow. That's huge. It's kinda hard to imagine *him* pouring out his soul to a stranger. I picture him sitting there with his arms folded over his chest and his mouth clamped shut while the therapist says, 'And how did *that* make you feel?' "

She laughs a little. "Well, he's gonna have to try," she says, "because I think, if he won't get help, I'm at the point of realizing that I might have to leave him."

"It's that bad?" My stomach drops.

She looks at me. "I can't live like this. Not for the rest of my life, I can't. If he's not going to do some work, then I can't pull him along any longer."

I put the turkey platter down and go over to her and hug her. She's stiff at first, but then she loosens up a little bit. I realize she's crying. And I hold on to her so tightly.

"Oh, Mags. I wish I could turn back time and be nicer."

"Oh, no need for *that*," she says. She takes a tissue out of her apron pocket and blows her nose. "I'm just telling you this so you'll understand why I might seem a little over the top about this wedding of yours. It's like a lifeline, planning this. It might be the last hurrah. I promise you I won't leave him before the wedding, no matter what."

"It's all going to be okay," I say, although I don't know what I'm talking about. "He doesn't want to lose you, Maggie."

"Well," she says and turns away from me. "We'll see, won't we? I don't want to talk about it anymore, so let's get the Christmas stuff out."

I look around the attic, like I'm seeing it for the last time. And then, having disposed of Thanksgiving, we very carefully carry Christmas downstairs.

That night, Bunny falls out of bed.

I wake up hearing a slight thump, and I scramble to turn on the light. There she is, lying on the carpet next to the bed, buffered by the pillows I'd placed there.

She doesn't get really hurt. Not only was her fall broken by the pillows, she landed just the right way. Nothing hurts her, nothing seems broken, her eyes look fine.

But, petrified, I stay awake the whole rest of the night and watch her sleep.

No way I'm leaving on Sunday, I say to Maggie and my father. I tell Judd that I won't be going back with him on the train, as usual; I'm going to stay at least through the first part of next week to make sure she's okay, and then I'll take her back to Hallowell myself, get her settled in.

"Okay," he says. "If you think that's what you have to do."

401

"I do," I tell him. "She's my *grandmother.* I have to take care of her, don't I?"

"Are you okay?" he says. He takes my hand, like a proper fiancé might do.

"Of course I am," I say. "It's just . . . everything, I guess." I let myself lean against him.

"Are you writing? Maybe you need to be writing. Doesn't that always make you feel saner?"

"Judd, are you trying to get on my good side or something? You never, ever ask me about my writing."

He leans over and kisses me on the cheek. "I know, and I'm cleaning up my act. And also, I just wanted to say that I had a good time with your family. And it was fun telling everyone about us. And I feel really good about everything, do you? Our plan? I think more than ever that it's the best thing we've ever thought of."

"Getting married?"

"*Yes,* getting married, you crazy. What did you think I was talking about?" He gives me a fist bump. "Remember when we used to do fist bumps all the time? And hip checks? You'd bang your hip into mine. Maybe we should bring those things back. I want to have little signs and signals with you. You know? I think that makes for a good married-people kind of thing."

I can't help it. I laugh. "Just go get on the train, will you? I'll see you back in the city."

He kisses me lightly exactly four times, gives me a fist bump, a hip check, and then he's gone.

As soon as he's completely out of sight, I call Darla.

"I can't come back until Thursday," I say. "There's been an accident at my house, involving my grandmother. She'll be okay, but I need to stay here with her for the time being. Get her resettled with her doctors and in her memory care unit. I'm sorry. Wanted you also to know that I spoke with Gabora, and she's fine. In fact, she isn't angry at all, and she even asked if I'd invite her to my wedding! So I think we don't have to worry anymore that there are going to be repercussions from what happened."

"Well," she says. "We'll see."

I swallow. "But also . . . well, I think I would like—well, actually, I'm thinking that I don't want to work with Adam anymore. It's not a good idea. No details that I want to share, but I'd like it if you could transfer him to another part of the company. Another imprint perhaps. Maybe before I get back. If you would do that. Thank you."

"I've been thinking the same thing," says Darla. "I was right about him, wasn't I? He's just not . . . fully adult somehow."

My hands are clammy and my stomach hurts by the time I hang up the phone.

• • •

Bunny and I sing in the car on the way back to Hallowell. I've heard that patients with memory loss still remember the music they once loved, and so I put on big band songs from Bunny's era, and sure enough, she sings along and smiles.

I stay and have dinner with her in the dining room that night. At first, I'm tense because it seems like full-blown chaos in there with the wheelchairs crashing into tables, and people trying to get served by the staff, all talking and calling out at once. But then I see that there's something really quite lovely about all of this. A woman wearing her napkin on her head is blowing bubbles with a little plastic wand, and a man keeps singing again and again a song he claims to have written for Frank Sinatra. A tiny, gray-haired couple tries to hold hands while they eat, and food keeps falling into their laps, which makes them both laugh. The staff members, whom I thought a moment ago must be harried and overburdened, I now see aren't feeling that way at all. They are smiling and indulgent and kind to their charges, and *all* of them—staff members and the old people at the end of their long, uncertain lives—are fully living just this moment before going on to the next.

My eyes blur with tears. I'm a mess. I've been so hard on everyone, so judgmental, so *grasping*. I've let so many moments go by without paying attention. I've kissed a man I shouldn't have kissed, and I've been thoughtless and hedonistic. I have to change. I decide right then: I'm going to make up for all the love I've squandered.

Bunny turns and smiles at me, happy like a small child is happy, for no reason. She leans over and whispers to me, "I am going to tell you a question," she says. "How did you get so nice?"

"Bunny," I say, even though I know she has no idea what I'm talking about, "I am going to try to be as nice as you think I am. I'm going to stop being selfish, and I'm going to marry Judd, and if he wants to, I might even move back home and help Maggie and my father, and I'm going to stop being a dumb, idiotic kid who thinks love is like some miracle that's supposed to come and save me. I am going to be the one who gives love. To everybody."

CHAPTER TWENTY-FOUR

By the time I get back to work the following Thursday, Adam's office is cleared out. I walk by it on the way to my own, and when I look in, I see that there's nothing there that would remind me of him. It's not until I go into my own office and open my desk drawer an hour later that I see that Gnomeo is lying facedown in my pile of pens.

I take a deep breath. Gnomeo.

There's no note.

I look through my desk again, just to be sure. Check under the blotter, under the telephone, and the computer monitor. I wonder if Adam was furious when he found out I'd had him transferred. Or was he sad? I hope he wasn't sad. Darla said she transferred him to an imprint in another building—the one called McCutcheon, which concentrates on fantasy novels. Perfect for him, she said. He's so . . . young. Everybody who works there is about thirteen, she told me. Rolling her eyes.

I sit there in my rolling chair, staring out of the window. I handled the whole thing so badly. Like, the worst kind of badly. Maybe I should just call him on the office extension and say—say what?

Thank you for the gnome.

Thank you for being the first person to hear about my novel.

I'm sorry I was so weird about kissing you, because I really did like it.

Maybe too much, but you probably already know that.

Anyway, good-bye.

I'm sorry for what I let Darla think, so good-bye, I'm sorry, good-bye.

I'm sorry.

Yeah, right. No. You can see why I can't call him. No. That would not be a cool thing to do. So here's my new plan: I am going to have a cup of coffee and then before the staff meeting, I am going to peek at wedding dresses online so that I can remind myself what my life is really about right now. And I'll text Talia and see if she wants to go help me try on dresses after work one day soon. And by the time I've done these two things, I'm not going to be thinking about him anymore.

Five more minutes, and then I'm officially over this.

It's good to have goals.

Anyway, it's likely that getting transferred didn't matter to him, one way or the other. A guy like that. This wasn't his career. He's just a guy bumbling around New York City for a while. Even if he was disappointed, even if he ends up leaving the company, maybe that's best for him. He didn't have any particular affinity for public relations after all; he'd said as much, hadn't he? He got the job almost by accident.

That kiss.

You know what it was? It was a longing for drama now that I'd committed to Judd.

Stupid.

At the staff meeting about new projects and whatnot, I notice that all his authors have been assigned to Mary Beth, who coolly reports on the progress she's making. No one looks in my direction; no one says, *Phronsie? So what happened?*

Maybe they think they already know. In which case, I would like to tell them that they are so wrong. Nothing happened.

It occurs to me that I have a friend, Leila, who works at McCutcheon. Anytime I want, I can call her and find out how he's doing. I won't do it today, of course, but sometime.

I put Gnomeo in my purse and take him home. He can't stay in the office anymore. Only when I get him home—well, what to do with him? It seems like he should stay with me as kind of a companion. He can't sit out on the table, where Judd would ask since when have I taken up with gnomes. Nope. He's a reminder of Adam that's just for me. I don't even know why, but I give him his own purse compartment—clear out all the tissues, pen caps, and old lipsticks in that one pocket. I think he'll be comfortable there.

That's what I'm doing when Judd calls me and suggests we meet at the diner as soon as he gets done with his eight o'clock client. He's got a hankering for some eggplant fries and hummus. I am so relieved. And so we go sit in our usual booth, and Alphonse swoons around us like we are rock stars, and we drink beer and eat our fries, and life is all back to normal. It's so normal that I smile and talk about Tandy's like it was the high point of my existence so far. Because Tandy's is Judd's favorite subject.

He goes on about different people's reactions to our news, and how everybody else is sick of their spouses, but how we're going to be different. How some people were actually envious when he explained our plan not to be in love.

Then he looks at me and licks his lips. Like he's maybe a little nervous all of a sudden. "Listen, I think we should go back to your apartment and go to bed." He arches his eyebrows meaningfully.

"Really," I say.

"Yes." He looks fairly certain. "You want to?"

"Yeah. I do want to."

"You're really sure?"

"For God's sake, *yes,* I'm sure. Are *you* sure?"

"Of course I am." He licks his lips again. "Hey, this has got to stop being awkward between us. Just because it's never been what we do, we've got to get beyond this point where it's weird. So to do that—we just have to make it happen. Like, often."

"I like the idea of often."

"Yeah. Regular sex is very good for people. Studies show that—"

I lean across the table and put my fingers on his lips. "Judd. No. No studies."

"Sorry," he says. "I'm just . . ." He slaps his hands down on the table. "You know why this is weird?"

"Because you aren't really attracted to me?"

"No." His face changes, and he reaches over to touch my arm. "No! Phronsie! Is that what you think? It's not that at all. Not even a little bit."

"Well . . . you don't *seem* like somebody who wants to make love all that much. And I don't *look* like the girls you've dated—"

"Please," he says. "Could we agree never, ever to mention the girls I've dated?"

"Well?"

"The truth is that I'm scared. Because you're my best friend. You're Hendrix's *sister.* And for my whole life I've worried that our relationship would go downhill if we . . . had sex. So I kept it out of my mind consciously. And I kind of can't get beyond thinking that, even though it's ridiculous."

"Oh," I say. "Well, I guess that's better than you not being attracted to me."

"All right," he says. He gives me a fist bump

and jumps up, and I watch him go to the cash register and pay the bill, joking with Alphonse longer than necessary, and then I gather my purse and sweater, and we walk to my apartment, hand in hand, ducking our heads in the late November wind.

My bed is filled with clothes from this morning's fiasco, when I tried to find something decent to wear. It's been a while since I've done laundry. Mr. Swanky is trotting along beside us, confused a little bit. He sits down at the door, whines. It's like he needs to point out that we're supposed to go into the *living room,* sit down on the couch, watch some Netflix. Also, we forgot the popcorn. Mr. Swanky loves the popcorn.

"Mr. Swanky thinks we've made a wrong turn," I say.

"Well, we didn't," Judd says. He starts unbuttoning his shirt. And then he takes it off. He has a beautiful body. Perhaps I've mentioned that. He cares how he looks. I shyly admire his muscles, which I haven't really given much thought to. I'm guilty of thinking of him only platonically. You know. Before now. He undoes the tie on his sweatpants and steps out of them.

"I guess I should get undressed, too," I say.

"Or I could help."

"I'd like that."

It's weird. He comes to where I'm standing and starts unbuttoning my shirt and then, once he's

411

taken it off, I reach around and undo the clasp on my bra.

Then he helps tug down my jeans, and I step out of them and then we're standing there in my bedroom in our underwear. I go over to the lamp to turn it off, because it's unbearable, this underwear business. I'm not wearing my best pair by any stretch of the imagination. It was so much easier the other night, in the dark, when he was already in bed.

It strikes me that when two people are in love, sex starts at an entirely different place—a sudden moment of being swept away. At least in my experience. That's how it was with Steve Hanover. Our eyes would meet, and then he'd be striding across the room, giving me The Look, and then in a matter of seconds, we'd be naked and clinging to each other.

And with Adam . . . oh God. We didn't even have sex, and yet even the air was electric.

Judd pulls down the bedspread and we get under the covers.

He says, "I like your pillows, but I thought maybe I'd bring one of mine over. You know, if I'm going to start sleeping here sometimes."

I stroke his chest tentatively. "Everybody in the world likes their own pillow."

"I was thinking I'd bring my second-best pillow because some nights I'll probably still sleep in my own apartment—you know . . ."

"Sure. Whatever pillow you want to bring."

He reaches over and touches me softly. Circling my breast. I take a deep breath. He closes his eyes, so I close mine, too.

He laughs a little bit. "Is this weird?"

"Well, a little. But we have to stop overthinking it."

"Right," he says. "Okay."

It's . . . nice. His touch. I see Adam's face rising up before me, and I remember how he said he didn't think I loved Judd. And then I'm back on the dance floor with his hand on my back and his nose in my hair, and my train of thought goes off the rails.

Paging Phronsie Linnelle! The present moment wants to have a word with you. Please return to your body as soon as possible.

I return my attention and find that Judd is making love to me. Kissing my collarbone. Sliding his hand along my waist. He knows what he is doing. All I have to do is let go and allow everything to work the way it's supposed to. All the parts, just like a normal couple. No awkwardness. We can do this.

I can do it, but I can't make myself open my eyes while I'm loving on him. He is good at sex, I'll give him that. He knows all the right spots to touch and for how long, and he smells good, and he cares about my pleasure. It's . . . good. Very good, even.

Afterward, he jumps up out of bed and starts putting on his clothes.

"What are you doing?" I say.

"I dunno. Just thought I'd take Mr. Swanky out for a pee. Don't you usually take him out about now?"

"Judd," I say. "Sit down on the bed. Swanks is fine. Let's hang out and talk."

"Okay," he says. He sits down next to me and smiles down at me in the covers. I snuggle down in the blankets.

"That was nice having our moms together planning the wedding," I say after a moment.

"Yeah. I never saw my mom like that," he says. "She and Maggie acted like they'd been born for this."

"True."

"I had to keep coming in from the man cave area just because I could hear them chattering and laughing. Very baffling and sweet."

He looks down at his hands. The conversation has run down.

"Why don't you lie back down next to me?" I say.

He does. We both lie on our backs, looking at the ceiling.

"Okay, now you have to come up with a topic," I say. "Now that we're done with talking about our moms."

"Um, okay." He makes a show of thinking.

"How about . . . the people who were the most surprised at our news?" He goes off on a long story about Tom O'Halloran dropping his beer on the floor when he heard. "Then he did a riff about the ol' ball and chain," Judd says, "which was totally inappropriate, and I told him so."

"Oh, but you know who seemed *really* surprised?" I say. I get up on one elbow and smile at him. "Karla Kristensen."

He colors just slightly and runs his hands through his hair. "Yeah, that was a little strange." He swallows. "Can I tell you something?"

"Yeah. Of course."

"First of all, we've agreed we're not going to do the whole jealousy thing, right?"

"Right."

"That's not our shtick."

"Of course."

"Well, she, like, came onto me."

"Oh my God. That's hilarious! Wow. She's still just the same, isn't she?"

"Yeah."

"And I'm sorry—but those boobs, Judd! The way she pokes them out at every opportunity. I think they have their own zip code. At the very least, they should be registered with the state." I flop back down on the pillow.

"It's pretty . . . pathetic. What she does."

"Oh." I punch him in the arm. "Uh-huh, buster. For a minute there I thought you were going to stop at, 'it's pretty.' The word *pathetic* was a long time coming in that sentence."

He laughs. "Well. For once, this time, I saw what was going on. I'm onto her now."

"So . . . um . . . what did you guys exactly do? Was there any . . . um . . . *contact for old time's sake?*"

He hesitates a beat too long. "Well, there was one kiss," he says.

"Are you kidding me?" I sit back up and look at him. "That woman is incorrigible where you're concerned! Was it . . . a big one?"

"Oh, it was a big one all right." He gives me a sly smile. "Some of her best work, actually. But I wasn't having it."

"Well," I say. "Full disclosure here: I kissed a guy in Charleston. And, also, just to be honest, a big one."

He makes his eyes bug out and then rubs them with the heels of his hands. "Get outta here! You *kissed a guy in Charleston?* No shit! A random stranger, was it then? Or was this just more online dating—number forty-five happening to be a Southern gentleman?"

"No. It was a guy I know. From my office."

"And . . . this *guy from your office* . . . is this a serious affiliation you two have?"

"No," I say quickly, too quickly. "In fact, he's no longer even working with me. That was it. A moment in time."

"Huh. Well, this is pretty interesting stuff." After a moment, he puts his hands behind his head, looking very satisfied with himself, and adds, "You know, case in point here. Not many couples could have a conversation like this one. Right? But it's fine because it's us. Right? Is this okay with you?"

"This conversation? Or the kissing we did?"

"The kissing we did *and* the conversation."

"Yeah. I am. It's fine."

"Me too," he says. Then he adds, "It's a gray area, admittedly. Not a lot of people would understand."

"Totally. Also, we're not going to do this anymore, though, like once we're married, right?" I say. "We agreed that there would be no cheating, and now that we've both kissed other people, I just wonder if that falls into any kind of . . . danger zone or anything. I mean, for later."

"Well, are *you* going to kiss him anymore? Because I'm not going to kiss Karla anymore. That's for sure," he says.

"No, I'm not. So this doesn't change anything. We still have a no-cheating-once-we're-married pact."

"Doesn't change a thing," he says. "Not in the least. Hey, we're very evolved, I think. We were just putting some things to rest."

"Totally."

Mr. Swanky gets up on the bed, sensing that

things have subsided enough that a dog would be welcome and perhaps even necessary. Judd idly scratches him behind the ears. "This is one of those times then? Where Mr. Swanky gets to sleep on the bed?"

"Oh, are you staying?"

"I thought I would. After I take him out. Why don't you come with me, and we can stroll around and see what's what in the neighborhood?"

"Okay," I say.

And we do. Because now we are officially an Engaged-Couple-Living-Together-Taking-the-Dog-Out-After-Making-Love. That's the kind of people we are.

"I guess it makes sense that when we're married, we'll live in your apartment if that's okay," he says.

"Sure," I say. "I do have that extra bedroom. For the baby's room."

We're silent, and I feel as though those words alone—*the baby's room*—have propelled us somehow into the next stage of our relationship.

"We can sublet my place, or I can let it go. Whatever you decide is best," he's saying, and walking along the sidewalk, listening to the sirens in the distance and seeing the garbage cans blowing about near the curb, I think that this is what life is going to be like: nice, civilized conversations with decisions getting made in such an organized, orderly way.

He says, "I was thinking I'd make a spreadsheet of all the stuff we have to do between now and the summer. You know, figure out whose health insurance we'll keep, and whose landlord to contact. Figure out what the deal is with life insurance, and of course, getting a marriage license."

"Spreadsheets!" I say, and he grins. I have made him so happy.

CHAPTER TWENTY-FIVE

"I have to tell you something," says Tenaj on the phone.

This is the fifth time she's called me since I've been back home. Apparently, since Charleston, I am taking her calls. I have to admit that it's kind of fun to talk to her. Especially since I don't feel like I'm twisting some invisible knife into Maggie anymore just by talking to my mom.

"Oooh. Tell me everything," I say. I'm taking Mr. Swanky for a walk, which means that I am mostly watching him inspect and rate the sidewalk detritus. Today's offerings, judging from the slow pace of our walk, are more intriguing than usual.

"Well," she says, and I can hear her suck in her breath, "yesterday I was walking, and I passed a construction site, and the light was red, so I stood there for a minute, and then I saw that all the men were kind of hanging out, like they were on a break. Some had hard hats on, and some were just lounging around, drinking from thermoses. I made eye contact with a few of them. One man lifted his hand like a wave, and there was something in his eyes. Well, it was love in his eyes. Not specifically for *me*. But love is a way of seeing the world, and sometimes you can see that in a person in just one instant, you know. And—well, I just got inspired to do this crazy *thing*. I had a book with me of Pablo Neruda's poems, and I took it out, and I went over to the fence and I started reading them poems out loud."

"You did?"

"I did. Through the chain-link fence. I read the one that says something about loving you as dark things are supposed to be loved. Do you know that one?"

"I don't." Mr. Swanky and I have stopped walking, waiting for the light. The dark thing in my heart maybe has sat up and is listening. The light changes at the corner, and I have to move again, nudged along by the New York people rushing forward. "What did they do?"

"Well, they did exactly what you'd think. Some of them listened. One man applauded, and then a few others did, too. The man with the love in his eyes smiled at me. His eyes said he needed to hear that. Some of them just finished their lunch in silence. And went back to work. We'd had a moment, though. That was for sure. It was the kind of thing that makes you know you're awake."

"As dark things are supposed to be loved," I say slowly.

"Yes," she says. "Wake up, wake up! Just connect. That's what I came away with." And she laughs, that same old tinkling sound from my childhood.

Mostly that's what these calls are like.

She always tells me something about her life. Like how she reads poetry to construction workers. And then we say good-bye.

Maggie says, "When you come for Christmas, maybe we could look at wedding dresses."

I laugh. "In Pemberton. New Hampshire? Wedding dresses? Really, Maggie? You do know that New York City has a couple of thousand dresses probably right on my block."

"Come on. Don't be such a snob. Lena's Bridal Barn has some nice ones in the window. Or we could go to New London. I just thought we could get an idea—"

"No, of course we *could*. God knows when the last time was that I was in a bridal barn."

"Oh, stop!" she says, but she laughs. "I suppose you're going to want to make this more complicated, aren't you?"

"I'm just saying . . . Lena's may not be able to compete with New York."

"Oh. Well, sure. If you think you need to look at *hundreds* of them."

I get it then. Maggie simply wants to *participate*. So I shift gears, the way the new me is trying to do lately. "Hey, listen!" I say. "After Christmas, maybe during the winter break, you could come to New York, and stay with me, and we could shop together. Maybe see a show or something. Have tea at the Plaza. Do wedding-y things."

"But your father—"

"No, no. This would be billed as a wedding preparation trip. Just you and me." I hesitate for a moment, wanting to ask her whether or not he's agreed to go to therapy. But not daring to. In case the answer is no. I'm so scared he won't ever go, and then what?

"We'll have fun," I say.

"I . . . I . . ." There's the longest of pauses, followed by a ragged breath. And I realize she's crying. Maggie, the strong, stalwart one, the person in my life who could face down any amount of rejection and grief and punishing looks I sent her way, is now crying.

"Aw, are you okay?" I say.

"It's just that—you and I—this moment, coming now, after all these years. Do you know how much I've wanted—? Well, never mind. I'm not going to go there." She takes a deep, shuddering breath. "Okay, I'm fine now. Sorry. Yes, to answer your question, I will come. The February school vacation. Now you're sure you wouldn't just rather do this with your girlfriends? Because I would completely understand if that's something you all do together, you know, for your weddings."

"No," I say. "*No!* They're all out of their minds.

They'd have me all costumed up like Samantha in *Sex and the City*, if I wasn't careful. It's you I want."

And I do. I want to see Maggie happy, to see her dab her eyes with a handkerchief when she looks at me in my wedding gown, and I want our heads bent over little tea cakes at the Plaza, like I've seen mothers and daughters doing. I want to be mothered. Maybe—this would be unprecedented—but maybe we could link arms when we walk down Fifth Avenue, and I could tell her how nice she looks, and she could tell me that I need a haircut, which I do, and we would go into a salon and maybe we'd both get manicures and look at the movie magazines.

This is what I'm signing on for: marriage and some collateral mothering. A quick nod to the Wedding Industrial Complex.

"I guess it's time I told you that a momentous thing is happening in my life," I say to Tenaj one day. It's a Saturday, two weeks from Christmas, and once again I'm taking Mr. Swanky for a walk. It's cold outside, and the streets are filled up with people rushing around carrying sacks of presents. Normally I'd be honoring my Saturday morning writing hours, but I can't seem to settle into it these days. Too much real life to think about, I guess.

"Well, if you've got momentous news, maybe

I'd better wave some sage around the room and sit down," Tenaj says, laughing.

"Ha! It's not that bad. It's that I'm getting married."

I may have said this a little too loudly, because, here at the corner, waiting for the light to change, several people turn and smile at me. I wave at them, shrug, do a little curtsy.

My mother, however, reacts without emotion.

"Again you're getting married? Why in the world are you doing this?"

She can't just let herself be like other moms, say, *Oh congratulations! Who's the lucky fellow?*

"You say that like it's something I do all the time."

"But you have been married before."

"Yes, I have. You're right."

"A really good-looking, sexy guy, as I recall. You loved him more than any human had ever loved another, you said. He had everything. Great sense of humor, gorgeous gray eyes, wonderful body—"

"Yes," I say drily. "Thanks for reminding me."

"Well? We need to remember our old selves, the way we once loved. You know, Pablo Neruda has lots of poems about that. In one of them, he says something about how he's forgotten the love itself, but says he glimpses her in every window."

"Yeah, well, this is not like *that guy* I married. This one is faithful."

425

"Faithful, got it," she says. "And are you in love with him?"

I laugh. "Who asks that question when somebody says she's getting married?"

"No. I thought not."

"Would you stop? We've known each other forever, for instance. He's a kid I grew up with on the farm. Judd Kovac. My oldest friend. We hang out together all the time."

"Listen to me. Don't get married to somebody because you've given up on love. There's a saying, you know, that you should never get married until and unless you're bowled over by your amazing luck. Or something like that. So are you bowled over by your amazing luck?" Then, before I can even answer, she says, "No. You're not."

"You don't know!" I say. "He's a good man. He'll be good to me. I've known him forever, and I'm going into this with my eyes wide open. Our marriage is going to be based on harmony and trust and affectionate friendship."

"Listen, sweetie. You may think I don't have any right to be talking about anyone's marriage ideas, being as how I've gotten married and divorced three separate times—but I just know that you're going to come across a man who's going to love you, and it's going to be magical. And I think you shouldn't stop until you find that man, that's all."

"Well," I say. "How do you know Judd Kovac isn't that guy? That's what I want to know. How you're so sure."

"Because I'm paying attention. People deciding to get married simply because they're old friends basing their marriage on harmony and trust, blah blah blah, sounds like a business arrangement to me."

"That's the way *you* see it," I say. "But you could be wrong."

"I don't think I'm wrong. And also, I now remember calling you one day because the universe wanted me to tell you to *not* do something you were about to do, and I just have a feeling this—getting engaged to this guy—might have been what it was talking about."

"I have some news for you. There *is* no universe that gives instructions. It's all just in your head."

To my surprise, she laughs. "Have it your way. If that's the way you want to see things, I'm not going to argue with you. My job, from now until the rest of time, is just to love you up. And not try to convince you of anything."

"Anyway. The wedding is going to take place in June. And Maggie is coming to the city to help me shop for a wedding dress."

So *there*.

"How delightful. And will the future Mrs. Judd Kovac be wearing white Chantilly lace?"

"Ms. Phronsie Linnelle-Kovac is going to fight like hell *not* to wear something that looks like a throwback to the 1940s, so no."

"That's my girl." Then she says, in a voice so casual I almost don't see it coming, "I'm actually going to be spending some time in the city, too. I'm teaching a couple of seminars at the New School. In February."

"Oh!" I say.

"And I would love to spend some time with you."

I have gone nearly half my life without laying eyes on my mother in person. And, for some reason, standing there waiting while Mr. Swanky executes his ninety-fifth pee of this walk, I am suddenly blinded by tears.

I don't even really know why. Only that it has to do with that girl I was, sitting next to her on the porch in Woodstock, dazzled by the love she seemed to generate all around her. And how after spending so many years with my heart turned against her, I realize I want to see her again. And that I'm also scared of seeing her, too. And in some weird way, these tears are for Adam, too. Telling me he'd be on Tenaj's side. Because he believed in love. And he was sure I did not.

I often think of calling him up, but then I push the thought aside. I'm sure I'm the last person he wants to hear from. But I so want to tell him that I haven't been writing my novel, and that maybe he was right that I need to let go of that story I was telling because it was holding me back. Maybe I could tell him that sometimes I wake up in the night and look over at Judd on the next pillow, and I want to get out of bed right then and go and write and write and write. About a woman who needs magic in her life. I feel that woman trying to tell me a story. I could thank him for putting that idea in my head. That's all I'd say. Nothing else. Just *thanks*.

The next Monday, during a lull time, I call my friend Leila, the one who works at McCutcheon. I'm sly about my intentions, just asking nonchalant questions like, "So, how's the new guy doing?"

Oh, she says, he's wonderful. Three of the women in the office have little crushes on him, she tells me. And he came to the Christmas party with some stunning young woman, breaking everybody's heart.

"Does he have gnomes?" I ask.

"Gnomes?" she says and laughs. "Did you say *gnomes?* No, he does not."

At the end of the call, she says, "You guys were so great to send him over to us. I'll tell him you said hello."

"No," I say. "No, that's fine."

Later, I realize that *of course* he doesn't have gnomes at work because they're all hibernating.

CHAPTER TWENTY-SIX

Christmas, New Year's. It all goes by in a blur. I'm busier than ever at work, organizing spring and summer campaigns for my authors: one who has written a craft book for children on their summer vacations; a couple of dystopian mysteries; a love story between two vampires. There are book tours, magazine reviews, staff meetings.

And I am on top of it all. Making lists, being efficient and organized. Judd and I are doing well. Also, he sleeps with me most nights every week, and we're getting a bit more practice with the lovemaking thing. Mr. Swanky is getting used to having both of us take him out on walks in the evening. We went to the usual round of Christmas parties and practiced being an engaged couple.

Talia said I looked radiant, but I am not radiant. I miss writing so much that it is like an ache in my chest. But I don't have time for that stuff now. I have to make lists and get prepared.

Then one night I have a dream about Adam, and it is so vivid that I snap awake in the morning fully expecting he'll be there in the bed next to me. I am a little startled to find Judd there instead, propped up in bed with his laptop, checking his spreadsheet for the gym. Year-end client totals. Bench press numbers. Who knows?

After I get off the subway that morning—well, I find myself walking to McCutcheon. Tiller has offices in two different skyscrapers, four blocks apart. I pretend to myself that I'm just going for a healthful walk before work, but it's thirty degrees outside, and the wind is blowing flurries, and the truth is, this day reminds me a little bit of the Snow Hurricane.

It's not that I want to see him. In fact, I'd be mortified to run into him. I just want to be in the vicinity, to see where he is.

I just want to see his face again. And then maybe I could tell him in person that I'm so sorry. I could tell by the way he looked at me if he really hates me.

I could give Gnomeo back to him. Because Gnomeo probably misses Juliet, who is hibernating without him.

But then before I even get to the building, I turn around. Because this is crazy, and it's unfair, and I don't have any right to know anything about him after what I did.

A new employee moves into Adam's office next to mine. She places a bunch of smooth river stones on the windowsill, and I can't help thinking that the gnomes would have found that delightful. They could have moved them around with their tractor, perhaps.

One day, near the end of January, Maggie calls to say I still haven't let her know about the font for the wedding invitations.

"Really? How many people are coming to this shindig anyway?" I say. "I pictured it being about seven, to tell you the truth."

"What? You don't want any more than that?" she asks.

"No, no, not at all! This is your show," I say. "As for the font, I agree with whatever you think. You have carte blanche."

"But I want you to care," she says. And then I know what she means. My father will never express an opinion on most things that don't concern him. I've watched over the years as she's tried to get his attention about the throw rugs, the geranium pots on the porch, the replacement linoleum on the kitchen floor. He won't care.

So I rustle up some opinions. I look at font styles online with her. I exclaim over the fun ones with curlicues. She says, in a worried voice, "But . . . should it be a more stately font, do you think? Maybe we need to pick out the dress first, and then we can decide things like which font gives the same spirit as the whole wedding."

"The dress will set the tone then?" I say. *Really?*

"Yes," she says. "We want consistency in tone, I think. I mean, don't *you?*"

"Absolutely," I say. Then I add, "Mags, I'm so glad you're coming soon. You can help me think about all these things I probably would never have known to think of."

"Yes, me too," she says. "I hope you're making a list of places we can go so we can be efficient."

"Definitely," I say.

"The Wedding Industrial Complex," says Judd when I hang up the phone.

"I just hope and pray we get a font that doesn't interfere with the wedding dress," I tell him, and he laughs. He's making himself a kale smoothie with strawberries before he heads out to the gym. People are working off their holiday cookies. And he needs to be on hand to make sure the old ladies are doing it just right.

"I'm surprised my mom doesn't want to come, too," he says. "Do it up *really* right."

"No," I say, "that would be breaking wedding protocol. The groom's mom gets a total pass. Apparently, according to all protocols, it would be highly inappropriate for her to express an opinion."

I say this, but you know what I'm thinking? That this is all unbearably sweet, that everybody's trying so hard on my behalf, and that—well, this is part of it, too—that I am taking my place in a long line of brides. Even at this late date in my life, I am being allowed to partake in the great pageant of matrimony.

Not what I would have chosen, or expected, but still, the closest thing I will ever have to being royalty.

Maggie arrives on a Friday evening in mid-February, one of those freezing cold nights when the Manhattan skyline looks like jewels against a black velvet sky.

I see her get off the train in Penn Station before she sees me, and so I get to observe her marching forward, grim-faced and holding a suitcase, wearing her tan puffy jacket and a plaid scarf, black pants and boots—and glaring at everyone around her as though she's sure one of them is about to jump in front of her and try to rob her of everything. The trip had been fine, she says in answer to my questions; yes, the seat was very comfortable, and a nice couple had sat across the aisle from her and told her it was too bad she didn't get to see all the Christmas hoopla on Fifth Avenue. The tall tree at Rockefeller Center was not to be missed.

"I told them, I've *seen* plenty of Christmas trees," she says. "I have a bunch of them right in my own yard. New Yorkers always think they've invented everything."

"They do," I agree. I take her suitcase, and we get a cab and take it back to the apartment, where we have cups of tea and make a list for tomorrow's marathon shopping event.

First stop the next morning is a small dress shop in Chelsea that Talia told me about. We have an appointment, and so we are given mimosas and some cookies while I try on one, two, six dresses, all of which will really do, but I watch Maggie's eyes carefully and don't see what I'm looking for yet: the amazed gasp, the tearful realization that this is *it.*

"Where to next?" Maggie whispers in the dressing room. "We don't want to make the rookie mistake of buying the first ones we see."

So we go to one of the warehouse-type places, where samples hang on hangers, and women move through the cavernous space fingering rows and rows of lace and tulle and netting. I am in row three, getting a little dizzy, actually, when I hear something—hands clapping from about fifty feet away—and I look up.

And there's Tenaj.

Freaking Tenaj.

So this is surely an illusion, one of those tricks of the mind. Because Tenaj has never in the history of the world just turned up in my line of vision like this.

And then she waves, and my stomach goes into free fall.

I look nervously over at Maggie, who is down the row, not four feet away from me, reverently

435

touching a dress that looks like it was made from a piece of satin with a tangle of shiny moon-beams stitched on it.

I feel the panic rising up in my throat as I try to reconstruct how this could have happened. I mean, sure, yes, I had *casually* mentioned to her the date of Maggie's arrival. And *yes,* I had told her we were going to be shopping for bridal gowns. But not where. Somehow she's got intuition for these things, and now she's walking toward me from the front of the warehouse, smiling, and as she gets closer, I think she seems longer, thinner, more determinedly avant-garde than the last time I saw her. Her hair is a glossy silver now, shining and curly. As she comes closer, I see the lines in her face, and I see she's still wearing clothing that looks like it was pieced together from old Indian pillows and saris. She has a bright orange beret, and a long lavender mohair coat over her patchwork mishmash of colors.

"Maggie?" I say in a low voice, not taking my eyes off Tenaj. "Maggie, honey."

"I know, it's not the right beads," she says from down the aisle, moving farther away from me. "I'd like this one, I think, but with pearls. I think they're so much classier, don't you?"

"Maggie." I move toward her, wanting to wrap my arms around her, protect her from what's coming. Tenaj is out of view now; I'm in a thicket of dresses. Maybe I could take Maggie by the hand, and we could hide, like children in a forest. Tenaj wouldn't find us.

"What?" Maggie looks up at me. "Are you all right?"

"There's something I want to tell you," I say. My tongue has thickened, like a piece of sausage in my mouth.

Maggie's eyes are round now. She's on full alert for trouble.

"It's Tenaj," I whisper. "Tenaj is here."

Her eyes cloud over, and her jaw tightens. I see it all flash past—the jealousy, the hurt—but then it passes, and she clamps down on all her feelings. She smiles.

"Tenaj—right here?" she says. "Oh, honey, you scared me. I thought you were going to say somebody had died. Or that the warehouse was on fire. Where is she?"

"She's . . . right here," I say.

Because she is. She has materialized next to me, and she's smiling. And Maggie smiles right back at her. I feel once again like the little kid here with my two moms, and we're back to it being a hot summer day, and I'm just the cargo being transferred from one car to another, from one life to another. With a stomachache. Looking from one of them to the other. Wondering if they're going to hiss at each other. Tension so heavy it's like gravity has doubled.

Only I'm thirty-six years old, and the two women standing on either side of me are looking at each other and sizing each other up but still smiling. Over the buzzing of my ears and a coughing fit that has suddenly seized me, I'm unable to hear anything, but I sense that the two of them are okay. They're adults saying hello. Tenaj is being all willowy and magnetic, her electric eyes looking kind, and Maggie is smiling stiffly, holding her ground.

As for me, I can't seem to stop coughing. Both of them look over at me with concern and start digging into their bags looking for a cough drop. Tenaj hands me a patchouli-scented handkerchief, Maggie has a lozenge of some sort, wrapped in cellophane.

At last my coughing subsides. Tenaj has asked a question, and Maggie seems to be politely showing Tenaj the satin number with the moonbeams. They both examine its fabric, shake their heads, look at me with some concern, and move on to the next dress.

"You know, I like the bodice of this one much better," says Tenaj.

"True," says Maggie.

I am incredulous. Are we—together in this?

"But are we absolutely committed to the white dress tradition?" Tenaj wants to know.

We? *We?*

Maggie says, "We didn't really talk about it. I

thought that was what she wanted. Perhaps you know more than I do."

"She hasn't told me anything," says Tenaj. "I'm just wondering: Is she thinking of going the whole nine yards? The veil and all of it? The train? The bouquet?"

They look at me, recovered now.

"It's fine," I say. "Sort of what I'd always pictured." My voice is all croaky.

Maggie shrugs. "Well. I'm open to anything," she says. "I'm just happy to be along looking at dresses, if you want to know the truth. This isn't something I ever thought I'd get to do."

I am so grateful to her just then that I want to hug her.

Tenaj says, "Well, then. White wedding it is. I like the *flow* of this one, don't you? The way it tapers, and yet if you gained two ounces from now until the time of the wedding, it wouldn't have to be remade."

"Well, that's certainly true," says Maggie. "I had a friend that happened to. Had to have the dress completely recut *twice* by the time the wedding took place."

They laugh. "Twice! God, what women do just for this one supposedly magical moment!" says Tenaj. She's looking restlessly around the warehouse, squinting at dresses as if she could materialize the perfect one.

"I don't really love it," I say. Being all

contrarian. "Too many seed pearls. I can see them all popping off if I laugh."

They regard me solemnly and go back to pawing through the samples.

"Now I really don't mean to intrude," says Tenaj, "*but,* as it happens, I know a little place in the Village that has some dresses we could look at. I mean, *if* we wanted. One of my Creative Mind students works there. And let me just say that I totally get it if you two want to go alone if you'd prefer. I didn't mean to horn in on your day. I was just passing by and wandered in."

"Passing by?" I say. "You were?"

She smiles. "Well. It's not as random as it sounds. Maggie, Phronsie here told me that you were coming to town, and I just happen to be in New York on a teaching fellowship, and this morning I woke up and thought, *I wonder if they're out looking now.* And so I was out . . ."

"No, of course, of course," Maggie is saying. "And you *are* her mother, after all."

Point Maggie.

"No, no, no!" says Tenaj vehemently. "Maggie, trust me. You are the one who raised her. I'm outmatched here, totally. I'll go. Just—it was nice to see you. All these years later. Water over the dam. Or whatever. You look great."

Point Tenaj.

"Well, as I said, I'm just happy to be in New

440

York," Maggie says. "I'll go anywhere and look at anything."

I'm a little dizzy with all this.

They look at me again.

"Well, if you're sure," says Tenaj. She turns to me. "So, Phronsie? It's up to you, kid. You want to see my student's store?"

"Okay," I say. "I guess there really isn't anything that's grabbing us here. Although there are about sixteen more acres of dresses to look at."

"Overwhelming, really," says Maggie. "You could get dress fatigue."

And then—well, the next thing I know, we're off to the Village. Tenaj hails us a cab, and we're whisked away. I sit in the middle between the two of them, and for a moment, it feels as though the earth's energy is shifting somewhere deep down below. I wish there was someone I could call to tell this to. Judd might be the one who would know how astonishing this is, and yet—even he wouldn't quite understand all the nuances here. Hendrix is working, and anyway, he wouldn't care. Not anymore.

It's Adam. It hits me that *he's* the one who'd love to hear this story.

Tenaj says, "So first of all, Maggie, I have to know, from *your* perspective: Just what is this lucky bridegroom like? Is he . . . dazzlingly sexy, or maybe is he . . . a brilliant intellectual? Scarily handsome? Dangerous? Or . . . ?"

441

Maggie and I look at each other. I shrug.

She says, "Judd? Well, Judd is a very nice guy, and he's dependable and funny and we've known his family for years. If I had to describe him in one word, I think it would be *comfortable*. People feel comfortable with Judd. Wouldn't you say so, Phronsie?"

"Comfortable!" says Tenaj, and her eyes are dancing even as they're boring into mine. "Well, isn't that something. Comfortable."

"He's also very handsome," says Maggie. Perhaps she's realizing she has damned Judd to the fires of Tenaj's judgmental hell.

"He is handsome," I say. "Really quite, quite handsome."

"Well, how nice is that!" says Tenaj.

They talk over me. Tenaj, waving her hands in the air, describes the nebulous, almost unexplainable creativity class she's teaching. Maggie counters with concrete stories about the need for algebra in the Pemberton school system.

When this runs down, Tenaj says, "By the way, how is Bunny? She was always so kind to me, even though I'm sure I wasn't what she had in mind."

"You weren't what *any* of us had in mind," says Maggie, and they both laugh.

"Oh, those days!" says Tenaj. "What a relief it is to be over all *that*." She reaches across me to pat Maggie's arm. "Maggie, I have often just wanted to tell you about a million things that need to be said. I must have started at least a hundred letters to you over the years, and then I've stopped because I didn't want to make any more mistakes. I mean, where to begin, right? But maybe I can tell you now. I'm just so sorry, so very sorry for the damage that was done."

"Really," says Maggie, looking out the window. "You don't have to say these things."

"I know I participated in your unhappiness. For that I'm sorry."

"Well," says Maggie stiffly. "He fell in love with you. What were you supposed to do about that? *You* didn't know *me*. For all you knew, he was free."

"Don't worry about me here or anything," I say. "I'm just fine."

They don't even pay me any attention.

"You know," says Tenaj, completely leaning over me to put all her intensity onto Maggie. "Maybe this is our chance to say some things. I *did* know about you, Maggie. He talked about you the whole weekend. How he was going to get married to you, and he was saving up some money, and that he was going to work on the farm, but he said he didn't really *like* the farm all that much, but he was going to do it anyway. For you."

"Yes," says Maggie. She has folded her arms now. I know that look.

"No. I swear to God this is true. He'd always go back to talking about you."

"Meanwhile, he's there, taking his clothes off," Maggie says tightly. "Please. You don't have to do this. I'm over it."

"It wasn't me he ever wanted," Tenaj says quietly. "I promise you this. There was nothing of substance there. Just a moment in time. Stuff happening that wouldn't have happened in any other time. It was never what was going to last. That's all I'm saying. You were the one he wanted."

"But then he stayed," Maggie points out.

"Oh, fuck, Maggie. He didn't stay for *me*. He stayed because he found out I was pregnant, and for some reason, his code of honor kicked in."

Maggie makes a little sound.

"Maggie, trust me, no other guy at the time would have done what he did—he didn't love me, after all—but he said he'd do the right thing. He was not happy about it, but he was going to be a man, and do what needed to be done."

"Could we—?" I say.

They get silent. And thank God the cab pulls up in front of the shop right then, and it's time that we sort ourselves out. I get out after Maggie on her side, and while Tenaj is paying the cabbie, I whisper, "I'm so sorry about this." And she shushes me: "It's fine. This needed to happen maybe. I don't know."

Tenaj comes around the back of the cab right

then, and we go into Glenda's Vintage Fashions, where in the window there are the most luscious boho dresses—lacy and old-fashioned and beautiful.

"A vintage shop!" says Maggie. "These are used?"

"Used *and* wonderful," says Tenaj. "A different outlook, perhaps, but think of it: it takes tradition to a new plateau . . . Hey, Miranda!" she calls, as a thin young woman with a long black braid comes out from the back, holding a toddler on her hip. "Namaste, sweetheart."

They hug and kiss, and Tenaj introduces us. "This is our daughter," she says pointing to me, and she winks at Maggie. "We share her, and now she's getting married."

"Oh, I love shared daughter situations!" says Miranda. She drags Tenaj to the back, and Maggie and I look around tentatively at the old oil lamps, lace tablecloths, Oriental carpets, and dresses—sexy and exotic—hanging on racks.

I pick out a filmy pink dress with a dropped waist and take it into the back to try on. It slides onto my hips, shimmers in the mirror, and the fabric, when I touch it, feels slippery and cool. I love everything it says, this dress. And when I come out of the dressing room and stand before my two moms, they both look surprised. Tenaj declares it wonderful.

"Do you like it, Maggie?" I ask, and she nods.

"It kind of looks like the wedding dress my mother was married in," she says. She touches it and frowns, like all mothers are required to do when confronted with fabrics. "Awfully well-made. But I wonder if you dry-cleaned this, though, would it fall apart? It's so old."

"Vintage," says Miranda, "and it's been cleaned. You don't have to do a thing to it." She turns back to Tenaj, and I swear I see her start to cry while they're whispering. The little boy she's holding pats her face.

"I think I'd like to get it," I say tentatively to Maggie. "What do you think?"

"Well," she says slowly. "I suppose. Funny, I hadn't considered a *used* dress, but this is . . . nice. I mean, if *you* like it. That's all that counts."

"It's not white, but it still looks very traditional to me," I say.

"Yes. It looks very nice on you."

I look at her closely. Something has changed in her face; she looks actually relaxed. Maybe Tenaj has soothed something that was ragged in her, with that story about my father.

"Okay . . . and then . . . shall we go get something to eat? Just you and me?" I tip my head toward Tenaj at the back of the store, now holding the toddler on her own hip and still curling her arm around Miranda. "We don't have to stay with her, you know."

"Whatever," says Maggie. She lowers her

voice. "I'm really fine with everything. You don't have to worry about me, you know. This is kind of a moment in time that you never would have thought could happen. It's kind of . . . eye-opening."

"You got that right."

"I guess I thought she would be . . . different by now, somehow. But she's . . . unbelievable."

I would love to know exactly what Maggie was picturing, but just then, Tenaj bounces back to us. "Listen, you two," she says. "Something has come up, and we're in for something of an adventure. Are you with me? Because I think this could be fun! Miranda here, Miranda is a flutist, and she's supposed to have an audition today to be in the orchestra of an off-Broadway show, a once-in-a-lifetime opportunity that the universe has tossed her way. But her sitter is in Brooklyn and can't get here, so I said I'd take Grover to the sitter's house. Now you don't have to join me, of course, but *Miranda* says that the sitter lives near this little shop she recommends, where we could look at veils and jewelry and such." She looks at Maggie and me with her bright, bright, talking-about-the-universe eyes, already sure of our answer.

I shrug and look at Maggie questioningly, and she nods. "Okay," she says. And just like that, it's settled. Miranda is so grateful. I pay for my dress, and the cab comes—and we jump in with

Grover, who has apparently only ever wanted to stay with his mom, and so screams for a while.

We all try to jiggle him and coax him into appreciating us, but nothing works until Maggie and Tenaj both give him their cell phones.

And then, in a move that could possibly win him a position as infant starting pitcher for the New York Yankees, Grover stops licking Maggie's phone and hurls it out of the car window, which I had just opened, trying to get some air. It goes flying, bouncing into the road.

It happens so fast that Maggie and I are speechless, but Tenaj bangs on the cab driver's shoulder until he agrees to pull over.

"Lady, I am not getting out of this car to run into traffic to get your freaking phone!" he says, once he hears what the problem is. "It's not even legal!"

Before the cab has even quite come to a stop, Tenaj jumps out. I see her running between cars, all of which are honking. Drivers are shouting at her out of the window, and she's like a gazelle somehow, dancing in between and smiling, holding up her arms like she might be channeling the pope.

Maggie has gone white, twisting around in the seat to see what's going on. "She's gonna get herself killed," she keeps saying in a low voice.

"No," I say, "she's not."

And sure enough, she swoops down and grabs

448

the phone, which had landed on the yellow line in the road, so it's still in one piece. She dances over to the taxi, triumphant, and slips inside next to us. She's grinning when she hands the phone back to Maggie.

"Whoo! That was such a rush!" Tenaj says. "I loved it!"

The cab driver loses his mind. "You!" he says to Tenaj, twisting around in his seat. "What are you thinking—running in traffic this way? You think these cars care about stopping for you?"

"It's not a big deal," she says. "It worked. Calm down." She reaches over and touches him on the arm. "I'm fine, I'm fine. Don't worry."

But now he pulls the car over roughly to the side of the road. "Get out!" he says. "I can't have this in my cab! You—all of you—go now."

We climb out of the cab—my two moms and me, the baby, the dress, the diaper bag. I am solemn, fearing the worst. But when I look over, Maggie and Tenaj are nearly doubled over, laughing, holding on to each other like they've been friends for life.

And that's how I know our day is spiraling into something unrecognizable.

"You know what?" says Tenaj an hour later, after we've deposited Grover with the sitter and checked out the veils and baubles shop, where I pick up a pink sunhat that looks better than any veil would. Sort of saucy and young-looking. "We should take Maggie for a walk across the Brooklyn Bridge and then have dim sum in Chinatown!"

Now see, this is crazy. It's February, for God's sake. We are carrying a wedding dress and a sunhat. Maggie is from out of town and she's probably tired. Also, I'm not sure that Maggie even knows what dim sum is. Or that she'd like it.

But Maggie says, "I'd like that."

"Which part?" I say. "Because we *could* just take a cab across the Brooklyn Bridge and admire the skyline that way. If it's skyline you're interested in." I switch sides holding my wedding dress plastic bag and my purse. Just to make the point, you know, that some of us are carrying stuff here.

"Great!" says Tenaj. "How often do you get to walk the Brooklyn Bridge in February?"

"I've gone a whole lifetime never doing it," says Maggie.

And that makes them laugh again. I swear, it's like these two are drunk. Maggie starts talking about a time she got drunk in college and climbed up on the cafeteria roof with a bunch of her friends. And Tenaj tells her about smoking dope in front of a cop one time and casting a spell on him so he wouldn't arrest her.

My two delinquent moms. Of course I can so

450

picture Tenaj doing that—hell, I may have even been there!—but Maggie? I turn and look at her.

"Maggie, what in the world were you thinking?"

"That it would be fun. I jumped off, too. And it was one of the high points of my life, I have to say."

"Being bad sometimes is," says Tenaj. "Unfortunately."

And they go off into peals of laughter once more.

"I think you two got drunk when I wasn't looking," I say. "And before I can walk across a bridge, I think I need some serious food."

"No, no, let's just get a hot dog off a cart!" says Maggie. "I've always wanted to do that."

And so we do. Hot dogs and a pretzel, cans of Coke.

Tenaj meets my eye and gives me a big, thousand-watt smile. I know this version of her. She is now in control, and she and the universe will be running things from now on.

I feel this impulse, seeing her this way, to tell her about Adam. I want to tell *both* my moms about him. I want to talk about him so much! Just to say his name out loud and to tell about the Snow Hurricane and the way we talked in the bar that day. How he knew so much about love. How he made me feel. I'd show them Gnomeo, still in my purse.

Tenaj tilts her head, questioningly. She knows I have something to say.

Then we walk through Cadman Plaza and down the path to the bridge. Its limestone arches frame the skyline. I take a breath in and don't say anything at all.

This day grows old and loose by the time we've made it across and have settled, tired and happy, in a divey kind of dumpling place in Chinatown, far from the crowds. It's starting to get dark, and we sit in a booth, drinking wine, like old friends.

"We need to have a toast," says Tenaj. "To the Brooklyn Bridge!"

"And to Phronsie and Judd, wading into the treacherous waters of marriage!" says Maggie.

"And God knows they are treacherous," says Tenaj. She looks at me meaningfully.

"Be quiet, you two," I say. "You're not supposed to be scaring brides. Even if you were married to the same man."

"Yeah, well, somebody should have scared *me* off from marriage," Tenaj is saying. "I got married four times—"

"Four?" Maggie and I say at the same time. I add, "I only know about three."

"Well, it was four," says Tenaj. "Which is the perfect number of times for me to know that I don't ever want to do it again."

452

"I don't ever want to do it again either," says Maggie, "and I only got married once."

We look at her. Maggie takes a sip of her chardonnay and puts the glass down and works her mouth around.

"Okay, I'm admitting it. I think I'm going to leave Robert," she says quietly.

"Oh, Maggie!" says Tenaj.

"You're really doing it?" I say. It's hard to breathe just now.

"Whatever it is that's gone wrong," says Tenaj, "we know it's not a failure of his wanting to be with you."

I think for a moment that Maggie would be justified in saying, *What do* you *know about it?* But she doesn't. She takes a deep breath and smiles at Tenaj. "Thank you for that."

"Who am I to know, but if I squint real hard, I see you and Robert hanging in until the very end because some miracle will come," says Tenaj, and I just want to reach over and shush her.

"Well, maybe, but *I* think it's not going to work out," says Maggie with a cheerful-sounding finality that surprises me. "I look at my life—what I gave up, what I do every day—and then I look at a day like today, that has about twenty-seven impossible parts to it and yet makes me laugh. And so many strangers! More strangers than I talk to in a year in New Hampshire. Like that little baby, going off with us just because his

453

mama said it was okay. And his mama trusted us to take him and keep him while she goes and tries to fulfill some dream and get herself out of a dress shop where everything she sells is about two hundred years old . . . and then . . . the bridge . . . this place . . . I just don't want to live like I do anymore, with a man who won't go for help. Goes to therapy and then just sits there like a lump when the counselor tries to help him."

"But he goes?" I say.

Maggie nods. "He goes, but he won't open up. And listen. Don't worry. We're not separating until after your wedding. We're going to hold it together until then."

"Maggie, I'm not worried about the wedding. I'm just thinking of you—and Dad."

Tenaj closes her hand over Maggie's. "I can feel his soul, and I see him letting all the joy go out of his life. Thinking he doesn't deserve all the abundance he has. All the love and respect he has. You know what? We've gotta love him back into health again. This is what we have to do! Come on, concentrate." She closes her eyes. "Maggie, you're going to love on him up close, hit him with all the energy and love you can muster, and . . . and Phronsie and I are going to beam love on him from afar. And he's going to be so flooded with all this energetic love that he's . . . he's going to go to therapy that works for him, and he's going to get himself all fixed up for the next third of his life. Which he will not want to waste.

"And you, Phronsie—" She turns to me, her eyes now wide and luminous. "You need to celebrate yourself the way you are right now, and, sweetie, you need someone who celebrates all of you, too, who doesn't just feel *comfortable* and inevitable. You think you're out of time, but, honey, you aren't. And I think when you're with the right person, it feels effortless. Not perfect maybe, but worlds apart from anything else you've ever known. So fall in love with your life, and you'll know the right thing to do, just like you knew the right dress to buy today."

Then she says she has to go because she has a class to teach tonight, this unicorn of love, but before she leaves, she takes Maggie's hands and looks into her eyes and says to her, "Everything always works out in the end. And if it didn't work out yet, then it isn't the end."

The next day—Maggie's last in New York—Maggie comes to her senses. We eat breakfast in the morning and then she insists we go back to Talia's friend's wedding shop, where, without fanfare, she buys me a traditional white wedding dress, with lace and sequins and seed pearls, as well as a fingertip-length veil. One of the ones I tried on yesterday. It's nice.

It's just the way things have to be, she says.

"I somehow think that other dress—and it is beautiful, make no mistake—just isn't you. I'm not really sure you won't have some regrets. I was awake all last night, tossing and turning, and I think it was the dress that had me going. It doesn't say *Phronsie* to me."

I don't protest. I see how she was just being generous all day yesterday, accepting my mother's eccentricities.

Later, while we're in the cab on the way to Penn Station, she says, "Your mother, oh my heavens!" She laughs this deeply fake laugh I recognize from nearly every evening of my childhood. "Interesting, interesting person, that one. But I'm going to tell you something: you live a whole life with a man, you know him a lot better than his weekend-turned-into-two-years *fling*."

"You were very nice to put up with all that," I say quietly.

"Well, she meant well. But I'm sorry, dear. Whether I stay or go from my *husband* is going to be based on a lot more than my husband's witchy ex-wife's *hunches*." She shakes her head and looks out the car window, like she's seeing New York back the way she always saw it before: dirty, noisy, scary, and filled with nuts.

"And as for her opinions about *your* upcoming marriage, let me just say that Judd is a lovely man. I noticed that she turned up her nose when we said he was *comfortable*. You and I know that's the goal of life: to marry somebody who gives you enough space and trust that your heart isn't being put through the wringer every damn day."

She lets out a big sigh. "Well. At least we found you a good dress," she says. "And you now have two to pick from."

That night, I'm lying next to Judd on my couch, and we're eating popcorn out of the bowl, and I try to tell him everything that happened. Which, of course, is impossible. I have to severely edit the entire day. Still, I make it into enough of a story that he laughs in all the right places. He's dutifully amazed at Tenaj being in the city, and then showing up at the bridal shop. I tell him about the trip to Brooklyn in the cab, the cell phone catastrophe, the walk across the Brooklyn Bridge.

"Did I come up at all?" he says.

"Oh, yes. Actually you did. She wanted to know what you were like, and Maggie said that you are *comfortable*."

He smiles. "I take it that Madame Tenaj DeFontaine didn't think that was such high praise."

"Ah, but we supplemented with your other charms. The way you can listen to me all night without fighting with me, and how you know instinctively just how much butter should go on popcorn, and you don't mind if Mr. Swanky sleeps on the bed, and you always want to be the one to do the dishes, unlike any other man who ever lived. And also you protect our old age by making us walk up the stairs, and we laugh together, and you have never cheated on anyone in your whole life, except for at Thanksgiving when you kissed Karla Kristensen. But I explained that was okay."

"Because you kissed someone, too," he says.

"Yes. Because I kissed someone, too."

"Holy God," he says. "Did you actually say that stuff?"

"No," I say. "Not a word of it. But it's all true."

CHAPTER TWENTY-SEVEN

Three months later, I am making dinner one night—pot roast with gravy—when Judd calls and says he's meeting some friends instead of coming home to eat.

"But I made gravy!" I say happily. "And guess what! I actually found a gravy boat in one of those little boutiquey kitchen shops today when I was on my lunch hour, and I went and bought it for us! And I don't think we should keep it high up in the cabinet no one can reach above the refrigerator either. It's going to stay with the regular dishes. Okay?"

I am ridiculously excited about this, in such an over-the-top way I know he'll relate to. It would have taken ten years to get across the hidden meaning of that one little symbol of home to a new partner. And that is the chief advantage of marrying your best and oldest friend. Steve Hanover never even heard me mention those words. Or Adam either, for that matter. Surprisingly, we didn't get to Symbols of Childhood Traditions in our one day in the snow. How a gravy boat signifies that you won't be alone.

"Wow, that's great," Judd says after a moment. "So listen, I'll see you tomorrow. I'll sleep at my place tonight so I won't wake you up."

"Okayyyy, but it'll be leftover gravy by then," I tell him in a singsong voice.

"So it'll be leftover gravy. Can we heat it up, do you think? Or is this magical, once-in-a-lifetime gravy?"

I come back into my right mind. "Of course we can heat it up," I tell him.

He's silent.

"Have a nice time tonight," I say.

He says he will, and I should, too. And his voice is clipped a little bit, which only means there are probably five things going on in front of him, and I'm his friend as well as his fiancée so I understand, but suddenly I also remember that he hasn't wanted to go to the diner in a very long time, and then I remember how we don't often have time for those long, analyzing conversations now that we don't have Dissect-A-Date to talk about. Which is crazy because Dissect-A-Date was about *other* people we were seeing romantically. But now I see that it was really about our friendship. We were having experiences so we could tell each other about them—it was all for the story.

And now we don't have those stories.

What we have instead is that we're *together* together. And we're too tired for the everyday stories, or like me, we leave stuff out. I'm always trying to fit into a role with him. The confusing role of fiancée and good-friend-not-in-love.

Then, because I've gotten on some long train of thought that I can't get off, I realize that he sleeps on the far side of the bed most of the time, not curled around me like I want, and he says it's because I'm like sleeping next to a furnace and so he has to move over where the sheet is cooler, and then there are lots of times he jokes that he needs to go see his first-best pillow, but why doesn't he bring his first-best pillow down here, which is supposedly *home* now. And he says well, then, because his second-best pillow would be the one he has upstairs, and then he'd miss *that* one, wouldn't he?

But what he means is that this *isn't* home.

I go sit on the couch and watch some stupid, nondescript romantic comedy that I can't even remember the name of. And at the end, when the man is running through an airport to beg the woman not to get on the plane and leave him, the whole scene looks so implausible and ridiculous and stupid that I think these kinds of movies should come with a warning label on them.

NOT. REAL. LIFE.

CHAPTER TWENTY-EIGHT

Real life is that we are getting married.

Yes, we are.

I know this because it is now June, and we are at the beach house in Wellfleet for what is turning out to be Wedding Week, my father and Maggie in one bedroom, me in another, and Hendrix and Ariel down the hall. Their boys are sleeping in sleeping bags on the sunporch. The dining room of the beach house is filled with stacks of linen napkins and candlesticks and tea lights and china plates and a whole bunch of wedding presents, all in piles on the floor because this is a legitimate, *real* wedding, the kind you'd see in a movie or something. Planned and executed under the able and eager hand of Maggie Linnelle, rookie wedding planner extraordinaire.

Everybody is acting exactly like themselves. Judd is staying in a different house with his parents, and they all come over and sweetly ask if there is anything they can do. And Maggie, bless her, allows Daisy Kovac to sort the silverware, which has been sorted a thousand times.

And my father and Hendrix and Judd mow the grass and trim stuff, and Ariel sets out flowerpots everywhere. Makes sun tea in a big pitcher and puts it out on the porch. The boys rake the beach. There will be a rehearsal dinner clambake.

My chest hurts. I watch Judd laughing with my father and brother. And I notice that he doesn't come over and sit with me on the porch, doesn't drink iced tea with me. Doesn't even look over and give me one of those fond, we're-about-to-get-married looks I was expecting.

My heart is hurting so much that I may have a fatal disease, and that will be so sad if I don't make it to my own wedding, I think. Maybe everyone will stay and have my memorial service on the beach instead.

Maggie, in her glory, is rushing around planning and executing things, calling this Wedding Central. Making phone calls, talking to relatives and friends who are in for the weekend, arranging brunches and hair appointments, manicures.

My father is trying very hard. Maybe he's just happy that a man he likes has agreed to take me on. Or maybe he knows that I'm really dying, and he doesn't want our last days to be spiteful. He comes and talks to me. He asks me bland questions about Mr. Swanky and about my job and about where Judd and I will live. He smiles more.

Maggie had told me that they are seeing a marriage counselor now. His idea. He wasn't getting much out of individual therapy. It's better for them to be working on things together. Again, his idea. He takes her out to breakfast on

Saturday mornings now, and he remembers to ask her how she's doing. He doesn't get so mad when he hears the construction vehicles anymore. They sit on the porch together in the evenings, holding hands.

So that's something. It's huge, in fact.

Over and over I say to myself: "Everything is okay. I am fine." I have heard that if you smile, it activates actual muscles in your face that improve your mood. Or something like that. Anyway, you should smile. Especially when you're getting married.

The other day, I was rummaging through my purse for my checkbook so I could write a check for the flowers I'd ordered—and who should fall out onto my foot but little Gnomeo. I think he *jumped* out, if you want to know the truth.

I packed him in my suitcase to bring to the Cape. After the wedding, I should probably mail him back to Adam in the inter-office mail. I'll seal him up and send him back.

I'll write: "Misses Juliet."

Finally, on Thursday, my friends arrive and move into their hotel rooms, and that night we go out joyriding to the beach, and then we walk along the sand, and I tell them that I am so crazy, and they say that everyone feels crazy in the forty-eight hours leading up to getting married. And

I say no, this is not that, this is a different kind of crazy, this is a what-am-I-doing kind of crazy, and they say what kind of crazy did you think we were talking about, of course it's the same crazy.

But no one understands.

I think the problem is the two wedding dresses, if you want to know the truth.

My two wedding dresses, which are hanging in the closet of my room. One for the Phronsie who belongs to Tenaj, and the other for the Phronsie who belongs to Maggie. But maybe that's too simple. And ridiculous, because both of them are the same Phronsie. And both of them are me. And I have now had four months since buying those dresses to figure out which one I am wearing to the ceremony.

I have also had four months to write my vows for Judd, and I haven't been able to do that either.

Finally I tell him we should just stick to the ceremony that the justice of the peace will read, and he reminds me that there isn't really a justice of the peace; it's going to be Russell, who got a special certificate or something from some kind of fake holy order church, and now he can do weddings. Which of course I already knew. I can't concentrate on all the details. But anyway, it will be Russell marrying us. Russell with the great hair. And Russell, as Judd points out, is a musician and doesn't *know* what to say, so we have to tell him.

Maybe he could just sing us a song. Sing us into our marriage, I say to Judd. Why not? Work some vows into a song format, and we'll answer, like a call-and-response, and then we'll be married. Signed, sealed, and delivered.

And Judd looks at me and then he purses his lips and goes out for a run, which is the way he deals with me lately. I don't blame him. I wish I could go out for a run to get away from myself, too.

And then—in what feels like a flash—it's Saturday. It's a bright blue day, with a breeze and a string of clouds trailing in the sky, looking like fine little feathers. The marsh grasses are blowing back and forth. The kind of day people would love to have for a wedding day.

Maggie is at my bedroom door, telling me that Russell is downstairs, wanting copies of the vows. I go downstairs to the too-bright kitchen, wearing my kimono, and I break the news to him, that I couldn't write anything. I tried, I say. Couldn't do it. Sorry.

"Maybe you could . . . write something now?" he says. He runs his hands through his glossy, beautiful hair, which is just how worried he is, because messing his hair up is a real sacrifice for him.

"Aren't there some standard lines you can say?" I ask him.

"Well, Phronsie, there may well be, but you see, I'm not really a *minister,* so they didn't let me in on the *words* they say in their special ceremonies," he says. "And somehow I missed the memo that I was going to have to infiltrate their ranks, and now it appears that whoops, I'm *all* out of time." He turns his palms up, empty-handed.

"Well, what did they say when you and Sarah got married?"

"Oh, who the fuck knows?" he says. He leans against the doorjamb and sighs. "You seriously don't know what you want to say to Judd?"

"That is correct. I seriously do not know what I want to say to Judd."

Maggie comes in, drying her hands on a dishtowel. "Russell," she says. "Why don't you come in here and let me know what you think of this fruit compote I just made? And we'll give Phronsie some coffee and send her upstairs, and maybe she can come up with some words you can use."

She is being so kind, Maggie is. I gratefully accept the coffee, and then I go back upstairs. She calls up after me, "Dear, the ceremony *is* at four thirty. So maybe put a tiny bit of a rush on it, if you can. Amber is coming by to do your hair at eleven thirty and it's ten forty now." I hear her say to Russell, "I don't see how she's going to do this if she hasn't done it already. Let's look

467

on the internet. See if there's something we could borrow."

I have no idea who this Amber is, or what is supposed to happen to my hair. Maggie knows all this. By the time Amber comes, I have written these words: "Hi, Judd. You and I have known each other for practically our whole lives."

But then what? I could talk about the great moments in our history together—the burping during circle time in kindergarten, the time I drove him to Canada when Karla Kristensen dumped him, and just listened to him blubber about her. When he drove me to the bus station the time I went to live with Tenaj. And the Dissect-A-Date moments. The diner. The eggplant fries.

These are not the moments one should talk about in a wedding vow. I feel a loneliness deep in the pit of my stomach. These are the only real moments that Judd and I have.

Amber comes in wearing jeans and a black T-shirt. She has swoopy black hair and false eyelashes that are so big they look like she's wearing tarantulas on her eyelids. Very disconcerting, I think. She says, "Do you want an updo, hon?"

"No. I'd like my hair to be down."

"Huh," she says. "Most brides get an updo."

"Not me."

"Well, I just said most, I didn't say all." She

lifts pieces of my hair and then drops them again. "It's curly," she says.

"Yeah."

"Not sure what you want me to do here. Curly hair is kind of a one-trick pony."

"Very true characterization of my hair. I've been saying that all my life. 'Hair,' I've said, 'you know only one trick.' "

"I can't do much with it then. You want it parted in the middle or on the side?"

"The way it is. The side."

"Okay then." She combs it, gently. "You know," she says after a while. "It's going to look pretty much the way it always looks. Is that okay with you?"

"Yeah," I say. "That's kind of what I want. This is a day like any other."

"Huh," she says. "I tell you what: You want I should put some glitter in it or something?"

"God, no."

After five minutes of steady, listless combing, she says, "Well, I think we're done here."

"Okay, thank you. Can I ask you a question?"

"Okay, hon."

"Do you ever see brides who change their mind right at the end? Who can't go through with it?"

"No," she says. She looks alarmed. The tarantulas on her eyes jump a little. "You'll go through with it, honey. You've just got the jitters. Everybody goes through with it, though."

● ● ●

I select the white wedding gown. Maggie comes in to help me put it on, and she brings a photographer named Elaine who takes moody pictures of us together, Maggie helping me with the veil. Maggie and me by the window, looking out, gazing soulfully into the future. Then me, looking in the mirror. Me, putting on lipstick. Me, from the back, my dress and veil making it seem I'm rising from a cascade of white clouds.

The photographer leaves to go bother some other people, all of whom are milling outside.

Maggie says, "You look—you look really nice. Even your father said so. He was going on and on about how nice you look."

"Can I tell you something? I feel like all this is happening to someone else. Like I'm in a play."

She shrugs. "Life's momentous events have a way of making us feel that way."

"You and Dad seem to be doing really well."

"Yes," she says. She looks at me for a long moment. "You want to know something crazy?"

"I need to hear anything crazy you have to say. Please! It couldn't be crazier than the thoughts going on in my head."

"Well, it's because of your mom."

"My mom. What's because of my mom?"

"That we've turned the corner. What she said to me. About how he always loved me, and he didn't really love her. It changed the past for me, really. I always thought I was second best, and I see now how I held back a whole lot of my heart. *I* was the angry one all those years. Furious with him. I pushed him away. I was there, doing all the work I was supposed to do. Did my duty. But not out of love. Nothing I did was out of love."

No, she did not do things out of love. I look at her and remember how tough she was. And how soft she seems now, in comparison.

She nods. "Ridiculous, isn't it? That I needed *her* to tell me." She smiles. "The marriage counselor said that sometimes we tell ourselves a little story, and we just hold on to it until it feels like it has to be true, and we can't switch out of it."

"Huh," I say.

"By the way, I saw Tenaj arriving a little bit ago. Shall I send her in? You might want some pictures with her, too, it occurs to me."

"Is she out there talking to everybody about the universe and how we all have to love ourselves?"

"Very possibly."

"Then I guess she'll come in and say all that to me. Who knows? Maybe it'll help."

"Maybe."

I am standing in a way that I can see my reflection in the mirror across the room. I look like somebody else. All of this is happening to someone else.

"Maggie, will you tell me just one thing?" My

471

mouth is a little dry. "What if Judd's only a story I kept telling myself, and marrying him isn't the right thing? There's something about it that isn't like . . . well, what other people have."

She gives me a long look. "I know that," she says. "But he's been your good friend for ages. He's got so many good qualities, and—" She stops, swallows, and looks at me. "Well, good qualities may not be the main thing. You have to figure out your heart, Phronsie."

"I thought I had."

"A lot of us think we have, and then we really haven't."

"But what if I figure it out wrong?"

"Then you can fix anything. Relax. Nothing is irreversible here."

I sit down on the bed.

"Phronsie, maybe I haven't said this to you, but I want you to know that even if Judd *isn't* the right one, I still love you. You're the one who's important to me here."

"But you've done all this work."

She stands there with her hand on the doorknob. "It'll be fine. You're the one I love. I want you to be happy. Okay?" She looks at me for another long moment. "I'll send Tenaj in."

I've collapsed on the bed when Tenaj comes in. She's a vision of boho lavender and pink, draped in silk and velvet. With wonderful cowboy boots.

472

"Wait," she says first thing. "Why aren't you wearing *the dress?*"

I'd forgotten this uncomfortable part of things. How Tenaj doesn't know what happened after she left Maggie and me, how we went to a regular wedding dress store like ordinary bridal citizens do.

"I got this one. I have both," I say listlessly. "Two dresses."

"But why? Whatever for?"

"It's hard to explain."

"Try."

"Okay." My voice feels thick, like it can't quite say it right. "Well, I have two selves. I'm pretty evenly split down the middle, you know. It used to be easier for me, when I was Phronsie sometimes and Frances other times. But now that we got Maggie to call me my real name, I'm Phronsie all the time. Except now. This is a Frances dress, isn't it?"

"It is definitely a Frances dress."

"Yeah." I look down at it, with all its stiff organdy-ness and lace. "Maybe if I put on the other one, then I'd be the person who could go get married."

"No pressure or anything. It's a beautiful day. People are just out there drinking cocktails and walking around on the lawn and going down to the beach."

"Where's Judd?"

"Is he the handsome one with the boutonniere?"

"Probably."

"He's talking to Hendrix. He seems fine."

"Okay. Well, I'm just going to lie here and think some thoughts."

"You do that. Think all the thoughts you want. Are you maybe going to change into your boho dress?"

"Not yet, I don't think. Just now I'm experiencing my Frances side." I look over at her. She's standing by the window, looking down at the yard. "Just tell me this. How many times of your four weddings did you think you might be making the worst mistake of your life?"

She laughs. "Um, none. I always believed in them at the time."

"Even to my father?"

"Especially to your father."

"Even knowing that he loved somebody else best?"

"I didn't really believe that. I thought he'd start to love me."

"Huh."

"Yeah, I'm optimistic about love. It's a character flaw."

"What about with me? Are you optimistic about this?"

She turns and looks at me with such wide eyes, such kindness. "No. But I'm optimistic about you."

"I wish I was."

"You know, there's a man out there who keeps looking up at this window."

"That's Judd."

"No. It's not Judd. Judd has a boutonniere. This is another man."

"Then it's Russell. The officiant."

"No . . ." She drops the curtain. "I met Russell, too. This guy is with an older woman who's hanging on him."

There's a knock at the bedroom door, and my father's voice. "Phronsie? Phronsie, it's past time. Are you coming out?"

Tenaj opens the door, and my father stands there, blinking at her. It's funny; I'd imagined this moment for so many years. The moment they would see each other again.

And now here they are, and even from the bed I can see that they are both taking in the vision of the other one right there, that it's one of life's big moments. He's wearing his best suit, and his hair is cut too short, and his face is all red. And she is looking at him with such a big smile on her face.

"Well," he says. "Hello, Tenaj." Some muscle twitches in his face.

"Robert! Come in and help us," she says. "I'm just in here trying to help our beautiful, confused daughter. Come in. Maybe we have some parental wisdom to impart together."

"Do we?" he says. "I just wanted to come up

and see if she might come down and get married soon."

"She's apparently still thinking that over."

"Why aren't you coming down?" he says to me. "Wait. Why are you lying down?"

I think he might be thinking that I'm a flake. That I'm like her. That he's washing his hands of the two of us. But surprisingly, he's got a little smile on his face. He comes over to the foot of the bed, and he reaches over and touches my foot, waggles it a little. I am wearing white nylons. I never wear nylons. Who is this person living in my body all of a sudden, a person who wears bridal-grade nylons?

"I'm coming as soon as I can pull myself together," I say. "I'm just having a little moment, is all. I'm deciding something."

"You're such a beautiful bride in your white dress. And didn't you already decide? I mean, this is Judd. You've decided about him years ago."

"Robert, the question about Judd may have changed slightly. From: Is he a good friend to Is this the person she really can love for the rest of her life? Is it enough?"

"Still," he says. "She did say yes. You're looking well, by the way. Unchanged in a Dorian Gray kind of way."

"Wait. You know about Dorian Gray?" I say to him.

"Phronsie, I did go to high school."

"My hair's gray, though," Tenaj says, patting it.

"Well," he says. "Anyway, you look nice." He looks back at me. "Phronsie, what's up, kid? What are we going to do here?"

"I'm thinking."

"She's thinking."

My heart is beating too hard. Maybe if I had a good cry, I'd know what I need to do. I could stop this hammering of my heart, get my breath fully back. I respect a good cry. But if I have one now, then when I go downstairs to get married, I'll have blotchy eyes and smeared makeup.

"But what are you thinking *about?*"

"I have two wedding dresses," I say. "They seem to sum up the problem somehow. In a way I can't describe."

"I don't really know why you went and got a second dress when the first one is so wonderful. And you're not even wearing it," says Tenaj.

"Listen," says my dad. "Wedding dress one or two doesn't matter. But if you know you don't want to marry Judd, I think you need to tell him. It might be kind of a hard conversation, but you have to do it."

"Daddy," I say. "Daddy." I start to cry. Big, blubbery tears. "Could you just come over here and give me a hug? Tell me it's going to be okay?"

"All right," he says, and he lumbers up to the

head of the bed. He's big and awkward. Bulky in his suit that doesn't quite fit him. I think it's the one he wore to Hendrix's wedding a million years ago.

He sits down beside me, and I sit up and put my head on his shoulder and cry. He's never allowed this. Even now I'm getting mascara on his suit. Which is bad to do. To deface a wedding suit right before its big moment in the spotlight.

"This is all I ever needed you to do," I say into the pinstripes. "To tell me it's okay."

"Oh, God, Phronsie. I always thought if I did that, you'd just cry more," he says. "You were such a weepy little kid."

"Of course I was! I missed my mom."

"Also, Robert, tears are not the enemy," says Tenaj. "She had lots of things to cry about. We screwed things up pretty badly, if you recall."

"Sometimes people cry and they might not be able to stop," he says.

"No, that's not true," she says. "People always stop. When they're done."

"Daddy," I say. I pull back and look at him. "I really, really don't think I want to get married to Judd. Do you hate me for that?"

"No, I don't hate you. I just—"

Tenaj says, "May I interject here? The correct answer is, 'I don't hate you, in fact I love you more than ever.' And then you tell her how

478

brave and authentic she's being, and how she's honoring her own truth, and you congratulate her. And then you go outside with her, and—"

"Do you mind?" he says. "I think I can take it from here."

"Well," she says. She winks at me. "It's been good to see you again, Robert. Phronsie, call me if you need more fortification." And she sashays out.

When she leaves, my father sits there next to me on the bed. He has his hands between his knees—his big old farmer hands, all rough and nicked and with dirt so deep it will never come out of the creases in his knuckles. His ears stick out, too, and they're reddened on top, like for good, and his face is all weathered now from all the years of sun. His blue eyes are permanently bloodshot.

"Here's what I want to say to you," he says. In his rough, gritty voice. "I'll love you whatever you decide to do. I—I'll love you forever. And I know I never said that enough."

"I know. I guess I've always known that deep down, but not on the surface maybe."

"Yep. I wasn't so good at the surface."

"I'm not so sure what this love covers though," I say. "Like what if I can't make up my mind for the rest of the day? Would you still love me then?"

His eyes widen a little. "Even if we have to

479

stay in here for the whole rest of the day while you make up your mind, I'll still love you." And he laughs. "It's actually what I'm *hoping* will happen. It'll cement our family's place in Pemberton as *the* craziest family."

We sit there in silence. And then he says, "I think you already know, though, so you might want to go tell Judd."

"Yeah. I suppose we don't *have* to be Pemberton's craziest family."

I stand up. I suddenly have a funny feeling in the pit of my stomach. Tenaj had said there was a man out there looking up at the window. And I suddenly know I need to see him.

I go to the window. People are walking around with drinks in their hands. They're all wearing nice clothes, except the ones who thought they were coming to a beach party. I see Karla Kristensen, of all people. Did Judd invite her? He must have. How did that get past me? But funny thing, I don't really care. I wonder if I ever would have cared before right now.

My eyes scan the rest of the crowd.

And then I notice that one of the most beach-partiest of the beach-partiers among them is a curly-haired guy wearing a Hawaiian shirt and khaki shorts, and my heart drops because he turns and smiles up at me. Waving at me with both hands. Then he points to his socks, which have gnomes on them.

Oh my God. My heart goes into free fall.

I shake my head. I'm laughing. "No!"

He points again. Does a little jig, gestures to each sock in turn.

"Oh my God," I say softly. "Oh my goodness. Oh my God."

"What in the *hell* is going on?" says my father from the bed.

"Daddy, you're not going to believe what just happened. There's a man—wait, he disappeared."

The whole scene goes wobbly on me, and then I hear someone running up the stairs and then there's a knock on the door, and I run over to open it.

And Adam is standing there in front of me. Adam! Crazy, smiling, tanned. Goofy-looking as hell. Hair a big ball of surfing beach hair. He just stands there, and I just stand there, and it feels like moments keep ticking past, and all we can do is look at each other. I may have my hand over my mouth.

"Gnome socks," he says finally. "I was showing you I have on gnome socks. How are you?"

"I'm terrible," I say. "Wretched."

"Because you're about to make the biggest mistake of your life?" He's smiling. He reaches over with his thumb and dries off some leftover tears on my face.

"Because I was, but now I'm not," I say. "I don't think I am anymore. I mean, I'm not."

"Oh Jesus," says my father, getting up. "Who are you, now?"

"Daddy," I say, "this is Adam Cunningham. And this is my father, Robert Linnelle."

"And Adam is—?"

"He's my—my—"

"I'm her disrupter," Adam says. He hasn't taken his eyes from my face.

"How did you know? How did you know to come here?" I say.

"I'm Gabora's plus one," he says. "She told me this was an emergency."

"Gabora!" My hands fly to my face. That's right; I had sent her an invitation at her insistence. "And where is she now?"

"She's in the old-lady section, sitting with your grandmother, I believe. They're discussing bunions and meat loaf and the true meaning of Thanksgiving and how great the Pilgrims were."

"What are you *talking* about?" says my father.

"It's all nonsense, sir. Just making things up." He keeps smiling. To me he says, "What do you think is going to happen next?"

"I think I have to have a very hard conversation next," I say. "With Judd."

"Yes, apparently you do," says my father. "So is this what it looks like?"

"Maybe," I say. I bite my lip. "Adam, will you stay? I have to tell you something about my novel."

482

"I'm staying," he says. "For the duration. I have some personnel issues I might want to discuss with you. And I do need to know how your novel is going."

"Oh, Adam. What a bad thing I did!"

"You had to."

"But I did it in the worst possible way! I'm so ashamed."

"We'll discuss all that. How's Gnomeo?"

"Good God almighty," says my father. "I'll send Judd up. Young man—Adam—maybe you and I should go outside and wait this one out."

"In a second, Daddy," I say. I can't seem to take my eyes off Adam. I reach for him, but he intercepts my hands before they reach his shoulders.

"No kissing," he says. "Not until you're not engaged anymore. I don't make out with engaged women."

I look over and see my father shaking his head. But he is smiling. "I'll send Judd up," he says. "Adam, son, you need to follow me out."

"Daddy, I just need to tell Adam one thing in private before he goes," I say, and my father shrugs and slips outside the door, and I turn to Adam. My head feels clearer than it has in such a long time. My face already hurts from smiling.

"Listen, I don't know what's going to happen here, and I can't quite put this into words that make sense, but . . ." I stop talking and stare at him. And then I start up again: "Listen, I don't care about figuring out the future anymore. I tried to pin it down, let it be recorded on spreadsheets, wrestle it into a kind of orderly submission: marriage, babies, safety, fidelity. And it gave me a big stomachache. That is all."

Adam is smiling at me, and he's holding both my hands.

"So that's all I want to say," I tell him. "I don't know what's going to happen here."

"No one does," he says. "We have eons to figure it out. Or not figure it out. Just going where it leads us. How would that be?"

I would like to tell him the part about how I really, really want children, and I might be running out of time, no matter what he thinks—but I realize that all I really want is to be with him. Just to see, you know, because I haven't felt so light in such a long time and that's worth checking out.

"I have to go talk to Judd," I say. "First I need to get out of this ridiculous wedding dress and put on my other one, the real dress. So I'll see you downstairs."

Judd knows. He knows. I see when he opens the door and comes in and finds me sitting on the floor. I'm leaning against the bed, with my head resting on my hands. He's looking stiff and overdressed in a navy-blue suit and a tie. His mother insisted he wear a suit to his wedding, Maggie had told me.

"Oh boy," he says. "On the floor, are we? What a picture this is!"

He closes the door. And then he lowers himself down on the floor across from me, tugging at his suit as he does, and he looks at me. It hits me that he hasn't really *looked* at me for more than two seconds since we made up this cockamamie plan.

"So is this what I think it is?" he says.

"Judd."

"I know," he says.

"What were we thinking, that we could do this without being in love?"

"Ah, shit, Phronsie. We said it was going to be better," he says.

"Blazing a new trail in relationships, we said. It will be perfect, we said. No jealousy, we said."

"Something like that." He laughs. "When did you know?"

"I think two minutes after you asked me to marry you."

"Then why the hell did you say yes?"

"Because I'm an idiot." I start to cry. "And because I wanted to believe in it. I got so hurt with Steve Hanover that I never wanted to feel all those things again. I didn't want to ever take another chance. Even those forty-four dates—deep down, I think I made sure they wouldn't work because I didn't *want* anything to work. But now I see that being safe isn't any way to live. Not really. And it's not fair to you. You deserve someone who loves you with their whole heart and soul. You deserve mad crazy love, Judd."

He nods and reaches over and wipes off my tears. My mascara is probably smeared.

"I knew this, too," he says. "For me, it was clear when I went to write vows."

"Oh God, yes," I say. "That. I never did do any, did you?"

"I figured I'd wing it. I was going to say something about how I knew we'd be friends when you laughed at my best burps in kindergarten."

"Huh. So rarely do burps get mentioned in vows. I'd considered putting those in, too."

"I didn't think beyond that. I scrapped the whole idea and made Russell look up something more flowery and marriage-y."

"And so not us."

"And so not us."

"You know what the worst part is?" I say after a moment. "If I'm just seeing you as Judd, my friend, I think the whole situation is kind of funny. But if I'm the one standing next to you, freaking *marrying you,* then I'm devastated."

"That is the worst part. You're right."

I feel my heart turning over. "I want to be in love. Really in love."

"Me too."

I look at him for a long time. His handsome face, which has been so closed to me. Turning away on the pillow. Never lighting up when he sees me.

And now he's smiling.

"You want to know something?" I say. "I think I like you so much better at this moment than I've liked you ever since we decided to get married. We kept saying we were best friends, but the truth is, we had even stopped being friends."

"I know," he says slowly. "It was so weird, really. We decided to get married and lost our friendship."

"So, then, we're calling it?" I say.

"Calling it. Let's go have a party." He does a fist bump.

"I see that Karla Kristensen is here. Does that mean what I think it means?"

"Phronsie. Don't make me tell you everything right now. The wounds may be . . ."

"There are no wounds," I say. "We've just got this one little thing to do—tell everyone out-side—and then we're having a massive blowout beach party. And then we're back to being best friends."

"Okay," he says. "I'll tell you later then."

And we shake hands. He kisses me on the forehead.

And we go outside to share the great news.

• • •

We stand together on the grass in front of the crowd of friends, both of us barefoot and holding hands. He's rolled up his suit pants above his ankles, and I'm in my boho dress with my hair looking just the same as it does every day.

I talk about the kindergarten day. (He interrupts me to tell them about the burps, and everyone laughs.) I tell them about our millions of conversations, about the Dissect-A-Date campaign, about the old ladies he helps.

And then I stop talking and look at him, smiling at me there, his eyes crinkled in the sunlight.

"It was a beautiful friendship," I say, "but it wasn't being in love."

"Because, no offense to the rest of you, but we said being in love might be stupid," he says.

"But it isn't. As it happens."

He nods so enthusiastically that people laugh. "And now," he says, "we get to be best friends again because we don't have to do all those pesky things like—"

"Never mind," I say. I put my finger on his lips. "Let's not kiss and tell."

"So we're sorry if we made you come all the way to Wellfleet thinking you were going to get to hear some lifetime promises," he says, "but maybe you can be consoled by the idea that you were here to witness Phronsie Linnelle and Judd Kovac saving their friendship from a dreadful fate. Marriage!" He shudders and people laugh.

"To friendship!" I say. Someone hands me a plastic tumbler of champagne.

"To friendship!" he says back.

"And may I just add one thing?" I say. I'm smiling at Adam when I say this part, but I give a glance toward Karla Kristensen, too. "I don't know this for sure, but I think it's just possible that after years of dating other people—that it was the giving up and deciding to marry each other that ended up being the secret to finding what we both wanted anyway. Here's to the law of relinquishment!"

"And to the magic of found objects!" yells Tenaj.

Because she always needs the last word.

"What the hell just happened?" I hear Daisy Kovac say.

And her husband says, "I'll tell you later."

"Was it a good thing, though?" she asks.

Maggie, standing nearby, goes over and takes Daisy's hand. "Yes," she says. "I think it might have been the best possible thing."

ACKNOWLEDGMENTS

Wow! What an amazing, unsettling time this has been lately—writing a book during the beginning of a global pandemic, during lockdown, when bad news seemed to be everywhere we looked. I felt incredibly lucky to have a deadline looming for this book, if for no other reason than it gave me permission to stop scrolling through the endless loop of news reports and remind myself that my job was to simply write my novel.

I owe so much to family and friends who helped make life possible during these last months of scariness. Thank you to my husband, Jim, who, working from home alongside me, kept my spirits up, as did our children, Ben, Allie, and Stephanie, even though often we could only be together remotely. And I offer so much love and thanks to their spouses, the best of the best: Amy, Mike, and Alex. Zoom calls with Charlie, Josh, Miles, and Emma were always lovely and crazy and made me laugh. And to little Mila, who was born right at the end as I was turning the book in. New life!

Thank you also to Kim Steffen, Leslie Connor, Linda Balestracci, Nancy Antle, Beth Levine, Alice Mattison, Holly Robinson, Deborah Hare, Andi Atkins Hessekiel, Mary Ann Emswiler,

Grace Pauls, Marcia Winter, Alice Smith, Marji Shapiro, Thea Guidone, and Sharon Wise, all of whom supported me with phone calls, snacks, socially distant walks, and often the willingness to read drafts over and over again. (I'm especially looking at you, Kim, Beth, and Nancy!) Bill Squier has earned my undying gratitude for telling me everything I needed to know about gnomes—and it turned out to be *a lot!* Thank you to everyone who told me their Woodstock stories. (I was too young to attend, but my Uncle Bob was in a rock group, Cat Mother and the All-Night Newsboys, produced by Jimi Hendrix in those days—and it's family legend how he and his band "almost got to accompany Jimi to Woodstock.")

And *huge* thanks to Darlene Faster Burmann, who once drove me all over the Northeast while we promoted a book of mine—and who took the time to tell me everything I needed to know about Phronsie's job as a publicist.

Fellow authors Kerry Anne King, Marybeth Whalen, Barbara O'Neal, and Nancy Star were always happy to jump on the phone and share stories. I am so grateful to have you four in my corner.

My editor, Jodi Warshaw, is absolutely the best any writer could hope for. Not only does she offer encouragement during the most uncertain times, but she's always available for phone consultations, plot talks, and a thoughtful analysis of where the book is going. Also, she is brilliant. I treasure our talks more than I can say. Christina Henry de Tessan is a tireless and wise editor who helped me shape the manuscript. My agent, Nancy Yost, offers guidance and wit and is always so much fun to talk to. Suzanne Weinstein Leopold is fabulous at helping me get the word out about my books. Kim Yau, my film agent, has been a tireless champion. And I'm sending so much gratitude to Danielle Marshall, Dennelle Catlett, Gabriella Dumpit, Jessica Preeg, and the entire Lake Union team for all their support and help.

Lastly, thank you so much to the readers who have not only bought my books but have also left wonderful reviews, invited me to talk to their book clubs, and have sent me their own heartfelt stories. I treasure each and every one of you. Please keep writing to me! Your words mean so much.

You can visit me at
www.maddiedawson.com,
or by emailing me at
maddie@maddiedawson.com.
Or on Instagram at @maddiedaws,
and Facebook at
www.facebook.com/maddiedawsonauthor.

BOOK CLUB QUESTIONS

1. Phronsie tells us that she was born to a witch and a farmer as an explanation for why she can't figure out love. Do you think that's the real reason? If not, what do you think is the real reason she's having trouble with her love life?
2. How do Phronsie's impressions of her parents' marriage and split-up differ from the story that has been told to her? Do you think she has any evidence for her theories?
3. How did Phronsie's marriage to Steve Hanover affect her future dealings with men? Did that have something to do with her failure to fall in love with any of the forty-four men she subsequently dated?
4. Judd offers her a marriage that's based on friendship, loyalty, and an agreement not to ever cheat. He says that being in love is overrated and in fact is the cause of the demise of most marriages. Does he make a strong case for this?
5. How important is romantic love in a happy marriage? Can best friends form a perfect union, do you think?
6. How did Phronsie's treatment of her stepmother evolve over the course of the book?

Was there any reason for her change of heart? Did Maggie make mistakes as a stepmother that made things harder?

7. Why do you think Tenaj stopped seeing her children? Did she have a legitimate reason?

8. How did Tenaj's explanation to Maggie of the Woodstock experience change things between them and between Maggie and Robert? Was she telling the entire truth?

ABOUT THE AUTHOR

Maddie Dawson grew up in the South, born into a family of outrageous storytellers. Her various careers as a substitute English teacher, department-store clerk, medical-records typist, waitress, cat sitter, wedding-invitation-company receptionist, nanny, day care worker, electrocardiogram technician, and Taco Bell taco maker were made bearable by thinking up stories as she worked. Today Maddie lives in Guilford, Connecticut, with her husband. She's the bestselling author of seven previous novels: *A Happy Catastrophe*, *Matchmaking for Beginners*, *The Survivor's Guide to Family Happiness*, *The Opposite of Maybe*, *The Stuff That Never Happened*, *Kissing Games of the World*, and *A Piece of Normal*. For more information visit www.maddiedawson.com.

Books are produced in the United States using U.S.-based materials

Books are printed using a revolutionary new process called THINKtech™ that lowers energy usage by 70% and increases overall quality

Books are durable and flexible because of Smyth-sewing

Paper is sourced using environmentally responsible foresting methods and the paper is acid-free

Center Point Large Print
600 Brooks Road / PO Box 1
Thorndike, ME 04986-0001 USA

(207) 568-3717

US & Canada:
1 800 929-9108
www.centerpointlargeprint.com